D0013900

The Mourning
PARADE

A Novel

Dawn Reno Langley

Amberjack Publishing
New York, New York

Therese ~
There's no greater
treasure than a friend
who accepts you as you are,
Thank you for that,
as well as for helping
me celebrate this
book. I hope you love it as
much as I loved
writing it.
Lots of love,
Dawn

Amberjack Publishing
228 Park Avenue S #89611
New York, NY 10003-1502
http://amberjackpublishing.com

Publisher's Cataloging-in-Publication data
Names: Langley, Dawn Reno, author.
Title: The Mourning parade / Dawn Reno Langley.
Description: New York, NY: Amberjack Publishing, 2017.
Identifiers: ISBN 978-1-944995-23-2 (pbk.) | 978-1-944995-30-0 (ebook) | LCCN 2016962238
Subjects: Elephants--Fiction. | Veterinarians--Fiction. | Asiatic elephant--Conservation--Thailand--Fiction. | Human-animal relationships—Fiction. | Mothers and sons--Fiction. | Children--Death--Fiction. | Bereavement--Fiction. | Love stories. | BISAC FICTION / Literary
Classification: LCC PS3612.A582 M68 2017 | DDC 813.6--dc23

Cover Design: Red Couch Creative
Artwork: Marco Smouse

Printed in the United States of America.

The Sanctuary

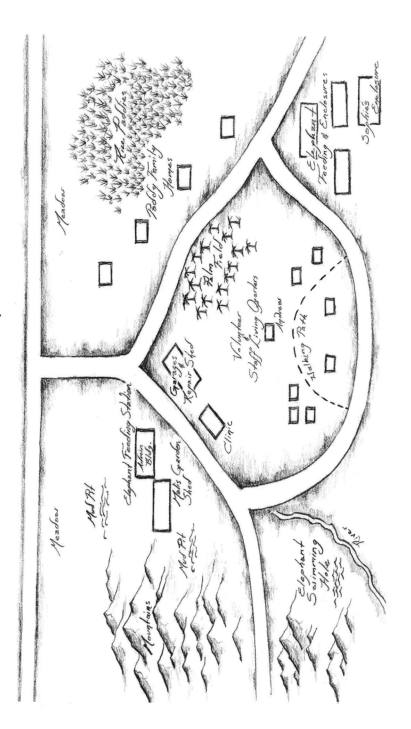

Meadow

Tree Pastures

Paddy Family Homes

Elephant Feeding & Enclosures

Sophie's Enclosure

Palm Field

Volunteer & Staff Living Quarters

Walking Path

Garages & Repair Shed

Clinic

Elephant Feeding Station

Admin Bldg.

Mali's Garden Shed

Meadow

Mud Pit

Mud Pit

Mountains

Elephant Swimming Hole

River

For my mother
Elaine Gordon Brander
(1929-2000)
and for my grandson,
Ryes Brander Wilson

And all my days are trances,
And all my nightly dreams
Are where thy gray eye glances,
And where thy footstep gleams—
In what ethereal dances,
By what eternal streams.

–Edgar Allen Poe

One

How had I come to be here
Like them, and overhear
A cry of pain that could have got
loud and worse but hadn't?
-Elizabeth Bishop

THE DOORKNOB FELT COLD and shimmied almost indiscernibly as the front door lock clicked. A definitive sound. Final. An ending. Natalie placed her right palm against the door and closed her eyes. *Breathe*, she told herself. *Just breathe*. Each sip of air required work. Thought. And though air meant life, breathing had become the hardest thing she'd ever done.

She slid the key under the doormat for the realtor who'd arrive after sunrise to put a lock box on the door. When she came home again, this house would no longer be hers. She'd return instead to her townhouse on the beach in Wilmington. This house, her family home, overlooked the Falls Dam, one of the prettiest spots in Wake County. She'd been approached to sell many times, but she'd always refused. She could afford a larger house and modern amenities like a gourmet kitchen or a screening room, but this old farmhouse was home. She knew every creaking floorboard to avoid when she wanted to sneak into the house unnoticed, and how to set the window in the corner bedroom just right so it would stay open to capture the river breeze on a late summer's night.

Years ago, when her ex-husband, Parker, and she had first seen the house, its view made buying it a no-brainer. It had been the right decision then, but now the house and everything around it appeared different. Her footsteps echoed when she came home late at night. The barn owls the kids loved to imitate had become an irritating noise that kept her from sleeping, and every shifting beam of light made the most mundane items appear sinister. Instead of being a balm for her soul, the view and the house itself only brought up all the memories of the years she spent here with her boys—and Parker. Even the happy memories were unwelcome now.

"You have everything, Miss?" The taxi driver who'd been silently waiting in the driveway startled her. His voice roused a pair of mourning doves nesting in the eaves above where the cabbie stood. They whirred into the sky.

No, I don't have everything, Natalie wanted to say. *I have nothing*. But she nodded silently instead.

As the driver maneuvered down the long, winding driveway, Natalie pressed her face against the window and forced herself to count the pine trees lining the road. In an hour or so, the road would be lined with media anxious to ask her how she felt now that a year had passed. She had chosen this early morning flight specifically to ignore such inane questions. Even in the dark quiet of this taxi, she didn't want to think about how she felt. If she concentrated hard enough, she could stop the scenes that played inside her eyelids like the twitching movements of a silent film. She couldn't drive when those moments arrived and stole her attention. In fact, it was after one of those blinding memories that she'd finally admitted she needed help.

She'd shared her deepest feelings about life and death with only one person in the past year: Sally Littlefield, her psychiatrist. She'd been too scared to share with anyone else the chilling thoughts she had late at night. The crushing fear that she might be losing her mind, and the realization that maybe being completely insane would be less painful than trying to pretend she could move on, made her lose her perspective. She'd told Dr. Littlefield during the first session that maybe it would be better if she had a complete breakdown. Then maybe she wouldn't know the guilt of living.

Dr. Littlefield attributed Natalie's roller-coaster emotions to post-traumatic stress, and she promised the drastic mood swings would eventually subside. Natalie wasn't so sure.

"It'll be most difficult for the first year," Dr. Littlefield had said. "Don't make any big decisions until you get past that first anniversary. And take care of yourself. Eat. Sleep. Nonstop work isn't going to make things go away. You have to feel your grief. Embrace it. Cry into your pillow until you have nothing left. Don't hold back."

Maman made sure Natalie ate. Too much. Sometimes she discovered two casseroles waiting for her in the refrigerator when she got home from work. Sometimes there was a cheesecake on the front porch. And she always insisted Natalie come over for Sunday dinner. Natalie ate in fits and starts, but she never got into the habit of three square meals a day.

She had listened, but the year was up now, and talking to Dr. Littlefield was no longer enough. Though the doctor didn't push, she made it clear that the only way to move forward was to put one foot in front of the other. "How?" Natalie would scream. "How the hell do you move on when both of your kids are gone, and you're still here? Who hates me enough to punish me like this?"

Dr. Littlefield said all the right things after that question. "You're not being punished. You might never have the answers to everything, but know this: nothing you could've said or done would have altered that day. Nothing. Be kind to yourself, Natalie."

It wasn't enough. It was never enough. Nothing stopped the pain.

Every time Natalie stepped back into the house, the memories flew at her from every corner of every room like thousands of hummingbirds, moving too quickly to catch, and poking their long beaks into her body, stinging her with images of her kids: Danny hanging off the side of the couch laughing, one tooth missing, upper right side, and beside him, Stephen, eyes crossed, wearing astronaut pajamas. She saw them doing their homework, watching television, baking brownies, making faces when she suggested the garbage needed to be taken out. She heard their voices and laughter so clearly that her heart quickened, and she nearly convinced herself the sound was real. But it wasn't, and in her heart of hearts, she knew it, so she'd push herself up the stairs past the memory of Danny, barely a year old, learning to walk, and she'd closet herself in her bedroom, door closed against the image of Stephen at seven, dancing down the hallway in his stocking feet. Only in her bedroom were the images stilled, so that's where she stayed, finally giving in and installing a microwave and coffee maker so she wouldn't have to go downstairs. She slept and ate there, wishing she found comfort in the house that had been home for so many years, but there was no longer any peace there.

Last night, she'd given in completely to the house and let it swallow her. She stayed awake all night to wallow in the past, opening each door of her heart as she opened every door and drawer in the house. Though her family and staff members at her equine surgery clinic would have helped, packing the memories was something she needed to do alone. She gently stored school photographs, report cards, and Halloween costumes in the last Rubbermaid crate at three in the morning, an hour before the taxi was scheduled to arrive.

During that last hour, in the quietest part of the morning, she curled into the couch on her back porch and listened to the night sounds as she stared into the blackness around her. She didn't need to physically see the pine trees to know they were there, or to trace the ebb and flow of the Neuse River that created her northern property line. She breathed in the scent of their existence, determined to capture the essence of the place where she'd spent the last fifteen years. The longer she sat on the porch, the more she remembered other sounds: the roar of a summer boat filled with teenagers screaming and laughing; the voices of children exploring their way down a woodsy path to the river-bank. An adult's warning: *Be careful. Don't go too far.* The child's response: *Don't worry, Mommy. I'm right here.*

She had seen the taxi's lights snake down the drive toward the house. Now she watched as the house receded in the rearview mirror. Its rooms would be empty soon. The boxes of items she couldn't bear to give away or destroy would wait for her at Easy Storage on Route 1 until she returned a year from now. In her suitcases, she had everything she'd need until then.

"So, where are you going?" The driver, a twenty-something, rangy kid wearing a Duke Baseball cap backwards, watched her in the rearview. His green eyes were friendly.

"I'm going to Thailand," she told him.

"Wow, Thailand. That's cool. That's where all those temples are, right?"

She smiled and met the cabbie's eyes in the mirror again. "Yes, that's the place. Some of them are even decorated with real rubies and emeralds." She didn't know why she chose to tell him that.

His eyes widened. "Maybe someday I'll get there."

They drove down I-40 and took the exit to the Raleigh-Durham International Airport without another word. It wasn't until he'd removed her third suitcase and closed the trunk that he finally asked. "Don't I know you? You look really familiar."

Her suitcases stood on the curb in front of the Delta terminal. Through the windows, the terminal was already busy with trav-elers though the night sky had barely begun to brighten. Her heartbeat quickened as the cabbie stared her down, curious.

"I don't think we know each other," she said, grabbing her receipt from his hand and replacing it with a hundred-dollar bill. Too much, she knew, but she would have paid ten times more to get out of the state of North Carolina without being recognized.

"Don't you want any change?" he asked.

"Keep it." She signaled to a porter pulling a trolley down the sidewalk. He loaded her three suitcases and headed inside.

Behind her, the cabbie called out, "Hey! I know! I know who

you are now. Not too many women with a waist-length, black braid like yours." He triumphantly grabbed the briefcase she held in her hand, brought her around so they were face-to-face. Her hands started to shake. "You're the horse doctor who took care of my girl's mare. Jodi Conchall. Her horse was . . . what the hell was her name? Starfire or Starlite. Something like that. Probably 'bout ten years ago. Both of them gone now. Horse is dead, Jodi's just gone. You might not remember."

She started breathing again. "I remember. Pretty little pinto. Heart problems." Yes, she remembered. That was the problem. She remembered everything.

A few moments chatting, and she freed herself. Entering the terminal, the harsh lights made her feel exposed. The Delta line was long. Families with bored kids, businessmen in gray suits and sensible loafers, hipsters on their way to someplace more foreign than the next guy. Natalie looked straight ahead, mentally counting the number of people in front of her.

But she couldn't help noticing the snaking tape that forced all travelers into lines. Her palms sweated. *Concentrate*, she told herself. *Count. Breathe.* But her vision swam, and the memory sucked her in.

Standing shoulder-to-shoulder with other parents and siblings, frozen behind the yellow caution tape, waiting. Waiting for the answer to the one-word question: why? Waiting with one beating heart between them and a chorus of soft sniffles and whispered worries floating in the air above them.

Hundreds waited with her for more than an hour at Lakeview Middle School, all standing behind the yellow caution tape, yet she couldn't hear a sound. No one spoke. Occasionally a moan or a sniffle escaped into the fragile silence, but it was quickly swallowed as if the person—mother, father, grandparent, sister—felt that releasing any grief too early would be traitorous. Bad luck.

After a while, the crowd deepened. Babies cried. Cell phones rang and were answered. Conversations were held in hushed tones.

We don't know anything yet.

No news.

The police are all over the place, but we don't know what's happening.

She'd been trying for a year to forget the eruptions. The cracks that split the air again and again. The gasps. The shrieks. The startled jumps from those in the crowd who stood, united by that yellow tape, as well as by those children in that school. Then the silence. The new and bone-chilling silence. So quiet that when the screams started exploding from the brick building, high-pitched and painful, they were a heavenly blessing. Proof of life.

"Dr. DeAngelo?" The attendant tapped Natalie's ticket on the counter. Impatient. How many times had she called her name? "Weight is five pounds over on this suitcase. You can either empty something out, or we'll have to charge you."

"Go ahead. Charge my card. I need everything I packed. I won't be back for a year."

"Doctors without Borders?" The badge on the attendant's jacket read: *Dolores.* The name fit.

"No, I'm a veterinarian. I'll be working at an elephant sanctuary."

"You can't get much more exotic than that," Dolores said as she slapped a ticket onto each suitcase. "I hear they're pretty smart and protective about their little ones. Strong mothers. My son, he's five, Alfie's his name; he loves watching the videos of elephants on YouTube. They're his favorite animal."

A stuffed pink elephant, three feet tall. Danny, two years old, sleeping against the elephant's belly every night.

Natalie swallowed hard. "My sons loved elephants, too," she managed. "My Danny wanted to free them all." She wondered if her voice sounded as strained to the attendant as it did to her.

"Be safe over there. They're always having some kind of revolution." The attendant handed Natalie her ticket and smiled.

"Exactly what my mother said." Natalie forced a smile in return, the same kind she wore every day when dealing with her clients. The horses she operated on were like children to their owners. All of them could be reassured with a compassionate smile. That came easily for her, but it also masked her own need for comfort and the reassurance that everything was going to be all right. She used to be pretty confident that she could handle any situation. Now she doubted her own ability to put one foot in front of the other.

Her grief was something she tasted in her mouth first, like the copper overtones of blood when she bit her lip. Then it moved to the back of her throat, threatening to cut off her windpipe. But even when she could breathe again, the grief was still present in the pit of her stomach like a basketball-sized sphere of molten lead. Some days the grief would take the form of a headache. Sometimes it would come as a heart-fluttering anxiety attack, but always—always—it was there. She had gotten used to it by now, and even welcomed the physical pain it put her in, because it felt like the punishment she deserved for being alive, for not speaking lovingly to Stephen that morning, for being overly concerned about being on time instead of giving Danny the extra five minutes he needed to finish eating his breakfast. Instead, he'd eaten it in the car on the way to school. For weeks after he was gone, she refused to clean the crumbs he'd left on the passenger seat.

A man with eyes like a cow's motioned her through security. She choked back the emotions, reminding herself that she had to breathe. *Just follow the people in front of you.* She kept her head down at Starbucks, ordering a grande decaf skinny mocha with whipped cream without making eye contact with anyone. She picked up the latest Chris Bohjalian novel at the bookstore, counting the number of pages she had to read before leaving it at the sister store at LAX. *No extra weight*, she'd promised herself. She kept her head down reading in the waiting area and took her seat on the plane without looking up.

Her seatmates soon arrived. He came down the aisle first: early thirties, trim mustache, dark brown hair that curled around his ears. Brown suede jacket. Loafers. Probably a teacher. He looked at Natalie, then the seat number overhead.

"I'm in there." He pointed to the window. "Jill, you're 14E, right? In the middle?" He glanced over his shoulder, then back at Natalie to make sure she was listening, and stared a little harder. He squinted, his brow furrowed, as if he'd left his glasses in his other jacket pocket.

A flurry of activity as he placed his suitcase in the overhead rack and then his partner's. Jill, a slight woman whose blonde hair was haphazardly gathered atop her head with an orange clip. They squeezed in, all the while apologizing for holding up the line—for making Natalie move—for having too much luggage. Then they were settled.

The two of them nodded at Natalie then looked at each other. Natalie leaned forward on the pretense of watching other passengers board and kept them in her peripheral vision as they whispered, then glanced at her again.

Shit, she thought and lowered her eyes to her book.

They were in the middle of beverage service when Jill leaned over and whispered to Natalie, "We're from Wake Forest. Our daughter goes to Lakeview Middle School. You're Dr. DeAngelo, aren't you?"

She had no choice but to nod. The woman was less than three inches from Natalie's ear. Her breath smelled of coffee and something fruity that turned Natalie's stomach.

"I can't imagine what you've gone through since the shootings. My God, I can't imagine losing my Amanda, but to lose two . . . I cannot imagine." She reached her hand to touch Natalie's. It was a light touch. Fingers cool enough to make Natalie flinch. "It was just about a year ago, wasn't it?"

Natalie pulled away. No one had to remind her that the Lakeview Middle School shootings happened a year ago. She knew. And she didn't want to hear the word "anniversary" used to define that day. "Anniversary" denoted a happy occasion, the moment you married, achieved a milestone at your company, or celebrated another year sober. It's never a word that should be associated with death. Never used to define that moment when twenty-seven men, women, and children came to an end. Two of those people were her sons. Danny, her always-questioning, symphony-loving, strident animal-activist. Her twelve-year-old beautiful boy. And Stephen, her fourteen-year-old. The teenager who tested every limit. Sullen, tortured, with a wicked sense of humor that he demonstrated in his brilliant graphic novels.

Two boys. No other parent had lost more than one child that day. She'd often told her boys that they each held half her heart. On that day, both halves were ripped from her chest. Now, only an empty cavern remained.

She had thought about violence a lot in the past year, and sometimes in very violent ways. She hated that a senseless act had taken her two sons, but she would commit an even more heinous act in a heartbeat if it meant she could bring Danny and Stephen back. Yes, she would kill to bring them back. Without a second thought or a bit of guilt. But that was something she'd never admit aloud. Her own mother didn't know that. No one did. Natalie had become an expert at hiding her emotions. Her mother also didn't know that the only reason Natalie was still alive was because she'd spent many hours teaching the boys that suicide was never the answer. She'd lost a friend at fifteen to suicide, and to this day she missed Claire and wondered whether she could have done something to convince Claire that her life would get better in time. Perhaps it was unrealistic, but she'd always feared one of the boys might fall prey to teenage depression and take their life as Claire had, so she'd started teaching them early, never thinking for a moment that she would face a worse tragedy.

She nodded at Jill, then turned away. The questions stopped. Natalie pretended to go to sleep. Part of her mind did doze, but she'd gotten used to surviving on very little real sleep, and as soon as they landed in Los Angeles, she quickly gathered her belongings and headed for the international terminal. With each step, she knew she succeeded in moving further and further from the non-stop reminders. Her mother had accused her of running away, but the only way being alive made any sense was doing something her boys would have been proud of: saving elephants. Perhaps she was running away from the place where it had happened, but she'd never leave the boys. Her sons would always own those halves of her heart.

She swiftly navigated LAX's busy corridors to the gate for her flight to Shanghai where she'd transfer to another one to Bangkok. She felt like Stephen held one hand and Danny the other. They excitedly whispered in her ears: *Elephants, Mom*, Danny said. *Remember to make sure they don't have those stupid chains on their feet.* The chains had made him cry each time they visited a zoo. *Kick butt and take names*, Dr. D., Stephen said. His flippant, high-pitched, teenage-boy laugh made her look around to see if anyone else had heard him. The family to her right continued to follow their dad like ducklings. The older couple on her left walked straight ahead, their eyes tentative, tightly holding each other's hands. In front of her and behind her, people talked and jostled and discussed their destinations. No one had heard.

Though Dr. Littlefield didn't agree, Natalie cherished these moments, even if they were hallucinations. Unbidden, yet comforting, they were the only moments when she'd ever see or feel her sons again. When they ended, she felt a disappointment that lasted until the next hallucination occurred. Her only solace was that no matter where she went, those vivid and substantial moments would accompany her like friendly apparitions.

Somewhere between Shanghai and Bangkok, she awoke with a start. In the darkened cabin, passengers slept. The flickering lights from the movie screens on seat backs created crazy shadows. She lifted a hand to rub her eyes and discovered her cheeks were wet, though she didn't remember her dream. Startled, she glanced around, but no one was watching. Her shoulders instantly relaxed.

She stared out the airplane window for a few moments and let the eggplant-colored sky play tricks on her. As the sky started to brighten, the engine's hum lured her back to a restless nap. The last thought she had before slipping into sleep was that she'd made the right decision to go to Thailand. The boys would have approved. For the first time in a year, she didn't have to watch the pity in anyone's eyes or answer unwanted questions. No one knew who she was. No one needed to remind her. Still, memories were the only thing keeping her alive, and the one thing that could kill her.

Two

Every experience, no matter how
bad it seems, holds within it
a blessing of some kind.
The goal is to find it.
-Buddha

NATALIE STEPPED OFF THE plane in Bangkok into oppressive summer heat that felt like a wet cloud she had to push through. As she followed the other passengers across the tarmac, it struck her that only a month ago she'd been in Atlanta at the Southeastern Veterinarians' Conference where she met Andrew Gordon, the philanthropist who convinced her to give up almost everything to move to Thailand for a year. He'd unwittingly offered her an escape from the media, as well as an opportunity to do something that would make a difference in the world, something that would make her feel worthy of life.

She shook her head now, remembering that she'd gone to the conference determined to take Dr. Littlefield's advice and find something—new research or a technique she could incorporate in her surgical clinic or a cause she could throw herself into. Anything that would keep her mind occupied.

"Your post-traumatic stress will continue if you don't make some sort of effort to move on, Natalie," Dr. Littlefield had said.

"I know that's difficult to hear, but you are alive. You're a brilliant vet, a valuable member of society. Your family—your parents and your brother and sister-in-law—love you. You owe it to yourself and to them and, yes, to your boys, to do something that will help you move forward. The nightmares, the feelings that you're having, they won't disappear by themselves. You need to do the work, Natalie. You alone must do the work."

At the conference, the white-haired Englishman, world-renowned for his philanthropic work on behalf of the world's dwindling elephant population, stared into the faces of hundreds of veterinarians and animal trainers in the audience. He wore a belted safari jacket with short sleeves and plenty of pockets over a pair of baggy shorts, as if he'd come directly from the savannah. At first, she'd thought him somewhat of a cliché, but that was before he spoke.

"I shall show you the devastation we face every day at my sanctuaries in both Kenya and Thailand. I shall give you the statistics regarding how many elephants live in the wild."

A giant screen lowered from the ceiling behind him. Natalie felt as mesmerized as she'd been the first time she'd taken the boys to an IMAX theater. Andrew Gordon's voice, growly and businesslike, told the audience, "I could tell you the whole story about our ellies and the thousands of others throughout the world who've been used and abused during their entire long lives, but instead I'm going to introduce them to you, and I'm going to let them do their own talking."

He paused again, and a low rumble came through the large speakers on both sides of the stage, then another sound: a higher-pitched rumbling reply. Behind him, on the screen, a ten-foot-tall elephant's eye came into focus. The lights in the auditorium dimmed.

"The rumbling you hear travels dozens of miles. One of the ways elephants communicate. They tell others of danger. They connect with family members and even find someone who's lost. Miles away. Their ways of communication are so complex that we've only started to figure them out. They're like dolphins, pinging messages like sonar, but I'm sure you know that. I'm not exactly speaking to grade school children here, am I?"

The audience laughed politely. Natalie leaned forward, riveted by both the elephants and Gordon. She'd known about elephants and their plight for years, had even done a short residency at a farm in the U.S. where circus elephants retired, but she'd chosen to work with horses throughout her career. This man and his elephants touched a chord deep inside that she'd almost forgotten.

The massive screen showed Gordon's "baker's dozen" (his words): his herd at Doba, the Kenyan Sanctuary. Still photographs showed several elephants so thin their skin hung from their bones like gray burlap curtains. Three had partial or complete blindness caused by the hooked poles used by their trainers to force them to behave for the humans in charge. One, trained as a circus performer, stood on her hind legs for so long that one of the legs was twisted awkwardly, deformed.

When the audience's gasps died down, one word floated on the screen: *After*. Photos of the elephants learning their new surroundings faded into photos of elephants feeding, rolling happily in a mud bath, swimming in the river. Elephants that had arrived malnourished appeared hardly recognizable. They had gained weight, no skull bones showed, their skin had tightened.

"What I want more than anything is your help." Gordon's voice lowered to a dramatic whisper. He spoke about the need for medicine, for more fencing, talked about buying some adjacent acreage so the sanctuary could expand and rescue more elephants to add to the dozen they now housed. He spoke of the research he could do with appropriate personnel, and he discussed the challenges he faced: the government, the daily costs of the sanctuary, the lack of qualified personnel. He wrapped up with a three-pronged plea: money, donations, and veterinarians willing to give a year of their lives.

When the clapping had stopped and everyone filed out the doors, Natalie fought through the crowd to speak to him, feeling a flutter of excitement in her chest. It had been an eternity since she'd felt anything resembling that emotion.

In bed that night, she thought about her spontaneous decision to travel to Thailand and work at Gordon's sanctuary, and she heard her boys' voices in the recesses of her brain, urging her to go on. The next morning, she called her mother. Surprisingly, Maman was the only person who tried to discourage her, but when Papa got on the phone, he told her not to worry about her mother. She would come around, he said. She hadn't yet, but Natalie accepted that, though she hoped that maybe here in Thailand, where no one knew her, she would be able to live a life that would make her sons—and her parents—proud.

The Bangkok airport terminal buzzed with high-pitched voices speaking a variety of languages she didn't understand. Natalie stretched to her tiptoes, searching the crowd beyond the new arrivals' rope until she finally spotted Andrew Gordon's white head. He held a sign with her name scribbled on it in red. She waved and moved forward.

"There you are, Dr. DeAngelo!" Andrew caught her in a bear hug and thumped her on the back as if they'd been friends since childhood. "I'm so glad you're here, love. Have a good flight?"

Moments later, she held onto the door handle of a crotchety Toyota truck that smelled of gasoline and animals as Andrew navigated Bangkok traffic with aggressive maneuvers that rivaled Italian drivers on the streets of Rome. His twists and turns were punctuated by curse words that would redden the ears of a rugby player. During one of their brief stops, Natalie wiped the sweat off the back of her neck with a flimsy piece of cloth she used to clean her glasses and took a deep breath.

All the while he was driving, Andrew chattered about the sanctuary and the projects he wanted her to spearhead, but she processed little of what he said and fought jet lag as the truck bumped along, dodging the bicycle-driven *tuk-tuks*, pedestrians, and vehicles coming at them from every direction. Her mind whirled, the result of both the twenty-plus-hour flight and the memories that haunted her. Slightly nauseous and overwhelmed, she put the back of her hand to her forehead.

At the next traffic stop, a group of people in red shirts filled the road until a herd of military ushered them out of sight.

"Bangkok's latest revolutionaries." Andrew shook his head and shoved the Toyota into gear. "This country doesn't know how to negotiate a political change without a revolution. Hopefully, they'll manage this one without killing anyone."

"If I'm not mistaken, a revolution had just been resolved the last time I was here about four years ago." Natalie's stomach lurched as Andrew maneuvered through yet another congested traffic stop.

"I swear there's one every other year," he said. "Makes for a very unstable government. Monarchy, but the king doesn't have much power. Democracy, but half the time the military's in charge. Don't get me started."

They passed through a neighborhood populated with storefronts filled with statues of religious figures: Buddhas of all types—sitting, reclining, standing, laughing; Kwan Yin, the goddess of mercy and peace; Garuda, the mythological bird man that stood as the national symbol of Thailand. Eight-foot-tall, emerald sitting Buddhas in one storefront. Cloisonné Buddhas and ginger jars to match in the next shop. A gold, reclining Buddha with a slightly drunk appearance in the store next to that one. Throughout the whole city block, each shop sold the same types of objects.

She knew she'd been here before.

Four years ago. May. The whole family had come to Bangkok for one of Parker's biomedical conferences. It was not a fun trip. She and Parker fought bitterly about everything: where to eat, what sites to visit, whether to take a tuk-tuk or a private car. On an excursion to find the perfect Buddha, they had a particularly volatile argument in this very neighborhood. Her kids had reacted as they usually did when their parents argued. Stephen retreated into his fantasy novel, inserting his earbuds and removing himself from the fray. Danny, tired and hot, plunked down on the dirty sidewalk next to a tiny Thai lady wearing a pink head scarf and round, black eyeglasses. All over the ground around her, piles of green bananas and lemon-yellow papayas were for sale.

"We should go back to the hotel," Natalie said.

Parker ignored her, stalking ahead.

Danny continued his discussion with the little Thai fruit-seller, learning the Thai words for banana and papaya, as well as "I'll make you a deal." Natalie heard his giggle as Parker finally turned around and said, "I give up. C'mon, Stephen. Danny!"

As they walked back to the hotel, Danny repeated his new words in his reedy voice, over and over. Parker spoke to him twice, and the third time, he lost his temper and snapped an open palm against the boy's cheek, silencing all four family members. Danny's stunned eyes filled with tears. He lifted a small, white hand to the red mark on his face.

Parker berated Danny all the way back to the hotel, in spite of Natalie's protests. "Don't ever hit him again. He's eight, for God's sake, Parker!" she'd said.

She knew then that the marriage was over, but she hung on. It was no great surprise when he announced a few months later that he was in love with the owner of Potts' Landscaping. What did shock her, however, was that after he disappeared with that woman one summer evening, he never once called or contacted the boys afterward. Not once.

"He's a narcissist," Dr. Littlefield told Natalie long after he'd gone. "He can easily disengage with anyone who doesn't meet his needs. In truth, he was probably a sociopath, a man with no conscience whatsoever. No empathy for anyone else. They're the nicest people in the world while they hook their victims. Compliments. Flowers. Specially-planned romantic dates. Every woman's dream man. Then they go for the commitment, usually early in the relationship. A month for you and Parker, right?"

When Natalie nodded, Dr. Littlefield smiled sadly. "If the victim pauses or says no, it excites the narcissist. They need—crave—the challenge. So, when the victim is hooked, when that woman (usually) falls for the incredible person who's showering her with attention, the narcissist closes the deal. They get married, or make some other type of commitment, and the victim's hooked, so the narcissist drops the façade. He's opportunistic, abusive, deceitful. The woman wonders if anything was the truth . . ." Again, she glanced at Natalie, and again, Natalie nodded.

"And kids are the strongest competition for the attention of the other parent."

The comment had hung in the air between them then. Dr. Littlefield sat in her chair, hands folded on her lap, waiting for Natalie's response. But she couldn't. The words kept repeating in her head: *competition for attention*. Had the boys been competing for hers, too? Is that why Stephen gave up after Parker left? Her eldest son had wanted his father, but Parker had absolutely no parental attributes.

Those words resonate even now. It was true, Natalie knew. Parker had not cared about the boys from the moment they were born. Though Natalie had tried to reason that he was jealous because they stole her attention, she knew now that it was more than that. Much more.

For the first month after his disappearance, Natalie had continued to contact Parker, left dozens of phone messages about the boys and what they were doing, texted him to arrange some kind of visitation with the kids. Not once did he answer her—or the boys. At first, she was baffled.

The kids didn't deserve to be abandoned. Then she became indignant, and then she started seeing Dr. Littlefield. It took two years, but she filed for divorce, and she asked her lawyer to ensure she had full custody. She needn't have bothered. Parker sent a lawyer to the hearing with explicit instructions not to share his contact information. They agreed to everything Natalie requested: custody, the house in Raleigh, as well as the vacation home on the beach, retirement funds, and some stocks.

Danny eventually stopped asking about his father, but Stephen retreated from Natalie as if she'd been the cause of his father's erasure from his life. He refused to hug her, ignored

Danny, and met life with a stony expression that pushed everyone else away. She waited patiently for Stephen to turn around, even enlisted a child psychiatrist, met with his teachers on a weekly basis, and occasionally, she'd see a glimmer of hope. But that glimmer was never fully realized.

When the story of the school shooting hit national news, Parker did not bother to call to express his grief. She hated him for that, even though Dr. Littlefield had warned her it might happen.

The media tried to find him for an interview but came up empty. Finally, the FBI caught up with him, but even Natalie didn't know what they'd asked. Natalie found out the news about her ex-husband the same way everyone else did: on TV.

Wrapped in her memories, Natalie caught herself against the dashboard when Andrew's truck came to a complete stop.

"Damn," he muttered, tapping his fingers against the wheel. "What the bloody hell? I'm going to see what the holdup is. You don't mind, do you?"

She shook her head, though it wouldn't have mattered if she had given her consent. He jogged up the street, weaving in and out of vehicles until she didn't see him anymore. Within a few moments, he was back, red-faced and sweating.

"We have a problem," he told her when he stuck his head back in the truck's window. "I need your help."

"Me?" She glanced ahead at the stopped traffic, sure there'd been an accident. "I'm a vet, not a physician."

"There's an elephant down. Grab the bag from behind the seat and follow me. C'mon. No time to waste!"

He disappeared into traffic once again.

"Christ!" she muttered, and reached with shaking hands for the old, black leather medical bag behind her seat. Traveling and a lack of sleep had finally gotten to her and her stomach rebelled, sending a mouthful of bile into her throat. She swallowed, chiding herself, knowing she'd be no good to Andrew or the elephant in her current condition.

Though she had no idea where she was going or what she'd

be facing, she followed Andrew and held her breath, trying to ignore the heat, the smells of spicy food, and over-heating vehicles. Rounding a Mercedes pickup, she spotted the hulk of a large elephant surrounded by a screaming crowd of locals, all pushing on the animal as if their frustration would compel him to rise.

Without even checking for a heartbeat, she knew the animal was gone, and their efforts were futile. The elephant's legs had buckled underneath the weight of an ornate wooden carrier strapped to its back. Its pupils were fixed and its large, pinkish-gray tongue lolled from the side of its mouth.

Andrew glanced back at her and slowly shook his head. He knew, too.

A short man with black hair that flapped around his head like wings circled around the animal. Tears running down his face, he muttered what sounded like prayers. Andrew approached him and said a few words in Thai that sent the man into fresh wails. He pounded his own forehead with the flat of his hand and his shoulders shook. Andrew continued to speak quietly and even though Natalie knew none of the language, she sensed the words were meant to console. It seemed that no amount of words would assuage the grief the man was feeling. Her throat constricted as she turned away.

On the way back to the truck, Andrew explained that the elephant and the man roamed Bangkok's streets daily, the elephant hauling giddy tourists for short rides. They returned every night to a dusty, small, side street where the man chained the elephant outside a one-room apartment, shared a few pieces of rotten fruit with the animal, and expected the elephant to perform the same tricks every day, no matter the weather or the abundance (or lack of) food. Though the work had torn the elephant's sensitive foot pads and the heavy weight of the carrier created permanent indentations in its back, the handler and his elephant were best friends.

"If we'd gotten here sooner, we might've been able to save him," Andrew said quietly, more to himself than to her. "We could've purchased the ellie, the man would've had enough money to take care of his family, and we could've brought the ellie to the sanctuary to live out the rest of his life. Ten, maybe twenty, years. In peace. Damn. Bloody hell!"

He didn't say another word during the long drive north to the sanctuary, and Natalie didn't mind. She felt his sadness and though she wanted to console him, waves of nausea made her want nothing more than to nap.

Staring out the window into the rain that now fell into the dark landscape, she wondered whether she'd made the right decision to come to Thailand.

Three

THE DAY WAS ALREADY beyond hot, well into the realm of heatstroke-inducing, when Natalie opened her cabin door a little after six in the morning. Her first morning in Thailand. She wanted to relish it, but her last conversation with her mother echoed in her mind, a remnant of last night's dream.

You're running away, Natalie. Sooner or later you need to face what has happened. Hiding with your animals will never help you learn what you really need . . . Natalie, are you listening to me? Will you ever learn how to communicate like a human being?

But I can't stay here, Maman . . . I can't.

Are you going to have cell reception, Nat? Will we be able to keep in touch? I want to know that you got there okay. There's always something going on over there in those third world countries. You need to make sure we can contact you.

Ignoring the echoes from home, Natalie took a deep breath and stretched her arms skyward, yawned, and filled her lungs with Thailand's mountain air. As she exhaled, she shoved aside yesterday's nightmarish elephant incident with a mantra she'd invented a year ago.

Concentrate on this, she told herself. *This moment. Everything begins now.*

During the past year, she learned to compartmentalize. She pushed her grief aside when she was at work. Performing surgeries on horses—whether they were pets or million-dollar breeders—required her complete control. She had another compartment for the anger she constantly carried. There were days she found herself in her driveway, no idea how she'd gotten there. But somehow, she moved through her life one heart-mincing moment at a time. At least—that's what everyone else believed.

No one knew how often the terrifying flashes of gunfire startled her at random times, or of her heart-pounding nightmares of seeing the boys slide off the edge of a cliff and being unable to reach them. No one could understand the bone-chilling shakes her body withstood whenever she imagined seeing her children on the street, then realizing they were someone else's. And she told no one that her flight to Thailand was a last-ditch effort to cure the paralyzing stress that often left her feeling it would have been better if she'd been one of the victims rather than the boys. The only thing that kept her going was saving horses' lives, and now, she'd be saving elephants.

She inhaled again. Slowly. *Concentrate.* Then exhaled. Long. Deep. *This moment.* She forced herself to focus and looked out on her surroundings. *Beginning now.*

So this is what the sanctuary looked like by sunlight.

Below the deck, a small, carefully-kept garden of yellow and orange marigolds and sunflowers bobbed with the early morning breeze. That little patch of flowers told her far more than Andrew Gordon relayed in the emails and photos he'd exchanged with her before she arrived. Obviously left by the last tenant of this cabin, the flowers spoke of the need to create a home, to care for this place and its mission. The flowers spoke of a full heart. As she stood at the door of the tiny cabin she'd call home for the next year, she knew that each day would be one of sensory overload.

She'd been to Thailand before, but she'd never really *seen* Thailand. Not *this* Thailand. Not the wild, feral jungles and open expanse of untamed meadows. Not the blinding night that thrummed with both the smallest insect songs, and the trumpet of the largest land mammal on earth. Not the steamy mist hanging over the Kwai river, creating a soft, magically green world filled with gigantic, gray ghosts.

Beyond the vibrant garden that edged the deck where she stood, rolled a verdant, lush meadow, acres and acres of gently-waving tall grasses. And beyond that, mountains. Kanchanbouri province's Khao Kamphaeng Mountains. So many different shades of green: emerald and lime and forest and absinthe and moss and olive. Not maternal and round and black-green as those she knew in North Carolina, but instead, emerald spikes jaggedly rising toward the sky like nature's cathedral spires. Odd angles. Sharp outcroppings. The mountains glowed an otherworldly light green, the color of Granny Smith apples, a beacon from the messy jungle that climbed up the mountains' otherwise intractable sides.

The air felt heavy with moisture and glistened with a rich, golden sunlight so thick she could have drunk it. The light moved with the trees, changing as the wind swayed the branches. The filtered sunlight made her feel as if her body itself—every vein and muscle—reached out to respond to its sensual warmth as well as the moist touch of the breeze.

Off in the distance, she saw movement, as if the horizon undulated, the heat creating an invisible wall of steam. She shaded her eyes and focused. And then she saw them.

The sanctuary's elephants.

The elephants moved slowly, stopping for long moments to feed on the supple, tall grasses. She counted eight, then another four, further away. The second group of elephants were smaller, the teenaged males Andrew had mentioned at the conference, she suspected. They would be less likely to stay with the herd, ostracized by the matriarch in order to prevent in-breeding. Nature's natural selection. The line of massive, grey shadows moved closer, and she realized they were coming toward the sanctuary's buildings. It must be time for breakfast.

Beyond her cabin, she heard the murmur of human voices rising above the birdsong and the rustling of tree leaves. She wasn't the only one awake and ready to start the day.

"I didn't think you'd be up so early." Andrew's quiet voice surprised her. He came from behind, a dark silhouette, then he moved through the shadows and became a pudgy square of white, dappled by the tree's leaves. His silvery-blond hair lifted from his forehead in wisps and caught the sun, creating a shimmering, backlit halo. He reminded her of a benevolent grandfather, a man she'd trusted the instant she met him. He was dressed all in white as he had been when he picked her up at the airport yesterday and was, surprisingly, still clean in spite of the brown dust that seemed to creep into everything. With a heavy hand on the porch rail, he glanced up at her, a smile on his thin lips and crinkles in the corners of his bright, blue eyes. "I bet you'd love a hot cuppa tea right about now, wouldn't you?"

His Liverpudlian accent masked the extent of his wealth and knowledge. He sounded oddly undignified, and Natalie supposed he fooled people the way some of her North Carolinian friends did. By maintaining their country accents, her friends created a persona that often worked when one of their Northern business partners wanted to negotiate a contract. "Never take my accent as an indication I'm a fool," a friend from Carolina once told her. The same was true with Andrew.

"Come with me," he said now, reaching out a fleshy hand. "I'll show you around my estate." He cackled, a humorously Draconian sound in this Garden of Eden. He reminded her of an old English version of Philip Seymour Hoffman, the brilliant American actor who'd died of a heroin overdose. Pudgy, ruddy-complexioned, and intense. The major difference between the two men was that Andrew made her feel protected. Safe.

They trekked over the same dusty path they had walked the previous evening but gone were the ominous shadows and eerie night sounds. Instead, their feet kicked up a reddish-brown cloud of dust that melted instantly back into the earth as if the humidity weighed it down, stopping it from rising more than a couple of inches from the ground. The road, smooth and packed and lined with trees, appeared shaven on each side as if by a giant set of shears.

The elephant road, she thought.

She smiled. Danny would have loved this. Stephen wouldn't have cared less. He would have rather been behind a computer writing and drawing than dealing with animals of any kind.

In the distance, an elephant trumpeted, and a deep male voice responded in what sounded like a command. Andrew continued talking as if he heard nothing.

"Almost fifteen exact square miles by American measurements." He waved a hand expansively and turned around, answering her unspoken question about the size of the sanctuary. "I know exactly what the bloody measurements are because we finished installing an electrified perimeter fence not a fortnight ago. About drained my supply budget, I'll tell you, but it's worth it. The fence protects the ellies by keeping them within a huge area where we can monitor them safely without putting them in small pens, or worse, chained. And it also keeps out human predators. Win-win situation. That scene you saw of the herd coming in from the Numong Meadow never would have been possible without that fence. Now the ellies can go wherever they want; they're almost as free as their cousins over there." He jerked a thumb over his shoulder, indicating the mountains behind them.

"Cousins?"

"A few thousand wild elephants living the way they should: in the jungle. Used to be more than a hundred thousand of them in Thailand, but through the years . . . well, you know how the elephant poachers work. It won't be long before they'll kill off the whole bloody population." He choked back some undefined emotion. Frustration. Anger. Grief. "This country reveres the elephant, but they also use the animal for their own benefit, training ellies for battle, or to carry the royal families, or haul logs off those mountains in the distance." He sighed. "They've helped farmers plow their fields and served humans in whatever other ways humans needed them until they were replaced by machinery. Then the ivory trade trumped everything. Human vanity." He shook his head.

She nodded. "My son Danny did a project in third grade on elephants and, at one point, I had to stop him from looking at the videos online. They broke his heart."

"Friggin' poachers. We battle them daily—both here and in Kenya. Not many know it, but the drug trade is heavily funded by ivory." He spat and hit the ground near a tree trunk.

Natalie hadn't known that, yet she wasn't surprised. Years of working with horses taught her way more than she wanted to know about the ways human greed destroyed magnificent animals. She'd had to euthanize many horses that had been pushed to the brink by owners who wanted them to run faster, leap higher, perform incredible feats. And when a horse died or was tragically injured, the owner would buy another one. Andrew was right: what happened to most animals was largely the result of human vanity.

Andrew continued, "Thailand's elephant herds dwindled from nearly half a million, both wild and domesticated, at the beginning of the twentieth century, to a total of not quite ten thousand at the present time. Can you believe that?"

She nodded again. One of the reasons Natalie had come to the sanctuary was because of their commitment to give some of those broken, blind, and dispirited elephants a chance to live the rest of their lives with the comfort and dignity they deserved. She had privately admitted to herself on the plane coming here that working to help animals in a country where no one knew her might help her heal. Now she wondered whether she might be wrong. Maybe being here would make her grief worse.

She forced her legs to move and followed Andrew. Clouds of dust filled her nostrils and clogged her throat. Coughing into her fist, she counted to eight then backwards, as Dr. Littlefield had taught her. *Concentrate,* she told herself. *Breathe.*

"Ah, here's the sanctuary family." Andrew pointed beyond the trees, and Natalie spotted the main building. The open veranda held a milling group of people, some talking quietly, dark heads together, while others clustered in small groups on the porch overlooking the meadow. Maybe twenty people in all. Several elephants stood leaning against the concrete pilings that supported the sprawling structure, resting their foreheads against the iron railings.

The smell of cooking lifted Natalie's chin. Though she couldn't identify the food, her stomach rumbled, and she realized suddenly that she hadn't eaten in almost twenty-four hours.

A tiny figure broke from the larger group and ran down the stairs, followed by two dogs: one large and black with long legs—a Shepherd mix, it appeared; and the other—white, fluffy, and scarcely larger than a Chihuahua. As the child sprinted toward them, raising mini, brown tornadoes in the dirt, it became clear that it was a little girl, shining black hair cut bluntly at shoulder length, barefoot and dressed in a bright orange, cotton floral dress. Her face sparkled with the largest gap-toothed smile Natalie had ever seen. The closer she came, the more Natalie realized the child was not going to slow down.

"My little whirlwind!" Andrew reached for the child as she leapt fearlessly into his arms and wrapped her legs around his waist. She hugged him tightly around the neck, chattering in a tiny, high-pitched voice. All the while, her dark eyes stared curiously at Natalie.

Natalie smiled at the child, but she simply stared back as if she'd been told not to trust strangers.

Andrew said something in Thai to the toddler then turned to Natalie. "This little darling is the camp mascot, Sivad. Her mother Mali works as one of the cooks, so this little one and her brothers live here. The mahouts and their families do, too, as well as the administrative staff. Those cabins around yours are for volunteers, but there's another set farther downriver where everyone else lives."

The dogs circled at Andrew's ankles, as excitedly as Sivad had greeted him, but Andrew ignored them, so they sniffed at Natalie instead. She patted their heads and watched two more join them:

a Golden Retriever mix and one that resembled a Beagle. All appeared healthy and clean. Unlike the strays she had seen on the streets of Bangkok, these were pets. Their little group grew larger by the second as more dogs arrived. By the time they reached the stairs, they had become a pack of six dogs and three humans. Buoyed by their cheerful energy, Natalie couldn't help but smile.

She mounted the stairs behind Andrew and Sivad and realized why she hadn't seen anyone else. *This must be where everyone starts their morning*, Natalie reasoned. Several groups filled the platform. People in their early twenties, probably volunteers, circled around one of the long picnic tables and spoke English, but the group of cigarette-smoking young men sitting and standing at the far end of the platform near the elephants spoke Thai. Under the overhang at the back of the building, a third group—three Thai women—bustled around an open cook-stove, clouds of steam rising above them.

No one paid attention to her arrival, which Natalie thought strange. Being ignored felt more uncomfortable than if she'd been ambushed, but perhaps they were used to seeing people arrive for daily visits and figured Andrew would take care of her.

"You'll meet the mahouts and the elephants they care for in a little bit," Andrew told her. "Each elephant has a caretaker, their mahout, and first thing in the morning, they have to feed the ellies, then take them for a mud bath. It's the busiest time of day. I'm sure you'll get right into the swing of things once you see how everything works." He reached for some overripe bananas and tossed them to one of the elephants. "You have so many skills we need, but you'll probably find there's lots to learn, as well. Like feeding these giant eating machines. These guys eat sixteen to eighteen hours a day, and most of them have special diets because of their advanced age or the various injuries they've suffered at human hands. We're too damn cruel." He shook his head, but it was a momentary pause before he grabbed her elbow and spun her around to face the group of people at a picnic table.

"Everyone, I want you to welcome Dr. Natalie DeAngelo just over from America. She's a fabulous vet with lots of big animal experience in North Carolina. She'll be here for the next year, so make sure to make yourself available. Answer her questions and all that." He smiled at her and patted her shoulder. "Now, let me introduce our crew. This," Andrew gestured to his right, "is Dr. Peter Hatcher. Been the resident vet for, what, eight years, Peter?"

Hatcher was a pale, blond man, tall and thin. When he shook her hand, his knobby wrists belied the strength in his grip.

"Welcome to the sanctuary," he said, his British accent far more clipped than Andrew's. "You here for the month or are you staying more permanently?" He gave her a tight-lipped smile, or at least she thought it was a smile. His eyes didn't light up at all.

"Clean the dust out of your ears, Peter! We're lucky to have Dr. DeAngelo with us. One of the brightest in equine surgery, she is. Not one of our university volunteers, though she certainly looks young enough, doesn't she? A bright little brown bird!" Andrew reached over and wrapped an arm around her shoulders like a great uncle. "She trained in North Carolina. Fulbright scholar for North Carolina State out of Raleigh. One of the best programs in the States. I respect what they've done with their husbandry program. Great work. I suspect she'll be a great help to us in the year she's here. I'm quite excited about having her."

"I'm surprised you didn't say anything to me, Andrew. We usually discuss such things." Hatcher's words dripped icicles as brittle as his pale blue eyes.

Andrew's grip tightened on Natalie's shoulder. "We can talk about this another time."

"Maybe we need to talk about it before Dr. DeAngelo—that's the name isn't it?—gets settled in." He nailed Natalie with a penetrating stare that made her pull her chin back as if he'd slapped her face. "You wouldn't have known that I know Dr. DeAngelo, unless you'd told me she was coming, Andrew, but since you didn't bother saying anything, I'll just tell you now." He turned to Natalie. "Do you have any idea who I am, Doctor?"

Shit, should I? Natalie felt her cheeks redden. She should have done more research, she thought, but getting everything wrapped up in the past month had left her little time to do any kind of research at all. Closing the clinic, getting the house ready, packing for the trip. That was enough. She flipped through the business cards in her mind. Had she met him at a conference? Had he written a book or an article recently? Made a breakthrough of some sort? She came up blank.

"Obviously, you have no idea." He drew himself up, straightened his shoulders, and huffed like a discontented Oxford professor. "Let me introduce myself. Peter Hatcher of Yorkshire. Trained at the Royal Veterinary College. Ring any bells?"

Everyone had begun listening to the conversation. A small group had gathered. All silent.

She shook her head, feeling absolutely clueless. "I've been to the Royal Vet, but that was many years ago when I was a Fulbrighter."

"And after you came home and continued your surgical work, did you have any connections with the school?"

"Peter, is this really necessary?" Andrew forced a smile but placed a warning hand on Peter's arm. Andrew glanced at the redness around Peter's hairline and the accompanying beads of sweat. For some strange reason, the man appeared ready to lose control.

"Yes, as a matter of fact, I did." Natalie pushed harder to remember a Hatcher from the school, but she couldn't place him. He was distinctive looking, tall with stringy muscles and a face quite sharp in its angles. She wouldn't have forgotten him.

"And you were one of the final readers for dissertations, weren't you? Never mind, you don't have to answer. I can tell by your face that you're starting to put two and two together. Listen closely, Andrew, because this is the kind of person you've just hired. I did my research work on formulating a cement we could inject into a horse's broken leg. It worked. It did." He pointed a finger into the air, as if to add an exclamation point to his comment. "We had plenty of studies to prove it, but when the dissertation got to Dr. DeAngelo, well, she became the fly in the ointment. She questioned everything we'd done. Every blessed report. Every statistic. Basically said we had not been able to validate our research and debunked my work completely." He laughed sharply. If possible, his eyes hardened even more. He stared directly at her as he continued. "I had to start again from scratch! Different topic. New study. Hours and hours and hours of work. And years of my time. Years! And you know what was so damned ironic? The cement worked. She started using it—my cement—in her clinic a year after she read my dissertation. A year after! And did she ever give me one ounce of credit? She never admitted to the academics who credited her with the glue that it wasn't her invention. This is the woman." He pointed at her and looked at Andrew. "This is the cheat you've hired."

As Hatcher ranted, some of the volunteers walked away, looking over their shoulders. Natalie remembered the dissertation. Yes, it had needed work, but she hadn't realized until much later that her questions had caused such an uproar. She remembered the research about eight months later when she was approached with a new product, much like the one discussed in the dissertation.

"Yes, I used the cement," she told Hatcher, "but I never claimed I invented it. Someone else sold it to me—a pharmaceutical rep from South Africa. The rest of the surgeons in the field had the option of purchasing it, as well. I was just the first to use it. I would never steal anyone's research, Dr. Hatcher. That's not the way I work. Honestly."

His eyes narrowed as he looked at her. "I don't believe you, and Andrew, I don't want to work with her. Period."

Someone gasped. Natalie felt a burning in the pit of her stomach and wanted desperately to escape, but the small group of people who were left tightened around her, as if in suspense about what Hatcher might do next. No one spoke for half a minute. Natalie glanced at Andrew, the only person at the table that she knew, and she didn't really know him all that much. Why would he believe her when Dr. Hatcher had worked here for years? She held her breath, wondering whether she would be on the next truck back to Bangkok, heading home.

Andrew twisted his mouth and let his hand drop from Peter's

arm, as if disgusted by his actions. Obviously, they had some history. "We'll talk about this later, Dr. Hatcher," he said in a voice low enough that only the three of them could hear. "For right now, you'll welcome Dr. DeAngelo. You and I will discuss your concerns after lunch. My office."

Though Natalie hadn't known the philanthropist personally for very long, Andrew Gordon had a reputation for being in control of his own ship. To her, that translated to keeping a close eye on his subordinates, especially those in charge of running any of his sanctuaries in Asia and Africa. But it appeared he was being challenged, and years of watching for signs of aggression in animals told her the two men could very easily have been facing off against each other as wolves often did. Years of experience also told her that this wasn't the first time these two men had confronted each other.

Andrew grabbed Natalie's shoulder, turned his back on Hatcher, and led her to an empty table in the middle of the expansive ten-foot-high concrete platform. "I'll get us some tea. You can take a peek at our residents." He swung an arm around, then retreated to a table where everyone had gathered to dispense their morning drinks.

All around the edges of the platform where she sat, elephants stood patiently waiting for their breakfast. Occasionally, one would grunt or snort or flap its ears, but otherwise, they were as quiet as apparitions. For a few moments, she studied the elephants' heads, noting the differences in their ears and their coloring. None of them were totally gray. Several were freckled, some pinkish, and others nearly white. Andrew returned with two cups of tea, as well as some *nam tao-hu*, a hot soy breakfast drink, and *pa tong go*, the deep fried bread sticks Danny had developed a taste for when he had tried them in the hotel in Bangkok.

"So, the story. Our story. We founded the sanctuary in 1989," Andrew began, a proud smile on his face. "Took this ten-thousand-acre trust, determined to make it home for abused elephants. The whole region is a mountainous jungle, as you can see, and the Kwai river gives us a headache when it regularly overflows its banks, but here and there, pockets of deep springs feed the river even during dry season and that gives us a constant source of water for the sanctuary and our elephants, which is incredibly important. Wish we had this river in Kenya. Water's always a problem there."

He took a sip of his tea and looked out into the distance, thoughtfully, as if seeing past the jungles and the river and its challenges. It was a few moments before he started again.

"That first year, when the sanctuary smelled of wet and rotten vegetation, a storm left the old-timers talking for months. That damn storm was so strong the river created new tributaries and moved buildings as though a colossal hand lifted them and plopped them—*kaput!*—right smack down somewhere new like they were the tiniest of frogs. God, that was bloody awful." Andrew screwed up his mouth and shrugged his shoulders as if disgusted by the memory.

He pointed to where Natalie guessed the buildings were and turned back to her, his mouth open, ready to speak, when a blood-curdling scream rent the air. She dropped her cup. A thousand prickles of fear brought every inch of her skin to life.

THE ELEPHANT, *the one they call Sophie, wants air. She gasps for it. Her life depends on it.*

But she can't. She can't breathe, and the fear pounds in her chest, drums in her middle ear, clouds her vision.

It's the pain that has taken her breath.

Her leg burns as if she's stepped into a giant fire ant mound, as if thousands of the biting creatures have crawled under her skin, snapping and burning at every inch of her leg. She tears at it with her short tusks, doesn't care that she's ripping the skin. She wants the pain gone. All of it. Now.

The elephant screams, vocalizing her pain with the trumpet, feeling the power of her own voice as it rides up from her belly to her abdomen to emerge in full force through her opened mouth. She lets the roar of her scream ripple into the jungle, climb up the mountainside, into the fish-scale clouds hanging low in the sky. And once the echoes stop, she screams again, and the sound acts as the key that opens up every other sensor in her body.

She opens her eyes and sees the crowd of humans around her. Feels their tension, their fear of her.

She smells the men. Their anger. Their distress. And something else. Something threatening. Cruel.

She hears voices yelling, the high-pitched sounds of human screams, the inconsistent orders from the mahouts. The sounds color the air with fiery streaks of crimson and orange that mimic the sizzling anger burning Sophie's eyelids.

She screams again, and this time, a glint of brightness catches her eye and stops her mid-bellow. A sharp pain in the wound steals her breath. A searing agony creates a fire from her knees up into her chest, into a set of lungs still tight, still unwilling to let her breathe.

She stumbles.

Her lips part. She feels her tongue loll. She stiffens her legs, forces herself upright again, because she's used to being strong. She's afraid of what will happen if she collapses to the ground.

The men. She fears the men.

Everywhere she looks, a human. Everywhere, the glint of that sun-dagger that split her skin. Everywhere, the acrid scent, the human life colors and sounds.

Now, they all jumble. The smells, the sounds, the colors. Too many men. Too much noise.

And the pain. Daggers of pain as large as mountains.

She bellows and lunges, snapped back instantly by the large rope at her ankle.

She wants to run into the rivers where the tide rises as high as the arms of the river trees. She wants to rut her tusks along the edge of the soft thick forest, ripping ravines into the mud that smells of other elephants' traces and thickens the air with its burnt and spicy odor. She wants to feel the strength in the legs that once could travel dozens of miles a day without a muscle quiver.

She wants the pain to stop.

For a very long time, she has lived with the burning flame in her leg. It engulfs her body with a heat that makes it possible to feel every pump of blood moving through her veins. The pain gives her no respite, no moment when she can breathe freely without the ever-present burn, no time when she can close her eyes and sleep for more than fifteen minutes without a jabbing reminder of the sore that has festered on her leg for all the days and nights of her time among humans.

She shakes her head, her giant ears flapping so hard that her teeth snap shut.

The men. The men cause the pain.

She tilts her head back to the sky, lifts her trunk and screams once more. A long, murderous scream designed to keep the men, those men who caused her pain, at a distance. A scream designed to warn.

Four

The spirit of a man will sustain
his infirmity; but a wounded
spirit who can bear?
-Proverbs 18:14

MAHOUTS SCRAMBLED TOWARD THE sound. Andrew sprinted along the length of the platform toward the commotion, as did everyone else, sweeping Natalie along with them. The trumpeting grew to a roar as they rounded the corner. People yelled. Her feet pounded in time with her heartbeat. Blood thrummed through her ears. Sweat dripped into her eyes. She realized she wasn't in the best shape for a sprint through one hundred percent humidity.

Within seconds, Natalie spotted the source of the roars: a group of mahouts struggled to contain a giant female elephant. The ellie's ears flapped angrily as she paced and charged. Backward. Forward. Her eyes rolled as the mahouts circled her, each holding a short hooked staff, an *ankus*. Her great feet shuffled, pulling the thick ropes that held her, and each time she reached the end of the ropes, she roared in full voice, a sound that literally shook the trees around them.

None of the other elephants had been tethered. The sanctuary staff prided themselves on letting their elephants roam free. Why had this one been hidden? She was obviously dangerous, but so much so that the mahouts needed *ankuses*?

The mahouts shouted commands at the elephant, none of which she obeyed. Instead, she roared her anger and wheeled on them. The ropes groaned and stretched. They wouldn't hold the big girl much longer.

A line of sweat popped out on Natalie's upper lip, and she checked for a line of escape, just in case. The PTSD she'd fought for the past year took hold. Her vision darkened, sounds sharpened. She heard the phantom gunshots, saw Danny's face in her mind's eye—imagining the awful, blank look on his face. Her hands shook uncontrollably. She shook her head to dispel the image. Started counting.

Several people knelt on the ground to the elephant's right tending to something she couldn't see. Natalie's head swam for a second, but then her veterinary training kicked in, and with one cautious glance toward the elephant, she headed for the group. She held her breath, hoping that the elephant hadn't killed someone. Her heart sank when the crowd parted for a second, long enough for her to see Dr. Hatcher's blonde hair, and between his knees on the ground, a yellow lab, its legs askew.

"He's still alive," Hatcher said to no one in particular. "But I don't know if his leg's broken. If that crazy elephant had been roaming free, this dog would be dead. No doubt."

Instinctively, Natalie pushed through the group and sank to the ground beside Hatcher. She ran her hands down the dog's forelimbs. "Broken in several places. Feels like the metacarpal and the radius." Her fingers moved swiftly but knowingly over the dog's torso, then along the spine. "I don't think there are any other broken bones, but . . ."

The dog whimpered softly, his large brown eyes watching Natalie as if certain she knew what she was doing.

"I need some splints. If you don't have splints, straight pieces of wood will do. And tape. Any kind. A gurney, too. Where's the clinic? We're going to need to get him somewhere I can set the leg. You have an x-ray machine here?"

Silence.

Natalie glanced around. Hatcher had stopped what he was doing and stared at her. His neck turned a bright red that slowly crept up his cheeks. Instantly, she realized that while her instinct was to jump into action, she'd inadvertently stepped on Hatcher's toes. She started to apologize but was interrupted by Andrew, who'd reached the scene right before Natalie. He broke into rapid Thai. Shouting orders, she suspected. Two of the mahouts leapt to their feet and jogged down the road. Hatcher moved away, heading for the elephant.

Within seconds, the mahouts returned with a small gurney for the dog. As they carried him away, Natalie watched Hatcher accept a giant needle from one of the mahouts. Three staff members had looped restraining ropes around the ellie and held her as Hatcher inserted the needle. *A sedative*, Natalie figured. The elephant's swollen front right leg was practically double the size of the left. A large open wound oozed a yellowish puss. An infection, for sure, but she had no idea whether the damage had been done a week ago or years prior. The elephant's giant ears opened wide and flapped, a sure sign she was in the anxiety red zone.

"That wound looks close to being septic. How have you been caring for it?" she asked. She meant the question for Hatcher, but he didn't answer. Perhaps he didn't hear her. Perhaps he didn't want to answer. Perhaps she shouldn't have pushed her way into the situation.

Sometimes she wished she were better at reading body language.

But isn't that why I'm here? Dr. Littlefield had said that to learn about yourself, you need to study how others respond to you. She'd given the task to Natalie as a homework assignment for the next year. "You've got to be your own therapist," she'd said. "Pay attention to yourself, as well as to the others around you." She'd urged Natalie to keep a daily journal, noting her own actions as well as others' reactions. "Connect to at least one person a day. The only way you'll learn to trust again is to open yourself to the possibilities. I know it might sound like a cliché, but you've got to lower some of the walls you've built. Trust your own gut reactions again."

"Damn dogs don't know when to keep their tails out of the way," Andrew said as he lowered to his knees behind her. "That blasted elephant is going to kill one of them someday. She's a malignant thing, as Shakespeare would say."

"Not if you let me put her down," Hatcher said. "She's a danger to everyone here, as well as herself." He knelt on the other side of Natalie. The mahouts had led the now docile elephant into a barn-like structure barely visible beyond the tree-line. Natalie watched as Hatcher examined the dog in the identical manner as she had. He bumped her out of the way with his hip.

"Feels like the metacarpal might have suffered a couple of major breaks," Natalie offered as she moved to her haunches and stroked the dog's head.

"We won't know until we take x-rays." Hatcher's manner was dismissive as if he couldn't be bothered listening to her. He turned his back to her.

"So you *do* have an x-ray machine."

He nailed her with a cold, over-the-shoulder stare and turned away once again.

She suppressed a sudden urge to slap him, but that would be entirely unprofessional, not to mention a sure way to get off to a disastrous start. She choked back her anger. There'd never been a time prior to being diagnosed with PTSD that she'd had a temper, but now the smallest thing could set her off. When her secretary sat Natalie down to point out the impatience that had pushed away most of Natalie's friends and co-workers, she realized she needed to get it under control. Obviously, there was still work to do.

Think it through, she told herself. *You're the new girl on the block.*

She needed to give Hatcher his space. And respect. After all, he'd been here for years, and she had scarcely arrived. Though she'd been trying to help, he might find her pushy. Not the right way to make friends, she knew, but he wasn't innocent either. A bit of manners on his part wouldn't hurt. She hadn't been bent on ruining his life so many years ago when she evaluated his theories, as he apparently believed. She'd been doing her job. Surely any educated person would understand that.

They made a small procession to the clinic only a couple of buildings away. Natalie could hear the elephant—*had they called her Sophie?*—roaring from the barn-like structure. She hoped they were able to control her and simultaneously prayed they weren't hurting her. No terrified animal deserved to be hurt. Yet, this dog was pretty damn scared, too.

Without speaking, Natalie worked on the dog with Hatcher as a team, stabilizing the right leg that had been broken in six different places, not the two or three Natalie had originally thought. The dog would be lucky to walk again without a brace.

When they finished splinting the dog's leg, Hatcher pulled off his gloves and tossed them in the trash, then turned back to Natalie. Everyone had left the clinic fifteen minutes before, so they were alone.

"Let's get something straight." A slight redness highlighted his cheeks as he pointed his finger at her. "I understand you've run your own clinic, but this one is mine, and if I'm not mistaken, your specialty is equine—not pachyderm—surgery, as mine is, so I might be able to teach you a thing or two."

She started to protest and to explain, but he held up a hand that effectively silenced her.

"I know Andrew thinks you're some kind of . . . *wunderkind*, as it were, and you might well be, but if we are to work together, you will follow my surgery's rules, and the first and most important one for you to remember is that you, my dear, are a volunteer. I am the full-time, paid member in this surgery. Not you. You take your marching orders from me. Things are done my way. Are we clear?"

Natalie had already risen, her hands shaking, a huge knot of self-doubt in her chest. How naive she'd been to believe this place and this experience would be the panacea for much of the pain and sorrow she felt. She kicked herself for having her head in the clouds, a fault Maman had always been quick to point out: *Dreaming of how things should be brings nothing but disappointment. Be ready for reality, and it will never hurt.*

The reality was that she'd come here in the hopes that she'd be able to successfully move past the worst of the PTSD by working so hard she'd fall into bed exhausted every night. Maybe she'd be able to conclude the most painful part of her grief. The reality was she wasn't alone in this place, and the others—especially Peter Hatcher—had their own agenda.

"Crystal clear," Natalie told Hatcher through clenched teeth.

She strode out of the clinic on stilt-like legs and gave serious thought to walking straight out of the sanctuary and thumbing a ride back to Bangkok. But that thought only lasted as long as the walk back to her cabin.

She'd never been a quitter. She wasn't about to start now.

Five

Man is an animal which, alone among
the animals, refuses to be satisfied by
the fulfillment of animal desires.
-Alexander Gordon Bell

"WE'VE BROKEN YOU IN right properly, haven't we, love?"
Andrew grinned at her devilishly as they ate their lunch. He'd
urged everyone to gather back on the platform for their afternoon meal, served banquet-style on one of the large picnic tables.
"Believe me, it's not always this exciting. Most of the elephants are
boring old dears. Sophie's the only one who's regularly a bother."

With the sun directly overhead on the end of the platform
where they sat, the day's humidity made North Carolina's summer
appear more like autumn. Natalie felt logy, unable to move. Her
t-shirt and shorts stuck to her skin like Saran Wrap.

After they finished eating, Andrew invited her to meet the
elephants that she hadn't met that morning. Their giant heads
bobbed at the edge, even with the concrete platform. She guess-
timated the platform to be a dozen feet off the ground. The herd
had wandered in from the meadow where they freely roamed
only an hour before. Now they waited patiently for their specially
prepared meals. Quiet. Dignified. Enormous grayish-pink ears
waving away insects. Shifting from one foot to another. Inquisi-

tive trunks reaching out like snakes. Large caramel brown eyes watching her passively.

"All of these lovelies have been abused. Humans train elephants to do things that they should never do," Andrew stated as he walked slowly in front of her, gently touching the trunks reaching out to touch him. "They are not meant to pirouette on their hind legs, yet circuses have forced them to perform that way for centuries. Their backs are not strong enough to withstand more than one hundred pounds, yet trekking camps outfit the ellies with wooden boxes that weigh far more, then they fill those boxes with humans. That's far more than their spines can withstand. And elephants do *not* paint. Whoever concocted that bloody ridiculous idea knew that these dignified creatures will do anything for their mahouts."

Natalie's mouth twisted. Physical abuse made her stomach churn. It enraged her. *Channel your anger*, she told herself. *Control it.* She'd come unhinged more than once during her career, and the aftermath of her rage was never pretty. She'd lost more than one client through the years. *Control it. Make it work for something good.*

"Some of our ellies are ancient: rheumy-eyed and slope-backed. Others, like that one to the right: alert and adolescent. None of them move very quickly, but they can, if they want to. I've seen some elephants sprint, so keep that in mind."

"I know. I saw them do that during the time I spent at the Wildlife Farm in Texas. That was about fifteen years ago, but I remember it well."

He stole a glance at her. "Then you know elephants charge anything they consider a threat, and though they appear benevolent and lazy now, you must respect their sheer size and powerful strength. Not only can they bring down a full grown oak, but they can topple trucks by simply leaning against them. They do it here all the time. And their trunks are not used only for eating, smelling, and drinking, but you know that, don't you?" He didn't wait for her to answer. "I've seen an elephant toss a guy who weighed more than two hundred pounds as if he was a piece of tissue paper. Broke his back, both legs and dislocated his shoulder. Poor bugger."

She groaned and sucked a breath between her teeth making a whistling sound that caused the large bull elephant near them to raise his head and look at her quizzically

"Make sure you stay where they can see you, love," Andrew told her. "They'll watch you. Size you up. If you're going to administer medicines or treat them, they will have to build a relationship with you first." He winked at her. "Some'll be more anxious to cross that bridge than others. Like this ol' flirt." He walked to the large bull whose enormous tusks rested on the concrete platform. The elephant rumbled contentedly.

"This is Ali. He's about thirty-two years old. He's a bit scarred from the way he's been treated over the years, but still quite handsome, eh? His mahouts weren't too kind to him when they were training him, yet he still loves humans. Amazing, huh? This guy does fine and loves the ladies. Don't you, ol' boy?"

Andrew reached into one of the large palm leaf baskets the volunteers placed on the platform and found a couple of small plantains. He waved them in front of Ali's trunk, causing the elephant's trunk to follow the snack like a cobra dancing to flute music. Andrew kept the bananas out of range for a moment before Ali greedily grabbed them.

Andrew chuckled and reached for more, then handed them to Natalie. "We all need to help at mealtimes."

Natalie gingerly held out the mushy, rotten bananas toward Ali.

"Make sure you stay where he can see you and hold the food close enough for him to reach. Believe me, he'll find it."

Sure enough, Ali stretched his trunk in her direction and grabbed the bananas. His trunk felt soft and wet but strong. When he wrapped the tip of it around her hand to grab the bananas, one of her rings slipped off her finger, and she watched it fly over the railing. It flipped to the ground, landing near the elephant's heavy foot.

"Oh crap, that's the ring . . . that's a special ring. Stephen—

my son—gave it to me." She hesitated, watching Ali's legs shift. She pointed to the mahout who sat near her on the crossbars above the elephant's head, pantomiming that she'd lost her ring and that it was on the ground. If Ali shifted even half a foot, he'd step right on it. As easily as a child shimmying down a tree, the mahout jumped off the porch, picked up the ring and hopped back up to where Natalie waited. She thanked him, and told Andrew she felt somewhat guilty that she'd made so much of it. In this country of Buddhists, such a connection to personal valuables was unusual. Sentimental value outweighed monetary value any time.

"No worries," Andrew answered. "I've kept every scrap of paper Sivad colors for me."

Natalie wiped the simple, silver ring clean and stuck it in her pocket, fighting back the memory of eight-year-old Stephen at Christmastime, so proud of his gift that he smiled, baring the gap where he'd lost his first tooth. Her hands trembled a bit when she turned back to the task of feeding Ali. Overly ripe bananas, some melons, small pomegranates, squash, and a few potatoes seemed an odd mix, but Ali didn't seem to mind. He grabbed each handful with his trunk, then leisurely lifted the pungent mush into his mouth, never taking his lushly-fringed brown eye off of her. She talked to him quietly as she fed him, making sure to remain in his line of sight, as Andrew had directed.

All along the platform, mahouts and volunteers mirrored Natalie's actions. The mahouts—young, fairly small, and agile men—laughed among themselves as they hand-fed their elephants. On occasion, one of them would shout a sharp command and though Natalie didn't know what they were saying, she studied the elephant's response and the techniques each mahout used to keep his charge in line.

"I wonder if some of the training skills we use with horses would work with the elephants," she mused, more to herself than to Andrew.

"Probably." Andrew watched her, smiling. "You always wanted to work with animals since you were a wee thing, didn't you, love?

She nodded. "I volunteered at horse farms long before I opened the clinic, and, even as a little girl, I'd sit for hours watching the horses and our dogs, learning their cues and reading their responses, mainly to keep from getting kicked or bitten." She laughed a little, remembering the day Dr. Slater, one of her favorite professors at NC State's vet program, told her in earshot of other students, "At least you don't anthropomorphize animals like ninety-nine percent of those other buffoons." They'd barely finished a particularly tough day that had sent three other students to the infirmary with damaging bites from the orang-utans they'd been studying. Only six students, including Natalie (the only female in the group) were left out of twenty-four.

"Animals are not humans," Dr. Slater told the group, "and the only good vet is the one who never forgets that."

He was so right. So damn right on the money. Yet, her deepest, darkest secret is that she talks to the animal she treats. She can't help it. She tries to think about her predilection in an intellectual fashion. She manages to occasionally convince herself that it's just the rumbling sound she makes when she talks that calms down her animals, but she knows the communication between species has many layers. It's deeper than just the sound of a human voice. It's inflection, emotion, delivery, and the actual words. She thinks often of Dr. Slater and whether he'd believe now that animals understand language.

With Dr. Slater still on her mind, she finished feeding Ali the last bits of fruits and vegetables in the basket. Then she sat cross-legged on the platform in front of him, patting his trunk as he inquisitively checked out her legs and arms, touching her softly, snuffling a bit as he did so.

"Your bristly hair tickles, buddy," she said, stroking Ali's forehead. "You're a big ol' boy, aren't you? You're going to be my friend, huh? We're going to get along fine."

Ali's long, gray eyelashes flickered as he watched her. He munched on some palm fronds, slowly and thoughtfully, as if considering whether to grant her his friendship. He reminded her of what the elephant version of Albert Einstein would look like:

intelligent and funny with gray tufts of wiry hair creating puffs around the tops of his ears.

She smiled—a comfortable, natural smile. It had been a very long time since she'd smiled without forcing it, but immediately following the smile, the guilt resurfaced. She had no right to feel any kind of happiness.

She could feel her cheek muscles slackening and her eyes turning down at the sides. It felt as if her skin might slide right off her bones. She'd forgotten how many muscles it took to smile and how few to be unhappy.

"Come meet the folks you'll be working with every day." Andrew offered a hand to help her to her feet.

She ducked her head as he helped her up, not wanting him—or anyone else for that matter—to read the emotions she felt. Often, she couldn't even identify them herself, but she did know one thing for certain. A bit of happiness and a spontaneous outburst of love for another being were feelings she hadn't had in a while. She counted her steps as she followed along behind Andrew.

They walked along the platform that stretched from the main pavilion to a smaller seating area with a roof made of roughly hewn posts supported by large steel trusses. Further in the distance, Natalie saw another, smaller building that might have been offices or a storage area.

"That's Thaya." Andrew pointed to the elephant standing about ten feet away, a bit smaller than Ali, with a freckled, pink trunk and ears. "She's afraid of the water for some reason, so we're trying to help the old girl get over her fears. Never any good to have an anxious animal around. Besides, she'd be a lot cooler for her if she'd come into the river. Right now, though, she's content with her mud baths."

He gestured to the right of Thaya and pointed. "Khalan, her mahout. He's Mali's middle son, and he lets everyone know that he's strong." Andrew snorted as if that was far from true.

Khalan, a head shorter than she and more muscular than the others, flashed Natalie a mischievous, movie-star-white grin that showed off his dimples, then put his hands in prayer position at chest level and bowed respectfully. "*Sawadee krup.*"

"*Sawadee ka,*" she responded. The Thai language was gender specific. She had learned the feminine response to Khalan's masculine 'hello' during her first visit to Thailand, and it was the only phrase she remembered.

Mali's middle son wore a fluorescent orange and green short-sleeved soccer shirt over a ragged pair of knee-length black pants. *It would be hard to miss him in any crowd*, Natalie thought wryly. With a shy grin, he nodded to her before flipping over the railing like an Olympic gymnast. He climbed nimbly on bare feet over Thaya's back, to straddle her neck. Yelling a gruff command, he dug his heels in and turned Thaya's head. A flourish of her tail, and they ambled away, with his knees tucked against her ears, his face bent toward her ear, talking earnestly to her as if she were a dog. They walked away, Huck-Finn style, as if they were strolling along the Mississippi looking for a good place to go fishing.

"I'm surprised he's riding on her back," Natalie said to Andrew. "I thought trainers were getting away from riding that way."

"As long as he's right at her neck, she's fine. The mahouts all know that. How ellies have endured everything that's been loaded onto their spiky backbones without becoming crippled is beyond me. But you know my concerns. I'm sure you know their skeletal system better than I do, and I've been working with them for years."

Probably not, she thought, but she didn't repeat that aloud. If someone quizzed her right now to name each bone, she'd flunk, but she did know that their dorsal vertebrae stood almost straight up, meaning those bones could easily be broken. A pachyderm's back wasn't meant to take any weight at all.

The other elephants and mahouts started leaving the platform area, creating a long, slow-moving line that appeared headed for the dirt road that led to the river.

"We'll meet the rest of them later," Andrew said. "They don't waste any time heading for their baths after filling their tummies.

Things are pretty quiet here when they're down at the river. Perfect time to catch up on administrative work we need to do. Let's go meet the people who make this place run like a well-oiled machine. You're going to need to know them. They'll get what you want when you need it."

He took her elbow and steered her back to the tables in the middle of the platform. A partial roof covered the area, creating a welcome piece of shade under the sizzling morning sun.

"This is Karina, my little sister." Blonde and sturdy, Karina greeted Natalie with a firm handshake and a once-over that made Natalie slightly uncomfortable.

In a pinched, gruff voice, Karina asked Natalie where she'd received her degree, and when Natalie answered, Karina asked again, as if she didn't believe a vet with a degree from the North Carolina State University School of Veterinary Medicine was good enough for the sanctuary. Though Natalie felt slightly offended, she responded each time with a smile.

"Karina grew up across the Channel in Belgium," Andrew said, giving his sister a squeeze that made Karina roll her blue eyes. "Not quite an English lass, but we'll forgive her for that. Right, sweet girl?" He laughed as his sister punched his arm as though they were still teenagers. "Karina cooks the books here. You'll be talking to her about supplies and purchase orders and forging checks." This time he ducked as Karina doubled her fist and swung at him like a drunk street fighter.

They bantered and teased each other a bit, but Natalie only vaguely heard their jabs. She thought about her brother, Stefan, and how he'd made it his mission as a child to find every slimy reptile in their backyard and hide each under her pillow, expecting her to scream. He gave up when the aquariums on her bookshelf became permanent home to the reptiles he'd "gifted" her: Freddy the frog, Thomas the garter snake, Willy the gopher snake, and Sylvia the snapping turtle. Little did he know she would actually enjoy the reptiles. After that, he left her alone.

Danny and Stephen had teased each other unmercifully, too. She often told them of their Uncle Stefan's tricks, but times had changed, and the boys were more likely to zap each other with video game weapons than to hunt down reptiles.

Andrew continued to shepherd her through the group of volunteers. She nodded and shook hands, but if someone were to offer her a million dollars to repeat the name of the last person to whom she'd been introduced, she wouldn't have had a clue. Part of her reasoned that it was all right not to remember since volunteers lasted a short period of time. Some came for a day, some for a couple of weeks, and only a select few stayed longer than that.

Then, one last person. "And this gorgeous woman is Mali. You met her daughter earlier. Sivad." He hugged Mali as he had hugged his sister, but Natalie sensed this relationship was far from innocent. Mali was definitely not a sibling. This was his lover.

Shorter than Natalie by almost a foot, Mali radiated confidence that drew Natalie in. The Thai woman smiled and a deep dimple accented her left cheek. She greeted Natalie with a *Wai*, both hands in the prayer position over her heart, she bent at the hips, her thin body as straight as a bamboo pole.

"Good morning. I hope you'll be happy here." Mali's voice, deep and modulated, carried only a trace of a Thai accent. Instead, she sounded as properly British as Peter Hatcher.

Natalie tried not to show her surprise.

"Mali's probably the smartest person at this camp," Andrew continued. "Whatever you need or want, she can either procure it for you or she knows someone else who can. She's the person who's been with me the longest, and I keep trying to promote her to administrative manager, but Mali's stubborn."

"No, that's not true, Andrew. It's simply that I like to cook." Mali tilted her chin in his direction.

"Are you English?" Natalie asked.

"Not exactly." Mali pulled off her apron, balled it up, and tossed it into an ever-growing pile of aprons and towels in the corner. "I spent most of my childhood there in a little town north of Liverpool because my father worked there. He was an attaché for the ambassador. Age two to twenty-two, I went to school at

Oxford because my father insisted. But I was born right here, about fifteen kilometers away, actually. I guess since I learned to speak in England, the accent simply never left, but I'm Thai."

"Mali's family has always raised ellies. They're Karen," Andrew answered.

"Karen?"

"The original elephant trainers," Mali said with a laugh. She pulled off her turban and roughed up her bluish-black hair with a sigh as if she'd been waiting all day to do so. "Our tribe lives on the Burma border, in the mountains. The largest group of peoples. The original settlers. Most of the mahouts here are Karen. They've come from generations of mahouts. Thousands of years. Some were involved in logging. All of my uncles, my brothers, and even my sons, are mahouts. They begin the process as children with elephant calves, and the two grow up together. Most of the chaps you see here at the sanctuary are Karen. I'm the only person in my family who went to university, and even I can't stay away from the *chang*."

Natalie assumed the word meant elephant.

"Master's degree in Psychology, and look at me, I cook for people who spend their whole lives covered in elephant mud." Mali's robust laughter brought smiles to everyone around them. She glanced up at Andrew, and her eyes softened. "But I wouldn't have it any other way."

For a brief moment, Natalie felt jealous of the relationship they had, but a memory of her husband Parker's flashes of temper with her and her boys intruded. She squeezed her eyes closed and replaced the memory with a reminder to concentrate on the moment. *Parker is the past. This is the present. Now is all that matters.*

Mali lowered herself to a bench and gestured for Natalie to join her. "Come, let's get to know one another. Andrew tells me you're from North Carolina. I've never been there, but I've heard the weather there's nearly as hot and humid as this."

"Not this warm." Instinctively, Natalie knew this woman might become a friend, someone to talk to, someone who might share some of life's treasured moments. That was, if Natalie could trust herself enough to let down her walls and let Mali in.

Six

All the resources we need are in the mind.
-Theodore Roosevelt

SLEEP DIDN'T COME EASILY that night. Natalie's internal clock was so far off that she wondered whether it would right itself anytime soon. When the sun went down, the workers at The Lotus Animal Sanctuary did as well. Natalie found herself wide awake, raring to do research in her tiny cabin, and frustrated that she couldn't. She longed to text home, but her cell didn't work. She thought about researching the elephant—Sophie—and treatment for her wounds. Her mind whirred, but that's all it could do.

So, she unpacked.

Within an hour, she had her clothes, books, and toiletries in their places. She sat on the edge of her bed and checked her watch. 8:35 PM. She took out a book she'd been reading on the plane, but her eyes wouldn't focus.

Jet lag, she told herself. *It'll go away.* But four hours later, her eyes were still wide open, and her brain hadn't even begun to shut down. It was like being high on speed.

At one o'clock in the morning, she talked herself into lying on the bed and made a game out of listening to the jungle's sounds. She'd always won when she and her fellow veterinary students had played "which animal made this sound" in college. She'd even taught the boys how to identify bird calls. Danny was better at it than Stephen, but only because he loved to sit and listen. Stephen would rather be talking than listening.

She closed her eyes and listened. Besides the elephants' grunting and an occasional barking dog, she heard a small monkey (she wasn't sure what kind, and that irritated her), several night fisher-type birds, and some rustling that could have been a rodent or a cat (she'd seen several on the grounds earlier in the day). She'd identified more than twenty-five sounds when her body finally relaxed into the bed, and the jungle sounds disappeared into the sleep world.

It was a light sleep. She remained aware of her body and that she was in a strange place, but dreams intruded on reality. Short snippets of voices, deep and far-away. An image of someone's hand, a small hand, reaching. The jolt of falling, then catching one's self.

She had the sensation of floating, then Danny's voice was in her ear. She sensed him nearby. In her dream, she reached for him, longing to press his skinny body against her, to hug him more tightly than she ever had.

She held her arms out again.

Mom, you remember the time we went to that zoo in, where was it? Asheville?

Asheboro, sweetie. It was in Asheboro. She knows she's saying the words aloud, talking in her sleep, and feels her consciousness rise a little, but she doesn't want to wake up. Not as long as she can see her boys.

I didn't like that place. Don't think the animals did either.

I know. That's why I'm here. I'm trying to make sure animals like those zoo animals have a better life.

An image of a carousel, a man selling pine cones nearby, the laughter of a young girl. She suddenly straddled a white steed, its mane festooned with carved wooden roses so real she could almost smell them. It was summer. She felt the sun's heat through the long filmy dress she wore. She watched its pink ripples flow beneath her, blown by the soft breeze across her face. In the distance, the squeak of a young elephant's trumpet.

She woke abruptly. Sat upright in the bed. The world around her was quiet. No animal sounds at all. She laid back down and closed her eyes.

The dream was still there. She slid into it, longing for her sons, calling Danny's name in her mind, but she wasn't near the carousel anymore. Instead she stood on the edge of an expansive meadow. Small white and yellow flowers blossomed at the top of hip-deep grasses that swayed like the waves of the ocean, mounding, then flattening and retreating.

She touched the flowers. They felt warm, as if some of the sun's rays had heated them. She moved into the grasses, felt their weight against her skirts, bent her head back to the sky.

Where are you? she called. The words expressed themselves, but this time she somehow knew she hadn't vocalized them. Her message would be heard, though. She knew that for sure. *Where are you?*

A cold wind whispered across her face.

She awoke once more, her cheeks wet, the corners of her eyes swollen, and with a sob in the back of her throat, she turned over and slept.

Seven

Blessings on thee, little man,
Barefoot boy, with cheek of tan!
-John Greenleaf Whittier

THE DOG GENTLY LICKED Natalie's hand and looked up at her with soft brown eyes. His tail thumped the steel table where she examined him.

"How's the leg, mister?" She tapped the cast, checking to see whether it had completely hardened, then touched the skin around the hipbone to satisfy herself that the cast wouldn't chafe. An infection could go undetected until too far gone. The dog could have been hurt much worse after a round with an elephant only a couple of days before. He would be fine.

She was about to lift the dog from the table and put him on the floor to assess his reaction to the cast when she spotted a little boy huddled in the far corner of the clinic. He seemed about eight to ten years old, a skinny little thing wearing a pair of red basketball shorts, a red and white t-shirt, and no shoes on his dusty feet. He anxiously pushed his shiny, black, chin-length hair behind his ears. Squatting against the wall with his arms wrapped around his knees, he watched her like a raven about to pluck a grasshopper into its mouth.

"And who are you?" Natalie asked. "What're you doing in the clinic?"

She folded the dog into her arms. He whimpered and the boy rose from his crouch. The dog wiggled, his nose stretching out toward the boy. Natalie adjusted her hold and lowered him to the floor.

"I get it. This is your dog, huh?" She smiled and joined the boy, so they could both watch the dog try to navigate with the cast on his leg.

For a few moments, they giggled as the dog slipped on the floor, then regained his balance like a newborn colt learning how to walk. The dog's eyes shifted to them every once in a while, as if he knew he looked foolish. He tried to walk on all fours, yet quickly learned the cast was a bit longer than his other three legs, so he stuck it straight out and maneuvered on three legs instead. The boy opened his mouth and gave a croaking laugh, an odd sound like a quacking duck.

Natalie smiled but kept her eyes on the dog, trying to figure out whether the cast needed adjusting. It always took a few moments for dogs to get their bearings when wearing a cast, but without exception, they adapted easily, and they never took offense if you laughed at them—though most raised an eyebrow and ducked their head as if embarrassed, as this one did. Finally, the yellow dog got into a rhythm and hobbled his way over to the boy. From the exuberant way they greeted each other, Natalie knew they belonged together. But why hadn't the child verbally responded to her questions?

The three of them sat on the floor together for another fifteen minutes, not saying a word. Then the door to the clinic opened. Hatcher came in, carrying a metal box and talking to someone behind him.

Natalie and the boy scrambled to their feet as though they'd been caught stealing the Crown Jewels. Even the dog paused, his nose twitching, his cast in mid-air. All eyes were on Hatcher and the woman behind him.

"Dr. DeAngelo." Hatcher acknowledged her and placed the

aluminum box he held on the counter and said something in Thai to the woman who accompanied him. She handed him the basket she carried, smiled shyly at Natalie, and scurried out the door.

"So you've checked our patient?" Hatcher motioned to the dog, who obediently hobbled to him, tail wagging furiously. The boy followed suit, standing next to Hatcher, his hand companionably on the dog's head.

"The cast hardened so I . . . I thought it would be a good idea for him to try it out." Natalie stumbled through her sentence, feeling as if she had committed some sort of a crime by coming to the clinic. Why in hell did he intimidate her so much?

"Not the first time this old boy's broken a bone." He checked the cast, patted the dog's head, then poked a finger against the boy's chest with a grin. "And my friend here slept beside him all night, didn't he?"

"I'm not sure if it was all night, but he was here when I got here." She moved forward, hoping that it wasn't her imagination that the ice in Peter Hatcher's eyes might have thawed a bit. She'd been prepared to pack up and go home today if things didn't get any better, but in the shower this morning, she reminded herself she wasn't here to impress any British doctors. She was here to help Andrew Gordon care for the animals at the sanctuary. And she couldn't deny her own personal reason: to heal. Those two reasons trumped any consideration for Peter Hatcher's feelings.

"They are never very far away from each other. Dog and boy. They kind of communicate telepathically," he said. "The boy, Anurak, hasn't spoken since he was born, but that mutt, his name is Decha, understands him perfectly. And I know Anurak understands us fine, too, don't you, laddie?"

The boy cocked his head and grinned.

"What happened to him?" Natalie asked. "Was he sick?"

Hatcher's face darkened as if it wasn't a story he wanted to share with her. He hesitated, then said, "I'm not quite sure, but from what we can tell, his birth mother's diet was low in iodine and that might have caused his mutism. She passed away shortly after he started to walk, and his father remarried, and moved further north. No one knows where, so I haven't been able to put the pieces together. I believe what happened to our boy here is quite rare. The child doesn't appear bothered by his inability, though." He reached out and high-fived Anurak. "He hears fine, is smart and comical, and certainly can communicate quite nicely. Just wish he'd tell Decha to stay away from Sophie. No matter how many bones she breaks, he keeps going back to tease her more. Dumb dog." Hatcher rose and spoke in Thai to the boy, then pointed outside.

Anurak shyly waved at Natalie, then he and Decha navigated the door together, the boy's hand on the dog's back, the dog adoringly staring into the boy's face. She recognized that look. Pure and unadulterated puppy love.

Hatcher busied himself with the box he'd brought in. With his back still to her, he said, "I suppose you want to learn the clinic and our routine. If you're going to stay, that is?"

Her shoulders stiffened. Did she read a bit of hopefulness in that last sentence?

"I'm staying." As soon as the words came out of her mouth, she realized they'd been a bit too forceful so she followed with, "So it would be good to know my way around."

He stopped and turned to face her. For a long minute, he stared at her quizzically as if trying to decide whether to say what he was thinking. She didn't speak.

In the silence, she studied the cracks in the floor, picked at a nail, thought about an exit strategy. She half expected him to argue that she needn't stay, that he had a truck at the front entrance to take her to the airport, and a return ticket in his pocket. And that would break her heart, because during the past couple of days, she'd found the girl she was at ten, the one who'd adopted the feral fox who lived behind her parents' barn and nursed that crazy red animal through a very difficult birthing of four black-pawed kits. The moment she looked into the animal's eyes, she saw the pain of another being and realized the fox feared that her kits would be hurt. That was the exact moment when she realized working with animals would be her life's work.

No doubt Maman abolished the adoption of anymore wild animals when the last kit returned to the wild, but Natalie found a three-legged dog on the side of the road the summer after. Then there was the thousand-pound pig the Stantons had given to her as a piglet when she'd reassured them that, yes, of course her parents knew she was bringing the piglet home. Finally, Pops convinced Maman that they might as well celebrate Natalie's ability to tame any animal—wild or domestic—and they contacted one of Maman's cousins, an instructor at North Carolina State. At thirteen, Natalie visited the campus and decided she wanted to be part of the Wolf Pack. No one questioned the odd animals in the barn after that point, and even Maman admitted a preference for the one-legged peacock who crookedly spread his fan, leaning against a tree or fence or lamp-post like "a drunken rainbow with eyes," Maman said.

Peter broke the silence. "Didn't Andrew give you a tour yesterday?"

"He started to, but then that elephant . . ."

"Sophie."

"Yes."

He placed the glass bottle he'd been holding into a white metal cupboard and gestured for her to follow him. Without another word, he guided her around the clinic, pointing out where he stored certain dry medicines, showing her recent medical records, giving her the password for the computer and the access codes for the high speed lab centrifuge, as well as for the refrigerator where he stored large amounts of amoxicillin, which "I use more often than any other drug."

Finally, they were acting like the professionals they were rather than teenagers. Hopefully, it would continue. She didn't have the energy for drama. Christ, that's what she came to Thailand to circumvent. It didn't matter whether the drama was hers or someone else's; she didn't want it in her life.

She asked about daily routines and drug availability, mentally noting some of his answers and jotting down the complicated ones in the small notebook she always kept in her back pocket. Even in the States where her colleagues relied on their cell phones, she kept a paper notepad, a habit which often proved wise, especially when she visited horse farms so remote that cell phone service was spotty at best. Besides, she found the pen and paper somewhat comforting. Reliable. She could sketch quickly, write prescriptive notes, and remind herself of tasks. That's all she needed. And she had it in her hip pocket, twenty-four-seven.

She asked him about the number of animals—besides elephants—that the clinic treated, surprised at the dozens of dogs, cats, birds, and even reptiles that Hatcher and the volunteers serviced every week. He impressed her by remembering each animal's name and detailing their histories.

"What about the elephants? We haven't discussed them yet." She helped Hatcher organize the bandages kept in a large woven bamboo shelf under one of the windows. He appeared to tolerate her assistance, yet she caught him straightening out the row she'd just arranged as if she hadn't done a proper job. The back of her neck prickled. She swallowed her frustration.

"Yes, the elephants," he said. "Their mahouts care for them, generally. I only handle emergencies or suggest some vitamin supplements when one develops arthritis or some such ailment. You've worked with ellies before?"

"Briefly. When I interned years ago, I did a couple of weeks at a sanctuary in the States."

"A couple of weeks?" He stopped and glared at her. In his eyes was an accusation: how dare she come here and step right in without the appropriate experience?

"I'm not incompetent. As a matter of fact, I'm quite capable of working with elephants." She caught herself starting to blather and stopped. Took a deep breath. Reminded herself that people could only make her feel the way she gave them permission to. She wasn't going to give this man permission to question her own capabilities. She'd always been a good student. She could become one again. But Hatcher had no way of knowing that. Best to butter him up. Take the high road. Apologize, even if he's wrong. Patently wrong. "You know, I have enough knowledge to get started here, and I have a lot to learn . . ." She swallowed hard. " . . . from you."

"Elephants are different from horses," Hatcher told her, "and a couple of weeks of training isn't enough for me to feel comfortable leaving you in charge if I have to. Christ, what was Andrew thinking?" He slapped a roll of gauze onto the shelf and rose to his feet. "Dr. DeAngelo, I simply do not have the weeks—actually, months! —it would take to train you."

"We have to start somewhere," Natalie said, forcing a stiff smile to her lips and hating that she felt compelled to use what some might term "feminine tactics." "Why don't you tell me more about Sophie? How are you treating that infection?"

Hatcher opened his mouth, then snapped it shut. His eyes narrowed as if he wanted to say something argumentative, then thought better of it. He rubbed his forehead.

"Sophie," he said. Both a statement and a complaint. The utterance of her name held a world of frustration and resentment within its two syllables. His eyes wavered a moment as if he was mentally reviewing the details of Sophie's chart.

"Sophie," he repeated. "That infection is one I've been fighting since she came to us six months ago. Sometimes I get it under control, then she goes on another rampage, and we need to restrain her, and it opens up the wound so we have to start all over again. To be honest, Dr. DeAngelo, I'm quite certain she's not going to be rehabilitated." He sighed. "I'm afraid she's getting worse. The wound is very close to being septic."

Natalie asked, "What caused the original wound? Had she been injured or was it just years of the chain? Do you know?"

"Being chained up every night after working all day in the logging industry. That's why Andrew refuses to use a chain, even though some of them don't know how to behave unless they're controlled, like Sophie," Hatcher replied. "Most of the ellies we have come from a local logger who finally realized he could no longer care for them."

"Did she come to the sanctuary with a family?" She remembered that Andrew had mentioned at the conference that he always tried to keep elephant families intact.

"No. She's probably the most antisocial elephant we've had. Andrew heard from the logger that Sophie had birthed several calves during her time with him, but there were no babies with the herd when we took Sophie on. Only her and three other females and one teenage male, Pahpao's son."

"Don't the people who capture elephants in the wild remove them from their calves?" Natalie asked, though she already knew the answer.

Hatcher looked at her askance. "I would have studied a bit more before coming here, Dr. DeAngelo." His voice had turned frosty.

She ignored his comment. "Couldn't that explain Sophie's rage? That and the infection? PTSD, perhaps?"

"It could."

"Maybe you haven't given her enough time, then. PTSD in humans often takes years to treat. It must be the same in elephants." She thought about sharing her own experience, but something told her Hatcher wouldn't care. That was just as well. She had a tough enough time talking about it with people she trusted. Holding the story close to her chest was safer. She'd find another way to make her point.

"I know that, but we can't lose any more animals because of her. She's endangering everyone's safety."

Natalie paused. "Do you think it's possible that the wound is making Sophie's PTSD worse?"

Hatcher's silence said volumes. He'd already thought of that, too.

Eight

My words fly up,
my thoughts remain below.
Words without thoughts
never to heaven go.
-William Shakespeare

NATALIE AWOKE SCREAMING AGAIN. Gasping for air. Fighting the mosquito netting over her head as if it were a giant spider's web.

As her eyes adjusted in the dark, she struggled to figure out where she was. Finally, the silence and darkness calmed her.

Thailand. The sanctuary.

Breathe.

Breathe.

One more night of nightmares.

She lay on the single bed, drenched in a thin coat of sweat. The faintest of breezes skimmed her body, wicking the moisture, cooling her. Calming her. She inhaled on the count of six and exhaled to the count of eight. Three times. And repeated. By the third cycle, she found her rhythm and knew she was safe. The worst was over.

She listened to the minute night sounds. An owl's soft hoot. The scritch-scratch of insects. In the distance, an elephant's rumble. She struggled to remember the dream that awakened her, but it had dissipated as soon as she opened her eyes. More often than not, she couldn't remember the nightmares.

Just as well, she thought. Sometimes the night terrors were twice as frightening when her eyes opened. It was a blessing when she couldn't remember the dreams, because the reality to which she awoke was worse and followed her throughout the day like specters with long bony fingers. She felt haunted, exhausted by the ghastliness of it all. She wished she could awake from that reality as easily as she did from her dreams.

There were times she longed to jump off a cliff, but she hadn't, and sometimes she thought it was simply because there weren't any cliffs available when she had the urge to leap.

She breathed again. Concentrated on counting. Something made her feel she was not alone. Comforted.

Another elephant rumbled.

The conversation she'd had with Dr. Hatcher earlier that day repeated itself in her mind. Had he been telling the story to elicit her help or was he showing off his firsthand knowledge of elephants?

She sat up on the edge of the bed and heard a short trumpet. The sound came from a different direction than the rumbles had.

Sophie?

Without hesitation, Natalie slid into a pair of shorts, pulled a T-shirt over her head, slipped on her sandals and left the cabin, carefully shutting the door so the sound wouldn't reverberate into the night.

The half-moon provided enough light to see the dirt road she'd followed the other day to where Sophie was tethered. In another hour or so, the sky would brighten. This very moment was the coolest and quietest of the day. She headed toward the sound and heard another trumpet, followed by some rumbles from the other direction. She stumbled over a root and righted herself.

The elephants' trumpets brought back memories of Billy Fribble, the owner of the sanctuary in Texas where she spent her internship. Billy was a small man, jockey-size, with a cloud of curly gray hair. She thought it ironic when she first met him that this tiny man could control such large mammals. One of the first lessons he taught her occurred right after she'd stumbled and fallen over a tree root like the one she'd tripped on.

"Think about an elephant's physical structure," he told her as they stood on the edge of the meadow where an old, retired circus elephant named Mildred grazed. "Their larynx is approximately eight times the size of a human's, so the sounds they produce can be below our range of hearing or extraordinarily high. If ol' Mildred over there adjusts her trunk or moves her tongue, she can make that sound different or louder. Or softer. And while she's making a sound, she might hold her head or her ears differently. You have to observe, Nat. Watch and listen. Use your human instincts to figure out what animals are telling each other. And us. You'll save yourself a lot of heartache if you watch them closely."

His advice had, indeed, saved her a lot of heartache. She hadn't been bitten by any dogs. No horses had nipped her or stepped on her feet. Most animals calmed perceptibly when she spoke to them. Now maybe she could get to know Sophie. Listening was always much easier when there weren't humans around, Natalie thought. No interruptions. No distractions.

She rounded the bend in the road, and Sophie's pen came into view. A large, clumsily-built structure with cement pillars, its roof rose high into the trees as if it was designed for giraffes rather than elephants. The elephant's head came up. She had heard Natalie. Sophie's ears waved, but she stood very still, her trunk pointing straight up in the air like a periscope.

Natalie stopped and turned to the side to make herself smaller so that she appeared less threatening. Speaking softly, she repeated Sophie's name. She had long ago realized that a soft, low tone was reassuring to animals, and it didn't matter what words were said. She repeated the name over and over again.

Sophie lowered her trunk, but still she watched, her body at attention.

Moving slowly, carefully, Natalie walked closer to the pen,

keeping an eye on Sophie's body language. The closer she came, the better. Natalie could determine Sophie's physical traits. She stood approximately eighteen feet tall, and her forehead was broad and flat, her skin a deep gray with freckles down her trunk. Her feet were as wide as Natalie's shoulders, and if she chose to, could easily crush a full grown, large dog. The elephant rumbled. She was curious but didn't exhibit any warning signs. Obviously, she was used to having people around.

Natalie strained to see Sophie's leg. She itched to examine the wound, curious to know whether it had responded to the treatment Hatcher administered. She moved closer, maneuvering herself so Sophie had to turn the damaged leg toward Natalie. Still, it was too dark to see it.

"Okay, no examination tonight, Sophie," she said quietly, "so let's get to know each other a bit. I'll sit here for a while, if that's okay with you."

The elephant rumbled again as if to reluctantly accept Natalie's company. They sat in silence, Natalie occasionally jotting comments in her notebook about Sophie's size, her markings and movements, or the sounds she made.

THE ELEPHANT *rumbles, reluctantly accepting the woman's presence. She watches the woman sitting against the big tree where the elephant—Sophie—likes to scratch her back. The woman is silent, writing busily. Now and again, she looks at the elephant. It is not a threatening look, but a curious one, as if she's trying to figure Sophie out.*

The curiosity is returned. The elephant reaches out her trunk, lazily sniffing the air around the woman's head, a sweet smell, something like the fruit every elephant (especially her) yearns for, the ripened papayas and bananas she could eat all day. It is not a man's smell, not the spicy smell they carry with them, not the smell of fear. It is still a human smell, but this smell is almost comforting.

The woman hands a banana to the elephant, repeats words she often says, but Sophie doesn't understand the woman. The voice is a low sound, almost a rumble from very far away, making Sophie's ears twitch with memories of other human voices. Not all the men have hurt her. Some have fed her sweet potatoes and doused her with cool water that eased the bites on her tender skin. Some have talked to her quietly and rubbed that special place at the base of her ear. But none of them have sounded like this woman or had her touch.

The bananas melt in Sophie's mouth. As she slowly circles her jaw, chews the juice out of the last of the skins, reluctant to swallow their sweetness, she watches the woman, never taking an eye off of her. The elephant wants more bananas. She moves toward the woman and reaches past her for the bananas, stretching into a sudden beam of sunlight. The woman turns, and she and the elephant are inches away.

Sophie rocks backward on her front legs. The woman laughs and reaches a hand out, touches the elephant's trunk lightly. Politely. There is no smell of fear in this woman, no hook in her hand, no harsh commands in her voice.

She quietly stands still and regards the elephant, calmly gazing into her eyes, and there is a peacefulness that fills the void between them. The elephant no longer reaches for the bananas. Instead, trunk still upraised, she exhales with a deep shudder and releases a billow of breath in the woman's direction.

The breath pushes the woman away, causes her to shriek so loudly Sophie, too, backs away. Then the woman laughs again, and Sophie cocks her head and scrutinizes the woman as if wondering exactly what is so funny. For another moment, they stare at each other, then Sophie's knee begins to throb, and she bounces her trunk against the sore, knowing what is coming. The pain. She lifts her leg a few inches from the ground, and the burning subsides momentarily, but she can't stand with her leg up in the air for long. The pain will return.

The woman, still watching, grabs her paper and pencil, scratches something on the page.

Then, noises from up the road. The scent of more humans floats toward where Sophie stands, one leg up, an eye on the distance. The tightness in the elephant's chest returns.

The woman hears the sounds, too. She swings her hair to her other shoulder and chews on the ends, then reaches up to pat the elephant's trunk before she turns and walks toward the men coming in their direction.

Sophie turns her head, but out of one brown eye, she watches the group of humans move away and listens for a long time until she can hear nothing except the calls of some monkeys in a nearby grove of trees.

Nine

> Friendship is unnecessary like philosophy,
> like art . . . It has no survival value; rather it is
> one of those things which give value to survival.
> -C.S. Lewis

"NERVOUS HABIT OR DOES it taste good?"

Natalie jumped and let loose an embarrassed yelp that sent birds fluttering through the trees.

Mali emerged from the shadows of a eucalyptus tree, laughing so hard and long that tears rolled down her face. She clapped her hands and tried to speak, but every time she opened her mouth, all she could do was giggle. Finally, she managed, "I'm so sorry, but if you could have seen your face . . ."

Mali's laughter was contagious and exactly the remedy for the tension she'd been feeling.

When her laughing finally subsided, Mali took Natalie's arm and looked up into Natalie's face, her mouth still upturned in a smile. Wearing a dark turban on her head, a food-stained long-sleeved black shirt, and an ankle-length multicolored skirt with a pair of old, dusty flip-flops, Mali was still beautiful because of the light in her dark brown eyes.

"So, why are you here? Sophie misbehaving?" Mali asked casually as if it were no surprise to find Natalie here so early in the morning.

"We were having a conversation about how to fix the world's problems," Natalie answered, returning Mali's grin. "Sophie has some wonderful ideas on how to achieve world peace, and she agrees with me that the economy could be fixed by printing some more money."

"I quite agree with you, Dr. DeAngelo," Mali said, sending herself into another peal of laughter.

Behind her, Sophie shuffled to the other side of her pen, favoring her leg a little but not acting as if she were in pain. Natalie stuck her notebook in her back pocket, determined to return later in the day to get a better look at Sophie's wound.

"I was heading for the greenhouse to get some vegetables for lunch. Want to come?" Mali tugged Natalie's arm.

Natalie nodded, grateful for the interruption, especially since Mali was the only person other than Andrew who'd been warm and welcoming.

They meandered down the path that wove through tall palm grasses, and Mali chatted about what she wanted to make for lunch and dinner, inane conversation that they would forget within an hour, yet Natalie felt a kinship she hadn't felt with another woman for a long time. She hadn't been close to anyone for more than a year.

Some of her best friends had opened up to the media, telling personal stories about Danny's childhood and the strong connection he and Natalie had. They shared anecdotes about Stephen. Treasured moments. They betrayed her, cruelly depriving her of her private grief. She shuttered herself from all relationships after that, wouldn't accept anyone's apology. Yet no matter what she said or did—or what she didn't say or didn't do—every move she made, every time she went to a celebration instead of to church, every moment she spoke out about gun control, every story about her daily life found its way into news reports. Grieving mother. Well-known vet. Divorced. The media was fascinated with the woman who'd lost both her sons in a school shooting. They made her boys their salacious headlines. Nothing hurt her more.

Maybe now, in this place, where she was only Dr. Natalie DeAngelo, the vet, rather than Natalie DeAngelo, the mother of two of the Lakeview School shooting victims, she could relax. Here she was simply an American volunteer instead of a victim. She wasn't the grieving mother here; she was simply Natalie.

And that's the way she wanted to stay.

Suddenly they were walking under a huge green netting Natalie hadn't even noticed until it replaced the blue sky. Mali walked ahead, into the midst of a huge nursery, at least an acre's worth of tender, green plants. A pungent and spicy smell assaulted Natalie's nostrils, damp and fermented, like the smell of a green lake overgrown with algae. Yet there was a biting fragrance to it so undeniably Thai that Natalie felt if she opened her mouth, she should have been able to take a bite out of the smell itself.

"How do you keep the elephants away from this?" They moved down the aisle between plants that ranged from bare-ly-sprouted seedlings to fully grown vegetables ready to be harvested. "Surely this would be dessert for them."

Mali picked a leaf off one plant, crushed it between her fingers and brought it to her nose. With a smile, she beckoned for Natalie to take a whiff. Spicy yet sweet. Pleasant.

"We have an extensive web of fencing around the perim-eter of the compound." Mali pointed outside the tent. "Andrew's design. It's been interesting to see the animals adapt to it, but they finally understand. Fence is bad. River is good. Before the fence, we never would've been able to raise these." She wiggled her fingers at the thousands of plants in front of them: yellow squash blossoms, cilantro and basil, reddish-green tomatoes, some white gourds Natalie had never seen before, and dozens of glossy purple and red peppers. The food grown here obviously fed the dozens of people who worked and volunteered for the sanctuary, and probably supplemented the elephants' diets, as well.

"The fence keeps them in and keeps others out." Mali motioned again, clockwise to indicate the larger world, then counter clockwise to indicate the smaller world that constituted the sanctuary itself. "We have a small banana plantation and some rice paddies, too. The little boy you met—the one who doesn't talk—his parents work the paddies for us."

"Does he understand English?"

"Oh, Anurak understands English fine. I've been speaking English to him since he was a baby. His parents—my cousins—speak only Thai. They're Karen, so he's bilingual. A bright little guy."

She continued walking down the aisles, deftly pinching leaves off various plants, releasing scents, some of which Natalie recognized: oregano, mint, cilantro. Some she did not. Mali plucked ripe peppers and long cucumbers, stretching her shirt out to create a makeshift basket.

"Can I give you some advice?" Mali's clipped English accent seemed so out of sync with the way she dressed and the exotic tilt of her head.

Though the question came out of left field, Natalie felt she had no choice but to say, "Of course."

"If you're here for the elephants, you should speak with one of the mahouts. They're the ones who know them best. Ask for help. Let yourself be taught. I respect your education and am certain everyone else does, as well, but the elephants will not know how many years you attended school. They'll be able to sense your insecurity before you step into range of them. What they need to know is whether you can communicate with them, and that doesn't happen overnight." She gathered a colorful cornucopia of bright red, persimmon, and lemon yellow vegetables as if collecting summer flowers into a fragrant bouquet.

Natalie pulled out the bottom of her own shirt like she did as a kid in her grandmother's garden, and Mali rewarded her with the heavy weight of a large head of broccoli and a royal purple eggplant. Then Mali glanced at Natalie sideways, her tongue caught between her teeth as if considering whether to finish her thought.

"My son—" Mali looked off past Natalie's shoulder as if considering a thought. "He could help you. Siriporn is a mahout.

He learned with my Karen cousins. And maybe it'll keep him busy. He's been spending far too many hours with the Red Shirts anyway."

Natalie remembered the rally she and Andrew passed on the way from the airport. "He's with the protestors?"

"My son is a dreamer," Mali added a sarcastic lilt to the last word. "He thinks he can change the world and doesn't realize how dangerous that is."

Natalie's smile melted from her lips, and she turned her head quickly so Mali wouldn't witness the tears that had unexpectedly sprung into her eyes. She had no right to feel angry but a small knot of fury filled her chest.

'My son.'

Mali had said it so easily. Nonchalantly. As if it was no big deal to have a son. As if he were no more important than one of her squash plants. She had said his name as if he angered her. Her eyes hadn't warmed. She hadn't added comments about his age or how he looked nor had she bragged about his talents. The tingles down Natalie's neck were because of Mali's omissions, and it wasn't the first time she'd felt the emotion. Natalie experienced it every single time someone talked about a son or a daughter in a way that felt too casual to her. It infuriated her that parents took their children for granted though she knew deep down in the most logical part of herself that she was being irrational. In her very soul, she knew Mali would feel as much pain as Natalie did herself if she had experienced a loss like Natalie's. But that part of her soul was tucked away safely and the emotions now coursing through her hovered right below the surface. They were the ones that protected her from the deepest part of her pain.

" . . . I could send him to introduce himself to you at dinner tonight," Mali continued. She had not stopped talking, Natalie knew, but even if someone had offered to give her boys back to her—unharmed—at that very second, she could not have repeated what Mali had said.

She turned back to Mali and forced a stiff smile.

"Do you have children?" Mali asked.

Natalie caught her breath, taken off guard by the unexpected question. "Yes," she said softly. "Yes. I had two boys."

It was Mali's turn to pause. From the corner of her eye, Natalie felt the burn of her surprised stare. "Had?"

Unable to speak because of the strangling lump in her throat, Natalie nodded.

For a moment, they walked in silence, then Mali stopped and put a hand on Natalie's forearm. "The Buddha said that 'every day we are born again. What we do today matters most.' Your boys would be proud of what you're doing, Natalie."

They stood on the path, Mali's hand still on Natalie's arm, its weight and warmth strangely comforting. Neither spoke. Memories of the boys filled Natalie's mind. Christmases. First days at school. Silly little moments that meant nothing: a giggle in the middle of a supermarket aisle, the crazy cross-eyed look Stephen gave her one night when she washed him in the bathtub, the first word Danny learned. "Ducky," he had said. "Ducky."

"They would have been," Natalie said, finally, and she put her own hand on top of Mali's. "They would've been proud. Thank you for reminding me of that."

Mali placed her fingers on her heart, then reached up to touch Natalie's. "I might have gone to university to learn about people's minds, but it's their hearts that truly matter. We are mothers. I understand. Believe me."

As they walked back to the pavilion where several women already stood at the cook-stoves, Natalie thought about Mali's advice to learn from the mahouts. Was it necessary? After all, she wasn't here to learn how to train an elephant. She was here to treat broken bones and diagnose illnesses and to possibly heal an aging matron with a horrible leg wound. That was what was exciting. Not elephant training. Other people could train animals. She was here to treat them.

But it was the right thing to do. The boys would have told her that.

Ten

Of all the animals, the boy
is the most unmanageable.
-Plato

FROM WHERE NATALIE SAT, she watched six elephants taking their baths in the filtered sunlight through the monkey pod, cashew, and breadfruit trees that lined the deep green hills and mountains around them. The constant hum of busy insects and the oppressive afternoon heat lulled her. She sat as still as possible, feeling the drops of perspiration lazily crawl down the back of her neck. It was useless to keep wiping them off. Though her body was still, her mind whirred with thoughts of Sophie and how to deal with her injury. The physical wound was the easy one to heal; the emotional one, lots tougher.

In the water, the younger mahouts played with their elephants, perfecting their dives and calling to each other as they hopped nimbly from one large gray head to another. The elephants joined in, spraying water from their trunks purposely toward the boys. The spray often floated Natalie's way, offering a pleasant mist on her arms and legs.

One of the mahouts—Chanchai, whose name meant "skilled winner"—had a reputation for being as sharp-tempered as any bad elephant the sanctuary had ever taken in. One of his wide-set eyes turned to the right, and so did the other. Whenever he looked at someone, he had to turn his head, which, ironically, caused the other person to shift out of sight. His pugilist nose told the tale of far too many fights on Bangkok streets, most of which (it was rumored) were with elephants. Mali told Natalie that morning, "If you sit and talk to him, he'll tell you about the many bones he's broken in his body and show you a few appendages that haven't healed quite straight. Even his voice seems broken. He either barks or squeaks."

He sat up now with one knee resting on Ali's head, gazing over at the other boys who laughed and talked as the elephants surged backward and forward in the clear, cool water. Ali, the first elephant Natalie had met, was also the largest bull in the herd. At thirty-two-years-old, he was known for his crazy temper when he went into *mustph*. The only ones who could control him were Chanchai and Mali's eldest son, Siriporn.

According to Mali, Chanchai had tried working with Sophie when she first came to the sanctuary, but Andrew had to rescue him when Sophie appeared determined to kill the mahout who was as mean as she. She did better with Siriporn and preferred him over and above anyone else at the sanctuary, though Siriporn couldn't give her all his time. He managed the mahouts, often taking on responsibility for any rescues the sanctuary did, then rehabilitating the new elephants.

Watching Chanchai in the late afternoon sunlight, Natalie believed that the mahout would have happily killed Sophie, too. Natalie couldn't quite choose the right word, but she sensed there was a cruelty to him that even he couldn't control. Like Sophie's. After all these years, it still amazed her how animals and humans who worked together often shared some of the same traits.

The rest of the mahouts pulled themselves up on the bumpy back of their dove-gray giants with arms like strands of twisted rope, bellowing in a language she didn't understand. Last night, she had heard Chanchai repeating the only American word he knew: drunk. Now, she heard it again. Over and over again: *Drunkdrunkdrunkdrunk. DRUNK.* Giggling uncontrollably, as if he were, indeed, drunk. His white teeth flashed giddily like bright slashes of sun against his brown skin.

During their conversation, Natalie wondered idly what the mahouts said now as they moved back and forth on their elephants, glancing in her direction every once in a while. The words seemed more than guttural commands. Gossip, perhaps. *But what did Thai mahouts gossip about? What they did with the kitchen girls last night? What their mother said about their dreams to move to India?* Several had told Andrew they were leaving at the end of the dry season.

As the late afternoon cicadas buzzed and the boys' voices blended in with that summertime sound, Natalie let her mind wander and noticed crazy details: how she couldn't stop twisting the candy wrapper she had pulled off a piece of soft chocolate moments before this drama began to unfold, how Chanchai raised his eyebrows when Ali's eyes widened and rolled back in his head like gray and white kaleidoscope circles, how the water eddied in patterns that caught the sunshine like a mirror, and how Ali, even though blind in one eye, had no problem finding his way around and acting like the big male he was. She thought about Sophie again, wondered how much of her lack of control was PTSD and how much was physical pain. She longed to get close enough to examine the wound and treat it. Though she had no doubt Hatcher had tried his best, she couldn't help but wonder if she might have better luck.

One of the mahouts yelled a warning, but it was too late; Ali rolled completely underwater taking Chanchai with him. They swam dangerously close to Kalaya, an old logging elephant, bringing screeches from the mahout atop her. For a long time, Ali remained under water with no sign of Chanchai. Natalie held her breath. She should do something, but what?

The only other person on the bank with Natalie was an older Thai woman who worked in the kitchens. No matter what the mahouts did, the Thai woman smiled, enjoying every moment as if it was a musical performance she'd waited her whole life to hear. Hardly the barometer for the fear Natalie felt.

But then the woman let out a yell.

Natalie glanced over to see the woman's eyes widen as she raised a hand and called out again. The situation had gotten out of control. Scrambling down the embankment, she knew she wouldn't be able to do anything about the elephant, but if a human needed to have mouth-to-mouth, at least she'd be close and able to help. She was about to dive into the water when Ali rolled again and came up for a breath, Chanchai still atop his back. Chanchai shook his head, his hair flipping side to side like a wet dog's, as he sputtered. Relieved guffaws and what seemed like taunting shouts rent the air. The other mahouts repeated, "*Ting tong, ting tong, ting tong*," over and over again. That was one phrase she knew. "You are very crazy," they told their friend. She agreed.

Shaking with adrenaline, Natalie crawled back up the embankment to where she'd been sitting. The mahouts laughed from behind her, and her cheeks burned with embarrassment, sure they were sharing a joke at her expense. Only after they filed slowly out of the river and down toward the large shelters to have their afternoon meal, did she rise to head in the other direction toward the clinic.

"Dr. Natalie? Dr. Natalie!"

She turned to see Mali's son, Siriporn, running toward her. They hadn't officially met, yet Andrew had pointed out the boy at breakfast that morning. He favored his mother, sharing her wide, dark eyes and infectious smile. He was smiling when he reached her and took off his baseball cap. He folded his hands in the *Wai* greeting, in prayer position in front of his heart and slightly bowed his head.

"*Sawadee ka*," he said. "Good meeting you! I am Siriporn. Want welcome you to Thailand." He nodded and bowed again, his megawatt smile never leaving his face.

She bowed back and thanked him. "Your mother has told me about you."

He nodded and laughed, a surprisingly deep and rich sound, unlike his tenor speaking voice. "She says I teach you about elephants, but I say my English not so good. Maybe she teach you?" He laughed again, and Natalie realized he was teasing his mother though she wasn't there.

They walked toward the clinic together, Natalie's sandals keeping time with Siriporn's bare feet. He spoke with his hands, gesturing toward the sky as he told her about his father, a respected mahout, who had died in an auto accident nearly ten years ago. Then he placed his hand on his heart when telling Natalie how proud he was of his mother and the loving way she raised him and his siblings. But his most expansive gestures accompanied his stories about the elephants he'd worked with throughout his life.

"Your English is fine," Natalie reassured him after he apologized for the fourth time when he couldn't think of a word. *It's actually quite endearing*, she thought, but she was surprised it wasn't better since Mali was fluent in English. *There's a story there*, she thought, instantly wondering whether Andrew had any part in it. Siriporn's words tumbled over each other in his excitement to share his thoughts. When she asked him about the individual elephants, his knowledge of each appeared far more comprehensive than Peter Hatcher's or Andrew's. They might know the elephants' illnesses or dietary needs, but Siriporn knew their personalities.

When they reached the clinic, she saw Hatcher's head through one of the windows. He appeared intent on examining something and didn't give any indication that he saw her.

"I need to join Dr. Hatcher," she told Siriporn, though she was reluctant to end their conversation, "but before you go, please tell me more about Sophie."

For the first time, Siriporn lost his smile. He shook his head slowly, then placed both hands on his heart. "Sophie in much pain. She want be good but she in pain."

It surprised Natalie that Siriporn's first comment was about Sophie's emotional state instead of her leg. She watched Siriporn's face in the changing shadows cast by the broad leaves of the cashew tree under which they stood. He thought long and hard for a moment, then continued.

"She very sad elephant. Work hard her whole life. No family. She very, very lonely. Siriporn work with her but no have time she need. She need friend. That make her feel better. And she need . . . how you say? She need . . ." He gazed up and squinted his eyes. "She need leg better." He shook his head and his frustration that he hadn't been able to help Sophie was evident. "She no like other mahouts. She no like Dr. Peter's needles. She no like dogs."

He scuffed his bare feet in the dust, crossed his arms over his chest and looked away. The collar of his t-shirt was frayed and the sleeve was torn, showing his bicep as it flexed a little, the muscle throbbing like a tick.

The unspoken resonated in Natalie's mind. She knew how Siriporn felt. There had been times in her career when she'd failed one of her animals, and the helplessness made her feel like she was walking on logs in a rushing river. The look on his face right now was one she'd worn in the past. She longed to reach for Siriporn and envelope him in a motherly hug. She wanted to remind him that there were often challenges in life that would cause him to grit his teeth and hold back tears, but all she could do was stand in the dusty road and listen to the distant barking of some of the sanctuary's rescued dogs.

"Is that all Sophie needs? Friends?" she asked, thinking that, between the two of them, maybe they could give her the time and energy it would take to start healing from her traumas, both physical and emotional.

Siriporn's smile faded. He shook his head.

"What do you think might make her feel better? Medicine? What kind of training?"

His eyes cleared. It was obvious he'd been thinking about this already. "She need freedom. Kindness. She need friend. Elephant always need friend."

Natalie nodded and smiled, then gestured toward the clinic. "I have to go to work," she said, "but let's talk again. And . . . maybe . . . can you meet me at Sophie's shelter tonight?"

His head bobbed up and down, and he thanked her over and over again as he backed away.

When she reached the top of the stairs to enter the clinic, she glanced back over her shoulder and laughed out loud to see Siriporn running up the road, occasionally jumping up to tap low-hanging branches as he passed underneath. She smiled to herself, thinking it was the first time she'd been able to enjoy a boy's antics without being concerned about memories of one of her own boys bringing her to her knees.

Eleven

No, my dog used to gaze at me,
paying me the attention I need,
the attention required
to make a vain person like me understand
that, being a dog, he was wasting time,
but, with those eyes so much purer than mine,
he'd keep on gazing at me
with a look that reserved for me alone
all his sweet and shaggy life,
always near me, never troubling me,
and asking nothing.
-Pablo Neruda

SHE WAS STILL SMILING when she entered the clinic, but that smile quickly faded. She'd forgotten that today was canine day. The clinic was filled to capacity with dogs on the first Wednesday of every month, Hatcher had told her. "Write it on your calendar and make sure you get here early. We're always full. Every hand is necessary, no matter what your skill level."

She didn't know why he had to add that last phrase, but he was right about the rest.

All of the sanctuary's resident dogs, plus most of the village's strays, filled the clinic's tables and kennels. Some came in for flea treatments, shots, checkups, and baths; others had continuing conditions that needed treatment. Every one of the twenty or so constantly-rotating volunteers was on hand, as well as the villagers who claimed one of the dogs as his/hers. Many of the dogs came from the same litters: obviously-related, large black labs with floppy feet and goofy smiles. Others were medium, sandy-colored mutts, and several small, curly-haired dogs that looked like they had poodle DNA.

All of the dogs barked or whined at a pitch so high and loud that the best way for Hatcher to communicate with the other human beings was via sign language. *When you have dozens of dogs all in the same building, you improvise,* she thought as he pointed and nodded at her.

"Take over on that," he yelled and pointed with his chin to the tray filled with vials of vaccines and flea treatment.

Nodding, Natalie slipped an apron over her shorts and immediately went to work, saying a silent thank you to the universe that Hatcher hadn't noticed she was late. In only a few moments, she got into the rhythm of vaccinating and giving each dog a quick check.

Anurak was an incredible asset on days like this. Normally it unsettled her to turn around and find him behind her, silent and smiling, his dark eyes twinkling with a secret to which only he was privy. Every time, he surprised her and she would shriek, which gave him a case of the silent giggles. He would slap his hand on Decha's head and open his mouth for a croaking laugh that Natalie could only imagine would be a braying howl of delight if the boy could speak. Even Decha would pull back his gums, show his teeth, and hang out his tongue, tail wagging so hard he lifted his back legs—complete with the heavy cast—off the ground as if enjoying the joke as thoroughly as his master.

But today when she turned around, Anurak stood there with an extra towel in his hands or a leash ready to slip over the next dog's head, as if he anticipated what she would ask him to do. He'd attach the leash and hold the dog still while she administered a shot or checked for ear mites. And Decha stood on the opposite side of the dog being treated, pressing against him as if providing the other dog a bit of canine comfort. Without the two of them, the day would have lasted twice as long with only half as much done.

When six o'clock in the evening rolled around and the last of the mutts had been happily released, all of the staff wearily found their way to the administration building and plopped onto the picnic benches for dinner and a beer. No one usually spoke on those nights—few had voices after yelling all day—and after eating, one by one they melted back down the road to their cabins to take advantage of a shower under cool rain water stored in barrels beside each building.

The quiet gave her time for reflection. Watching Hatcher during the day, she had to give him his props for putting events like this into place. By immunizing, sterilizing and protecting the local dogs, he saved their lives and, conversely, cut down on over-population. A win-win situation. It broke her heart to know that the dogs found on the street never had a chance. No homes—temporary or otherwise. She'd been horrified the first time she saw a truck filled with dogs. Live dogs. Piled ten deep atop each other, heads poking through the wire cages into which they were crammed. They were on the way to market. After the truck passed, she vomited. Then she became angry.

"We have to be part of the solution," Andrew often said. Every time he saw another problem, he employed everyone who worked for him to discover a solution. His actions bought life for more dogs (and elephants) than he had ever imagined. In less than a year, he'd not only saved the dozens of dogs they worked on today, but hundreds more. Hatcher had been part of that success.

Natalie nursed the last of her beer until everyone except Hatcher had left. It felt like this was the right time to approach him.

"We did some good work today," she said. He sat a table away from her, but she didn't move from her own seat. Truth be told, she was simply too tired to get up and join him.

"Thirty-eight vaccinations, twelve dogs spayed and god-knows-how-many flea treatments. Good day, but the tip of the iceberg, I'm afraid." He lifted his bottle and polished it off, then rose to place his dishes in the wash bucket.

Encouraged by the interaction, she rose and emptied her dishes, as well. "Must seem like an impossible task sometimes. To take care of all the strays as well as the abused elephants, I mean."

He nodded. "Quite different for you, I'm sure."

"True. There aren't many stray horses in North Carolina, though I've seen my fair share of abuse."

"No comparison, is there?"

As they walked to the end of the platform and down the stairs, Natalie chose her words carefully, hoping she could find some common ground with him. "It is quite different, but one of the reasons I came here was for that very reason. I admire what you've done for Andrew, and for all of those animals. I've already learned a lot from you."

Hatcher stopped mid-step. "Why are you buttering me up? You needn't bother. I trust my first impressions of people, and the one I have of you won't change."

"Buttering you up? I'm not buttering you up. It's the truth. But I also think I could contribute something, as well. I've had a few ideas about Sophie—"

"Stop right there." He halted in the path and turned on her, a flush coming up in his pale cheeks. "I appreciate your experience, Dr. DeAngelo, but I have far more years with elephants than you do. I'm happy to listen to your ideas about dogs or cats or . . . horses." He stressed the last word. "But the elephants are mine."

He stalked away. She wanted to chase him down and defend herself, but instead, Natalie straightened her shoulders and shook off her anger. Once again.

Still, she didn't want to follow him so she turned right to take a path she'd seen Mali take.

"I'll deal with you another day, Dr. Hatcher," Natalie muttered as she fought her way through short palm trees that dug into her calves with the ferocity of a feral cat. She lifted her legs and slammed them down, breaking branches and leaves like a stampeding bull. Determined to find her way back to the cabin, she ignored the stinging cuts in her legs and concentrated on her anger at Peter Hatcher. "I'm not giving up on Sophie," she announced to the dark night sky. "Whether you like it or not. I'm not giving up on her until she gives up on herself. And, even then, I'll fight you, you bastard."

Twelve

Beyond plants are animals,
Beyond animals is man,
Beyond man is the universe.
-Jean Toomer

"ARE YOU READY?" HATCHER asked Natalie.

Behind him, the mahouts Khalan (Mali's middle son) and Jabari, who had been in the river with his elephant the day before, yelled harsh commands and waved their arms frantically at Sophie. She stood in front of them, wide ears flared and her trunk raised to the sky. Backing up as far as her tether would allow, her white-rimmed eyes grew twice their size, a sure sign of her fear. She trumpeted, long and loud, an abrasive sound that slithered down Natalie's backbone. Natalie knew that sound. Sophie was angry. Again.

Natalie glanced apprehensively at Hatcher. He stood to her right, fully composed and focused on Sophie and the mahouts. The mahouts moved closer, carefully monitoring Sophie's every move, talking to her, commanding her to stay still, and using their *ankuses* to hook her by the ear and turn her so that Hatcher could examine her festering leg.

Natalie assisted Hatcher, responding to his needs of antibi-otic-filled needles and giant swatches of white cloth that he used to wipe the wound. The fetid smell told Natalie volumes. If the elephant didn't submit to the antibiotics, the infection would spread even further, and she would die.

She sighed deeply and shifted backward. Hatcher abruptly stopped mixing the ingredients for Sophie's afternoon medicine and pulled his glasses down so that he could peer at Natalie over their rims. He scrutinized her through his virtually non-existent, white-blond eyelashes.

"Are you ready?" he asked again. Quietly. Evenly.

They had agreed yesterday that she and Siriporn would be on hand for the treatment so Natalie could assist and Siriporn would translate the mahouts' commands when they moved Sophie. So far, confusion reigned and all Natalie had learned was to stay out of the way of Sophie's flailing trunk. But now Hatcher expected her to assist. She could not only assist; she could do the work herself, but the look Hatcher shot her now made her feel he truly expected—and hoped—that she would fail.

Her body tensed up every time they shared the same space, even when there were many other people included in their group. She found herself waiting for a judgmental comment or a sarcastic jab. He didn't want her there. Period. He didn't bother to try to hide it. His anger was a thick, dark mask he wore like a steel cage over his fair and otherwise innocuous features. Dr. Peter Hatcher liked to be in control and when anything arrived that threatened that control, he lost his composure.

His icy eyes now sharpened like a camera lens suddenly in focus. If she wanted to offer a suggested treatment for Sophie, she would be facing his wrath. She kept her mouth shut. It wasn't a good day to take on Hatcher's anger. It was more important to tend to Sophie's infection.

She sensed movement behind her and turned, expecting Siriporn, who'd been with her only a moment before, but it was Anurak, his fingers wrapped around Decha's ear. He stood only a couple of feet away from her. Both the boy's and dog's eyes intently focused on Sophie. Natalie's first instinct was to move them out of harm's way, but they appeared ready to bolt the second Sophie flicked an eyelash, so she let them be. Anurak smiled shyly, lifting a hand in greeting. He wore the same ragged red basketball shorts and red-and-white t-shirt he had worn when she saw him last. As she waved back, she wondered if they were the only clothes he owned and made a mental note to ask Mali if the boy could use some new ones.

A shuffle and a sharp cry returned her attention to Hatcher and the mahouts. Hatcher crouched next to Sophie's leg, his hypodermic needle inserted right above the infected area. Sophie growled and trumpeted, tossing her head, but the mahouts caught her with their *ankus*es, stopping her trunk when it whipped dangerously close to Hatcher. Natalie gasped and started forward, but the mahouts waved her back.

"Move right," Siriporn ordered her. He reappeared on Natalie's left, but his eyes were not on her. Instead, his attention was on Sophie and he watched every nuance of the elephant's body language. "Sophie nervous. She know Dr. Peter will stick needle in. See her left leg?" Siriporn spoke without taking his eyes off Sophie. One arm kept Natalie back; the other was flung wide to keep his own balance.

Sophie's leg lifted, and she flicked it backwards.

"Damn!" Hatcher darted forward but not in time to complete the injection before Sophie moved away.

"Let me help!" Natalie said. "Pass me the needle." She took a deep breath and shouldered her way in to squat next to Hatcher.

"Christ, no! She's not a horse, Dr. DeAngelo," Hatcher snapped. "And I don't have time to train you right now. Get out of my way!"

Natalie knew that it was now or never. Either he had to accept her help, or she needed to book the next flight. She planted herself and grabbed a couple of disposable gloves, slipping them on her hands, before picking up the large bottle of antiseptic at Hatcher's feet. The next time Sophie swung around, Natalie shot the infection on Sophie's leg with a squirt of antiseptic, then got out of the way so Hatcher could inject the needle. He took her cue, stabbed the elephant's leg with the hypo and injected it while the mahouts used every bit of their strength to hold Sophie in place.

Hatcher pulled out the needle after the medicine had been delivered and skipped out of the way the next time Sophie's head lolled in his direction. Wiping his hands on his shorts, he stepped back and watched her as if pleased with himself. He glanced at Natalie and nodded. A simple nod, not a word of encouragement, but it was enough. At least he'd acknowledged her.

"How often are you planning to do this?" Natalie asked as they stood about ten feet away and gathered Hatcher's medicines and needle packs into his bag.

"Every six hours, if she'll let us. It's gotten so that she knows why we're bringing her into this building, and she's truly afraid, but this is the only place that's large enough to hold her so we can inject medicines and check her vitals. The worst part is she needs two rounds: one above the infection, another closer to her heart. Now that she's had the first round, she'll feel a bit of relief, and it's easier to give her the second round. If we don't get this infection under control, it'll spread quickly throughout her system and we'll lose her. Their skin often heals over the wound, so I've been trying to keep this wound open until the infection calms down."

"Let me give her the next round," Natalie said quietly, not taking her eyes off the mahouts.

"You've never done this . . . She's unpredictable. No. I'm afraid I'm not going to let that happen."

"Listen, I've given more rounds of antibiotics than I can count. Horses. Cows. And, yes, when I was interning, even a few elephants, and one time, a rhino that had the toughest hide of any animal I've ever shot."

Hatcher opened his mouth to argue, but she stepped forward and put her hand on his arm. "I can do this," she said quietly.

Without another word, he handed the hypodermic needle to her. The mere weight of it in her hand reminded her how much larger this animal was than the horses she regularly medicated. She felt a strength within that she hadn't embodied for a very long time. A welcome feeling, she moved with it as confidently as she would respond to a horse she'd been riding for years.

With one eye on the mahouts, she silently synchronized her movements with theirs, as Siriporn had encouraged her. Any quick or jerky movement on her part would alert Sophie to her, and the elephant would swiftly lower her massive head or swing a heavy foot, could reach out her trunk and grab the nearest body part, then easily fling Natalie so far that every bone would be shattered.

Natalie knew that, and because that image was as real as the hairs standing up on her forearms, her sense of timing became as natural as any other animal's. Part of that sense came from years of working with horses and connecting with a hoof one too many times. She knew several clients who had lost family members because of accidents with horses. That horrible knowledge taught her to be cautious, quick and alert to the signals animals telegraphed before they reached what she called the red zone. Besides, no heightened physical danger could be as horrifying as sitting alone and thinking of her boys. Her sons, her lost loves. Her body and her mind now belonged to this one elephant rather than to her own self.

As soon as the mahouts caught Sophie's attention and the large gray head began to swing in their direction, Natalie plunged the foot-long hypodermic into Sophie's upper leg and delivered another round of the antibiotics into her system. The elephant bellowed and lifted her leg, but Natalie skirted out of the way, twirling like a ballerina. Sophie's leg and trunk missed her by a mere two inches. Sophie bellowed again, but this time, it was born of frustration rather than surprised pain. She wasn't used to being caught off guard. The mahouts caught her head with their short wooden prods and diverted her attention.

Hatcher stood aside, a shocked expression on his blond-whiskered face.

From the corner came the sound of clapping. Natalie had forgotten about Anurak and Decha. The boy gave her a big grin, and Decha, as if he knew what had happened, yelped and wagged his tail. Sophie roared and charged forward, but she couldn't go far.

Natalie sprinted to Anurak, lifted him off his feet, and ran with the dog and child out of the building and into the sun. Sophie was still trumpeting when Natalie, out of breath, stopped by a monkey pod tree and leaned against it. Decha held his cast straight out, his tongue drooping from the corner of his mouth in a lopsided dog grin. Anurak looked at his dog, then up at her, and silently began to laugh. Suddenly, she realized that the boy and his dog had made a game of taunting Sophie, and if it continued, one of them could be Sophie's next victim.

"You're going to have to stop doing that," she told Decha, shaking a finger in his face, "and you, too," she told Anurak as sternly as she could. "Stay away from Sophie, okay?"

She wondered if either of them understood.

THERE ARE *so many humans Sophie cannot see them all. They flash by in colors like the sun and the river. Though she hunkers her head down, leaving her peripheral vision open to see those flashes of color and people, those brief warnings of danger, she concentrates instead on using her other senses to determine the direction the men are moving.*

First, they're in front of her, and she can see their scowling faces and the swirls they create when they pass in front of her or wave their arms like the river birds. Then they hover behind her legs like flies do after she rolls in the mud.

Some of the men flit to her right, and one has zigzagged behind her left hip. She's surrounded. Her heart starts beating more quickly. She needs an escape. She must find a way out of this rapidly-tightening circle.

The woman is to Sophie's right, her voice calmer and lower than the mahouts. She holds herself straight and wide, and she's taller than the men. They listen to her. They watch her, and so does Sophie, because the woman is trying to control the yellow dog. In and out of the woman's legs, the dog weaves, in and out. Then he's dashing in and out of Sophie's sight, charging forward to bark, then pulling away when the boy who doesn't make sounds grabs the dog's ruff. The woman commands the dog, yelling at it the way mahouts yell at Sophie. The dog sits and stares directly into the woman's face, and it's clear the dog understands and will obey her.

Sophie cannot be sure. She cannot trust.

The elephant slams down her back feet, lifts her front leg up and, growling, slams it down. She's afraid. She's telling them: do not come near.

The yellow dog is unpredictable, and though Sophie can see him sitting at the woman's command, it is the dog she must watch. He is the danger. His claws ripped the skin of her leg, split it open to burn anew. She must not let him close enough to do the same again. She will kill him if he hurts her again.

Sophie's ears twitch, begin to flare out. She flaps them, a sure sign she is threatened. The woman calls to the dog as if she senses what Sophie feels. Then she pulls the boy and the dog to the side and talks to them before turning to the other humans with a voice that sounds like a growl. She flails her arms, gestures for them to leave, pushes against them. She looks over her shoulder, says something to Sophie, but the words are lost. Sophie cannot hear them above the men's yells. So much noise. So many voices.

Sophie grunts, shuffles backward.

Too many humans.

She raises her rear foot, turns it like a small radar. Lowers it to a hairsbreadth above the ground. Dust clouds skitter on the earthen floor, particles really, tickling her sensitive foot pads. She knows without turning her head that the human behind her is moving away. It was a man, the mahout who rides the young female with the high-pitched trumpet that shakes the palm leaves whenever she shrieks. He moves up the road, joining the man who smells of red meat. As they disappear into the dust, they talk loudly, throwing their words to the ones left behind.

The woman continues to move around the circle, speaks to each man, to every mahout who had been around Sophie. The woman sounds angry. She growls like a jungle cat. Urgent. Commanding.

She speaks to each of them, one by one, until she has reached them all, and the waves of her fury appear stilled. They leave, the men, disappearing into the trees like gibbering monkeys, chattering and pushing each other until they are well out of sight.

Only then, when all sound vanishes into the tree branches and she no longer smells the man smell close by, does Sophie feel she can totally lower that rear foot. She settles it down so gently not even one speck of dust is disturbed.

The boy and the yellow dog hug the woman's shadow, following so close on her heels that she stumbles. She lets loose with a sound, but she laughs. It's a sound of relief after what could have turned tense.

And, still.

The dog eyes Sophie, and she stiffens, immediately alerted. Vigilant. They stare at each other, daring the other to make the first move. Sophie thinks of the pain. If the dog moves, Sophie will lift him with her trunk and slam him to the ground.

When the woman speaks to the boy, the dog cocks his head, pants with a long pink tongue and wags his stiff sliver of a tail. The woman points toward the dwellings up the road where the others live, and the boy and dog follow her command, sprinting away through the low, sour bushes that lead to the river.

Relieved that the dog is gone, but unsure whether everyone has left, Sophie raises her head, lifts her trunk, scents the air. Only the woman is still here. She stands near Sophie's head, gazing off into the direction of the river. She reveals no anxiety, no tensions, no rage. She breathes deeply and with regularity. Sophie can sense the beating of the woman's heart.

She settles her rear leg back to the ground, satisfied. It's safe.

The woman is safe. She has not caused any harm. She will not hurt Sophie.

But Sophie knows: being alone is always safest.

She looks toward where the sky meets the mountains and watches the last of the sun's appearance for that day.

Thirteen

Until he extends his circle
of compassion to include all
living things, man will not
himself find peace.
-Albert Schweitzer

THE LITTLE, RED TRUCK pulled up to the sanctuary's main
building and the driver hopped out to let down its back gate.
Surely they aren't all supposed to fit in the open back, Natalie thought
as everyone moved forward to climb aboard.

Ten people had gathered to take the excursion to Damnoen
Saduak, the floating market. Mali told her that the trip would
take at least two and a half hours one way. Natalie squirmed at the
thought of being crammed onto the truck's bed, sitting on a hard
plank seat with ten other people, on this hot and sunny morning.
Even after a couple of months at the sanctuary, she still wasn't
used to the relentless shirt-drenching heat. Surely six would be
the maximum allowance in the back of the truck, but no, everyone
piled in, giggling and teasing and squeezing onto the plank seats
like schoolchildren on their way to a fun field trip. She climbed
in behind the last of the group, unable to resist smiling at the
delighted faces surrounding her.

On the way to the market, Natalie shifted from side to side, unable to get comfortable, but no one else seemed to have the same difficulty. They teased each other, chatted to their friends, or like the teenager to her left, hung their heads over the sides of the pickup, relishing the breeze, however hot and wet.

About an hour into the trip, she realized she might as well relax and enjoy the ride as everyone else was, so she did. She concentrated on the warm wind in her face and purposely took a couple of long and deep breaths, forcing herself to relax and to find the good in the situation. She was with happy people. The day sparkled with Thai sunshine and clean air. She was embarking on another adventure, and it would be fun.

Her mouth eased into a smile.

Mali sat next to her, cradling a sweet grass basket on her lap as if it were a baby. "I'm hoping to find a woman who sells rare spices," she told Natalie over the truck's rattle. "Different farmers come every week, so I'm never sure who'll be there. They all work out of *ruea hang yao*, you know, those long-tailed boats."

"I've seen photos of them," Natalie said. "They're quite colorful."

"Tourists love them," Mali said, holding her basket tightly as the little truck sped around a corner. "Usually I don't even go on these excursions, but it's hard to get the spices I need for *Tom Yum Hed* and *Gang Ped Fug Tong Mungsavirat*. Andrew loves my soups and vegetarian curry."

At the other end of the bench seat, Hatcher hung his head out over the side of the truck like a dog and watched the scenery race by. He'd mentioned yesterday that he had an appointment with someone he called "the old medicine man," a person who regularly supplied him with vitamins that the sanctuary vets mixed in with the elephants' food on a daily basis. Most of the powdery mix was calcium, Hatcher told Natalie, and the mixture was adjusted for each elephant. He had yet to share exactly what the other vitamins were, which she found odd but not unusual for him. He liked keeping secrets.

Opposite him, Karina sat with her knees together, feet planted securely on the floor. Her thin lips pressed firmly into a straight line as she watched the mahouts' wives teasing each other like a disappointed school marm. Every time Natalie saw her, she shook her head at the thought that she was Andrew's sister. They couldn't have been more different if they'd come from planets on the opposite end of the solar system. From the first moment Natalie had met her, she had never smiled. But Natalie felt willing to bet her last dollar that Karina was a bit sweet on Peter Hatcher from the way her eyes softened whenever he came near.

They'd make a good match. Natalie smothered a giggle at the thought and looked over her shoulder at the verdant jungle and jagged mountain peaks they passed through. Surely there were times when this part of Thailand appeared dim and unattractive, but even during the rainiest of days, she found something marvelous that took her breath away. Thailand and its people and its animals filled her heart with their natural splendor, and she couldn't imagine any other place that would come close to its beauty. With a sigh, she luxuriated in the view and the need to do nothing at all but enjoy it.

The road twisted and turned through sky-high trees wound up in climbing vines, past terraced rice paddies sculpted like stairsteps against the mountainside. Occasionally, the dense jungle separated, and she'd spot the blue river snaking its way alongside the road, or a small hut selling local products like palm oil or bananas. The air smelled green, heavy with the scent of dirt and mango, spicy live cloves, and a faint muskiness like patchouli.

Soon the scenery became less jungle-like and more civilized. Small huts with cars and trucks parked in the driveways dotted the road. Open-air shops sold produce, honey, coconut art, and Buddhist statues. Traffic thickened and the occasional stoplight gave Natalie a chance to check out the small towns they passed through. Streets lined with car shops and supermarkets; small, vibrantly-decorated temples next to taxi offices emblazoned with neon signs. Women shouldering baskets full of orange sweets they sold to passersby. Sleek ninja motorcycles competed for parking spaces with Vespas. And every once in a while, a reminder of home: a 7-Eleven sign or a red-white-and-blue Pepsi banner.

They'd been in the truck for nearly two hours when the driver pulled into an Esso station complete with a 24-hour store and a Burger King. Natalie stretched her arms above her head and yawned as she followed Mali to the restrooms. A group of school-girls discharged from a tourist bus raced in circles around her, their ear-splitting shrieks reminding her how quiet the sanctuary was, even on its noisiest days. She'd take elephants bellowing over teenage shrieking any day of the week. Though she could under-stand very little of what the girls said, it was easy to tell that they were flirting with some of the boys who had streamed off their companion bus in a much more leisurely fashion. She watched their interactions.

Across the sidewalk, Hatcher stood outside the store, a cold drink to his lips, his eyes focused on the same group of flirting pre-teens. He caught Natalie's eye, shook his head as if commenting on the silliness of young love, and smiled.

Natalie took a step back as if he'd pushed her. It was such a tiny moment, minuscule really, but she felt as shocked as if he'd dumped a bucket of ice water over her head. She laughed aloud. *So it took a trip out of the sanctuary for him to act like a fellow human being.*

"Where's the river?" she asked Mali.

"What river?"

"Isn't the Floating Market on a river?"

Mali laughed. "Not the type you imagine. Technically, it's the Mae Klong that flows through Ratchaburi, but the boats pull up between some buildings on what's basically a skinny little canal, barely wide enough for a couple of boats to pass by each other. You'll see. Come on. I'll point you in the right direction and see you in an hour or two."

Mali took her friend Hom's arm and the two of them walked away, heads together conspiratorially. Natalie envied the friend-ship and the obvious need they both had to spend time alone without Andrew around. He'd stayed behind to take care of administrative details, and Mali had seemed pleased she'd get to spend the day alone.

Natalie was left alone with Hatcher, who glanced at her and adjusted his sunglasses. "I have to see the apothecary . . ."

"You don't have to explain. I can explore on my own. I'm a big girl." She pulled her hair back and tightened her barrette as he walked away, then suddenly realized she had no clue where to go. "Wait! Wait a minute!" Jogging the few steps to catch him, she broke a sweat even though it was not yet nine in the morning. "Where's the Floating Market? All I see are buildings."

"Go into one of the entrances and have a look." Hatcher waved an I-don't-have-time-to-take-care-of-you hand at her and melted into the throng.

She entered the nearest open-sided metal building, instantly grateful for the shade it provided. This time of day felt stagnant, when the only wind that moved was an artificially-produced breeze from an overhead fan.

For a moment, she oriented herself and took in all the sights and smells. The building teemed with booths that catered to the tourist: bamboo hats shaped like umbrellas, orange T-shirts emblazoned with elephants, garishly-designed pocketbooks, wooden Buddhas, golden-red Thai puppets, fake silk scarves, cotton balloon pants in all colors and sizes, intricately-woven white lace blouses, and red and yellow carved wooden children's toys.

It's a flea market like the one in Raleigh at the State Fair Grounds, Natalie thought, *except this one is full of goods created in Thailand for tourists.*

Beyond the food booths cooking steamed rice and spiced meat or offering frozen bananas and fruit drinks, the canal Natalie had been hearing about separated one building full of tourist kitsch from another identical to it, and on the canal: the long, canoe-like boats.

Each boat brimmed over with fresh fruit and vegetables like yellow-and-green papayas, while another held crescent-shaped bunches of bananas, and yet another was loaded with gold-en-green watermelons, rumored to be more delicious than any back home. Boats floated by filled with piles of neatly-stacked, hand-crafted bamboo pocketbooks, cerise and aquamarine silk scarves like the ones being sold inside the buildings, carved wooden elephants that fit into each other like nesting dolls, or funky coconuts shaped like monkeys. The female boat owners, wearing wide-brimmed bamboo hats over their sun-lined faces and sporting knee-length, colorful aprons to hold their change and tools, piloted their canoes in and out of the canal with long bamboo poles. They reminded her of the stories Mark Twain told of the Mississippi, except she couldn't understand a word these women said.

People called out the prices of their merchandise, customers haggled about what they would pay, store owners enticed buyers into their stalls or to the pier where boats rested to sell their goods, and everyone raised their voices to the highest decibel.

Natalie stood for a while watching the organized confusion and shook her head, amazed at the ancient use of the canal as the conduit for sales of goods that not everyone in the region could grow. *The Thai version of the Walmart Superstore*, she thought. *Much better than the Walmarts in the States. At least this type of economy thrives on individual ownership.*

From down river, she heard a familiar voice and without so much as a glance, realized it was Mali negotiating a better price for something she was purchasing from a vendor in the canal. Natalie headed in her direction.

"Oh, there you are, my dear." Mali straightened up, shoving the small greenish fruits she'd purchased into the cotton bag she had slung over her shoulder. "What do you think of this Floating Market? Pretty unique, eh? Have you seen Siriporn? I asked him to find the spice woman for me."

Natalie shook her head and inwardly chuckled. What teenage boy would want to be seen with his mother? Surely he'd disappeared with his friends rather than do Mali's bidding.

Mali glanced around her, more concern on her face than the situation warranted. "Someone said there's a Red Shirt meeting nearby," she muttered. "If he's involved with them again, I'll . . ."

An ungodly scream ripped through the marketplace. The same sounds Sophie made when she could no longer stand on her infected leg.

Natalie's hair prickled along the edges of her scalp. Without thinking, she turned and instinctively ran toward the sound. People scattered in front of her outstretched hands. A woman stumbled. Natalie stooped to pick her up, then heard another scream.

An elephant in pain.

She moved faster, pushing her way through the shopping crowd to the end of the football-field-length building. Sweating and breathless, she emerged into the white-hot sunlight onto a tiny side street, temporarily blinded. She stopped for a moment, shaded her eyes and scanned the street. A small crowd had gathered past the little bridge that spanned the canal. Above their heads she saw the gray hump of an elephant's head. On its back, at a precarious angle, hung a garishly decorated covered seat large enough to hold four adults. The seat itself weighed between fifty and seventy-five pounds. Add two or three adults at an average of a hundred and fifty pounds each, thus the elephant might be forced to carry between three and five hundred pounds.

Her stomach turned as she shoved her way through the throng. A woman hawking pencils shaped like palm trees stuck a handful of them in Natalie's face, "You buy some for your chillen, lady?"

Natalie waved her away.

She stood close enough to the elephant now to smell the fear. A mahout poked the screaming animal with a pointed pole, digging it again and again into the ellie's delicate eye socket. The elephant rocked backward with each new jab, rivulets of blood and pus running down its face as it tried in vain to back away from the abuse. The top of the *howdah*, the wooden seat the elephant carried on its back, slammed repeatedly against the building behind it. She had nowhere to go. Trapped. Terrified. And from what Natalie could see, the elephant was probably blind. And in serious psychological distress.

"Stop!" Natalie grabbed the mahout's shirt. "What the hell are you doing? You're killing her."

The mahout spat at the ground and rattled some Thai curses. Natalie had no idea what they meant but the mahouts at the sanctuary used the same terms with Sophie. However, this mahout didn't smile when he spoke the words. Instead, his eyes gritted shut, and when he opened his mouth to let another tirade fly, he appeared toothless. He wore a threadbare blue and white shirt and shorts made of rags. On his feet, he wore a pair of red flip flops at least three sizes too big. She instantly realized he was one of the men Mali had told her about: an elephant owner who took his animal to the same streets every day so that she could earn money for him by giving tourists the exotic treat of a ride on her fragile back. Animals mistreated like this ended up at the sanctuary with such damaging injuries that they couldn't turn their head from side-to-side or walk straight.

"Okay, old girl, okay," Natalie murmured as she moved closer to evaluate the elephant's condition. Runny sores around the elephant's eyes and ears spoke of years of being poked and prodded mercilessly. The pads on her feet were worn and bleeding as a result of spending long hours on unforgiving cement. Her skin hung off her skeletal frame in folds, and her knees practically knocked against each other.

Natalie shook her head. Even though most of the elephants at the sanctuary had major health issues caused by human handling, she'd never seen one this bad. It brought tears to her eyes.

"No animal is ever healed by a vet's tears." A gruff voice she instantly recognized spoke in her ear.

She turned to see Peter Hatcher and Mali approach with several others from their group close behind.

He slid in front of her so that he stood between the elephant's mahout—who seemed to be getting angrier by the moment—and Natalie. Mali moved to stand by his side. Slowly, in halting Thai, Hatcher addressed the mahout.

At first, Mali stood silently, but when Peter glanced over at her as if questioning a word he'd spoken, she chimed in, her Thai natural and relaxed, though her tone sounded strident. Natalie understood nothing except their body language. Peter held his arms open, gesturing toward the elephant who had now begun rocking side to side. The seat atop her back tilted, even more precarious than before. In the back of her throat, she keened and rumbled sadly.

The mahout balanced on one foot, stamping the other occasionally into the ground as if doing a strange traditional dance. His voice varied between a scream and a demand. Mali kept her own voice even and quiet; whenever she spoke, both men had to listen. All around them, Thai people stood in small clumps, whispering behind their hands and watching the drama unfold in front of them.

Fifteen minutes later, the mahout spoke calmly and quietly with Mali as if they'd grown up together, and Peter turned, took Natalie's arm and walked her away.

"What happened?" she asked.

"We offered him some medicine for the elephant, and Mali's going to keep trying to talk to him about surrendering the elephant, but this is his living. It might not work." He glanced back over his shoulder and kept his hand on Natalie's arm as though sensing that she still wasn't convinced. "You must not be cheeky when dealing with an owner. In spite of the way it looks, he's doing the best he can. Most of these guys have had elephants in their family for generations. He doesn't think what he's doing is . . . wrong. He's simply making a living for his family."

"But that animal is dying . . . he's killing her!"

Hatcher's blue eyes darkened. "You know that and I know that, but that chap has no clue. You can't come over here and all of a sudden expect years of tradition to change because you have one encounter with a mahout-owner. Sometimes you have to back off a tad. Don't be a bull in a china shop."

"And let the animal die? I can't do that. And you can't either, can you?"

"We're not letting the animal die. We'll get the owner help in order to understand how to deal with her, and slowly, but surely, we'll convince him there are other ways to make a living besides using her to trek tourists around, but we have to be respectful."

"Can't Andrew do something? Buy the elephant? Bring it to the sanctuary?"

"Ultimately, that may be what happens, but Andrew's not here right now. It's only us, and drawing a crowd in the middle of the Floating Market doesn't make the locals look upon us very favorably. You can't barge in there and simply . . . well, scream and shout. You need to think before you react."

"When it's an emergency situation, you react. You move. You do what needs to be done to save the animal. You know that. You've been a vet as long as I have."

"Yes, that's true, but I've lived here longer than you have, and I learned the hard way that you don't butt into their business. There are other ways to handle the situation."

Across the street, Mali smiled and bowed to the mahout who had taken the rope around the elephant's neck and was leading her away. The ellie followed him slowly, her gait unsteady and wobbly. Then, out of a side alley, a man appeared with a hand-made ladder. The man spoke briefly to the mahout, who leaned the ladder against the elephant and climbed up to the wooden seat, unleashing it from the elephant, and with the help of the man on the ground, lowered the seat off the elephant's back.

"See?" Hatcher said into Natalie's ear. "One step at a time."

Mali strode across the street. "He expects us to come to his farm next week," she told Peter. "And he's ready to give the old girl up if Andrew can come up with enough money, but I fear that ellie's not going to last another week or two."

He nodded, then released Natalie's arm and told her, "If you want, you can come with me next week. For now, this is all we can do."

"At least the mahout took the seat off her back," Natalie said as they all started walking back toward the truck.

"Small victory," Mali muttered, eyes straight ahead.

In the truck, Mali, Hatcher, and Natalie sat together, talking about what had happened. At the other end of the truck, out of earshot, Karina shot Natalie venomous glances as if suspecting the conversation was a romantic one. Natalie longed to tell her she had absolutely no interest in Peter Hatcher. If Karina wanted him, bless her, but he was not on Natalie's agenda.

Siriporn had boarded the truck at the last minute, sporting a new, red T-shirt. Mali was right. He'd gone to a political meeting. Mother and son studiously ignored each other, their angry silence more damaging than an outright quarrel. Natalie watched silently, wishing they knew how silly the argument would feel in the future. They should treasure each moment, for the future wasn't promised. All they had was now.

Once they were on the road, the truck's noise prevented everyone from talking, so Natalie watched the scenery go by. Immersed in her own thoughts, she realized she'd acted like her old self during the crisis with the street elephant. No flashbacks. No PTSD. She breathed deeply and a film rose over her eyes as the city streets faded to jungle. An unexpected feeling of guilt overwhelmed her. She hadn't thought of the boys for hours.

Fourteen

When elephants fight, it is the grass that suffers.
-Kikuyu Proverb

THE PIGLET SQUEALED AS though its life was coming to an end that very second. Though Anurak held on to the wriggling, little, pink mass with both hands, it seemed to Natalie (and to everyone around her, most of whom howled with laughter) that the boy was losing this battle. Finally, Anurak grabbed the piglet's front legs in one hand and turned the rear end toward Natalie with the other. With a triumphant toothless grin, he nodded at her.

Natalie brushed her hair out of her eyes, took a deep breath, and shoved the needle into the pig's thigh. One last squeal from the piglet, and she pulled the needle out and nodded to Anurak, who'd been acting as her assistant all morning. He placed the squealing piglet on the ground where it promptly scurried back to its mother and the dozen siblings that had already been vaccinated.

"That's the last one," Hatcher announced. He stood next to the sanctuary's truck, his hand atop the valise he carried with him every time they did these runs.

This trip to the local village was the third Natalie had joined in since coming to Thailand. Each time, she learned more about the local people, the Thai language, and the customs of the surrounding villages. On today's visit, they had vaccinated this farmer's pigs against parasites, viruses and bacteria, then she splinted his dog's foreleg and checked on his pregnant cow.

The voluntary visits were Andrew's way of supporting the community. He had started the tradition years ago, only a few months after the sanctuary had opened its gates, and though the visits were meant to keep the community's pets and livestock healthy, they also cemented the relationship Andrew had with his neighbors. The farmers donated any leftover produce to feed the elephants and would help repair a section of fence around the sanctuary's five-mile perimeter because Andrew continued to help them. Everyone won. Animals included.

Natalie speculated that Andrew wisely realized he wouldn't be able to conduct his work without support from the locals. Not everyone agreed with treating animals so fairly, but the Buddhists in the neighboring communities accepted Andrew as one of them, and though he never talked openly about his religious beliefs, Natalie thought there might be more truth to that than fiction. He understood the Thai people and dealt with them in a quiet and unassuming way. He was careful not to take advantage of any people who worked for him, and as a result, everyone connected with the sanctuary shared Andrew's philosophies, from the way they ate (most followed a vegan lifestyle) to their commitment to the animals.

"Andrew puts people out of business," Mali said. "The elephant is royal in Thailand, but they've also been a beast of burden, helping human beings by doing the heavy work. A family who owns an element can hire it out or use it to do farm work or logging. Makes them pretty valuable. Andrew's had to be quite diplomatic when explaining what we do."

Peter, Andrew, Mali, and Natalie climbed into the back of the truck with very little discussion and took the forty-five minute ride home in bone-tired silence. The morning had been a long one, and it sapped all of their strength to wrangle the piglets and ensure that all of the other living beings on the farm were healthy. Anurak and Decha had tagged along so Anurak could visit his teacher for a sign language lesson. Decha shared the lessons, as much as a dog could, and filled the role of therapy dog though no one had trained him as such. They rode in the cab of the truck with the driver, Anurak's uncle.

Natalie idly picked clumps of dirt from under her nails and tried not to doze as the truck bumped its way down the rutted two-lane highway. All she could think of was how good it would feel to take a shower back at her cabin. Sometimes it felt like she hadn't been clean for days, and she often found herself fantasizing about a scalding hot bubble bath she could sink into up to her neck, but she'd come to the realization that as long as she stayed at the sanctuary, both hot water and bubble baths would be at a premium. No matter, though. She felt happy and satisfied. She could deal with taking cold baths as long as she had soap—and her mother had sent her a new supply that arrived yesterday.

The movement of the truck lulled her, and she finally submitted and closed her eyes. Half asleep, she listened to Andrew and Hatcher arguing about their favorite soccer players. Andrew followed Manchester United, and Peter staunchly supported Chelsea. From the sounds of it, they were fierce rivals. In the background, Mali sang softly, her voice sometimes drowned out by the truck's squeaks and rattles. In her semi-conscious state, Natalie felt like an interloper to their conversation, almost invisible to the others. No one expected her response or attention, and the privacy and freedom felt almost euphoric.

Before long, the truck pulled onto the long dirt road that led into the compound. Natalie stretched and opened her eyes. Hatcher and Andrew gathered their things and quickly sketched out their plans for the rest of the day. Mali gazed toward the kitchen area as if wondering whether the prep work had been done for the evening's meal. Natalie grabbed her knapsack so she could hop out quickly and head for that shower before dinner.

They rounded the corner to the parking area, and the truck came to a screeching halt. Natalie fell to the floor with a thud. Rubbing her butt, she stood up and followed the others as they scrambled out. In front of the truck, debris littered the road. Where there had once been a gravel driveway now stood half a wall from of the side buildings used to house garden equipment. Beyond the wreckage, Natalie only saw sky. Mali's nets over the vegetable garden had disappeared.

"What the bloody hell . . ." Andrew's mouth was open as he stared at the wreckage.

"Was there a wind storm while we were gone?" Peter asked, though none of them could answer his question.

"More like a hurricane," Natalie said. "Only it doesn't look like it rained. The ground is completely dry."

Andrew went down on his knees, inspecting what appeared to be fresh tracks. He spread a clump of grass with his fleshy, liver-spotted hand, and swore under his breath.

"Mali, find Siriporn," he said, his voice low and controlled.

Mali scampered toward the mahouts' sleeping quarters, and returned less than a moment later with Siriporn at her side and two of the other mahouts behind them. All were out of breath.

Andrew rose from his crouch and now stood with his hands on his hips, his attention on the mahouts. "What the hell happened here?"

The boys looked as guilty as if they'd thrown a party in the family home while their parents were on vacation.

Siriporn stepped forward. Thinner and taller than the other young men, he wore an uncharacteristically serious expression on his face. "We tried to stop her, Mr. Andrew. She running quick and quicker. Mahouts run. Cooks run. Everyone run."

"Who?"

The mahouts' furtive side glances told a story their words could not.

"Who, I asked!" Andrew leaned closer, pulling himself up to his full and imposing height to tower over the much shorter mahouts.

None of them spoke for a long, uncomfortable minute, then Siriporn piped up in a small, embarrassed voice, "Sophie. Sophie got away from mahout. She much strong. She broke wall."

"That damned elephant! She's going to kill someone as sure as I'm standing here. Where is she now?" Hatcher said, his lips compressed into a solid line. A spot of red burned on both of his cheeks as he scanned the horizon, his hand shading his eyes like a sea captain.

The mahouts looked at each other then lifted their arms to the side in unison.

"You've got to be fucking shitting me," Hatcher spat. "How the hell do you lose a friggin' elephant?"

If not for the destruction surrounding them, Natalie would have laughed at Hatcher's atypical outburst, but she knew that giggling would be misconstrued, so she choked it back. Instead, she caught Mali's eye and said, "Why don't you and I go toward the greenhouse area, and you two"—she pointed at Andrew and Peter—"go to the clinic. Siriporn can head for the perimeter. The others can cover the river and the rice fields. Maybe if we bring Ali, Sophie's more likely to come to them. If we spread out, we can find her more quickly." Other mahouts and workers had arrived upon hearing the commotion, and with military precision, they all followed Natalie's suggestion and headed in various directions to hunt down Sophie.

Natalie glanced back over her shoulder and caught Anurak's eye. He stood next to his uncle. Decha sat close by his side, tongue lolling out. She nodded toward the cabins surrounding the rice fields and pointed in that direction, signaling for Anurak to go home and to stay there. If Sophie was on the war path, Decha would only anger her further. She didn't need to tell him twice. He trotted down the dirt driveway, Decha right behind him. They had far too much experience with Sophie's anger to tempt their luck.

Mali and Natalie made their way toward the greenhouse, speculating about what might have happened. As they drew closer to Mali's vegetable gardens, they both fell silent. The gardens were unrecognizable. Totally destroyed. It appeared the elephant had run back and forth through the netting and eaten most of the vegetables that had been close to harvest while trampling everything else. Mali swiped at a tear as she pulled some of the netting from a large pumpkin that had somehow managed to stay intact.

That one tear tugged on Natalie's heartstrings more than a full-blown sob would have. She knew how hard Mali had worked to make this garden flourish, the hours she'd put in weeding and watering and urging blooms to grow into squash and pumpkin and zucchini. Now crushed tomatoes lay underfoot and made a squishing sound that Natalie ignored as she walked over them. She wound her arm around Mali's shoulders, allowing Mali to lean into her.

"We'll replant everything," Natalie said, "and pot whatever we can save. Don't worry. I'll help you."

Mali simply nodded and sighed. Her shoulders slumped as her eyes filled with tears. "If it hadn't been Sophie, one of the other ellies probably would have found this soon enough. I always feared it didn't have enough protection."

They walked through the mess, lifting plants and picking up a vegetable or two. The smell of veggies just beginning to rot in the sweltering sun told her that the destruction had probably occurred early this morning. In the distance, mahouts yelled to each other as they searched along the tree line. Within only a few moments the calls drifted away, and Mali and Natalie were left in the quiet of the destroyed greenhouse.

"We should help them look for her," Mali said as she brushed off a large yellow squash and added it to the small pile of undamaged vegetables she balanced in her arms. "We can't do much here."

"Let's take this stuff to the kitchen, and we'll come back." Natalie turned and started back to the main building, checking over her shoulder to see whether Mali needed help. Satisfied Mali had her veggies under control, Natalie moved forward and suddenly felt like she was being watched.

"Sophie," Natalie whispered.

Behind her, Mali came to an abrupt stop.

Only a dozen feet in front of them, the errant elephant stood in a patch of tall grasses, quietly pulling them up with her trunk and eating them. She eyed them curiously but made no move toward them. They were close enough to hear her satisfied breathing as she munched the tender grass shoots.

It dawned on Natalie that she and Mali might be downwind or that Sophie now knew Natalie's scent and was fairly comfortable with her. On the other hand, Natalie and Mali had spent the morning on a farm and had not yet had the chance to shower, so maybe they smelled like animals. Whatever the case, Sophie acted as though they posed no threat to her.

"Mali, can you hear me?" Natalie whispered, not daring to turn her head or to move.

"Yes."

"Move backwards toward the greenhouse, then head to the river. Find the mahouts. I'll stay here with Sophie."

Mali didn't respond, but Natalie could tell from the swishing grasses that she had done as requested.

As Sophie moved forward to reach a patch of grass with her trunk, Natalie cocked her head and saw that the elephant dragged the five-foot-long heavy rope that normally connected to an O-ring in the ground to keep her safely anchored. Each time Natalie and Peter administered Sophie's medicine, she wore one rope on her front right leg and another on her back left one, both connected to the O-ring. The mahouts would take opposite sides so that they could ensure that she didn't grab anyone with her trunk. But right now—as she dragged the rope behind her—she didn't seem dangerous at all. Natalie wondered, *could the rope be what's fueling her anxiety and stress?*

"Maybe you need to be trusted, huh, ol' girl?" Natalie said softly, inching closer.

Sophie raised her head and stared at her for a moment, but soon went back to eating.

Natalie tried a few more steps. Again, Sophie raised her head, acknowledging Natalie's advances but returned to eating almost immediately. She seemed quite content to be out in the sun, unimpeded, as free as any other elephant at the sanctuary.

It was the closest Natalie had been to the elephant, and she was about to advance a few more steps closer when she heard voices coming up the road. Sophie's head lifted. She heard them, too, and low rumbles escaped her throat. A warning sound. The sound of an animal in defense mode.

"It's okay, girl," Natalie spoke softly and lifted a hand. "I won't let anyone hurt you."

The small group of mahouts, led by Hatcher and Andrew, came into sight. They spotted each other at the same moment but their eyes quickly looked past Natalie—at Sophie. Hatcher threw up his hand and the group came to a halt.

Natalie raised her own hand in silent warning and glanced back at Sophie who had stopped eating to watch the approaching humans.

What the hell do I do now? If I move, she'll move. If I stay still, we'll never get her back to her building.

The vegetables Natalie had been carrying weighed heavily in her arms. She shifted and balanced them more evenly in her T-shirt. Sophie turned her head, and her eyes focused on the pumpkin on top of the pile. She glanced back at the group, then at the pumpkin again.

"Andrew," Natalie called out quietly. "Please keep everyone out of the way. I'm going to try to walk her back to the building."

Andrew started to protest, but Hatcher stopped him and placed his hand on Andrew's arm. The thought immediately went through Natalie's mind that Peter Hatcher would love nothing more than to see her fail at this attempt. Even the suspicion that he'd be so crass made her more determined to prove herself to him. She knew it didn't really matter whether or not he acknowledged she had some finesse with the animals. What mattered was whether she could help Sophie. *Fuck the ignorant Englishman who wouldn't let go of his grudge.*

Reassuring Sophie quietly, Natalie took a step toward her. Sophie raised her head and her big eyes blinked slowly as if she understood Natalie's plan. A hushed argument took place in the group of mahouts, but Siriporn's voice rose above the others' and they moved away as Natalie had requested. She took a moment to balance the vegetables in her shirt so she had one hand free and then lifted the pumpkin toward Sophie.

"You want this?" She dangled the pumpkin from its stem.

Sophie reached out her trunk. The end of it wriggled, opening and closing like fingers.

"Follow me, and I'll give it to you." Natalie took a few steps toward the dirt road that led down to the river and to the back of the camp where Sophie had been housed. She walked confidently, close enough for Sophie to smell the food, but far enough that Sophie had to reach. Natalie had no idea whether this would work, but there was no harm in trying. "C'mon girl."

Sophie took one step, then another. The tip of her trunk continued to reach toward what Natalie held. "You're being very patient," Natalie said as she gave Sophie the pumpkin. Sophie popped it whole into her mouth, chewing on it luxuriously.

Success!

THE WOMAN *pulls a long zucchini from the basket and waves it around Sophie's trunk, so she can smell it. Sophie reaches for it, grabs it with the finger-like tip of her trunk, deposits it in her mouth, and chews, watching the woman all the while. Whenever the woman moves and the elephant follows, she is rewarded with another zucchini in her mouth. It's become a game. Is the woman deciding to give a zucchini to the elephant, or is Sophie determining whether she's hungry enough to follow the woman for the zucchini? It doesn't matter. There's never enough juicy fruits and vegetables.*

"Sophie, want a zucchini? Come, Sophie." The woman produces another squash, then another zucchini. The words are different, but the elephant understands the meaning. She comprehends that the words are an invitation and the vegetables are the prize. She has been taught this response many times in her life, by many different men. She knows what to do.

With each piece of food, the woman moves backwards, slowly. She entices Sophie to follow her, to come closer if she wants the reward. The elephant is hesitant, at first. Usually, there is a punishment as well as a reward. She's learned that, too. And for that very reason, she doesn't trust men.

This is a woman who smells safe, though. Non-threatening. Her voice lacks the roughness, the sharp edge, of the mahouts'. Even her touch is different—warmer—as though her body temperature is several degrees higher than her male counterparts'.

She holds only vegetables. No poles or ankus in her other hand. She beckons the elephant forward once again.

Sophie swings her head from side to side, glances behind her, unsure of her feet. It has been a long time since she's walked freely. Her legs wobble a bit, but their path is following the river now, and she smells the water beyond and becomes excited, lifts her trunk, produces her version of a delighted trumpet.

Even though excited, she moves slowly, careful with her leg, feeling with the other for holes and fallen limbs. Every once in a while, she grabs a low-hanging branch and nibbles at a newborn leaf, taking the chance to rest her leg for a moment.

The woman walks to the elephant's side, talks quietly, gives a command, offers the food. Sophie immediately understands: If a word is spoken and Sophie responds, she gets food. If she does not, she gets no food.

She crushes a particularly juicy zucchini in her mouth.

Still, she has not taken her attention off the woman. If the woman raises her voice, Sophie will halt in her steps and refuse to respond to another command, no matter how softly it is spoken. She will never trust the woman again. She will reject the woman, because she knows from long years of experience that human beings can inflict horrible pain.

But her senses say this woman is not going to abuse Sophie. The woman will never use an ankus. She's a firm mahout, and her commands are clear. Sophie is beginning to learn this woman's heart. She tastes the compassion in the woman's essence, she hears it in her voice, sees it when they look into each other's eyes. The woman's touch is as delicate as new summer grasses, light and healing. But the elephant remains guarded.

Somewhere nearby, the men watch. Sophie can smell them, but she knows from the way their scent lingers in the air that they aren't moving toward her or the woman, so she relaxes a little and concentrates on the food.

"Good girl, Sophie. Here's some carrots. Good girl." The woman walks ahead, Sophie following, her large ears billowing back and forth with her frustration. She wants those carrots.

From the corner of her eye, Sophie spots the man's blond head. She pauses, momentarily forgetting the carrots, and reaches her trunk out to check his hands for ankuses or needles or bottles. Whenever he is near, there is pain. He equals pain.

She sees nothing, but she moves into the enclosure, reaching out behind her to grab the carrots out of the woman's hand. Still, watching him, her ears twitching, shifting back and forth but seeing no way out, feeling trapped.

The man gestures to the woman. The woman nods and continues backing into the building. His eyes shift to the side, and his scent is tinged with something acrid that burns the end of Sophie's trunk. She senses that it's not only unsafe for her, but this man means harm to the woman, too.

The elephant feels something solid against her back leg and knows she can go no further. It feels unfamiliar, so she reaches her trunk out to touch the steel gate and the bars on both sides. She has not been under this roof before, but something tells her it'll be safer than near the man.

The woman sucks in her breath and keeps motioning Sophie forward. She produces a squash from a bucket beyond the bars. A surprise. Sophie had thought the food was gone. She continues shuffling toward the woman, blocking her into a corner.

From outside, the elephant hears the man yell, a warning sound, but the woman shows no fear. Instead, the way she looks into Sophie's eyes relates a sense of trust, and somehow Sophie knows she will not get poked or prodded. Sophie knows the vegetables in the basket are hers, and that's all she wants, there is nothing else more important or dear to her, and she will find a way to have them.

"Okay, old girl," the woman says quietly as she closes the large steel gate that will keep the elephant in the enclosure. She says something else that Sophie doesn't understand, but her voice is soothing. She touches the elephant softly, telling Sophie to move to the right, and offers a squash which Sophie takes and lifts into her triangular mouth while shifting her hips to the right, giving the woman enough space to slip out.

As the woman leaves, talking to the man who walks ahead of her, Sophie circles the enclosure, smells the pile of vegetables the woman left right outside the gate. She reaches for them, stretches her trunk completely to its tip and leans forward, almost stumbles before realizing that no ropes are tied to any of her ankles. She can eat as much as she wants, so she does, and after the pile is depleted, burping loudly, she leans against a cement pole and takes a contented nap.

Fifteen

We are the children of our
landscape; it dictates behavior
and even thought in the measure
to which we are responsive to it.
-Lawrence George Durrell

To Natalie, there were few things more satisfying than
having a breakthrough with an animal. Whether that meant
finding a way to halt an aggressive cancer in a British Mastiff,
saving a beautiful thoroughbred's leg, or getting an elephant to
trust her—it didn't matter. All she wanted to do was to find an
answer to a problem. She thought about that with her feet planted
shoulder distance apart, feeling rooted to the earth as the luke-
warm shower water pounded her from above. She liked having
answers that made sense, and she felt most vulnerable when she
had unanswered questions. Questions unbalanced her. They made
her feel as though one leg was stretched high into the air while the
other tried to maintain balance on a log spinning in a wild river.

As she walked to the big building for supper, the fatigue
of the day rolled off her shoulders as easily as the soapy shower
water had. A layered fuchsia, watermelon, and robin's egg blue
sunset sky revealed its richness along the far edges of the meadow.
She stopped to breathe it in for a moment. In the distance, a dog

barked and an elephant answered with a long rumble. It was a sound she'd heard often, but this time she wondered idly whether it had been Ali and was surprised that she'd begun to identify the elephants by their sounds.

Mali had brought whatever undamaged vegetables and herbs she could find to the kitchen, demanding they be used as quickly as possible. Some of the cooks teased that there would be no meat for a week because that would be how long it would take to eat all the veggies.

Mali caught Natalie's eye and smiled. "Perhaps it's time to stop eating meat completely," she said in English, then she turned to the cooks and volunteers and repeated the comment in Thai. Natalie guessed from the looks on their faces that they weren't sure whether that was a good idea.

Natalie found a seat at the same long picnic table where Andrew, Peter, Karina, and some of the volunteers sat. She smiled across the plates and bowls at Karina on the other side. That was a mistake. Karina instantly averted her gaze and switched to sit on her right hip so she could continue talking to a volunteer who'd arrived from Germany the night before.

Natalie moved to the other end of the table and put her tray down next to Karina's knapsack. Everyone picked up their conversations where they'd left off, ignoring her. Was that a sign that she was accepted? They didn't have to pay attention to her? Or were they purposefully ignoring her? She squirmed a little in her seat and looked around, but no one paid any attention to her, engaged in their own side conversations, or simply gazing into the distance.

She took a spoonful of food, telling herself she was making too much of it, but from somewhere in her teenage past came a memory she'd long forgotten of being ignored by Carrie and Sabrina and Jill, the girls she'd been friends with since grade school, and the same familiar stab of betrayal came back to haunt her, coupled with the unanswered question: *what did I do?*

She shifted in her seat, realizing how ridiculous it was to revisit the same question at this stage of her life and even more ridiculous that her first inclination was to run away from the situation. It took all of her willpower to anchor herself to the seat and act nonchalant.

Andrew was the first to break the uncomfortable silence. "Peter, Natalie, Mali, and Siriporn: When you are done with dinner, we need to meet. Be at the long table in half an hour." He rose as he spoke and made eye contact with everyone before taking his dish and moving to the sink to rinse and stack it.

Mali followed close behind and spoke with him quietly before walking with him to the end of the patio where several of the elephants waited patiently for their evening meal.

Natalie silently swallowed her food and watched Mali and Andrew, deep in brow-furrowed conversation. They were an odd couple in so many ways: he, tall, broad and blonde, a no-nonsense Englishman with a few rough edges; Mali, small, slight, and dark, exotic yet European, intelligent and cultured, and able to straddle the diversity in the camp as well as in her personal life. Siriporn, her eldest son, personified Mali's Thai life, while Sivad, the youngest of Mali's children and Andrew's daughter, resembled her mother in more ways than the two others, yet it seemed that she might have more of a challenge than the others since she had a fair modicum of Andrew's stubbornness. She ran around camp free as a butterfly, often getting into places and things that she shouldn't. Khalan's eyes were a different shape than either of his siblings', and he was smaller in frame and height than Siriporn, but they had the same broad mouth. All three of Mali's children had her smile.

Natalie liked Mali, and though she often felt she'd never truly know her, the irony was that the two of them had one major factor in common: they both loved their boys way too much. Natalie knew by the way Mali talked to Siriporn that the two of them were bonded more strongly than Mali was with Khalan. Though most mothers wouldn't admit it, there was always one child who needed more attention, more mothering, more love.

Danny had been that child. Everything Danny had done delighted her. And Mali looked at Siriporn with the same kind of wonder. Seeing the raw maternal emotion wash over Mali's face often felt like too much to bear. Natalie turned away, overwhelmed, and fought it with every ounce of her energy. It would never end. This pain. The only thing that helped was to find another focus. She blinked hard and forced herself to watch her new friend.

Mali stared at Siriporn as he approached her and Andrew. It was an odd moment. Andrew ignored Siriporn. Mali glanced back and forth between her lover and her son as if unsure to whom she should pay attention. In that blink of an eye, Natalie understood Mali better than she understood herself. She watched as conflicting emotions chased each other across Mali's face as she fought being caught in the middle. After a few moments of talking, they all turned and glanced at Natalie. Something in their gaze stirred her and diverted her from the jealousy she'd begun to feel. Just as well. The envy connected to that deep well of grief she couldn't afford to plumb right now.

Mali lifted a hand to her mouth, her eyes still focused on Natalie. She spoke to Andrew, who nodded and walked over to the table where Natalie sat. For no other reason than an instinctual and powerful feeling of dread, Natalie felt that the world as she knew it would soon change.

"Listen up, everyone," Andrew called out. "Natalie, Peter, Siriporn, and Mali, gather around. Everyone else, you need to find something else to do. We need this space for a private meeting. Now."

The volunteers gathered their plates and cups nervously, chattering among themselves as they moved toward their cabins. The kitchen staff moved more slowly, straightening up their work spaces before meandering off in the direction of one of the big trees where they took their breaks. Karina lingered longer than everyone else, as if expecting that Andrew would suddenly remember that she needed to be part of the meeting. When he didn't, she slapped the table and stomped away.

Finally, the five of them were alone. Hatcher sat across from her, playing with a paperclip as if it was the most important thing he'd ever done. Mali and Andrew sat next to each other, and Siriporn slouched against the table instead of finding a seat, a worried expression on his normally smiling face.

"I wanted to talk among us before I make this announcement to everyone else, because all of you are going to play a role in what we have to do." Andrew folded his large hands on the table in front of him and stared down at them solemnly. "You all know what Sophie did, and all of us—with the exception of Natalie—realize that kind of destruction has been Sophie's modus operandi since she came to us a year ago. Peter and I talked last night, and I spent the whole night pondering this issue. I don't think it's going to end. She's costing us way too much in stress and medicine and, now, damages. I'm afraid that the next thing she's going to do is to physically hurt someone. Peter believes we need to put her down."

Hatcher flipped the paperclip into the air.

Siriporn pushed off the table and folded his arms across his chest.

Natalie couldn't move.

"That's it? No talk about it?" Siriporn glared at Andrew.

"Do you have a better idea? You're the one who's been dealing with her all this time. Have you seen any changes in her behavior? Anything for the better?"

Andrew's question stopped Siriporn. He pushed a hand through his hair and muttered something unintelligible.

"We can't put her down." Natalie realized the moment she spoke that she had no idea what else to do, but somewhere deep down, she felt like the decision wasn't a wise one. "There's got to be something else. Something that hasn't been tried." She directed the last comment to Hatcher, who hadn't looked up from the paperclip he now twisted and turned.

Mali rose and put her arm around Siriporn. Her head reached his shoulder. She spoke to him quietly. His deference for her was evident in the way he leaned in to hear her speak.

Andrew glanced up from his folded hands at Hatcher, then to Natalie. "If there's another way, I'd certainly like to hear it. I'm the last one to get on board when it comes to putting an animal down. But I have to listen to the veterinarians that I hire to give me good advice, and Peter—"

Natalie's chest tightened as she searched for words. "She followed me back to the holding area. All she wanted was food . . ."

"She certainly ate plenty when she destroyed my gardens." Mali plunked herself down at the end of the table next to Siriporn. "We all know elephants are voracious, but most of them are not vicious." She avoided Natalie's gaze. "But we have plenty of others that need our help and are more likely to be rehabilitated."

Mali fell silent. For a moment no one else spoke either. Hatcher kept his eyes on the paperclip. Andrew studied his fingernails, and Siriporn stood, arms folded, looking into the meadow as darkness descended on the elephants grazing beyond. Natalie looked at each of them for a long moment, one at a time, wondering what was going through their heads.

"I can't believe you don't think she's worth saving." Natalie shook her head and sighed long and deep. No one answered. Silence descended and lingered for several moments. Finally, she could stand it no longer. She stood, leaned over the table to look directly into Andrew's somber face. "Please do me one favor. Give me a day to consider our options. I didn't come all the way to Thailand to put animals to death."

He leaned back and rubbed his forehead. The lines around his eyes had deepened since the day before. "You know, my dear, one of the reasons I brought you here was because of your commitment and the second reason was because you seemed a quick study with a lively curiosity. But I'm afraid you might be too sensitive." He paused and drew his hand across his mouth. "I hope I'm wrong."

Natalie twisted her mouth and paused for a moment. She had to answer him. She had to win the argument. This argument, in particular. "Give me a couple of days. Let me do some research. I'm sure you'd rather save Sophie than lose her."

He squinted his eyes looking up at her, bringing his bushy

white eyebrows together to create one chalky line across his brow. He pursed his lips as she had seen him do during his presentation only two months ago in the States. Though they had interacted almost every day, she had come to think of him as a kindly older man instead of the philanthropic millionaire who moved as easily and freely around the globe as some did around their tiny neighborhoods. He was used to launching arguments with governments. The defense of her own dissertation was the only argument she'd ever given that wasn't personal, and that was more than a decade ago.

"Just a couple of days," she repeated. "Please." Tears burned at the back of her eyelids.

Andrew and Hatcher exchanged a long, probing stare but no words.

Finally, Andrew broke the stare and glanced at Natalie. "Two days. And if she does anything else—anything at all—during that time, I will have to make the decision to keep my people and the other animals here safe. You know that 'oftentimes excusing of a fault doth make the fault the worse by the excuse.'"

On the walk back to her cabin, Natalie mulled over Andrew's Shakespearean quote. How could one blame Sophie for her actions when human beings were at fault? If she had not been abused, she wouldn't be defensive. If she wasn't defensive, she wouldn't tend toward violence. No one had given her a chance to recuperate from her PTSD and until that was cured, she wouldn't trust anyone to treat her physical injuries.

Catch 22.

She kicked the dirt, feeling angrier than she probably had a right to be. The night wind rustled the trees a bit, making them whisper as though warning her to relax. She gazed upward, catching a glimpse of the moon through their waving branches and fought a sudden wave of homesickness.

If Sophie were a horse in her care, Natalie would not have hesitated to call for help. There were five or six people she counted on. Horse whisperers, others called them, specially-trained professionals who retrained animals that had become dangerous. She had no connections here. No team on which she could rely. No network of trusted colleagues.

She'd have to take on the fight alone. She'd have to find a way to help Sophie.

But how?

Sixteen

We are weighed down, every moment,
by the conception and the sensation of Time.
And there are but two means of escaping and
forgetting this nightmare: pleasure and work.
Pleasure consumes us.
Work strengthens us.
Let us choose.
-Charles Baudelaire

THE DREAM SWUNG BACK and forth in time, as it always did when she dreamt about Danny. One moment, he was a baby, and the next, he was a married man introducing her to her first grandchild. She heard his loving voice and his proud laughter. She felt the warmth of his breath on her cheek, the power of his brief and intense hugs. If anyone had asked her when she awoke about the content of the dream, she'd have been hard pressed to find a storyline, yet she could detail the gamut of emotions she'd ridden in every nanosecond of time that was the gift of seeing her younger son again.

When she first opened her eyes, the moon still shone through her window, telling her it wasn't even close to sunrise. She tossed and turned on her thin mattress, finding no comfort in the waves of homesickness that washed over her. Homesick for her down-filled, king-sized mattress, for the promise of a piping hot shower every morning, the aroma of freshly-brewed tea, the scent of pine trees after a light rainfall, the crackle of autumn leaves underfoot. She even missed the little arguments her parents had whenever she went to their house for dinner.

Nighttime was always the worst time. It reminded her of her solitary life when the dark silence enveloped her. The sadness she knew during the day could be dampened with activity, but at night, that grief fed on her heart. She wished she'd never known love. Love brought pain. Heartbreak. Fear.

Finally, she fell back into a fitful sleep. This time, the dreams changed. She still saw Danny, but he wore a white lab coat, and they were going to the movies together. That made no sense, and even worse, throughout the movie, he repeated over and over again: "The cows. Temple's cows. Watch the cows." By the time he'd repeated it half a dozen times, Natalie wanted to retreat somewhere where she would not hear his voice or the nonsensical phrase he repeated. "Temple's cows. Temple's cows."

Then the dream ended abruptly, and her eyelids flew open. Sunlight spilled into her room like overripe lemons, telling her it was far past sunrise, her usual waking time. She sat up on the edge of the bed, groggy. Dreaming often felt like a theft of sleep to her instead of a rejuvenation. She needed down time for her body to recoup after working long days. If she didn't get it, she moved through the next day in a fog. This would be one of those days. Yet, as she slapped some cold water on her face and readied herself for work at the clinic, she remembered the research she needed to do in order to keep Sophie alive, and Danny's words from her dream repeated themselves in her mind: "Temple's cows."

What exactly did that mean? The thought rotated in her mind over and over again as she dressed, pulling a pink Sanctuary t-shirt over her head and slipping her legs into her khaki shorts. She found her laptop under a pile of nutritional health white papers she'd been studying to determine whether they were feeding the older females enough calcium to supplement what they'd been missing in their leafy diets. She'd done the research several days ago when she had a few hours to sit on the platform. The only time she could use the laptop here at the sanctuary was when she physically sat at one of the tables where they ate their meals. Connectivity was non-existent in her cabin, away from the wireless router. Even when she sat near it, she might only have Internet service for half an hour or so in the afternoon.

Temple's cows.

She walked up the dusty road, past the fields of palm grass that had been partially harvested to feed the elephants.

What kind of temple shelters cows? An Indian temple? Why would my dream be telling me about cows in India?

She ate a couple of pieces of toast and sipped a cup of bitter black tea while trying to get on the Internet. When she finally found a weak signal, she Googled "Temple's cows." Eighteen million hits, most of which pointed to Temple Grandin, the autistic woman made famous for her inventions for moving cows through slaughter houses in a humane fashion.

Of course.

Natalie had read some of Dr. Grandin's articles on reducing animal stress years ago, but once Natalie focused on equine surgery, her energies were concentrated on that field of study and her research turned to other specialists. But somewhere in the back of her mind, she must have stored Temple Grandin's story. And perhaps she'd shared it with Danny at one point.

She scanned the list of online articles for the legitimate and academic papers Grandin herself had written.

An hour and two more cups of tea later, Natalie lifted her head and watched the horizon for the elephants she'd heard trumpeting. *Temple's invention . . . the hug machine.* Grandin's machine was meant to be used on cows heading for slaughter. The machine squeezed cows from both sides as their heads hung through an opening in the front of the box. When she saw them settle down after being in the "squeeze box" for a little while, she adapted it for herself. As an autistic woman, Grandin never wanted to be touched yet desperately needed that physical comfort people get from hugs. The box worked to soothe her, and

131

Temple used it to control the anxiety she often felt during her years away at college. The deep pressure the squeeze box provided had a calming effect that Grandin could not deny and both animals and human beings benefitted from it.

"That's it!" Natalie whispered. She reached for her notebook, sketched out a box-like structure that would immobilize Sophie so that Hatcher could medicate her and make her feel safe so Natalie could also start training her using protected contact and positive reinforcement. Zoos and other animal sanctuaries had been using the protected contact technique for years to manage captive elephants. Instead of poking elephants with hurtful tools like hooks, caregivers and trainers stood outside fences and elephants could choose to freely approach humans for treatment or treats. Safe for both mistreated elephants as well as the humans caring for them.

Natalie wrote in her notebook:

> *Combination of:*
> *1. Grandin's squeeze box*
> *2. the protected contact technique &*
> *3. positive reinforcement = a safe Sophie.*
> *Add time = recovery from PTSD.*

She felt a bit giddy. *It might work. It HAS to work.*

For the rest of the day, her mind buzzed with the details of putting her plan into action. The steel bars already in place in the holding pen where they worked with Sophie could be simply moved inward to give Sophie enough room to fit inside, yet allow her access to everything she needed—food and water—and to give Natalie room to work with the elephant. The training might take time, but it would be worth it. Others had already proven that it worked. Keeping Sophie in a smaller area encased in widely-spaced steel bars would keep both elephant and trainer safe. Natalie would have access to the animal, and Sophie would have some freedom. No ankle chains or ropes around the neck. No need for three mahouts to help anchor her during the time

Sophie needed her meds. No negative treatment for the elephant so clearly traumatized.

It might work.

By the time everyone gathered for dinner, Natalie had a proposal ready for Andrew.

"I think we can adapt her shelter fairly easily." Natalie passed a copy of her sketch of the design for a squeeze box big enough for an elephant to Andrew, Hatcher, and Siriporn.

They sat quietly during her presentation, listening without interrupting as she detailed her idea. She'd been excited to talk to them about the new technique for Sophie, figuring they'd all be on board since their commitment to rescue animals was as strong as hers. But Andrew continued eating while she spoke, Hatcher gazed toward the other table where the volunteers gossiped and laughed noisily, and Siriporn simply smiled, making her wonder exactly how much he understood.

She paused for a moment. Andrew was the first to meet her eyes.

"I'm sure you feel this will work, Natalie, but have you given a thought to the cost? Most of the funds we currently have available must go to keeping our animals fed. Crikey, I've been trying to raise money to repair our exterior fence for the past year. Ask Karina. She's been struggling to balance the books with very little luck. Don't get me wrong. I applaud your creativity, but I'm not sure we can afford it."

"I think I can do it with what we have," Natalie said, only half sure it was true.

"Even if we could," Hatcher added, "who's to say it would work? Or that Sophie's the one to spend the time, effort, and money on? There are three other elephants with major medical issues that need attention. All of them need constant medication. And none of them are violent. That friggin' elephant has cost us more in the past year than all of them combined."

"Not quite what I meant, Peter, ol' chap," Andrew interrupted. "If we had the funds, I'd do whatever it takes to rehabilitate Sophie, you know that."

"I thought we agreed the best solution—the most humane thing to do—is to put her down." Hatcher turned to Andrew, leaning forward, his platinum eyebrows arched. It was obvious to Natalie at that moment that it wouldn't have mattered if she had a magic wand she could wave over Sophie. Hatcher would say the fix was quackery, anything to disprove her. Even if it meant killing an animal she might be able to save.

"The infection is persistent," he continued. "It's eventually going to take the whole leg, and I'm certain the pain is driving her insane, which is why we can't get her under control. You know damn well, Andrew, that we've tried everything medical that I know of. You can't fix her psychological problems until the medical issues are addressed successfully. She needs to be put out of her misery."

"I've thought about that, too," Natalie said, flipping open her notebook. "We could treat her more aggressively, try a different antibiotic cocktail, and if that doesn't work, I can research that new procedure being used on bacterial strains in AIDS patients."

Everyone silenced. Hatcher shrugged and played with a paper clip.

"Are you volunteering to take her on?" Andrew leaned back, her sketch still in his hands.

She paused but only for a heartbeat. "Yes. I'll do it."

"That still doesn't give us the money we need to create the damn contraption!" Peter's voice had risen, become strident. His jaw hardened.

"True," Andrew raised his hand to silence anymore of Peter's arguments. "But before we go farther, Dr. DeAngelo needs to put some time in with Sophie. Siriporn has already started working with you anyway, hasn't he?"

She nodded. Siriporn smiled at her. Sometimes she believed he understood English better than he spoke it, but other times, she wasn't so sure.

"Okay, I'll give you some time," Andrew said as he rose. Behind him, Mali had come to the table and now stood silently. "But if anything else happens . . ."

"I understand," Natalie said, fighting hard to keep the excitement she felt from showing on her face.

Seventeen

My family history begins with
me, but yours ends with you.
-Iphicrates

SOPHIE SWAYED GENTLY IN her stall, still munching on the last
hand of bananas Natalie had fed her. Each day began exactly the
same: Natalie rose at four in the morning, fumbling in the dark for
her T-shirt and shorts before finding her way down the path to the
elephant barns where she prepared Sophie's breakfast and fed her.
Alone. Siriporn joined her around sunrise to start the day's lesson,
but for a few hours, Natalie and Sophie had time to bond.

On the first day, Sophie slapped her trunk on the dirt floor
of the enclosure, refusing everything Natalie handed through
the steel bars. Pomegranate, squash, persimmons, palm fronds,
bananas, potatoes. It didn't matter. Sophie wanted none of it.

Puzzled, since food had always worked as a training device
previously, Natalie watched Sophie's movements closely, writing in
her small notebook she kept with her at all times.

*What am I missing? What signs can't I read? Keep track. Every
detail: the number of times Sophie slaps her trunk on the floor, whether
she stares at me or looks away, how Sophie moves—side to side, foot to
foot.*

It didn't matter what the movements or reactions, even if it was the flicker of an eyelash. Natalie wrote it all down.

Sounds were important, too. Natalie had heard plenty of trumpeting and growling in the short time she'd been at the sanctuary, but she now recognized a variety of other sounds: chirping and tweeting and calls that sounded like birds. Rumbling. Roars. She recorded some of the sounds with her cell phone (which never had enough signal to make a call or send a text anyway) then realized unless she could pair the sounds with Sophie's movements, they were useless. So she video recorded everything instead.

At night before she fell into her twin bed, every muscle in her body stressed to its limit, Natalie watched the videos she'd made that day. Late into the night, she reflected on the new insights she'd made about Sophie's personality, and she combined her handwritten notes with the medical records Peter Hatcher shared with her. He'd changed Sophie's antibiotic cocktail, and both he and Andrew agreed that it could work. Time would tell.

Sophie's hunger won out when Natalie handed a particularly pungent piece of watermelon through the bars. She not only ate the watermelon but everything else Natalie gave her that day. A small success, but an important one.

I'll understand you if it kills me, damnit, Natalie thought when Sophie rumbled quietly. Content.

By the twelfth day, Natalie realized that understanding Sophie might be the death of her. Even though the elephant had allowed Natalie to feed her the day before, she wanted nothing to do with her once again. Fighting to keep her frustration in check, Natalie forced herself to sit quietly on the sidelines as Sophie paced and trumpeted.

During the third week, Siriporn had shown up at the enclosure on Wednesday morning. Natalie half expected to be upbraided for what she'd done on her own, but he looked at her and said, "Sophie quiet." It took her a while to realize that "quiet" meant "behaved." That, she suspected, was a high compliment from Siriporn.

That Friday afternoon, she received a letter from Maman, as

well as one from her sister-in-law, Kerry.

> We all miss you," Maman wrote. "The winter is promising
> to be a long one. So far, we've had two ice storms that
> totally shut down Raleigh, and you know how much I hate
> ice. We're not prepared for it.

Natalie shivered involuntarily then glanced around the area where she sat reading Maman's letter. The bougainvillea crawled up the side of the cabin and spilled over the side of the porch. The scent of ginger blossoms filled the air. She'd been watching a black-backed kingfisher all morning, listening for its high-pitched call as it flew above the elephants swimming in the nearby stream. No ice here. Thank God for that.

> We're starting to plan for Christmas—only a month
> away—and Stefan and Kerry are coming for Thanksgiving.
> Will you miss my cinnamon rolls and deep fried turkey? As
> I sit here writing this, I hear you groaning about our weird
> French-Southern-Italian Thanksgiving dinner, but I bet you
> miss them as much as we miss you. I've shown everyone
> that I see the pictures you've sent of Thailand and your new
> friends and the elephants. Everyone agrees that this is the
> best thing you could have done for yourself—even though
> I don't particularly agree. Pop and I still miss you horribly.
> We wish we could have been with you last week. I'm sure
> getting past his birthday was difficult for you.

The rest of the letter blurred. Natalie read something about people looking at her house and maybe there'd be an offer on it before the holidays. Then Maman was on a roll about North Carolina politics, and Natalie was lost.

Maman knows Danny's birthday. How could she have gotten it wrong?

Shaking her head, she folded the letter and shoved it back into the envelope. Patting the flap a bit, she closed it as if giving a blessing. Then she slid one finger under the flap of her sister-in-law's letter, hoping that reading it would make her feel better than her mother's had.

Kerry repeated the same news about the weather that Maman had. (*Did North Carolinians always talk this much about the weather? Funny, Thai people never mention the weather at all, yet the heat is often unbearable and when it rains, everyone and everything living is affected. Life moves on, and Thai people barely acknowledge the weather at all.*)

Then Kerry wrote:

> Listen, Nat, I want you to hear this from me before someone else tells you. One of the TV anchors did an interview with the kids' teachers about the first year after the shootings. Horrible. All about how people are trying to move on, even though their hearts are broken. Some of them talked about giving their time and energy to fighting for gun control. They're saying all the parents and family should be using their voices to make a difference. Someone mentioned your name, and it's all over the place that you're not in the Raleigh area anymore. I know you don't want to hear this, but like I said, better to hear it from me.

Natalie folded the note and put it back in the envelope wishing she'd never read either letter.

His birthday.

Maman had it wrong. This was October. Danny's birthday was in March. She had never been good with dates. When Natalie turned eleven, she arrived home one afternoon to balloons all over the porch and a huge "Happy Birthday, Natalie" sign fluttering in the wind. The only problem was that her birthday was a month later. It had become a family joke, and Natalie never minded because she'd celebrated her birthday twice that year.

Yes, Maman was horrible with dates.

Still, the thought that she would ever become so engrossed in her own life to miss an anniversary of Danny's life was unacceptable—even if it was untrue.

Natalie smacked the edge of the desk with her hand, instantly wishing she hadn't hit the right hand, her operating hand. Tiny shocks ran down the side of her hand and up into her forearm. Even thousands of miles away, Maman made Natalie doubt herself. That was nothing new. No matter how accomplished or successful she'd become, Natalie felt six years old in her mother's presence and part of her would always be that hurt, insecure child—even when her mother forgot her birthdays or couldn't tell anyone what day of the week it was. Pops might think it was cute—Maman's forgetfulness—but it had long passed into the realm of pure irritation for Natalie. She had lost her patience with her mother the first time a teacher had suggested Natalie had strengths in math and science but couldn't complete a literature project. All Maman needed to hear was her daughter's deficiencies. After that, the strengths didn't matter. The world might welcome a female who knew how to calculate algebraic equations and how to name all the bones in the body, but if one didn't know literature, Maman thought that person stupid. So that's what Natalie became in her mother's mind: stupid.

Enough.

Natalie turned to the window. Storm clouds gathered, dark and foreboding, above the monkey pod trees. It was time for Sophie's afternoon snack, and if a storm was coming, Natalie needed to feed the elephant before the thunder started to rumble. Siriporn would be coming down the road any moment with Ali. She'd wait for him on the porch so they could head down to Sophie's enclosure together.

The letters still on her mind, Natalie haphazardly gathered a bucket of vegetables for Sophie and placed it on the ground near the enclosure, then turned to put on a pair of plastic gloves. She'd come to the conclusion that keeping Sophie's food as clean as possible would help the infection heal more quickly, so she'd started feeding Sophie by hand. The constant contact between them was building a level of trust.

When she turned back around, Sophie's trunk rooted around in the pail.

"No!"

Natalie's cry startled Sophie. She tossed the pail into the air, bringing it down with a ferocious thump on Natalie's head. She slumped to the ground, her leg buckling at an odd angle under her.

Sophie watched Natalie try to stand, as if she couldn't believe she'd had anything to do with the accident. Natalie lowered her left foot gingerly. A sharp pain burned up her calf. She moaned.

"Damn, Sophie. You shouldn't have done that."

In the distance, the sky roared. A storm, winding through the mountains. Sophie's trunk lifted straight into the sky. The air crackled and the smell of sulfur filled the air. Through the ground, Natalie felt the rumble of the storm, and in that very moment, she had a sense of what Sophie must feel through the pads of her feet. Somehow she could tell that the storm was too far away to matter, and this particular storm would skirt the mountains, but there were others behind it. Stronger and more dangerous storms.

Natalie turned her torso, but still couldn't stand completely upright. She moaned again.

Reaching out with her trunk, Sophie found Natalie's arm and traced without actually coming into contact with her skin. The hair on Natalie's arm stood straight up, the sensation more visceral than the hot throbbing in her ankle. But Sophie's tender touch was soft—took away the pain—made Natalie believe it was temporary. Everything is temporary.

Eighteen

Too much politeness conceals deceit.
-Chinese proverb

By the middle of the afternoon the leg felt strong enough that Natalie walked up the dirt road toward the kitchen. She checked her watch: 3:12 PM. The kitchen staff would be gone home or sitting on the platform to relax for a while before starting to prep for the evening meal. If she was lucky, no one would be there, and she'd be able to raid the ice chest for a plastic bag of ice. She'd take it back to her cabin and sit with it for the rest of the evening. It should take down the swelling.

She'd taken some ice out of the vintage fridge and found a plastic supermarket bag to put it in when she heard voices coming toward the kitchen. She held her breath, recognizing one of them as Andrew's. Thinking quickly, she knew she'd have to lie about the ankle, and she simply wasn't good at lying. Still, she would have to.

She hobbled over to a stool and put her leg up on it, then took a swig out of the Coke bottle she held in her hand. Forced a smile on her face.

That smile turned into a grimace when Peter Hatcher came into the kitchen. Close behind him was Andrew. They were in a deep discussion about what they needed for supplies and when they could take the ride into town to get them. At first, they didn't even notice she was there. Then Hatcher gave her a curt nod and said, "Hi, how're you doing?" before continuing his discussion with Andrew.

Andrew smiled in her direction, without stopping his conversation, grabbed a Coke out of the fridge, then followed Peter back out to the platform. Their voices drifted away, then she heard the truck doors slam and the truck fired into gear. Only then did she exhale the breath she'd been holding.

With the ice bag in her hand, she found her way back to the cabin and stayed there, icing her ankle for the rest of the night. It wasn't until after nine that she finally paid attention to Sophie's trumpets and limped back to the enclosure to feed her. But as she neared the enclosure, she spotted Peter walking away into the darkness. Obviously, Sophie's cries were not ones of hunger. She'd been angry about Hatcher's nocturnal visit.

Curious, Natalie opened her mouth to call to him, but she shut it quickly. If he saw her limping, it would only raise questions.

Sophie silently reached out her trunk for the calcium, sweet potato, and rice mixture in Natalie's pail. Her eye hovered at the same level as Natalie's. For a moment, they stared at each other, and Natalie felt Sophie asking the same questions she was.

"Why was he here, ol' girl?" Natalie whispered as Sophie's big brown eye blinked. "What was he doing to you?"

Nineteen

Animals make us human.
-Temple Grandin

MALI'S FEET DANGLED OVER the side of Sophie's newly-re-modeled enclosure, and she gestured once again to Siriporn, who was on one side of the enclosure. The steel bars had been adjusted, according to Natalie's specifications, so the enclosure was now a larger model of Temple Grandin's cow hugging machine. Though large enough for Sophie to move around, the enclosure was small enough to keep her quiet and calm. It worked better than Natalie would have suspected.

Mali, her glossy black hair in a braid down her back, wore a white T-shirt and loose white cotton pants. She looked like a schoolgirl instead of Siriporn's mother, yet she now shouted orders to him loudly and rapidly in Thai.

Natalie listened to the two of them as she fed Sophie, surprised that she occasionally caught the meaning of a phrase or two. She smiled at the way Siriporn slapped his baseball cap against his open palm repeatedly as he tried to make his point. Still, Mali appeared to be winning their argument about whether he could spend the weekend in Bangkok.

Though Siriporn had been teaching Natalie what he knew of being a mahout, it was difficult since he spoke broken English, at best. There were details Natalie was missing, so she asked Mali for help. Though Mali was still upset that Sophie had ruined her garden, she had agreed. For the past two hours, the humans worked as a dysfunctional trio.

Natalie's ulterior motive was that she needed Siriporn to teach her the commands Sophie already knew. Once she could get Sophie to follow the basics, protected contact training would go more smoothly. Moving her in and out of the holding area safely was the most important factor, and she was pleased with the way it had been rebuilt to her specifications. The hydraulically-controlled gates could be lifted or lowered, making it easy to maneuver Sophie into place for her treatments without endangering any of the humans who had to work with her. No more ropes. No more chains. Sophie handled the transition well, welcoming the absence of the *ankus*. But the most important part of the training method was to utilize the same personnel. Natalie and Siriporn, and occasionally Peter, were the only humans who worked with Sophie. Others might come to watch, but they weren't allowed to work with her.

When Natalie had Sophie alone, she worked with the elephant in the steel cage, prodding her with long, padded contact poles she had modeled on the ones used in some progressive zoos that had reported great success with the technique. With the poles, she could move Sophie backward and forward without causing any undue pain. Natalie contacted some of the pioneers in the technique and one of them had sent her his dissertation on the subject. It was invaluable, even though it took hours to print it from the office computer. She'd read it deep into the night, making notes in the margins, highlighting whole passages, and underlining the phrases that made her think.

With consistent use for the past couple of weeks, Sophie was starting to move in the direction Natalie wanted or to lift a foot with a simple touch of the pole and a voice command, followed by a food reward. Sophie's quick response made Natalie believe the elephant really did want to learn, and, more importantly, that she wanted to please Natalie. The moment she realized that

Sophie was like any other domesticated animal who recognized human beings as the alpha—the one with the food, the caretaker—was the moment Natalie knew she had made the right decision. It would take time and effort, but it would work. She felt it in her bones.

Of course, Siriporn didn't understand what Natalie was doing at all and expressed his frustration. Why didn't Natalie learn to ride Sophie, he wanted to know. How could she expect to be a mahout if she didn't establish herself as the rider? Did she expect this animal to simply understand the words without using the *ankus*? Impossible, he would say, and each time, he'd take off his cap and slap it against his hand for emphasis.

Mali didn't understand Natalie's philosophy either, but Andrew had told everyone to cooperate with her, so Mali did as Andrew asked. She reminded Natalie, however, that Andrew had put a deadline on Natalie's work. Three months, he'd said, but if anything—any little thing—happened before that deadline was up—if Sophie harmed another being or maliciously destroyed another piece of property—she would be put down. So far, Sophie cooperated as if she knew this was her last chance. Still, Natalie always worked with her safely, and in the back of her mind, she realized that Sophie's life was in her hands.

Siriporn still brought Ali back to the barn after everyone else left the river and the four of them could have the water to themselves. Natalie and Siriporn watched Sophie closely, still not completely trusting her, but hopeful because at least Sophie wasn't throwing animals up in the air and destroying buildings. Ali, the old bull, waited alongside the barn now, out of sight.

In the barn, all had quieted down. Natalie grabbed some of the bananas from the food pail, handing half of them to Siriporn. Together, they silently fed Sophie until the pail full of goodies had disappeared.

"She need medicine." Siriporn pointed to Sophie's leg and the still-weeping wound.

"She had some this morning. Dr. Hatcher will be back later with another dose. We need to wait." It wasn't easy to convince

Sophie to let Hatcher stab her with a needle, but they had no choice. Until the wound stopped weeping, the shots would continue. "I think I'm going to keep her here today, Siriporn. The wound is too open. Why don't you come back after you take Ali to the river?"

Mali slid off the steel bar where she sat and watched Siriporn command Ali to bend on one knee so he could scramble up to sit astride the bull's neck. As they lumbered away, Sophie groaned a couple of times, a low, almost mournful sound, and leaned against the bars as if longing to follow them. Ali had disappeared into the tree-line when the calls of several other mahouts echoed down the road. Obviously, the other elephants had joined Ali and Siriporn. The group's laughter receded into the distance.

"He's a good boy, your son," Natalie said as she swept the area clean of leftover food.

"Yes, as long as he's with the elephants. When he's with the village boys, he's a different Siriporn. Very different." Mali kept her back to Natalie. "Jung said, 'I am not what happened to me, I am what I choose to become.'"

Natalie leaned on the broom. A trickle of sweat crept down her back. A swim would have felt good. "What do you mean?" She knew exactly what the quote meant, but could Mali be referring to her? The quote hit a little too close to home. It was one Dr. Littlefield used regularly.

"I mean I think my son has chosen to be a dissident," she snorted, as if amazed at the irony. "Siriporn remembers when he was a child, and his father and I talked about politics all the time, never realizing the small child at our feet heard everything." She shook her head, turned, and smiled. Rueful.

"You should have seen him at that age, Natalie. Shiny black hair, the brightest eyes. Ran everywhere. Never walked." She leaned her cheek against her broom and her eyes became distant, she didn't move for several long moments.

"Too much talk about politics. Questioning the king. Making trouble. It worries me." Mali shook her head; her braid swung back and forth. "A government official came the other day asking about Siriporn and the group he joined. Andrew diverted his attention, but . . . I worry Siriporn's getting in too deep. He's always been cheeky, but I fear he's gone too far. He's too much like his grandfather. He talks too much." She gazed into the distance, a film over her eyes. "I worry."

"What worries you?" Hatcher's voice startled both women. He laughed at their reaction and swung himself up on the bars where Mali had been sitting. He wore a pair of cutoff scrubs brown with mud, yet the line where his shorts ended and the tanned part of his legs was still pinkish-white.

At the sound of his voice, Sophie shifted her weight away from the bars closest to him and moved as far as she could to the other side of the enclosure. She associated him with the huge hypodermic regularly thrust into her skin.

I'd back up, too, Natalie thought. *Hell, I'd break down walls if I saw that needle coming!*

She wondered if it would be rude if she asked why he was there. Then realized she didn't care. "Is it time for her shot? You're early, aren't you?" Her throat tightened, making her voice high-pitched like what Pop would call a "fisher wife."

"Wanted to see how everything is proceeding and whether you need any help. I'm sure this protected containment thingy is proving to be a mite more than you bargained for, eh?" He stared past Natalie and studied Sophie intently but kept his distance, which was probably smart. The only male Sophie trusted at all was Siriporn and only when Natalie and Ali were there. "You need to give her antibiotics twice a day," he said.

"I know that." Natalie fought the urge to tell him to leave. She put the broom in the corner. Mali moved toward the road as if she knew where the conversation was heading and didn't want to be involved.

"Are you going to tell me what's wrong? What you're worried about?" Hatcher fell in beside Mali. Natalie caught up with them, feeling like Hatcher had no business poking his nose into Mali's conversation, but she was a big girl. If she didn't want to answer him, that was her decision.

Together, the three of them scuffed their way up the dirt road.

"It's Siriporn. His politics. You know." Mali gazed up at Hatcher, sheltering her eyes with her hand. A burn striped the back of that hand, a red slash that needed treating. "He doesn't understand what he's getting himself into. It's dangerous. People have died. For what?" Her voice rose an octave. "The Yellow Shirts will always be in power. The poor never win over the rich."

Hatcher shrugged. "Ah, so that's what it is. Mother doesn't want to let go. He needs to discover for himself, though, don't you think? He's old enough to make those decisions about his beliefs. And if his political leanings get him into trouble, he's old enough to get himself out. Let him ask the tough questions. Let him explore. You're probably making more of it than you need to."

Mali grunted non-committedly and looked down at her feet. "Were you living here the last time there was a coup?"

"Not living here, but I had visited that year. About eight years ago, correct?"

They continued talking, but Natalie's mind was elsewhere.

The trees rustled above, and she glanced up to see an osprey winging toward the glistening river in the distance. The predator's magnificent arched wings, extended wing 'fingers,' and white underbelly made her catch her breath. She followed the graceful bird's flight, until it knifed its wings and flew downward, out of sight. Papa had taught her the names of birds when she was little, and it wasn't until she started veterinary school that she realized he knew the most common ones but wasn't familiar with the rare or soon-to-be extinct. Still, the moments she spent walking with him while he tended to his small garden were precious. She often wondered whether Danny and Stephen missed having their father around after he left for simple reasons like learning the names of animals and birds. She sighed.

As they passed the river, three elephants—Ali and two younger cows, the sisters Kalaya and Anugraha—splashed and squirted, dousing mahouts who sat or stood atop them, daring each other to dive off. Could Sophie hear them? Did she long to be with them? She was her happiest, it seemed, when she rolled and submerged in the cool water. Natalie felt guilty that she hadn't brought the elephant to the river today, especially since it would have meant she would have missed bumping into Peter.

"Natalie?" Mali touched Natalie's arm. "Are you with us?"

"I'm here," she answered.

"You were deep in thought," Hatcher said.

She simply nodded, embarrassed to be caught ignoring them both.

"Can I ask a question?" Hatcher pointed to Natalie, his eyebrows arched, as if half expecting her to say no.

She nodded again, though she feared what his question might be.

"Do you have any idea how much this protective containment costs?"

"It's protected contact, Dr. Hatcher." She hated that her voice sounded haughty, but it seemed he found every excuse to poke at her. It was getting tiresome. "And right now, the cost is minimal because the structure was already built. All we had to do was to move the steel bars in closer and fashion some long poles."

"What about the labor?"

"Siriporn volunteers his time, as do I." Narrowing her eyes, she thought a moment. "Is there a reason why you want this to fail? It seems that you truly expect Sophie to go on a rampage and kill half the people in the sanctuary."

"Maybe it's because I've seen elephants rampage in the past. Have you?"

"You don't have to actually see a rampage to know about them, Dr. Hatcher." Again, her voice sounded haughty, but this time she didn't fight it. "And the point of using protected contact is to make sure Sophie feels safe enough with us not to need to act out." Prickles of anger crept up Natalie's neck. "Exactly why are you so reluctant to let me try this?" *It can't just be the dissertation,* she thought as she physically bit her own tongue. A coppery taste filled her mouth.

"You want to know why? I'll tell you." Hatcher's cheeks reddened. "Because you're a bleeding heart American taking some time off to come help the poor elephants. You're going to go home and tell everyone what a *mah-velous* working vacation you had while the rest of us remain here to try to repair your lame attempts at fixing the savage beast." Hatcher's nostrils flared and his fists clenched.

"I'm not here on vacation." She wondered the instant she said that why she felt the need to explain to him. "I have a surgical clinic at home that's running half-time because I made the choice to be here. I'm volunteering my time and expertise for a year. Not a couple of weeks. This isn't a lark. And you don't have a clue who I am or what my motivation is, but you know what? That doesn't really matter. What matters is Sophie, and I don't think you give a fuck about her! I think it would be easier for you to let her go and move on to the easier cases."

Hatcher stepped closer until she could literally smell his breath, a weird combination of coffee and garlic. Natalie stood her ground as he ranted, only understanding every other word of his rapid-fire diatribe, until Mali pushed herself between them.

"Stop it! Stop it right now!" Mali yanked Hatcher, still sputtering profanities, away from Natalie. "Both of you are here for the same reason, don't you realize that?"

"She's a goddamn diva." Hatcher flailed his arms trying to lose Mali's grip. "Comes here all jacked up about the best way to do things, talks Andrew into some cockamamie treatment, and that elephant is no better now than she was weeks ago. What the hell!"

Natalie pointed a shaking finger at him. "How in the hell would you know? You come by and stick a needle in her leg and leave. You have no idea whether she's improving. You don't even know her."

"And you do? Seriously, Dr. DeAngelo, you need to step off that pedestal of yours and see the writing on the wall. That elephant is dying! Keeping her alive is only serving one thing: your vanity!"

Without another word, Hatcher turned and stalked toward the cabins, leaving Natalie and Mali standing in the middle of the road, their mouths hanging open.

THE WOMAN *sits next to Sophie's leg that night, talking to her for a long time. The words string together, sounds merely, for they make no sense to the elephant, but she listens anyway, and after a while, she hears the same two sounds, the same two words over and over again: Stephen. Danny. Danny and Stephen. Danny. Danny. Danny. Stephen and Danny.*

Though the elephant doesn't understand the meaning of those two words, she does understand the emotions that color the words every single time the woman utters them: grief. Sadness and despair. Heartbreak.

Throughout the long night, the woman does not raise her voice, though Sophie can tell she's raging against some horrible agony that only a human understands, and only an hour later, that she's overwhelmed by a knee-crumbling sadness. The woman's body throbs. Her head hangs to her chest. She gasps for air.

Sophie grumbles and, often, trumpets when the woman sobs. Straight, high-pitched, short bursts that echo the woman's pain, empathizing with the emotions that appear to sweep through the woman like a tidal wave.

The hours pass by, and the woman still leans against Sophie's healthy leg. They arch into one another, drawing support from their angles. But the wounded leg begins to ache and the elephant sways, side-to-side, agitated, uncomfortable. The ache tells her there's a storm nearby, and the pain in her leg always intensifies during and after a storm. The only thing that brings relief is rocking, swaying back and forth.

The woman's unceasing chatter transforms into a soothing piece of music, weaving in and out of Sophie's consciousness. The voice vacillates between high tones and lower, climbing up and down like the mountains around them. Occasionally, the woman quiets, her breathing becomes even, and she sleeps.

The elephant stays very still during those times, moments only for the woman doesn't stay asleep long. Part of Sophie is afraid to move, afraid to wake up the woman, to disturb her. She feels a strange maternal urge to care for and protect the woman like she would her own calf, an urge she sees reflected in the woman's eyes. She can practically smell the woman's need to care for a child of her own.

The woman, restless, wakes, in the middle of a dream, and looks immediately at the elephant, as if she wonders whether Sophie understands her purpose. Sophie's baleful eye stares back at the woman unwaveringly, reassuringly. The elephant can understand emotions, especially raw emotions, but she has to decide whether this human is trustworthy. In Sophie's world, actions tell her the truth. An angry dog will attack an elephant whenever given the chance. She has seen that first hand, has experienced a dog attack, so she knows the truth of that statement. Her instincts are good, and they tell her to stay away from dogs. If she does, she feels safe.

This woman doesn't create a fear inside this elephant like a dog does. The woman has not hurt Sophie and every indication is that she won't. That is Sophie's truth about the woman.

The woman rouses again. Again, she talks. Quieter, this time. Sorrowfully. Sophie loops her trunk over the woman's shoulders, offering comfort. As if she had been waiting for Sophie's support, the woman continues to speak, her voice getting stronger, calmer as the night darkness breaks to dawn.

Twenty

We are not human beings having
a spiritual experience.
We are spiritual beings having
a human experience.
-Pierre Diehard de Chardin

"Siriporn told me you wouldn't let Dr. Peter near. He said, 'Dr. Peter do exam through bars. He says the leg still infected, and he put Sophie down tomorrow." Natalie imitated Siriporn's voice, deeply concerned, and rightfully so.

Though Natalie had hunted for Peter for more than an hour, she hadn't been able to find him, so she went to the pen where she now knelt in front of Sophie. Every muscle in her body ached.

"Sophie, you must help me convince him. Give me something. Show him what you've shown me. Please. We have to convince him this wound is healing. That you're healing. He thinks you're dying, Sophie."

The elephant's trunk came through the bars, snuffled Natalie's hair.

"I can't give up, old girl. You can't either. We have to fight back."

Sophie flared her pink-tipped ears and huffed.

The two of them stood and watched each other for several

moments. Natalie wondered what the elephant was thinking. She'd often wondered during the first months working with the horses under her care. After a while, she knew by the way a horse neighed or whether its nostrils flared or how it pawed at the ground whether it was ill or a good candidate for a certain pharmaceutical rather than surgery. It became second nature for her. But now, here, she needed to learn and recognize signs and elephant language. It was like becoming a vet all over again.

"We'll do it, Sophie," she whispered, reaching a hand up to touch the elephant's bristly trunk. "We'll do it together. We'll prove him wrong."

The next day, before Hatcher arrived, Natalie attempted to treat Sophie's wound herself, and the old girl allowed Natalie to do so. He had no choice but to let Natalie keep treating Sophie, though he wasn't happy she had shown him up once again. Now she wondered whether he'd ever respect her work.

Sophie trumpeted, one short blast, probably in answer to something she heard in the distance. Natalie glanced up and realized that in her daydreaming, she hadn't even noticed how close they were to each other. She ordered Sophie to back up. Sophie did so immediately.

"Good girl, good," Natalie said quietly.

She went through their training commands, as they did every day, but this time she recorded them using the video camera on her cell phone. Sophie responded to each command without pause, something she had not done before. Normally, one or two had to be repeated several times. Natalie kept the video going as she opened the door to the inner enclosure, moving toward Sophie's leg to get a better shot of the wound. She didn't have time to react before Sophie's trunk reached out for her old tire, the "toy" she could push and pull while in her enclosure. As it passed by Natalie's head, her braid wound in the tire and yanked her with it. With a quick whip that tore her shoulder, she flipped onto the ground and found herself on her back, looking up.

Sophie, standing above her in the enclosure, glanced down, as surprised as Natalie. But Natalie couldn't move and being on her back looking up at Sophie wasn't where she wanted to be.

With a groan, she rolled to one side, trying to get away from Sophie's reach. "It's okay, girl. I know you didn't mean it."

Another groan. She pulled herself to a seated position. The cell phone had fallen and shut off. *Small favors*, Natalie thought, reaching for it and shoving it into her pocket.

Sophie's trunk reached out and touched Natalie's leg. Natalie froze, waiting for the elephant to take advantage and flip her again. But Sophie simply explored Natalie for a moment as if apologizing and checking to see if she was okay, then Sophie withdrew her trunk.

Natalie rolled her head, tentatively feeling for any dislocation in her shoulder, surprised to find none. But every part of her head hurt from having her braid yanked. She'd certainly have a headache that would last for days. As she struggled to her feet, she giggled. If anyone saw her right now, covered with straw and bits of mud, her hand on her back like an old lady, they'd be certain it was Sophie's fault. The elephant even *looked* guilty. But it was Natalie's own damn fault that she'd gotten caught up. She made a mental note to quit daydreaming when she took care of Sophie. If anything else happened, she might not be so lucky to be picking herself up.

She found herself sleeping in the enclosure hours later, awakened by voices nearby. Siriporn and Chanchai. Dusting herself off, she pulled some hay out of her hair and glanced into Sophie's pen. The elephant's massive behind faced her. Natalie darted away just before Sophie doused the ground with a stream of piss.

"Dr. Natalie?" Siriporn, his Yankees baseball cap on backwards, dodged Sophie nimbly. "You sleep here?"

"Not on purpose," she answered, rubbing her stiff shoulder. "I guess I dozed off."

"Miss Karina looking for you. She want you come her office."

"Why?" Natalie had little to do with Andrew's sister, and that was fine with her. No love lost.

Siriporn shrugged. Chanchai had slung a leg over the lower part of the enclosure and busied himself giving Sophie some treats. She never turned down a piece of food, even from the mahout she liked least.

"Will you two feed Sophie while I go find out what she wants?" Natalie knew they could take care of themselves, but she had promised herself to stay by Sophie's side until she could edit last night's video to show Andrew how well she was doing. He was the only one Hatcher would listen to, so she had to get to it first in order to convince him how wrong Hatcher was. Sophie was improving, not dying.

Karina was sitting at the picnic table near the building's overhang, taking up the only space on the platform that always had shade. She peered at Natalie over her glasses and managed a smirk that Natalie guessed was the closest thing to a smile Karina had. She wore a clean Sanctuary t-shirt, a loose gauze skirt and a pair of sandals. Karina was the only person at the sanctuary who stayed clean, no matter what.

Natalie nodded at her. "Mind if I get some tea? I spent the night at the enclosure and haven't had breakfast yet." *It wasn't lying if she didn't tell the whole truth, was it?*

Karina flickered her fingers, as if regally giving permission.

When Natalie returned, cup in hand, Karina stared intently at her laptop screen, not acknowledging Natalie for several moments. Her blonde hair curled in damp ringlets around the edges of her smooth, round cheeks. In another era, Karina would have been considered attractive in a voluptuous, milk-maid fashion, but in today's world, she was overweight and dowdy.

Natalie was halfway through her cup of tea before she finally interrupted Karina and asked, "You wanted to see me?"

"The enclosure." Karina's Belgian accent sounded like rough French. Anything with a "th" sounded like a "z."

"The enclosure?" Natalie asked.

"The elephant? Sophie? Her house. It will cost many *baht*." Karina's eyebrows arched above her gold, aviator-framed glasses making Natalie feel responsible for bankrupting the sanctuary.

"Andrew decided to build the enclosure. I just designed it." Natalie shifted so she could see Karina's laptop. She'd been studying a budget spreadsheet, but why would Karina need to talk to her about budgets? Andrew made all the money decisions. As his chief accountant and bookkeeper, Karina knew that.

"Andrew say you made the plans for the enclosure?" Karina still had not met Natalie's eyes.

"I made some suggestions, but why are you asking me this? I'm sorry. I don't understand."

"Sophie, she needs to move out. Another elephant will be arriving soon, see? I think you know this one. From the floating market, yes?"

"Yes. The street elephant. I remember. But why would that elephant need Sophie's enclosure? And why are you telling me this? I would think that Andrew and Dr. Hatcher would make the decision, not me. Besides, if Hatcher has his way, Sophie won't be around after today . . ." Her voice cracked, and her throat tightened.

From a distance, she heard someone calling her name. The voice came closer. She rose from her seat, upsetting her cup.

Chanchai pounded onto the platform, out of breath. He grabbed her hand and pulled her. "Dr. Natalie! Come! Come! Dr. Peter. Kill Sophie. Come!"

In a split second, she put the pieces together. Hatcher had planned to put Sophie down while Karina kept Natalie occupied. She shot Karina a glance that expressed exactly how much she hated her in that very moment. It didn't surprise her to see a smirk form on Karina's tight mouth.

Natalie sprinted along behind Chanchai, hoping the brief meeting with Karina hadn't given Peter enough time to administer a sedative—or worse, the potassium chloride that would bring on cardiac arrest and death.

She ran harder.

They rounded the corner to the enclosure in time to see Hatcher, syringe in hand, having a heated discussion with Siriporn. She silently blessed Mali's son for having the courage to interfere though she knew it would probably cost his—and possibly hers and Chanchai's—job.

"What the hell are you doing?" She flung herself between the two men. Out of the corner of her eye, she saw that Sophie had backed herself into the furthest corner of the shelter, as far from Hatcher as she could possibly manage.

Natalie grabbed Hatcher's wrist. He pushed against her. The needle dropped. Natalie dove for it as a first baseman does a ground ball, then rolled away, kicking her leg up to knock Hatcher to the dirt.

"You're a crazy woman!" Hatcher rose and dusted himself off. "I told you I was going to . . . put her down. It's the only humane thing to do."

"Humane? Or selfish? What's the real reason? Does she look like she's in agony, for chrissakes?" Natalie's braid fell across her face, blinding her momentarily. She grabbed it and pulled it back, inadvertently reminding herself of the accident with Sophie the night before. She hoped the video had shut off early enough so there was no footage of her being knocked to the ground. She'd need that video now to prove that Sophie was beginning to heal. It would take time for the wound to heal completely and for Sophie to recover from her PTSD—even partially, but time was the one thing Natalie had to give. He couldn't take that away.

"We've talked about this, damnit," Hatcher slapped his hands as if he was done with this conversation. Done with her. "The wound's not healing. This isn't your decision."

"It's not yours either." She placed herself between Sophie and Hatcher, standing as tall as he was, fists at her side. She'd never been so sure of an argument she needed to win. "The sanctuary's guidelines say two vets have to agree when euthanasia is suggested. I read the guidelines cover to cover when I first got here, and I do not agree with you. Unless you can find another vet, we're at a stalemate, Dr. Hatcher."

Their raised voices had drawn a small crowd of mahouts and elephants. Hatcher eyed them all cautiously, then turned back to Natalie. "You may have me outnumbered now, but this isn't over," he said quietly.

"Not by a long shot. Come hell or high water, you'll not put this elephant down unless we've tried everything possible, and she's in pain. I'll make sure of that."

As Hatcher limped away, Natalie caught Siriporn's eye. She'd never seen him smile more widely. She wasn't the only one rooting for Sophie. Why, then, did she still feel so uneasy?

Twenty-One

Music is the universal language of mankind—poetry their
universal pastime and delight.
-Henry Wadsworth Longfellow

THAT NIGHT, VERY LATE, when there were no sounds at all
in the sanctuary—no elephants rumbling, no crickets, no human
voices—Natalie woke up abruptly. She thought she heard echoes
of voices in the night air. Whispered moments amplified by
silence. She imagined she could see the words in the ebony darkness, could touch their density. Then she realized what she heard
was the leftover filaments of her dream.

Breathing a sigh of relief, she remembered that Sophie had
been given a reprieve. Still, she'd sleep next to the elephant from
now on.

She stared into the darkness, thinking of her life. The painful
pitfalls and the soaring bliss, the days she would always remember,
the days she longed to forget. She saw in her mind's eye the brilliant Carolina blue, cloudless sky that greeted her the morning she
married Parker. In a surprising rush, she remembered the powerful
well of love that arose when she saw his nervous face, his hands
twisting, his tongue flicking out to wet his parched lips. She had
loved him. That had been the best moment of her life, until the

moment Stephen decided to end her 26-hour labor and come into the world, a perfect little pink body topped by a slick head of black hair that her mother swore had caused the horrible heartburn Natalie experienced for the last three months of pregnancy. And when he started to cry, his lower lip quivered, and his love put a permanent imprint on her heart.

An errant tear ran down her face now. Raising her hand to wipe it, she rustled the bed covers, and out in the darkness, she saw Sophie's open eye. The elephant rumbled softly, as if half awake, then shifted her huge body and inadvertently leaned on her infected leg. She let out a bit of a moan, a small cry, and immediately shifted back. Sophie had begun rocking in the past couple of days like Natalie remembered her mother doing when the arthritis in her back got to be too much for her. She was doing it now though the steel enclosure didn't let her move too far. Natalie knew the rocking was a way of reaching out for another elephant, something Sophie never had to worry about in the wild, but when she was contained, she couldn't reach another in her herd.

How long has it been since you've been a member of your own family? Natalie silently asked the elephant. *Would you recognize them if you saw them now? Would you know your own calves?*

According to the mahouts, Sophie had given birth at least once before being caught and forced to work, so Natalie had been right to assume a couple of births after her initial exam of the elephant. Now, watching the old female moving back and forth in the shadows, posing no threat to anyone, a pained soul trying to get some relief, Natalie's heart clenched. Sophie had momentarily let down her guard, revealing that she really wasn't mean or broken but simply that the pain in her leg had changed her. Natalie wondered whether Hatcher had been right, that Sophie was in agony, then pushed the thought aside. Uncomfortable, yes, but not in agony. Natalie knew that discomfort could be healed. Healing agony was far more difficult. And she knew how an animal in agony acted. Hatcher was wrong.

She slowly rose from her cot and moved soundlessly on bare

feet toward the elephant, determined not to make any sudden moves and keeping within Sophie's line of sight. About eight feet away, she stopped and so did Sophie. Through the darkness, Natalie sensed Sophie reaching out, as if attempting a telepathic message. When the wet tip of Sophie's strong trunk accidentally touched Natalie's arm, both elephant and human froze. Something told Natalie to hum. Softly. Even though it made little sense, she followed her instinct. Throughout her life, instinct seldom led her astray, so she trusted it.

Sophie responded with a low, long rumble, barely audible.

Natalie hummed again, and again Sophie responded, as though the sound were comforting. She kept her trunk on Natalie's arm. Heartened, Natalie started singing softly, simple, nonsensical words that felt like a lullaby.

Sophie's ears moved, a tiny bit of a shimmy, like radar fine-tuning to pick up a faint signal.

Natalie took a slow step back, uncertain whether the sound had irritated Sophie, but the elephant kept gently moving her trunk. Now it hovered about six inches from Natalie's face.

Instinctually, Natalie wanted to hold her breath, but she knew better not to show or feel any fear at all. Yet Sophie was unpredictable and Natalie counted her steps to the door, just in case.

The nonsensical lullaby grew a little louder, a hoarse whisper, and Sophie again acted as though it comforted her. She regarded Natalie with one watery eye, then turned her head and reached back to touch the steel bars with her trunk as if asking for them to be removed.

Show me I can trust you, ol' girl.

The words to one of her favorite Eagles' songs came to mind, and she sang it softly to Sophie.

I love to watch a woman dance
She bows her head and lifts her hands
Her hips begin to circle slowly
Her eyes half closed; her face is holy
She holds the whole world in a trance

Sophie swayed a bit more from side to side but didn't take her eyes off Natalie. Natalie sang a little louder, more confidently, yet still low and soft. The waltz rhythm of the song felt like a heartbeat. She twirled a little, her white cotton nightgown lifting a bit. Rising on her toes, she spread her arms out and closed her eyes, imagining the sound of accompanying instruments.

She remembered first hearing the song when she bought the Eagles' album after a particularly melancholy period when she thought she needed a man in her life. Its poignant melody moved her to tears, reminding her that there were men in the world who truly loved women. She listened to it over and over again, celebrating her grandparents who had loved the Eagles, and taught her to dance to the very early albums when she was only eight or nine years old. The music brought back memories of growing up in North Raleigh, spending summers at her grandparents' place under the pungent fir trees on Falls Lake where her cousins would challenge each other every year in a swim race across the mile-wide portion of the lake. She never won, but the annual barbeque was chockfull of love and gales of laughter and warm hugs from people you only saw on special occasions. Her Aunt Lee, a short and rather ungracious woman prone to gossip, sharp comments, and J. Crew shirts with khaki shorts, loved Natalie more than her mother and grandmother combined. And she acted. Natalie could hear Aunt Lee's dramatic thespian voice as clearly as if she sat right beside her. "Natalie Renee DeAngelo, you remember this now, sweetie. You're the most exotic flower in the bunch. I look at your friends and they're all daisies. You're a freaking perfect damask rose! A gorgeously deep and musky red-black rose. Don't ever forget that. Ever!"

She likes the slow songs of love lost
They take her a million miles away
'Cause to dream, sometimes, is the only way
To go to places you can't get to any other way
Our eyes connect; she takes my hand

I love to watch a woman dance

For years, Natalie had been too embarrassed to ask what "damask" meant, but when she turned fourteen, she finally realized she'd look it up herself rather than ask.

Natalie paused her dancing for a second. She had never felt comfortable enough to be herself with Parker. He wouldn't have understood the deep and rich well of emotion that must be plumbed in order to live fully, to completely sink one's self in the detail of one brief and romantic moment, such as the Eagles did in this song. She doubted Parker ever simply watched her at any time in their marriage. He might not have ever realized her eyes were the color of polished copper—at least that's what Pop had always told her. "In the middle of your eye is the heart of the fire." That comment made her feel beautiful, but that was Pop. He loved her unconditionally.

That song.

So we danced together, close and slow
So slow we're almost standing still

That song. The lyrics made her feel worthwhile. When she first heard it, she felt it fill in the holes of self-doubt that had pitted her psychological armor. Parker's exit from her life and from her children's world rocked her trust in her own judgment. He disappeared and never looked back. No phone calls, no visits, no birthday cards or Christmas presents. Gone. That had been the ultimate child abuse. And for her, he cemented a wall in her heart. Between the part Parker had closed and the whole halves of her heart that were her boys, she figured she had minus nothing.

After that, everything in her life felt as uneven as a rock trail. No foot forward to solid ground. A difficult struggle. Having an anthem, a song that proved a man out there somewhere appreciated women enough to write such gorgeous lyrics, helped her go through a stage in her life where she could build the bridge to move forward, not worrying about or needing anyone else in order to be whole. She felt strong then. She'd always wanted to have that feeling, yet in order to feel a groundswell of strength and self-confidence, she also needed to go through the negative, the defeats, the disappointments.

And then the shootings . . .

She stopped twirling. Her cotton nightgown floated down and settled at her knees like a heavy cloud. In a blink, she realized where she was. Thailand. In a barn. At an elephant sanctuary. Sleeping with an elephant. Suddenly aware of exactly how close she was to Sophie right now, she felt the heat of the elephant's skin.

She avoided Sophie's eye, and the whole time she did, she continued to sing. Then the music paused, and though it was the briefest of moments, Natalie and Sophie connected, eye to eye, creature to fellow creature, and the moment became so magical that Natalie caught her breath and reached out a hand. Sophie didn't move, as much in a trance as Natalie, but the second Natalie's hand touched the elephant's trunk, both of them started as if they'd experienced an electric shock. Natalie checked herself. She hadn't felt this calm since sharing the same space with Sophie. The elephant rumbled a little as if in reply to Natalie's thought.

"Do you want me to keep singing?" Natalie's spoken voice cut through the silence, a much more intrusive sound than her singing. As soon as the words echoed and died, she started singing again.

Sophie swayed slightly and rumbled low and long, as if letting loose with a sigh.

WHEN THE *sweet sound stops, the echo of the woman's singing*

continues for long moments, growing softer and softer as the echo loses intensity. It becomes part of the air, and Sophie lets her body sway. She flaps one ear after the song ends, searching for the woman's sound again. Her eyes close halfway, and she lets herself relax. She longs for the sound to resume. The woman's sound reminds her of the murmuring sands on the great dry river bed the herd crossed each season. It was the season of no water. The land was cracked, one crack so large an infant fell through to his death.

The herd, led by Sophie's grandmother, headed along the river to the deepest point where she knew they could find fresh water. A few days' trek. The old mothers surrounded the herd, keeping the young ones between them, protected from both the winds and predators. They knew the way, they'd made the trek before, they knew how to adapt to the weather, and they were stronger than any predators. But the babies had neither knowledge nor strength.

Sophie, young then, remembers the sound the river bed made. A song like the woman sings. A call of the wind, the moan of an animal, the sound of a voice in a storm. The desert's song. But in that sound, she also hears her mother's shuffle, a percussive that maintains a beat— two hard steps, one lighter, then a double step. The irritated grumbling of the oldest female in the herd, her back leg dragging behind her, the ankle mangled by the young female lion that lived up-river. The others had seen the cat, too, and circled around Sophie and the other young elephants, but the old female wasn't fast enough to escape the lion's claws. They fought the cat off together, but now the old female lagged behind, a place she wasn't used to occupying.

Sophie's cousin, three wet-seasons younger than Sophie herself, trotted next to her, her infantile shrieks demanding the nannies' constant attention, often inserting herself between their legs, tripping them. The little one still had no control over her trunk and whipped it against Sophie's leg. Too tired to play, Sophie lowered her head and bumped the calf.

That sound, that whine of the wind following the riverbank, that's part woman, part wind, all natural phenomenon. It curled around Sophie's ears, turned her head. She could smell the dust, feel its stinging in her trunk and on the edges of her eyes. Even now, she can taste the *dryness that closed up the back of her throat. Even now, she can hear the sound that made her ears ache.*

That was the day the herd ended.

Twenty-Two

What shall the world do with its children?
There are lives the executives
Know nothing of . . .
The other world is like a thorn
In the ear of a tiny beast.
-Robert Bly

THE MIST CUDDLED THE mountaintops in the distance like gossamer shawls. All sounds fell away, muted as if the mist actually had some weight. A high had moved in overnight, dissipating the heat of the previous day. Every living being responded to the change in temperature. Flocks of birds chirped and crowed and fluttered as if happily renewed. The sanctuary's dogs tumbled over each other, invigorated and acting like puppies, even old Huey, the hound who'd grown fat from lying in the sun, his black face gray with age. Even the elephants came in from the meadow for their early morning meal with more gusto than usual.

Mali and Natalie sat at their favorite table near the elephants' feeding station, sipping their morning tea and talking quietly, as had become their habit.

"Andrew began packing last night for Kenya," Mali said. She stared straight forward, studying the rising mists in the meadow beyond. Her voice was quiet, almost as if in respect for the morning stillness around them. "I feel kind of guilty because I'm not happy about him leaving right now. Selfish, I guess. I worry about Sivad. She crawls up on Andrew's leg whenever she can, screams for her Papa when he leaves eyesight. She prefers to ride on his hip rather than to walk with me. Her mother."

She sipped her hot tea. Natalie didn't feel the need to reply. She watched the far corner of the meadow where the mist shifted like silvery-green clouds and waited for Mali to continue.

"Each time he leaves, it's harder on her. The last time he left she was barely two. She's three now. She can count the days. She asks questions about where Papa is going. How can I explain to her, Natalie? What can you say to a child who really doesn't understand logic? She thinks in emotions." Mali took her teabag out of the cup, placed it carefully on the teaspoon on the table, and sighed.

"All children are like that." Natalie's voice was sandy, gritty. "When I first started the clinic, Stephen was in second grade, so we went to school every day on the bus, but I had to take Danny to pre-school, and he cried every single day. Broke my heart." She'd just bought the clinic and had been so pleased with the new building and her name on the sign. She'd sent out more than a thousand invitations for the open house, yet only two special visitors really mattered: her sons.

"She's so attached to him," Mali continued. "I think this time will be the worst. She's probably going to cry for days, like your Danny." She wrapped her small hands around the cup and took a sip. She sat sideways on the bench seat, both legs tucked under her long, black skirt, and her eyes focused on the clouds near the mountaintops, as Natalie's had been a moment ago. "The psychologist in me knows she'll be fine as long as she has a solid base of love and self-respect and knows her father's coming back," Mali continues. "But the mother in me worries. I guess it's true that it's what we do."

"I understand, believe me. It's not going to be easy on you either."

A long pause. Mali breathed noisily, a long inhale, then an even longer exhale. "You sound like you've got some experience with this kind of problem."

"A little bit. Maybe." Natalie turned away so Mali couldn't see her face. The conversation was hitting too close to home. Her throat tightened.

"I've never asked you. What happened to your husband?"

The question took Natalie aback, but she knew Mali wasn't probing. They were simply having a woman-to-woman conversation. It was safe. "He left," she said with a shrug. "Disappeared one day, and we never heard from him again. My friends said he left with another woman, but I don't know for sure. Don't even know if he's still alive."

"Was he with you when your children passed away?"

It's a simple question, a reasonable one, but it stopped Natalie for another long moment. "No, he'd already left."

"And after?" Mali's questions were phrased as if she'd been wondering how to ask, how to get Natalie to talk.

"If you're asking whether he came home after the boys died . . ." The word still stuck in her throat a bit. "No, he didn't." Natalie clamped her teeth tight.

Talk about your feelings, Dr. Littlefield had told her. *Don't hold back. Your anger is poisonous. Let it out.*

"He must be dead, then," Mali said matter-of-factly. "No parent would stay away from their children's funerals."

Natalie loved Mali in that moment. "No normal person would," she said, nodding emphatically. "I wouldn't have thought a parent could desert the kids he'd helped raise, but he did. For that, and so much fucking more, I'll never forgive him. But he's got his own issues, so I've tried to understand."

"Issues?"

It was Natalie's turn to sip her tea. As she gathered her thoughts, she realized Mali might understand far more than many others, even those who knew Parker personally. "Yes. Big issues. He's a narcissist."

"Ah, that explains it. What's the saying? He wined and dined you from the beginning, right?"

Natalie nodded again.

"And when you fell for him completely, he didn't want you anymore?"

She remembered the moments when Parker coldly turned away from her, the moments when she needed him most. But he'd change his tune completely if she was the one to shut down. When she was angry or turned him away, he turned the charm back on full force, and she fell in love all over again.

"Jekyll and Hyde. I wonder sometimes how we could have had two kids together. By rights, we should've split up the first time he cheated on me. We all would've been better off."

"But he would have had to concede defeat," Mali said, clinking her wedding band against the cup for emphasis. "Narcissists always want to be the winner, the good guy, even though they're anything but."

"My kids didn't deserve the way he treated them. And even though his . . . his disappearance from their lives hurt them both, I must say I wasn't sad to see him go." The truth was that Natalie spent years dreaming about what would be the magic elixir to make her family whole again, but she never shared that irrational longing with anyone. She may have harbored the emotion, but she couldn't admit that obvious character flaw out loud. How could anyone love a person so devoid of love themselves?

"Can't say that I blame you. My kids' dad wasn't much, but at least he was there. Then he died—heart attack. He'd smoked since he was ten. Siriporn was barely a teenager, but he stepped in and became the man of the house. I guess I'm the only one who still sees him as my baby." Mali clucked her tongue and laughed softly from the back of her throat as if she knew how everyone else saw her and accepted it, but that wouldn't change how she felt.

"Mine will always be my babies," Natalie said. "Isn't that the case for most mothers? Our babies are always our babies."

Mali reached for Natalie's hand and held it without saying a word. They sat there quietly. In the distance, an elephant trumpeted and a dog barked, as if in answer.

"I don't know what I'd do if I lost a child." Mali turned to face Natalie full on, her eyes filled with tears as if she knew exactly what had gone through Natalie's mind. "I think that's what gets to me most about working here. So many of these elephants had babies torn from them, and they mourn those babies like we do. I love Andrew, and I know his compassion runs so deeply that he'd lie down and die rather than give up his work, but there's something about being a mother that he'll never understand. The bulls have great memories, but their social connections are different. The matriarchs, they hold the herd together."

Natalie choked back a sob and squeezed Mali's hand.

"We don't have to talk about it anymore, Natalie, but know that if you want to, I'm here. Okay?" Mali rose from the table and brushed herself off with a businesslike efficiency, as she might have when she had an office and clients who came to her for the same kind of advice she'd just given Natalie. "Now I think there will be a whole gaggle of hungry mahouts descending upon us momentarily, so I'd better start cooking some breakfast. You alright, my dear?"

Natalie forced a smile and nodded. Sometimes she felt as though she'd known Mali for years.

Mali's crepe-soled shoes barely made a whisper as she walked away.

Halfway down the road, she heard a tree rustle behind her and turned to see Siriporn atop Ali. The silence of an elephant still surprised her.

"*Sawahdee krup*, Doctor Natalie!"

"*Sawahdee khaa*, Siriporn. Have you already had breakfast?"

"Thai people, we snacking a lot. We always eat. No worry." He grinned. The brightness in his eyes must have been his father's, and his crooked smile marked with a big dimple in the lower part of his right cheek was not Mali's. Handsome. For a younger woman, he would be a great catch, yet he didn't seem interested in any of the younger Thai women nor in the volunteers who always hung around, waiting for the mahouts to share some down time.

It was easy to return his smile.

They walked side by side for a while, he still riding on Ali, his legs astride the bull's neck, and Natalie with one hand on the upper part of Ali's leg. Though Ali's skin was thick and wrinkled like dove-colored leather, she could still feel the muscles rippling beneath as he took one ponderous step after another. He looked down at her from beneath a long fringe of eyelashes, his mahogany-colored eye regarding her as if curious but completely confident he could take care of himself. She felt a great sense of peace when the big bull hovered silently nearby, as if she could trust him to take care of anything in that ponderous, quietly commanding way of his. She thought of him as the father of the herd, though only two of the elephants—the sisters—were actually related, and they weren't his progeny. The elephants had all arrived at the sanctuary at different times, which was often problematic. Elephants didn't automatically bond the way other animals did. Put a group of dogs together and one of them might not take to the pack, but most of them would be fine. Not the case with elephants, yet Ali got along with all of them. Even Sophie.

"Dr. Natalie?"

Glancing up, Natalie was temporarily blinded by the sun right behind Siriporn's head. She shielded her eyes and squinted. Both elephant and mahout were silhouetted in the afternoon sun. A golden haze highlighted the trees in the distance.

"Can I ask question?" he continued.

"Of course."

Natalie sensed him trying to put his words together in English. He needed patience, so she gave it to him, though she often thought he knew more than he let on. Sometimes it felt that he used language as an excuse that Mali didn't understand him. Siriporn had chosen to start training to be a mahout early in life, so he was not regularly exposed to Mali's English. Instead, he, like his father, uncles, and grandfathers, worked with elephants and maintained a traditional Thai lifestyle.

"Believing is important, no?" A shadow cast by the trees cut off the sunlight. Siriporn peered down at her earnestly.

"Yes, I think so. What are you trying to ask?"

"I . . . believe government wrong. Mother say I wrong. What

you think?"

Natalie's gaze fell to the little puffs of road dust her flip-flops kicked up. Each step, another tiny cloud. Right foot, then left, and right again. It dawned on her that she hadn't been truly clean since the first day she'd arrived, but it didn't matter anymore. There were far more important things to consider than whether you had dirt under your fingernails. She took a few more steps, considered how to answer Siriporn's simple, yet extraordinarily complicated, question.

"Sometimes we need to make our own decisions," she started, speaking slowly and thoughtfully. "But we always need to remember how our decisions will affect others. Especially those we love. Think about how elephants act, right? The herd always supports each other. They're stronger when they act as one. They need that community, because they know each other and take care of each other, keep each other safe. Mothers always protect children; boys are independent. All together, they are supposed to learn how to govern themselves." She checked herself and thought for a moment before continuing. "I think what I meant to say is that is how everyone wishes a government would operate, but the truth is that there are a lot of different kinds of governments. You know that."

He nodded, his face solemn.

"I believe, as an American, that we should believe in our traditions and our country, as a whole, but I'm also the first one to question the government any time I feel that it could be doing a better job. That's my right as an American." Taking a deep breath, she thought, *this is where I need to be really careful.* "But it's different in other countries. Look at China's ability to curtail the Internet, and other places where the rules about who you can marry or what you can wear is legislated. People are jailed—and worse—for speaking out against their governments. Who would know better than you—and your family?"

"Mm mm . . ." Ali moved slowly, Siriporn's body swayed with the movement of his elephant's steps. "But if government hurt people we love, what then?"

She thought for another moment. "You're Buddhist, right?"

He nodded and looked straight ahead. He knew where she was going with that question.

"You know the answer, then. We must think of others before ourselves," Natalie said. She immediately wondered whether that answer was enough. The Buddhists she'd met were some of the most sensitive, thoughtful, and compassionate people she'd known. They thought long and hard about decisions that would affect other living beings. One of the reasons this country remained one of the most peaceful in the world was because the majority of its citizens were Buddhist. Yes, they weren't perfect. Yes, they often argued, and even overthrew the government on occasion, but they believed in peace. And their belief system determined the way they dealt with each other. She admired them. Their philosophy remained one of the soundest and most sensible of any she'd known. They counted on each other as human beings rather than on a god they couldn't see. That made them accountable, and though they had not written the golden rule, they lived by it. Every day.

Together, Siriporn and Ali and she walked down the rest of the road in silence until they came to Sophie's enclosure. She trumpeted in welcome. Ali rumbled back. Siriporn lowered himself to the ground and for a moment, Natalie and he spoke silently with their eyes.

Then Siriporn said, "You are my friend, Dr. Natalie, like Ali is Sophie's friend. Funny friends." He laughed a little. "Girl and boy elephant do not live together. Boys live with boys. Mamas and sisters and daughters live together."

Natalie returned his smile. He didn't want or need any more than that, it seemed.

"Dr. Natalie, please help me explain how I feel to Mother. I don't want hurt her."

"I know, Siriporn." Natalie fought the frustration of being caught in the middle. She sympathized with Mali as a mother, but she also understood Siriporn's need to be his own man. "I'm not sure I can help you, though. I don't understand the politics here completely. All I know is that your mother is worried about you."

He watched Ali amble to Sophie's enclosure. The elephants raised their trunks and explored each other briefly, then Ali leaned against the steel bars like a cat rubbing a scratching post. They knew their schedule. It was time for their daily walk to the mud pit.

Siriporn turned back to Natalie. "This my country. My people. We want freedom. Old king will die. People must rule people. Like America. America no want English king, yes?"

"Yes, that's true, but I don't think it's the same, Siriporn. Your king is from your country. He lives here. During the American Revolution, a whole ocean separated the new land from England."

In her peripheral vision, Natalie spotted Sophie bouncing her head against the bars, anxious to be free. This discussion had to wait.

"Listen, Siriporn, I'll make you a deal. We can talk about this later, discuss the American Revolution all you want, but do me a favor, ok? Remember your mother loves you and don't do anything crazy, alright?"

Sophie trumpeted. Natalie and Siriporn moved toward the gate to let her out, but before they opened it, Natalie put her hand on Siriporn's. "Promise me?"

He paused, shifted a moment as though she had asked him something far too difficult to decide in a moment, but then he nodded.

As they walked to the mud pit with Sophie and Ali, Natalie realized that Siriporn's promise had been given too quickly. She made a mental note to talk to him again. This time she would ask about his plans.

The elephants lumbered into the river and immediately submerged themselves. A cool breeze rattled a nearby breadfruit tree. She pulled out her notebook and settled beneath the tree, and within moments, became engrossed in the tangle of data she'd been amassing for weeks. It was time to make sense of all of it.

Twenty-Three

> It is a fine seasoning for joy
> to think of those we love.
> -Moliere

NATALIE TRIED HER BEST to ignore Christmas. Four months, she'd been here. A year and a half since the boys died. Her second Christmas alone.

She spent the whole day with Sophie, working on commands, moving her in and out of protected contact, practicing lifting her feet, making sure Sophie felt comfortable with Natalie's hands in her mouth, taking multiple trips to the mud baths and the river. Anything to stay busy. Anything to push away the clouds of doubt and the streams of memories. Anything to quell the homesickness.

Cicadas buzzed as the sanctuary's dogs chased each other in a game of rough-and-tumble tag on the platform. Most of the volunteers had returned home for the Christmas holidays, leaving for the month of December to return in January, if they were to return at all. A skeleton crew remained so that the administrative duties would be accomplished. All of the Thai staff were still in place since the majority of them were born in the area and Buddhist. Of the non-Thai staff, only Karina, Hatcher, and Natalie stayed to celebrate the Christian holiday. Andrew, still in Africa, probably wouldn't return until February. Andrew's absence provided a stay of execution for Sophie and gave Natalie more time to work with her.

But it still wasn't enough.

Whenever there was a thirty- or ten- or even a two-second lapse in activity, memories cropped up in Natalie's mind: Danny's first Christmas when he stared at the lights, fascinated by their brilliance. That simple act thrilled all the adults around him. He had been the center of attention since birth, a happy baby who giggled constantly. Even two-year-old Stephen got a kick out of the baby's wide-eyed staring at anything that twinkled or sparkled.

By his third birthday, Stephen understood Christmas and Santa Claus, and he begged her to take him to see the "toeman" (his way of saying "snowman") in the yard around the corner, and he never understood when she tried to explain that the eight-foot-tall blowup snowman lit up only when it was dark outside. Each night when she picked him up from daycare, they came home via another route so they could see different decorations, but he wanted—and expected—to see that "toeman," so she finally gave up on everything else. And he smiled and laughed every time they did see that "toeman." He told Santa Claus that Christmas that he wanted the "biggest blue bike," and when Natalie asked him why, Stephen answered in his best three-year-old serious voice, "Because blue bikes are the fastest, Momma."

"He would've loved you, Sophie. Both of them would have," she whispered into the elephant's ear as they walked back from the river.

In the distance, she heard laughter coming from the administration building and realized with a start that it was dinnertime. She imagined Hatcher and Karina at the table with a bottle of wine and the Christmas chicken they'd talked Hom, Mali's friend and one of the cooks, into butchering for their holiday dinner. For a long moment, she and Sophie stood silently in the road, listening to the echoes of the conversation. Natalie considered getting Sophie settled and going to join them. Perhaps it was time to put differences aside and celebrate the holiday the way it should be. On some soundless nights, the loneliness for home and familiar things manifested as a physical weight on her chest. Tonight's weight felt astronomical. She'd stay alone tonight. Being around others would only accentuate the depth of her loneliness.

Still, she was hungry and it certainly would be nice to at least have a festive dinner—even though she had no desire whatsoever to break bread with anyone—least of all, Hatcher and Karina.

While she fed Sophie back at the enclosure, she fought with herself about sharing dinner with the others. She sang a Beatles' song to Sophie as her stomach growled again, and Sophie farted in response.

"Thanks, Soph. God! Talk about curing someone of their hunger." She backed off and waved her hand in front of her face. She could have sworn Sophie grinned, having a good joke on the stupid human. "Okay, I give. I'm leaving."

In the dark, she found her way to the back of the administration building, hoping she could find the kitchen door and beg some food from Hom. She knew the women in the kitchen would think it strange, especially since she'd never been to the kitchen's back door before, but she really didn't want to be forced to share an uncomfortable meal with Hatcher and Karina. A faint light from inside beckoned her.

Female voices and laughter floated through the kitchen's screen door as she drew closer. One of the voices sounded like Hom's. Her high-pitched giggle rose in octaves depending upon how tickled she felt, and right now, she seemed breathless. Natalie felt a little twinge of jealousy that she'd been left out of moments like this, but it passed as quickly as it came when she caught the unmistakable fragrance of green curry chicken and another scent—pungent and spicy. In the dark, she couldn't identify the plants and bushes, but she suspected the scent came from one of them, then she bumped into something wooden.

A box set up above the ground. Her fingers explored the side of the box, and she wound her way around it until she faced its front. The scent came from the box, not the kitchen. A yellow light streaming from the kitchen door highlighted the box, which she now realized was a Buddhist spirit house, the center of which held a sitting statue of a Buddha. An altar shelf filled with half-burnt candles and small mementoes: a statue of a little man, a car, a tiny doll, some beads, and what appeared to be a dozen eggs. The spirit house, shaped like a temple, had probably been built at the same time the main building was erected.

The incense. That's what I smelled.

She'd seen spirit houses throughout the country: on street corners, in funny little alcoves outside convenience stores, at entrances of parks, or in doorways of apartment buildings. Wherever there were people and homes, the spirit houses were there, too, to pay homage to the land and to the ancestors who owned it.

On the opposite side of the box: a color candid shot of a little boy around six years old in full head-thrown-back laughter. She could practically hear his delighted chortle and imagined him trying to get his favorite dog to behave. She lifted her fingers to smooth the photograph's edge. A lump rose in her throat. She turned away.

The screen door slammed. She heard a match strike and a cough. She spotted Hom.

They both jumped as if they'd seen a spirit and shared a good belly laugh with each other. When the giggles died down, Natalie pointed to the photo of the little boy, then to Hom.

"Is he yours?" she asked.

Hom looked at her blankly. She knew very little English.

Natalie pantomimed rocking a baby, pointed to the photo, then to Hom. This time, Hom's face brightened.

"Your baby?" Natalie asked.

"Beebee, beebee." Hom pointed to her stomach, then rocked an imaginary child and pointed to the photograph. The light from the kitchen door framed Hom's round face. A definite resemblance, she seemed to say. Hom smiled, somewhat reassuringly, and reached out to touch Natalie's arm.

"*Aaa-haan-meuu-yin*? Dinner?" Hom asked, pantomiming a

plate and moving her hand from the 'plate' to her mouth, then pantomiming the act of chewing. "Yum, yum." She rubbed her stomach, motioning for Natalie to follow her.

Inside the small kitchen, three women bustled about, cleaning up pans, sweeping the floor, putting food back into the industrial sized refrigerator. One large stove took up one wall, the sink and refrigerator against the other. An amazingly small kitchen for the amount of food that they produced every day. And it sizzled inside the little room. But it didn't seem to matter to the women. One of them, whom Natalie had never seen before, handed her a disk full of chicken and rice and vegetables that smelled so spicy it made her mouth water. She started walking out the door, intending to take it back to her cabin, but the woman pulled over a three-legged stool and motioned for Natalie to sit and eat. So she did.

She ate her Christmas dinner as if she hadn't eaten for the past three days, all the while watching the women as they moved confidently around each other, wrapping up leftovers, cleaning the only counter in the kitchen and scrubbing the remaining pots. By the time she finished eating, they had completed their tasks, so they all left the kitchen together. Hom shut off the kitchen light and, in complete darkness, the trio of women moved off into the night, heading for the enclave of cabins located on the other side of the administration building. The opposite direction that Natalie headed.

After they walked away, the surrounding vegetation swallowed whatever sounds they might have made, leaving Natalie in silence under the stars. She took a deep breath and tasted the chicken's spices, a very different taste from what she would have eaten any other Christmas night.

In her ear, Danny whispered, "What an adventure you're having, Mommy."

She felt a faint brush of wind, as soft as a breath, and reached her fingers up, knowing she wouldn't catch it. But she smiled anyway. It was okay. Everything was as it should be.

On her walk down the road back to her bungalow, she found

her voice and lifted it clearly to the stars.

> *You'd better watch out.*
> *You'd better not cry.*
> *You'd better not pout.*
> *I'm telling you why.*
> *Santa Claus is coming to town.*

Danny's favorite.

She lifted her head to the sky. Thousands of stars dotted the heavens in familiar constellations and unfamiliar clusters. She'd never been an astronomy buff—she was lucky she knew how to spot the Big Dipper—but she loved looking at the sky. In the moment and more than a little buzzed from the wine, she shut off the lantern and let the night settle around her. Gradually, her eyes adjusted and she discerned the shapes of trees and the roof-line of one of the cabins to her right. For several long moments, she stood there, staring into the night sky, not thinking, simply breathing. Then the sound of the sanctuary's phone ringing in the near distance broke the silence, reminding her she hadn't ventured very far from the platform.

After the third ring, she heard Hatcher's gruff "hullo." Amazed she could hear him so clearly, she remained anchored, wondering who'd be calling so late. Then she fuzzily realized it had to be a long distance call. Another time zone. Part of her hoped it was her mother: it would have been good to hear from home, but Maman wasn't prone to unplanned phone calls or visits. Natalie knew when Maman would call because she wrote to let Natalie know weeks in advance. Natalie often teased Maman that mail actually did arrive within a week to ten days, and if Maman wanted to reach Natalie sooner, she could email. But, no, Maman was very old school: paper letters—hand-written—and long, newsy phone calls.

"No, I'm alone right now," Hatcher said. "How are things in Kenya?" His voice floated through the clear night air as though he held a microphone. It had to be Andrew calling. "Things are going well, for the most part. Running a skeleton ship here, you know. Everyone's gone home for the holidays . . . yes, yes, yes, most back in January . . . no, we'll be fine. All the mahouts are still here . . . yes, yes, that's fine . . . she's still here . . ."

For several moments, he only murmured or huffed, then, "You have a lot more faith in her than I do . . ."

Natalie's ears pricked up. Was it the tone of Hatcher's voice or the words he used that told her he was talking about her?

"Do you realize how much money we've spent on her little experiment? Nearly seventy-five thousand American dollars!" Another silence. Hatcher kept trying to speak, but Andrew must have been having his own say on the other end of the line. "We've never spent this much on one elephant. If we have a medical emergency anytime soon, we're royally buggered."

Natalie sucked in her breath. Hatcher was lying through his teeth! The expenses were minimal. *Where the hell did he get that figure? Whoa, wait a minute. Karina.* Natalie wished she could hear Andrew's response.

"Sophie's a serious waste of time and resources, Andrew, and you know it. She'll come only so far, then something will push one of her buttons, and she'll blow her cork, like before. We need to cut our losses . . . I know . . . I know . . . No, I don't think that'll work. You know how I feel about this!" Hatcher's voice became more strident. He liked having his own way, and right now, it didn't appear that was happening. "She's going to hurt someone, and we'll end up being sued . . . I know, you must under—Don't worry. I won't." He grunted a few times. Listened.

Deep down, Natalie felt a guilty pleasure hearing Hatcher bumble around and was glad she hadn't butted in when she heard him lie. He'd entrap himself without her help. She had become so used to his bullying that his failings were a relief of sorts. Made him halfway human. A contradiction, of sorts.

"All the other ellies are fine. Yes. Dogs, too . . . yes, Mali went to her sister's for a couple of days. Should be back Saturday . . . okay, I will . . . don't worry, I won't say anything . . . Andrew! I said I wouldn't say anything . . . you know I don't like the woman . . . It's more than the dissertation, Andrew. You know that . . . But we're supposed to discuss these hires before you bring them onboard. If you'd talked to me . . ." Silence again.

The hair on the back of Natalie's neck bristled.

"Yes, I understand that." Hatcher's voice grew quieter, like a schoolboy answering his teacher. "I do understand, but I wish we had." The conversation stopped right there.

Afraid to breathe, Natalie waited a couple more moments, then realized Andrew must have hung up. He had a reputation for ending conversations where he wanted them to end, often spinning on one heel and walking away, interrupting the other person mid-sentence. Even Mali complained of his tendency to be curt. Knowing that Andrew had cut Hatcher's conversation short gave her an even greater sense of satisfaction than she'd felt listening to Hatcher stumble over his own words.

A cough echoed in the night air. Footsteps. Hatcher came down the path toward her. She turned and walked quickly toward her cabin, feeling with her feet for the path, keeping her lamp unlit and hoping she didn't trip on the way.

The smell of ginger blossoms suddenly turned sour.

Twenty-Four

I was once like you are now,
and I know that it's not easy,
To be calm when you've
found something going on.
But take your time, think a lot,
Why, think of everything you've got.
For you will still be here tomorrow,
but your dreams may not.
-Cat Stevens

NATALIE HAD AGREED TO tutor Mali's sons in English, science (particularly biology), and mathematics in exchange for a year's worth of Thai horoscopes. It didn't really matter that she wouldn't be able to cash in on all of them because she'd be leaving in less than a year. Truth be told, she didn't really care about the horoscopes and would have tutored the boys anyway because it filled some tiny void inside her soul to be around them, but Mali's offer of the horoscopes was her way of paying Natalie. Afraid of breaking a cultural rule, Natalie simply went along with the agreement, and Khalan and Siriporn came to her for lessons whenever she was nearby. Surprisingly, she saw each of them at least twice a day.

And in spite of the fact that the horoscopes didn't matter, she listened when Mali already said she'd been born in the Year of the

Tiger. "People born in the Year of the Tiger are brave, intelligent, powerful, but on the other hand, they can be bloody arrogant and painfully short-tempered. You should probably not have a relationship with another person who is also a Tiger. You'd probably bludgeon each other to death!" She laughed, poking fun at herself, and teasing Natalie.

Natalie felt strangely empowered, as if she embodied the tiger's spirit, and her interest grew until she looked forward to discovering what other predictions Mali would conjure.

The horoscopes were far more pleasant than bacteria and phylum or the sets and graphs Natalie created for the boys, who often didn't want to sit still for their lessons. She taught them in English, as Mali suggested, and she watched their eyes glaze over if she spoke too quickly. And she learned quickly that a lesson delivered while walking was more often remembered than one delivered in a classroom. So, their classroom became the jungle and the river and the tree stumps along the side of the road. Anywhere they were.

Surprisingly, Sivad, the little, black-eyed magpie, sat in on the lessons and sponged up everything. She now babbled in English about the dogs and the elephants (she had renamed each of them) and she detailed what she had for her last meal to anyone who would listen.

Siriporn had requested Natalie teach him the history and philosophies of the most famous of the world's non-violent protestors: Gandhi, Martin Luther King Jr., Mother Theresa, the Dalai Lama, Henry David Thoreau, Rosa Parks. She felt inadequate at first, but the more they talked, the more she found herself more knowledgeable than she'd originally believed. Siriporn's knowledge of the English language now included words like "humanitarianism" and "peaceful activism" and "righteous dignity."

Khalan, Mali's second eldest, was more interested in learning about animals so the words he knew weren't likely to be used in common conversation. He wanted to learn quickly—which meant learning in Thai from the other mahouts in the village and then bringing that knowledge to her for translation. It wasn't the most academic type of education, but Natalie wouldn't give up. Besides, she had an ulterior motive. She soaked up every piece of native teachings or ideals. Who would know their elephants more than the people who'd lived with them for centuries?

It was past two in the afternoon, the hottest part of the day, and Natalie's patience had worn thin with Khalan. They'd been working on mathematic equations, his weakest area, and at it for almost three hours, sitting on the platform, shifting seats when they lost the shade that gave them a bit of respite from the relentless heat. They'd hit a wall and for the past couple of moments, Khalan had been staring into space, completely uninterested, and at this point, she didn't blame him.

Though she had promised Mali that her son would be well-prepared for his last year in school before heading to university, at this rate, he wouldn't make it. Sadly, it didn't seem to make a difference to him. He'd rather be right where he was.

Natalie wondered if any of his teachers had ever felt this level of frustration.

"See if you can tell me about what you see over there," she told Khalan and pointed to an Oriental pied hornbill with a brightly-colored bill who'd flown past the platform where they sat at one of the picnic tables. The bird landed on the edge of the overhang where several elephants milled about waiting for their trek down to the river with the mahouts.

"Bird," Khalan said.

She had hoped he would remember that they'd named various birds yesterday, especially since she'd imitated their calls so that he'd be able to differentiate between them (and so he'd pay attention). She wondered how teachers did it every day: presenting dog-and-pony shows to students who couldn't care less.

"Yes, it's a bird," she said now, hiding her disappointment. "It's an Oriental pied hornbill. Can you say that? Hornbill?"

He looked at her mouth. She said it again, and he imitated her.

"Good!" They high-fived—something Khalan never failed to

laugh about—and Natalie took the opportunity to squeeze some more new words into the lesson.

They were almost done for the day when she heard footsteps and voices behind them. Khalan lifted a hand in salute as Natalie turned to see who was coming.

Karina, a clipboard in her hand and a scowl on her face, walked toward them. She had gathered her frizzy blonde hair up with a clip atop her head. Her chubby feet were stuffed into sandals way too small for her, leaving her toes to hang over the edge by a good inch. The outline of Karina's bra created rolls of fat where the straps cut across her back.

"English lessons today?" she called from where she stopped at least twenty feet away. "Nothing to do at the clinic? Sophie still in her enclosure? Her muscles must be atrophying by now with the lack of exercise she's getting." Karina lifted her pen and the clipboard as if about to check off Natalie's answers to her rapid-fire interrogation.

Natalie hid a smirk. "Khalan's doing well with his lessons." He still sat next to her, though Natalie suspected he wouldn't need much of an excuse to escape. She smiled at him, knowing he understood at least a part of what she said even though he might not respond. "Dr. Hatcher didn't need me at the clinic today, and Sophie's been getting plenty of exercise."

Karina twisted up her mouth. Her eyes shifted to Khalan, then back to Natalie as if she disapproved. "I didn't realize Andrew paid you to tutor the help."

Though Natalie bristled, she forced herself to smile. "Oh, but he doesn't pay me, Karina. I'm a volunteer, remember?"

Karina huffed and bent her head to her clipboard.

Natalie took her opening. "Any chance you can schedule someone to clear out Sophie's enclosure? That's not in my job description."

Khalan chuckled, hiding his mouth with his hand, his brown eyes glittering like a child who'd been caught with a secret. The little bugger understood more than he let on.

Another set of footsteps. Natalie peered over her shoulder.

Hatcher. She tried to hide her feelings once again. In that second, it dawned on her that she'd come across the world and still found a fair modicum of drama. Humans, they couldn't live without their drama.

"Boy, you're a busybody," Hatcher said, looking directly at her when he reached the table.

"I'm not sure that's the term I'd use," she answered as she gathered the paper and books on the table. It was time to "exit stage left," as her brother would say. She had no patience for Hatcher right now.

Khalan stood, looked at each of them uncertainly, as if trying to figure out what the *farang* (the Thai name for foreigners) were going to do. But the way his brows knit together, it appeared he didn't want to hang around.

Telling herself to ignore the comments and the undercurrent of sarcasm, Natalie made a pretense of putting her papers in order and kept her eyes down.

"I asked Siriporn whether he was working with you and Sophie today, and he said you gave him the day off. That true?" Hatcher asked.

Natalie glanced up to see Hatcher's eyes on her. Behind him, Karina held her clipboard to her chest with a smug expression on her face.

"Yes, that's true. Sophie and I were going to work alone today."

"Is that safe?" Hatcher actually managed to sound concerned.

"Absolutely, we've been working alone a lot lately. She's fine with me. The only time I really need another set of hands is when I'm giving her an antibiotic or checking her foot pads." It was true. Sophie's demeanor had become calmer, more docile, in the past month. If Natalie hadn't had a veterinary background, she'd swear it was because she now sung to the elephant every night. But she knew better. The leg wound was healing, and she would only need a couple more rounds of antibiotics before the infection would be cured.

Hatcher raised an eyebrow skeptically and swung his

eyeglasses in a circle by their arm as if he didn't know what else to say. "Good, then we can put her back in general population soon."

"As long as she's not near any dogs and we keep the protected contact training program going . . ."

"Let's get her back with one of the other mahouts. It's time for you to work with me on the other tasks at hand. I need to return to regularly visiting the villages, but I can't do that because there's too much to occupy me here. I need another set of hands." He paused for a moment and gazed toward the jungle in the distance. "This elephant has taken up too much of your time. Time to tend to everything else that needs doing in this . . ." He raised his palms to the sky, twisted his mouth, and said, "sanctuary."

Speechless, Natalie watched him descend the stairs and disappear down the pathway that led to the clinic. His bony shoulders hunched up a bit, drawing his T-shirt into wrinkles. If he didn't have a belt on, he would have lost his shorts, she thought. He had no butt whatsoever. But his long legs were well-muscled and he strode with strong steps and a sense of purpose.

In a thought that surprised her, she wondered if, in another life, at another time, she might have been attracted to him, or at the very least, they might have been friends. But at this point, she wasn't even sure she respected Peter Hatcher. He'd decided long ago that she was the enemy, and now she knew she felt the same way about him. She had no patience with people who were so hardheaded.

But all of that had to be put on the back burner. Right now, Sophie's fate was far more important than the war with Hatcher.

No matter how good Sophie was doing, Natalie didn't want to leave her with a mahout. None of them knew the protected contact procedures, nor had anyone—except Siriporn—seen it in use. Besides the training, Natalie strongly suspected Sophie had been abused by some men in her life, because she had an altogether different way of responding to the men than she did toward women. All of the women who'd come by the pen had been allowed to approach Sophie, even to touch her. But the only man she tolerated was Siriporn—and only when Ali remained nearby. Natalie felt fairly certain that being poked by an *ankus* or ridden by a mahout would throw Sophie right back into the same constant state of fear she felt several months ago. She wasn't willing to take that chance.

Time to go over Hatcher's head and call Andrew.

She was so immersed in her thoughts that she didn't notice Mali until she turned and almost tripped over her.

"Might I ask what that was all about?" Mali pointed to Hatcher, already halfway down the road. Behind Mali, Karina suddenly reappeared, then back-stepped and whirled around to flee to the office as if terrified by the much smaller and less intimidating Mali. Natalie thought that was strange, yet she sensed a history existed between Mali—Andrew's lover—and Karina—his sister—that only they were privy to. And Natalie really didn't want to know. She had enough on her mind.

"The usual," Natalie answered with a dismissive wave of her hand. "Nothing really. By the way, do you know when Andrew's scheduled to call again? I'd like to give him an update on Sophie."

Mali paused for a heartbeat as if she had been about to say something then thought better of it. "I believe he's going to call tomorrow night around six o'clock our time. If you stick around after dinner, I'll make sure you get the phone. He's been asking about you anyway, love, so it would be a super idea to talk with him straightaway."

She motioned for Natalie to sit, then slid onto the bench next to her.

"How's my boy doing?" Mali kept her voice low since Khalan was at the next table and engrossed in conversation with another mahout about Khalan's elephant, Pahpao.

Natalie sighed and mentally slapped herself for doing so when she saw Mali's eyes flicker in surprise. "He's not doing badly," Natalie said. "I only wish he'd study more between lessons. He struggles a bit."

Mali shook her head and glanced at her middle child who

had begun feeding the ellies some fruit. "My lazy one. The boy would rather swing in the hammock all day or play with the animals than to do any kind of work—school or otherwise. I don't know what I'm going to do about him."

"He's young yet," Natalie said, simultaneously thinking he sounded a lot like her. Growing up, she'd much rather spend time with her animals than do homework. "Let him be. I'm sure he'll find his way."

With a start, she remembered her father saying the exact same thing about Stephen.

Twenty-Five

Lives of great men all remind us
We can make our lives sublime.
And, departing, leave behind us
Footprints on the sands of time.
-Henry Wadsworth Longfellow

SIRIPORN STOOD AT NATALIE'S side, his thumbs tucked into his pockets, his baseball cap on backward so his view of Sophie would not be obstructed. "Deeper, Dr. Natalie, deeper." He was in his element, sure of himself, the teacher rather than the one being taught. More than two months into training, and he was not quite satisfied with the authority Natalie exerted when she commanded Sophie.

"Hou!" The Thai command for 'stop' and the gritty way she had to pronounce it razor-scraped against the sides of her throat. She'd been hoarse for days but determined to get this language down. Now Sophie watched Natalie intently whenever she raised her voice. Natalie had to admit it made her proud to see Sophie responding as well as she did without the need to lift the training baton she used in protected contact. The long pole had made Sophie nervous at first, but Natalie had rubbed the rounded cotton tip with some banana and left it where Sophie could smell it. Eventually, Sophie's fears eased, then Natalie got her used

to being touched with the pole. Hours of that training before Natalie coupled some commands with the pole. Then she was able to back Sophie up to get her medicine or to be examined. It had been going well. But no matter how well the training went, Sophie would never like dogs, and since the dogs at the sanctuary were used to roaming freely, Natalie felt fairly certain she'd always have to ensure that Sophie had a human escort nearby. Right now, that human escort was Natalie.

"*Sok*," she told Sophie, and the elephant backed out of the pen. One more command—*Phae*—to come, and Sophie followed Natalie freely, peacefully.

They rewarded her—and Ali—with a visit to the mud pits. Siriporn and Natalie sat on the cement fence posts, giggling as their charges rolled and splashed mud on themselves and each other, so happy in the mud pit that they trumpeted with pure pleasure. Natalie and Siriporn chatted, as they often did, about the other elephants, about the weather, and about the people they knew. Siriporn gossiped nonstop, Natalie had discovered, and because he delighted in shocking her, she now knew that Chanchai dated Jabari's sister and that Jabari had been caught drunk at least three times in the past month on rice whiskey that he made and sold to the other mahouts (and that his mother had thrown him out).

But what Siriporn liked to talk about more than anything else was politics. During the past couple of months, his English had improved by leaps and bounds. Now when he told Natalie about his beliefs and asked her about the United States' democratic system, he added new words to his vocabulary every time they talked.

"If the Thai government run in democratic way like U.S., we vote on laws, yes?" Siriporn asked.

She nodded. It was hot, and they'd had this conversation before, so she was only half interested. She had never been a political person, and truth be told, she'd rather hear the latest gossip, but Siriporn was such an earnest young man and had taught her so much that discussing the political system in the

States seemed a fair way to repay him.

"And military? They ruled by president?"

"Ultimately. But there are military leaders and they listen to the secretary of defense who listens to the president."

Siriporn took a stick and started drawing a pseudo pyramid on the ground. He pointed to the pinnacle. "This the president?"

She nodded, already seeing where he was heading with his organizational chart. Ten minutes later, they had written it all out on the ground: the executive branch, the legislative, and the judicial.

He nodded and looked at the diagram one last time as if memorizing it, then he dusted his sandals over it, wiping it out.

They called the elephants back, and as the lumbering mud-covered beasts reluctantly left the pit and began walking back to Sophie's enclosure, Siriporn turned to her. "Andrew come back, you know."

She was surprised. "I thought he wasn't coming until next week."

Siriporn shrugged his shoulders. "He come tonight."

Sophie touched Natalie's arm with the wet tip of her trunk and rumbled gently as if sensing Natalie's concern. She had hoped she'd be able to give Andrew another report on Sophie before Hatcher got to him. Now she wondered how much poison Hatcher had already poured into Andrew's ear. Surely Andrew would talk to her directly. Surely, he'd come to see Sophie himself and would be able to figure out that she wasn't the same elephant she'd been when he left. Surely, he'd give her another chance.

Or not. He'd known Hatcher longer than he'd known her, probably trusted him, and he had a history with Sophie.

They arrived at the enclosure and got Sophie into her pen. She didn't even need to be led in anymore. The pen was like a security blanket for her, and she knew when she stepped into it that she would be fed. Sophie would do anything for food.

As Natalie shoved her hands into the large bucket full of sticky rice mixed with a calcium supplement, some sweet potatoes and squash, she thought about what she'd say to Andrew.

She wished she could be completely honest and warn him about Hatcher's tendency to be cruel to the volunteers, workers, and to her, but she was fairly certain Mali had already done that for her. Mali had phone conversations of her own with Andrew and had shared the details of some of them with Natalie. Mali had had several run-ins with Hatcher in the past couple of weeks, and though she didn't have it in her to be nasty, she also didn't let others bulldoze her. And she wouldn't hesitate to share the truth with Andrew.

Siriporn called for Ali, commanded the bull to lower his head and then scrambled astride to sit with his legs behind Ali's ears. He'd already taught the other mahouts that the only way they could ride their elephants was on the strongest part of their necks. Personally, Natalie would rather they not be ridden at all (she refused to get on Sophie's neck), but she didn't push the issue. At least, not yet. If she'd learned one thing while being at the sanctuary, it was that it wasn't home, and she had to respect the Thai way of doing things, no matter how much she disagreed. Siriporn silently watched Natalie for a few moments as she fed Sophie, then told her he'd see her at dinner.

As Siriporn and Ali ambled down the road, Natalie realized he was probably headed back to the big enclosure to drop Ali off before he left the sanctuary for another of his Red Shirt meetings tonight. She wondered whether she should say something to Mali, but as she handed another sticky ball to Sophie, she decided not to. No, if Siriporn wanted to tell his mother, he would. In the meantime, she wouldn't get in the middle.

Twenty-Six

Let us alone. Time driveth onward fast,
And in a little while our lips are dumb.
Let us alone. What is it that will last?
All things are taken from us, and become
Portions and parcels of the dreadful Past.
-Alfred, Lord Tennyson

ANDREW'S OPERA ENDED ABRUPTLY, and a screen door slammed. Natalie exhaled the breath she'd been holding and waved at him standing on the porch. "Don't you love Don Giovanni?" he called out. "No one does it better than Renee Fleming!" He smiled and began walking toward her.

Perfect, she thought. Her timing couldn't have been better. She could get a few moments of precious private moments with him before he headed for his office. She wondered whether he'd seen Peter yet.

Andrew's hands flew around him like a bird's wings, conducting the opera still soaring in the background. The aria ended, and he looked disappointed. "Radios were free when I was growing up. My ol' dad always said classical music and opera would make you smart, so that's what we listened to. Don't know if it worked, but I do so appreciate the drama." He laughed, struck one hand out to the side, then up into the air in a triumphant flourish.

He blasted opera on his stereo every Sunday. Natalie was never sure which one he was playing, but he sang along loudly enough for the whole sanctuary to hear. And badly. So badly, it was humorous.

As the music beckoned her up the road, Natalie remembered how much Danny loved the symphony. One moment, in particular, one precious night they went to the North Carolina Symphony alone, just the two of them. The memory, as brilliant as a ten-carat diamond.

Danny sat in the symphony hall after the lights went down, his dark head bent, nose flaring as if breathing too hard, lips tight and intent. Hands folded like a cathedral spire in his lap as he peered over the railing of their first balcony seats as the tympani pounded and cymbals clashed during the final movement of Tchaikovsky's Romeo and Juliet Fantasy Overture. His feverish eyes alit and his little fingers twitching as if playing the tympani, and when the string section swelled for that romantic crescendo, his eyes filled and he swiped at them as if embarrassed to be so emotionally swept away.

To this day, she cannot hear that overture without falling to her knees in spasms that literally feel like they will crack her rib cage right down the middle. Each time, she can see his face. His dark eyes focused on something deep within the orchestra that no one else saw but him. He lived between the violin strings. His heart entwined in each pluck of the harp. His soul pounding with each beat of the bass drum.

Andrew's booming hello brought her back to Thailand and the dirt road and his hut in front of her. Reluctantly, she pushed the memory aside.

"Welcome home!" she said as they hugged. "How's everything in Kenya?"

"Three new elephants." Andrew was proud of every animal he could rescue and she had no doubt he would be just as committed to his cause even if he was completely broke. There were some whispers that his vast estates were drying up because of recent fluctuations in the market, but at least for the moment, his philanthropy was healthy.

"But there's been a spate of poaching, and we lost an entire family on the northern boundary of the reserve." His voice broke, and he fought back tears, as he always did whenever one of his big lovelies fell to poachers. "The new elephants blended in well with the herd, even though they've been witness to the horrible murders. And you know what that means. We'll be dealing with PTSD for a while. However, my big cows are stepping in as nannies, and I think one of them might have known the other ellies. Gives this ol' limey a warm feeling in the cockles of my heart when their social structure is repaired."

Andrew wearily pushed a thick hand through his shock of white hair, but he must have felt Natalie's eyes on him because he gathered himself and looked at her. "So tell me the news about our ol' Sophie girl. I hear you've made quite a turnaround with her. What kind of magic are you weaving?" He waggled a finger in her face as if he knew all of the details already.

"No magic," she said. "Simply perseverance and a bit of empathy. Oh, and a lot of consistency. We work on moving her around, getting her to obey simple commands, over and over again, building her trust. That might seem rather simplistic, but it has worked. Also, I think it makes a difference that I'm female. Whenever there's a guy around, she seems tense."

Andrew chuckled and patted her on the shoulder. "Sometimes animals do have a gender preference. Would definitely explain a few things wouldn't it?"

They sat companionably on his porch steps, and for a brief moment, everything was quiet. No birds, animals, leaves turning in the breeze. A pause of life. She took the moment to gather her thoughts about what she wanted to say.

"I've written up all of my reports about her, Andrew," she began. "I've been keeping track of all pertinent data in my notebooks since I got here, and I've recorded the data into spreadsheets now. I know we have a small sample for the testing, but using Sophie as a case study, I think what I've done with her can be compiled into a white paper I'd like to deliver at the next

World Veterinary Association congress. That is, of course, if you agree."

"Impressive! I'm amazed that you've found time to think about that, what with all the rest of the hubbub. You've been burning the midnight oil, haven't you? Bravo, my dear, bravo." He patted her awkwardly on the shoulder, as if he'd decided a hug was too much and a handshake too impersonal. "Can you forward the documents to me so I can look at them more closely?"

She agreed to load them on a jump drive and give them to him, then he asked more about Sophie.

"She shares your love for music," Natalie said, "and the combination of mahout training along with the protected contact techniques has made her more confident. Having Ali around seems to help, which kind of surprised me. I thought she'd get along better with the females."

"I'm not surprised," Andrew said. "Sometimes it all depends on how they were raised. Since Ali was a loner, and so was Sophie, and Siriporn has dealt with both of them, they might be more comfortable being together in this type of situation, even though it would be totally different if they were in the wild. Both of them—Ali and Sophie—are probably picking up on your comfort level. Ali's laid back. Sophie needs that calmness, and she feels that with you. Siriporn's got a natural way with the ellies, too. He's a lover not a fighter."

They laughed. "I see it at the sanctuary in Kenya all the time," Andrew continued. "Ellies build relationships, both with other members of the herd as well as with humans."

She filled him in on the antibiotics she'd given Sophie for her leg infection.

Andrew slapped his leg. "I'm excited. The possibilities . . . we can incorporate the same type of treatment with some of the other elephants—both in Africa and here in Thailand." He gazed off into the distance, as if considering the next step.

Not once did he mention the costs of such treatment or training, the way Hatcher had, perhaps because he realized that what she had been able to accomplish in a short amount of time was only the tip of the iceberg.

"Write up a draft of a paper, Natalie," he said as he rose and stretched his arms above his head. "What you've learned, love, could help many others. Now, time for lunch, my dear." He shook his legs out and made his way down the stairs.

"There's one more thing," she said, still sitting. "Can you give me a couple more minutes?"

His eyes narrowed a bit as if he suspected he'd have to spend more money, but he sat back down. "Of course. What's up?"

"It's Dr. Hatcher," she began. "I know he's been here a lot longer than I, and I truly respect his expertise, especially when it comes to pachyderm veterinary treatment . . ."

"I hear a 'but' in there."

She smiled a little and nodded. "I need your advice."

He leaned forward, attentive, his large hands folded on his knees.

"When I first started working with Sophie, I think Dr. Hatcher questioned my intentions," Natalie began, "and though I tried to reassure him, he didn't seem . . . well, happy with my expertise. He asked several times whether I'd been delivering the medicines Sophie needed, he's been concerned about the amount of the budget that's been going into Sophie's care, and I don't think he agreed with the way I've concentrated on her rather than spreading myself out more thinly and working with the rest of the animals here. But the biggest issue . . . my greatest concern . . . is that he tried to put Sophie down without consulting me." She paused a moment and checked Andrew's face. He lifted a finger to her as if encouraging her to continue.

"Forgive me if I'm wrong," Natalie's voice quivered, "but I thought sanctuary policy states that euthanasia takes the agreement of two vets."

Andrew held up his hand. "Stop right there. That's true, but as I understand it, he saw the error of his ways, correct?"

She nodded.

"Sophie's alive, she's healing, and we now know how protected contact works. Sounds like a win-win to me." He rose, using his imperious height. The thinness of his smile showed that his pleasure in the conversation had quickly faded. If there was anything Andrew hated, it was personal drama.

She rose, too, several steps above him, yet still not equal to his height. She'd made a mistake, she knew now, and she was sorry she'd brought up the personal issues she'd had with Peter Hatcher. Her throat constricted and the space behind her eyes burned with unshed angry tears. She swallowed hard. "I'm sorry to bring you into it. I just thought you should know about his dealings with me and some of the other people here."

"Don't worry. I know." Andrew closed his mouth and glanced away, focusing his attentions on something in a distant tree. "Let's leave it here. Concentrate on what you've discovered during the time you've spent with Sophie and continue to document what works with her and what doesn't. Let's work together to bring the world's attention to our elephants rather than expending your energies on a bloke who has his own work to do."

His statement made, he turned and started walking up the road toward the main building and his office.

THE BROAD-LEAFED *trees cast a tiny patch of afternoon shade in front of where Sophie stands. She longs to reach it, but even more, she longs for the mud pit, longs to throw some cool dirt over her back, longs to immerse herself in the hole. The day has been brilliantly hot, the sun boring through the breaks in the overhead leaves like small flumes of fire burning down into the ground. It's time for the mud pit. Time for some relief from the tightened web of her sagging skin.*

She and the woman are working in the enclosure and have been for far too long. Though the woman has brought plenty of food— pumpkins and knobby squashes, zucchini and sweet potatoes—Sophie longs for a bucket of water. A roll in the mud-hole. The river. Anything to cool her skin and to rid herself of the biting flies that have started to inflame the wound in her leg.

But the woman won't let her out of the enclosure.

The elephant moves from one column to another, from the set of bars near the woman to the opposite side of the enclosure near the gate, trying to find an exit, but they are all blocked. Each time Sophie finds herself blocked, the woman is there, offering a treat, forcing Sophie to remain calm, talking to her, asking her to move or allow her to check the wound. Sometimes they are successful; other times, Sophie won't submit.

The woman is on the other side of the bars now, moving Sophie back and forth with the soft-tipped poles. Each time Sophie moves, a new zucchini comes through the bars and she takes it, but her thirst for water is greater than her need to please the woman.

She's growling now.

Irritated.

Still, the woman repeats words that the mahouts use, asking once again that Sophie move in and out of the enclosure, backward and forward. Tired, Sophie still lifts her feet at the woman's commands. Over and over. The constant movement begins to pull at the wound on the leg that has only a few days ago begun to heal.

She plants her feet, tosses her head, trumpets. Irritated. Finished.

The woman steps back, watching, assessing. "It's okay, Sophie. It's okay."

She says something else that the elephant doesn't understand but the emotion she senses is the same weariness and exhaustion she, herself, feels.

She wants to lie in the cool river and let it run over her hot body.

Now.

She ducks her head and pushes it against the woman's back as she would a young elephant. A gentle push. The woman glances up as if she knows the elephant is trying to tell her something but she doesn't quite understand.

Sophie clicks in the back of her throat. A plea.

The river.

"You're a good old girl." The woman reaches into the bucket and *offers Sophie some sweet pink fruit that tastes like a mouthful of sweet, cool water. Delicious, but still not what the elephant needs.*

The afternoon gong sounds, which means the humans go to the big building, and the animals are left alone. And that means the elephant will not go to the river until the woman returns right before the sun goes down.

The woman leaves, following the rest of the humans as they walk up the road, snaking toward the scent of cooking food.

Sophie trumpets in the woman's direction. She wants water. The river. The mud bath.

Water.

She trumpets again. Louder, this time. She shakes the enclosure gate with her trunk and tastes the sweetness of what's left of the woman's handprint on the iron bars. The elephant still smells the woman's presence. Sophie shakes the gate again, then throws her head back and roars.

The sound is still echoing through the enclosure when the woman begins running in Sophie's direction. Sophie throws herself at the wall, still roaring.

The woman calls out and starts running back toward the enclosure. Sophie can hear the pounding of her feet as she comes down the road. Other voices follow her. The men.

Sophie backs into the enclosure when the red and yellow and orange shirts jumble together at the gate. The mahouts have ankuses in their hands. She trumpets again, this time from fear mixed with anger.

The woman orders the elephant to stop. The mahouts pause, each poised to come into the enclosure, each prepared to do what Sophie already knows will hurt. The woman moves closer, says the elephant's name, speaks quietly, reassuringly.

"Look, look, look, Sophie," she says, and Sophie does.

But the elephant is not only tired and thirsty now, she's afraid and angry. She watches the woman closely, but she's fearful of the men. When she shakes her head, her great ears flap. Dust sprinkles down onto the woman's hair.

"Leave," the woman tells the men. She tells them to go, then says something else the elephant doesn't understand, and waves them away.

They return to the road, talking amongst themselves, glancing back over their shoulder at the elephant and the woman in the enclosure.

Sophie relaxes her ears, shifts from side to side, and looks at the woman.

The woman makes a big circle around the elephant, checking her body, touching near the leg wound, and then she returns to stand in front of Sophie's face and looks into her mouth, checks her trunk and her eyes.

"Better now?" the woman asks. She stands with the elephant for a long moment, hands on her hips, head cocked as though she's thinking. Then she opens the gate and motions Sophie forward.

"You're a good girl, Sophie," she says, and they head in the direction of the river.

When Sophie sinks into the cool water, she rolls forward, an elephant's version of a somersault, then curls onto her side, trunk spouting bejeweled water into the hard afternoon sunlight.

Twenty-Seven

Our daughters and sons have burst
from the marionette show
leaving a tangle of strings
and gone into the unlit audience.
-Maxine Kumin

NATALIE KNEW THE INSTANT she woke up that today would be hellish. Danny's fourteenth birthday.

As she swung her legs over the side of the bed, she thought they might have planned a trip or a special dinner. He probably would have reminded her how old he was, that he was a teenager, not a little boy. She brushed her teeth and refused to look in the mirror. That woman in the mirror might have surprised her son with a birthday party for all his friends.

"He'd always been well-liked. Everyone loved Danny," she told Sophie as she fed her. She walked up the road intending to have tea with Mali as she did every morning, even though the thought of trying to sit and be normal quite simply would not work today.

Halfway to the administration building, she passed her own cabin and could go no further. Without another thought, she turned around, mounted the steps, went inside, and closed the door behind her. She leaned against the doorjamb for a long moment, her weary shoulders bowed forward with the weight of her memories. She forced herself to take the five steps to her bed, crawled under the mosquito netting, and curled up into a fetal position.

That's where she stayed the rest of the day, in spite of Mali's three visits: the first to see if Natalie was okay, the second to deliver lunch, and the third to deliver dinner. The two trays sat on her desk, uneaten.

She lay on the bed the whole day. Sometimes she slept. Sometimes she stared at the ceiling. Twice, she tried to write a letter to her mother, but she never got past writing the date. Surprisingly, she didn't cry, even though everything felt heavy: her arms, her legs, the shirt on her back, the hair on her head. She couldn't move. And she didn't bother trying.

She napped on and off while thinking about reading the three-month-old veterinary journals Maman had sent in her last package. Natalie had dubbed her mother's "care pack-ages" as "Survival Packages." Capital letters. Somehow Maman instinctively knew that Natalie wouldn't be able to find Old Bay seasoning or barbeque sauce in Thailand. The cooks relished the evening lessons in Southern cooking that Natalie gave them after receiving the latest Survival Package. And how did Maman understand that the specialty soaps she bought at the Wake Forest Farmer's Market would be the perfect mix of lanolin and shea butter to remove layers of caked-on mud? Maman also made the occasional mistake, though. She sent chocolate chip cookies that arrived a melted mess. And issues of *People* magazine that Natalie refused to read. She had even refused to stock them in her waiting room at the clinic back home. But Mali had a weird predilection for them, so Natalie simply passed them along.

Staring up at the line of laundry she'd strung from the window to the door, Natalie thought about the latest box Maman had sent and how she'd spread the goods across her bed the day before. A package of hair clips, always useful; two leather journals embossed with scenes of the Eiffel Tower and Big Ben, perfect for those times they had no Internet service; two packages of Lorna Doone cookies—a staple, as far as Natalie was concerned;

three bath-size towels; three new magazines—the *Cosmopolitan* would go to Mali; two medical journals; three new mini recorders (she'd asked for those); and ten new flash drives. A treasure trove.

Every time she woke up, Natalie listened for Sophie, but even though she could hear the elephant's lonely trumpet, she couldn't move.

When the next morning came, she felt oddly surprised. It seemed brutally unfair that the sun shone and the sounds of the sanctuary were cheerful, optimistic. A gloomy storm would have been more appropriate. She lay in bed for a few moments, then forced herself to swing her legs over the side and act as if yesterday hadn't happened.

An hour later, her wish for a storm was granted as she and Sophie left the river.

The monsoon's raindrops blossomed into frogs that danced across Natalie's path. She trudged along the dirt roadway that, within moments, became a brown rivulet. Sophie brought up the rear. She never wanted to leave the river even if the rain became torrential and had a way of sulking as she walked that made Natalie chuckle. She never thought an elephant could sulk, but Sophie did her best impression, actually sticking out her lip and hanging her head.

Working with Sophie that morning quickly made the previous day a memory, and Natalie concentrated "on the now," as Mali often encouraged her to do. It was April, the 12th day of rainy season, the 128th day of her time with Sophie, the 182nd day of her time at the sanctuary, which left 183 days before the year ended. She trudged some more, the sucking sounds of her feet in the mud keeping time with the mental math calculations that occupied her brain. She counted things a lot lately: days, hours, the number of times she'd repeat the same command to Sophie. The repetition of it all, the predictable routine of it all, lulled Natalie into a state that she didn't even understand sometimes. If she were asked to define her emotional state to someone back home in the States, she'd be inclined to call herself vigilantly cata-tonic. Yes, an oxymoron, but it explained how she felt. Cognizant of everything around her but unable to react.

She stopped under a banana tree for a moment and cupped one of the largest leaves to create a type of straw for Sophie. The rain poured down the spine of the giant rubbery leaf, and if Natalie held it just so, she could give Sophie an extra special drink. They stood there now, both human being and elephant totally drenched, but not caring. Sophie's head tilted back like a pachyderm screen star as she captured the rainwater in her heart-shaped mouth. Natalie stretched to her highest height in order to tilt the leaf.

Though Sophie hadn't exhibited any recent anxiety, Natalie still had to remind herself of the large elephant's history of erratic behavior. That was hard to imagine right now when Sophie appeared to be approaching elephant nirvana. If she could purr, she would have.

Idly, Natalie wondered what her cabin would feel like in another couple of weeks. Already there were three leaks in her ceiling, and she'd fashioned makeshift "catches" for the rain that drooled into her room via the roof holes, crawling down the walls or dripping from the ceiling. One leak now watered a gardenia she had potted. Another was redirected (via an improvised pole) into her bathroom sink ,and the third dripped into the proverbial pot: a clink-clink-clink sound that lulled her to sleep every night.

When the season began, she still slept in Sophie's enclosure, but that ended the first time the monsoon rains drenched her and her bed (and bed covers, sheets and pillows). She moved back into her cabin—shivering and wet—that first night, certain she'd hear Sophie bellowing in protest at some point during the evening, but she'd been wrong. Sophie had slept clear through the night and greeted Natalie with her usual chirruping the next morning as though she hadn't noticed her "roommate" was not there all night.

It had been time to wean Sophie from the constant contact they'd had with each other anyway, though from Hatcher's point of view, sleeping in the elephant's barn was not the healthiest way to carry on a mahout/trainer role (she didn't agree with him). But maybe this time he'd been right, Natalie begrudgingly admitted to herself. On the other hand, being alone with Sophie had been peaceful, without the human drama both of them could do without.

Natalie left Sophie at the platform for a moment with several volunteers and picked up her mail, happy to see a letter from her sister-in-law, Kerry.

Why the old school handwritten letters, Nat? Can't you send me an email, or do you not have service way out there in the jungle?

The question bothered Natalie, and while the volunteers took care of Sophie, Natalie grabbed a pen and a piece of paper and started an answer to Kerry:

We get service—it's not great, but we do. It seems more thoughtful and personal, and I don't know the word I want . . . connected, maybe? . . . If I sit on my porch with a pad of paper and a pen to write you about what's going on in my life. Life here is slower. It makes sense to write letters the "old school way.

Don't get me wrong, it's not that nothing happens here. On the contrary! There are small dramas every day—sometimes every hour on the hour.

For instance, yesterday the rains washed one of the smaller huts right off its stilts and the family that lived there—father, mother, fifteen-year-old daughter, thirteen-year-old boy, a set of five-year-old twins, and a baby barely walking—tumbled over and over each other as if in the spin cycle. When they were finally retrieved, they ended up in our vet's clinic where Dr. Hatcher and I patched them up the best we could.

And on Wednesday of the week before, a woman bullied her way into our pharmacy, demanding to see me. From what we could tell, she'd heard that my horoscope was in line with hers and nothing could convince her that I was not a medical doctor licensed to treat human beings, thus I wouldn't be able to deliver her baby. We had to send Anurak to get my friend Mali so she could translate. (Anurak is the boy whose dog, Decha, was the one Sophie almost killed when I first arrived. Remember I told you about that? They come visit me every day, but Sophie still doesn't like the dog, so we sit on my porch at the cabin and chat—or at least I chat. Anurak doesn't talk.)

Finally, after almost two hours, the woman seemed calm enough to leave the sanctuary.

Damn if she didn't return the next day! Walked all the way from her village and came to the clinic to find me again. But I wasn't there. I was with Sophie—and nothing Dr. Hatcher said to her would convince her that I wouldn't be in the clinic at all that day. He was fuming. Mali told me later. She thought he would literally drag the poor woman all the way out to the road—almost two miles!—and give her a boot in the ass and tell her to go home.

I feel bad for the poor woman, but I have to tell you that Mali and I laughed all night long when we thought of the woman arguing with Hatcher. I wish I'd been a fly on the wall! I must admit, on a more somber note, that's the only way I would ever have any insight into Dr. Peter Hatcher. Maybe that's fine. He's not necessarily someone I feel the need to understand on a much deeper level. Know what I mean?

Kerry, you know Maman often said men have no clue about what goes on in women's minds, but I think it's just the opposite. Hatcher is a closed book to me. I haven't a clue why he can't let go of the dissertation debacle and move forward. God knows I never tried to hurt him (though I must say, at this point, that I wouldn't mind letting him figure it out on his own). I want to simply be me. I've tried with every ounce of my inner strength to ignore him when he gets on my case, but there are times when I would literally like to strangle him. He frustrates me more than any human being alive. The only person who I can talk to about him is Mali, and she feels the same way I do. Should I address him about it or should I completely ignore him and move on about my own business?

Change of subject: how are things there? Have you had a chance to visit my clinic to see how everything's going? Tell them all that I send my love and any time they see any articles I should read, they should drop them into the mail and let me know whenever they see a conference I can attend. I still have so much to learn!

Well, Kerry, kiss and hug everyone for me. I love you and miss you, but Sophie's calling. My "boss" is hungry again!

~Nat

Twenty-Eight

It is not light that we need, but fire;
it is not the gentle shower, but thunder.
We need the storm, the whirlwind,
and the earthquake.
-Frederick Douglass

NATALIE REREAD THE LAST sentence of the paper she was going to submit to *The Journal of Veterinary Science*. It was the result of all of those notes in her notebook, the spreadsheets she had created and analyzed, the hours of late night typing.

"Best I can do right now," she pronounced and closed her laptop. She had spent the whole morning trying to finish the paper. She tried to push it out of her mind as she readied herself for the day, but it kept sneaking back, so she kept one more small notebook in her pocket and jotted down her thoughts, intending to do a final rewrite later before sending it off. She had a pile of notebooks atop the table in the corner of her room. Thankfully, Maman had more coming in a box already on the way.

Siriporn had fed Sophie and taken her to the river while Natalie wrote, so she anxiously wanted to hear how Sophie had done with the other elephants, though she sensed it must have gone well. If it hadn't, the whole sanctuary would have heard about it by now. It didn't take long for news to travel.

Mali was still in the kitchen when Natalie arrived at the platform, so she made a cup of tea and sat quietly at a table, watching angry gray storm clouds gathering above the mountains. Everything smelled like rain. The elephants huddled in a tight group at the far end of the platform. The whole baker's dozen of them: trunk to tail to trunk.

They must sense another storm coming, she thought as she sipped the bitter and hot black tea. Elephants heard rain and wind more than a hundred miles away, often pointing with their trunks in the storm's direction, Andrew had said in his lecture at the conference where she met him. African herds migrated at the end of dry season because they knew there'd be fresh water if they moved toward the area most likely to get rain. Meteorologists could put away all their fancy equipment if they learned to read animals, Natalie thought. Crossing her ankle over her knee, she once again marveled at all she had yet to learn about animals even after many years of schooling and many more of daily experience.

A breeze picked up and blew her napkin across the table. She wore long cotton pants for the first time in months and folded her arms to her chest to make up for the flimsy t-shirt she wore. The temperature had dropped ten degrees since she awoke, but she laughed when she realized it felt chilly though the temp hovered between eighty-five and ninety degrees Fahrenheit. Nowhere near the chilliness of a North Carolina winter.

A pair of feet came into her line of vision—dirty, missing two toenails on the right foot. Siriporn's feet. She glanced up at his smiling face.

"In old day, instead of saying 'Saw-a-dee,' we ask 'have you eaten yet.' Show we care for you." He plopped down next to her and folded his hands on the table. "So, have you eaten yet?"

She lifted her cup in answer. "Only this."

"That not food. You too skinny. Voice not deep enough to command Sophie. Eat more!" He pounded his chest in a comical Tarzan imitation.

She laughed and shook her head, remembering her mother accusing her of being anorexic. Little did she realize that no matter how much Natalie ate, she didn't put on a pound. "You have a hollow leg," her father would say. Natalie laughed again. Siriporn seemed pleased to make her smile.

"How did Sophie do this morning?" she asked.

"Eat first. Then talk." He padded toward the kitchen, his bare feet slapping against the cement. She watched his strong, walnut-colored calves, wondering idly whether hers would ever be as strong. When he returned, he held two bowls of rice and placed one in front of her.

In silence, they ate for a little while, Siriporn scooping the rice with his fingers, the Thai way. Natalie gave him the respect he requested and waited for him to finish before she pointedly raised an eyebrow and asked again.

"All the ellies play in the mud with truck tire. Sophie watch, then she play like schoolgirl. That's why her job perfect."

"Her job?"

"She's one of oldest females. Should teach younger ones. Good for her. Make her feel better."

Natalie pondered Siriporn's statement. True, Sophie had improved tremendously in the past couple of months, and she always got along better with elephants than with human beings and dogs. Could it be time to start putting her back in with the herd? The only thing stopping Natalie from doing so were the dozens of dogs who roamed freely throughout the sanctuary. If Sophie ran into one, Natalie had no idea what the elephant would do. PTSD could rear its ugly head at any time, and Sophie could easily kill any dog that irritated her. On the other hand, Siriporn could have suggested the very thing Sophie needed in order to take her next step in recovery. Giving to others worked for Natalie. Why not for Sophie, too? Perhaps Siriporn made a good point. Maybe they needed to try.

They spent the next half hour planning how to re-introduce Sophie to the herd, and when they were done, Natalie headed for Andrew's cabin to ask him whether he could have everyone rein in the dogs and keep them confined to one area of the sanctuary for the next couple of days while she and Siriporn worked with

Sophie.

It was the first time she'd visited his cabin since the day he'd upbraided her about complaining about Peter, and though she didn't look forward to talking to him, she knew he held no grudges and would probably concentrate on the task at hand rather than bringing up what she'd said. She knocked on his door and waited a minute, hearing a bit of a scuffle like a chair being pulled back from inside. When he didn't answer the door, she knocked again.

"Coming!" he said. Then the door opened and he stood there, red-faced, white hair wild, his shirt half-buttoned. "Oh, Natalie. Ummm . . ." He glanced over his shoulder, then back at her, all the while buttoning his shirt. His feet were bare, and she suspected someone else shared the cabin, but she didn't want to know who. Especially if it wasn't Mali.

"Sorry to interrupt, Andrew, but Siriporn and I were just talking about Sophie and planning on reintroducing her to the herd and we wanted . . ." She rambled through the plans they'd discussed and asked about the dogs, wondering as she spoke whether he heard anything she said because he appeared thoroughly disconnected. Though he nodded as she spoke, he wasn't looking at her. Instead, he stared over her shoulder and cocked his head as if trying to hear any noises coming from within the cabin.

"Sounds good, sounds good," he finally said and she heard a brushoff in his tone. "Let's get together and talk about it at dinnertime, say? And why don't we talk about your article then, too."

She nodded, and he closed the door. In her face. Before she headed back down the stairs, she heard a woman's voice from inside. Mali's voice.

That was strange, Natalie thought as she headed for her own cabin. Why wouldn't Mali say hello? She shook off her curiosity, certain she'd interrupted something.

By the time she'd reached her own cabin, she'd thought more about the article and had made a few more mental notes. Actually, it would be good to talk to Andrew about the paper she'd written about Sophie and how she'd worked with her, combining old mahout techniques with Protected Contact. She'd started sending out queries about it several weeks ago, and one of the international veterinary medicine journals had already expressed interest. It had been a long time since she'd published, so opening the email to read of the editor's fascination with her project had given her a thrill. Unfortunately, she couldn't share her excitement with anyone yet, because it wasn't officially accepted. She'd probably push the "send" button on her rewrite late at night. Today was the first chance she'd had to speak with Andrew. Though he wasn't a vet, he'd have some great input, for sure. She'd concentrate on that rather than her odd interaction with him, she decided.

She caught a glimpse of herself in the small mirror hanging by her door. Her dark hair was a mess, frizzy around her hairline from the humidity of the day and caught in a long tangle of braids that fell to the middle of her back, but her brown eyes were bright and her smile wide. She almost didn't recognize herself. The shock made her step back and re-examine the image in the mirror. How long had it been since she'd actually looked at herself when she combed her hair or brushed her teeth? She didn't have a mirror above the bowl she used for cleaning every morning. A previous owner had left this tiny mirror behind, and she had to be honest with herself: this was the first time she'd actually peered into it.

Now she stepped closer and examined herself. No makeup, no long hours spent working the frizz out of her hair, no monthly appointments for facials. This was her. Fresh. Simple. Unadorned. Her skin: blemish-free and browned by the hours she spent in the sun. Her eyes: clear. No dark bags underneath as there had been during the year after Danny's and Stephen's deaths. She slept every night now. Sometimes she didn't dream or even realize she was falling asleep. She'd simply lie down and suddenly she'd be conscious again, and it would be the next day. And even though she felt like she'd never get rid of the dirt under her fingernails, she didn't look dirty in her mirror. She looked . . . what was it?

Happy? No, not happy. Content. In spite of all the stresses of working with Sophie and the other animals and the tension with Peter Hatcher, she was content.

She stepped back and laughed. Content. No shit.

Twenty-Nine

One touch of nature makes the whole world kin.
-William Shakespeare

WHEN NATALIE SPOTTED THE bottle on her desk, she muttered aloud, "Another gift?" Mali's friend and fellow cook, Hom, kept expressing her eternal thanks after Natalie saved her dog. Hom brought the dog to the clinic with a snake bite the week before. A vial of anti-venom and the dog was fine. No big deal, Natalie had thought, but Hom went out of her way to thank Natalie every time they saw each other—literally dozens of times a day. She had bought gifts for Natalie, as well. It was becoming embarrassing. She talked to herself all the time these days and found it helped her figure out problems or reminded her to do something later on or helped her vent, as she did now.

Natalie was surprised to see that it was brandy. The type of liquor that would roll smoothly down her throat, leaving a little trail of tasty fire. God, she loved a good glass of brandy, and she hadn't had one since leaving the States. But how could Hom have known that? And where did she find a bottle of this quality? Where did she get the money for it?

Then she saw the white envelope. No writing on it. *Odd*, she thought. She slid her finger along the flap and opened the letter, fighting the mouth-watering taste for the brandy. If the brandy *was* from Hom, she'd return it. A bottle of this quality would be the equivalent of three months' salary, minimum. Even if she had saved a member of Hom's immediate family, Natalie didn't expect a payment like this.

One eye on the burnished bronze bottle, she flipped open the sheet of paper and began reading. Andrew's handwriting. "Congratulations," he began, "your article on Sophie will soon be published. One of the editors is a friend of mine, and he called me tonight to ask more details about your work. He was quite impressed, young lady! You deserve a congratulatory drink. Cheers!"

She plopped into the desk chair, the letter still in her hands, a shocked grin on her face. She reached for the bottle, cradling it in her hands reverently.

"Damn it, you're right, Andrew," she said aloud in the quiet cabin. "I have a cause to celebrate. So I'll start now. This very moment."

It took a few moments to find something sharp enough to break the seal on the bottle and another moment to find a water glass to pour the precious brandy into, but when that liquid honey fire crept down her throat, she groaned like a woman climaxing.

She'd thank Andrew tomorrow. Tonight she'd enjoy this gift from the gods.

An hour and two drinks later, she brought the bottle and her glass down the moonlit road to Sophie's barn. The elephant was sleeping on her side when Natalie arrived, but when she called out her name, Sophie raised her giant head and lumbered to her feet, instantly reaching her trunk out to touch Natalie's arm.

Natalie put the bottle down and opened the door to the enclosure. Sophie rumbled softly, the greeting she always made when Natalie came near.

"You're going to be famous, old girl," Natalie said softly as she came abreast of Sophie. She leaned her forehead against the elephant's lowered head and stood there silently for a moment wondering exactly when the two of them had come to this point of comfort with each other. She totally trusted Sophie now, and she knew the elephant felt the same way. It had taken many hours and days of work, but it was worth it.

Through the years, Natalie had owned dogs, trained horses, rescued more cats than she could count, but she'd never had a more profound relationship with any animal than the one she shared with this elephant. She knew now why mahouts were so happy. Sometimes it felt like Sophie actually realized and mirrored the emotions she felt.

She pulled her head back and looked into Sophie's good eye. Sophie chirruped and reached her trunk towards the bottle Natalie had set on a bench. She chuckled. "I'd love to share a drink with you, Soph, but I'm afraid you'd drink the whole bottle, and god knows what kind of a drunk you'd be, so you'll have to be content with a few bananas."

She found some in the storage bin and fed Sophie, who shifted from side to side and tried to back up as she did when Natalie took her down to the river for a bath.

"No, we're not going out right now, girl. It's night-time."

Still, Sophie backed up.

Natalie looked up the road, well lit by the moon. The night remained balmy and clear. The crickets had long since stopped. The only sounds breaking the silence were the ones she and Sophie made.

"Ah, what the hell. Let's take a walk. But we're coming right back, okay?"

They strolled silently side by side down the road. Natalie with her bottle, Sophie with as much spring in her step as an elephant could muster. Her version of wagging her tail.

Natalie watched Sophie frolic in the water like a huge moonlit shadow, rolling over and over and shooting fountains of river water into the air. The gentle splashes of water and Sophie's occasional delighted shrieks echoed in the tiny canyon created by the surrounding hills. In the dark spaces cast by the moon's light, Natalie imagined she saw movement or eyes watching them, but she brushed away the specters and found her thoughts easily diverted.

With the bottle cradled between her legs, she thought about what would come next, delivering the paper in front of an international group of her peers, and the feeling of dread at being in the spotlight again made her fingers tighten on the bottle's neck.

No need for panic, she told herself sternly. *Nothing's happened. And this isn't the States. The media's far more interested in the revolution here than the story of some American woman who lost her children in a school shooting thousands of miles away. And no one's going to send the paparazzi to hunt down a veterinarian who wrote a journal article about how to treat elephants with PTSD.*

But she couldn't stop her hands from trembling, couldn't stop the fractured scenes from flashing in front of her eyes. She knew she was in Thailand, could feel the night air around her, but her vision was stolen and replaced with the scene in front of the school, borders of yellow tape, small groups of people huddled together. She saw the ambulances arrive, seen their spinning roof lights, heard the police's orders as they tried to clear the parking lot where she'd come every morning to let the kids off. She smelled the Indian summer heat, knew even then that there'd been an afternoon thunderstorm that would wash the area clean of important evidence. And she must sit down because the vignettes come faster. She hears the questions from reporters and judges and lawyers and family and from herself. Questions that could never be answered. Questions she never wanted to hear again.

The scattered images blur her vision even more, blend in with each other, and time passes. She remembers the days after the shooting. The funeral plans her family made for her boys because she was unable to. She doesn't remember the funerals, not one moment, but she sees herself in bed for weeks, remembers the heaviness of her head against the pillow, and doesn't quite know how she rose from that bed, how she even functions today so far from home and all that was painful. Still, today, how does she function with both of her children gone?

She breathed into the fear which sat, fist-like, in the middle of her chest, convinced herself she'd feel better after taking another sip of her brandy. For more than an hour she sat on the riverbank nursing her drink before sleep crept over her and made her eyes droop. She called for Sophie, who didn't argue and followed Natalie back to the enclosure.

It was past one in the morning when Natalie finally set the half-empty bottle back on her desk and fell into bed. Her last thought before passing out was that she had forgotten to write home.

Thirty

Women and elephants never forget an injury.
-Saki (Hector Hugh Munro)

When Mali put the soup down on the table in front of her, Natalie gazed into the *kway tiew nahm sai* and swallowed hard.

"This noodle soup is spicy," Mali said. "The Thai cure for a hangover. Believe me, love, it'll cure that pounding headache." She mimicked the feeling by bulging her eyes and opening and closing her hands beside her head like a fireworks display. "And that queasy stomach." She pointed to the bowl, and the smell wafting up practically burnt Natalie's nose hairs.

"I'm going to puke," she said. Never again would she drink liquor. Ever.

"You're enjoying this a bit too much!" Natalie called, and instantly winced.

Mid-morning. Everyone at the sanctuary was either working or, like the kitchen staff, taking a break before the second part of their day began. Being alone at this time of day felt like a blessing, though Natalie hadn't really raised her head high enough to acknowledge the peace and quiet since falling into bed in the wee hours of the morning.

She hadn't even had the stomach to feed Sophie this morning, so she flagged down the other mahouts as they made their morning trek to the mud pits and asked Khalan to feed Sophie her bananas and squash breakfast. Siriporn had taken a few days off to go to some of his political meetings (in spite of a heated discussion with his mother), but Sophie seemed comfortable with Khalan now, so Natalie decided to trust him. She had no choice. She couldn't have walked down the road if someone paid her this morning.

"I see you found the bottle," Andrew chuckled as he straddled the bench beside her. "It wasn't necessary to guzzle the whole bloody thing in one night."

"I didn't. Just half." Natalie's stomach lurched. He smelled like bananas and coffee. She closed her eyes and wished he'd go away.

"That's enough to give *anyone* a hangover." He chuckled again, then put a hand on her knee and forced her to look into his baggy blue eyes. "You'd better be back on your feet by tonight. I'm expecting company, and they're going to want to meet you."

The thought of carrying on a conversation with anyone right now elicited another moan from Natalie. She held her head in both of her hands, once again, and hoped he'd go away.

No such luck.

"Still have some of the bottle left, don't you?"

She nodded. Even the slightest of movements made her feel like her brain had become untethered within her skull. *Would the queasiness never leave?*

"Drink a quick glass then. Hair of the dog!" He slapped the table, causing her to groan again, then he wheezed as he hefted himself off the bench and called for Mali.

"We're going to have company tonight, and I want you there, Natalie, so get yourself together."

Together he and Mali brainstormed a meal for the evening while Natalie sat there, still cradling her aching head in her hands. Each time they mentioned a new dish, her stomach lurched. Trying not to appear obvious, she slid her fingers into her ears and hoped they'd be done soon so she could figure out what to do next. She wished with every fiber of her being that could summon the ability to teleport herself back to her cabin. Unfortunately, she couldn't.

Finally, Andrew and Mali left. Natalie glanced down into the brown soup once more. She lifted it and thought about it for a moment, then tilted the bowl and poured the stuff down her throat. Sour bile immediately arose, and she gagged, but forced herself to keep it down. She broke out into a sweat, but clamped her jaw closed, and sat with her hands tightly folded on the table.

Miraculously, about fifteen minutes later, the headache vanished and the queasiness abated. She was about to find Mali and declare her a goddess when she heard some childish laughter and a male voice coming up the road.

Craning her neck, she saw six of the kids who lived at the sanctuary—children of the kitchen staff and mahouts—and right in the middle of them, Peter Hatcher with a big smile on his face. Even from this distance, she heard the kids calling him "*Khun* Doctor, *Khun* Doctor," a term of respect. She watched him lift one of the little boys into the air. The child giggled until he couldn't catch his breath. Hatcher gazed up at the child and smiled from ear-to-ear. Natalie's eyebrows arched in amazement. She had never seen this side of him before.

Because none of them knew she was watching, she felt granted an unspoken permission to be a voyeur. Taking advantage of it, she tucked her legs under her and wrapped her arms around her knees, feeling like that silly long-legged felt elf that almost every family owned among their Christmas decorations. Like the elf, she sat silently, a painted smile on her face, eyes wide open, and watched. She longed to be part of the imaginary world that children—no matter where they lived—created. A world that did not include pain or heartbreak or death. At that age (the children playing with Hatcher were no older than six), they didn't know the incredible pains and heartache they would most certainly encounter later in life. Children that age were infinitely capable of reminding adults (even serious adults like Peter Hatcher) of what it took to embody happiness and joy and lightness in their lives.

True, she had never seen him smile and laugh as he did now.

Though it might seem that he was the one in control of the children's playtime, Natalie knew the children's innocence stripped the scrim of anger away from his personality and temporarily replaced it with the carefree laughter she heard now.

Danny had giggled excitedly like those children. Yet he could be extremely logical and serious. When he was in the fourth grade, he told Natalie he thought the planet Pluto was actually the largest in the solar system.

Everyone had lied to him, he told her. "It looks small because it's really far away," he said in that breathless way he had when he was so excited his words tumbled over each other like puppies. "When you get up really close, it's gigantic. Bigger than all the others put together! And you know who can prove it? Superman, that's who. His planet, where he lived with his dad before they all blew up, it's really close to Pluto. They go there all the time for vacations like we go to Disney World. Pluto's really special, Mom," he said seriously. "All the kids are blue and the parents are brown so you can tell them apart. But when Superman and his family go there, they're green like Kryptonite. So you can tell them apart, too."

When she cocked her head at his explanation, he'd giggled like crazy as if he'd pulled the biggest practical joke on her.

"Well, all parents are someone's kids," Natalie told him, "so wouldn't they be blue, too?"

Danny paused, looked down at his black and white Converse Chucks as he slapped them together. He thought for a long and quiet moment. "When you have kids, you change color," he finally said. "So that's why some grownups act like kids—like Mr. Matheson. They never had kids."

She shook the memory and watched Hatcher playing a rough and tumble game of soccer with the kids. But it wasn't more than five minutes when the monsoon threatening the mountains and jungles with rumbles and thick, round, black clouds for the past couple of days suddenly arrived, unloading sheets of gray rain interspersed with cracks of thunder and tree-splitting lightning. The elephants had alerted every one of the storm days ago, giving the sanctuary enough time to put up their storm shutters and to lash everything down that might go flying. A twenty-pound object hurled by a gust of wind could kill someone. But the kids had continued playing their games, never paying attention to the shift in the wind. Now they screeched and cleaved to Hatcher as if he had become a magnet and the kids were flakes of steel. Natalie could see them moving into the clinic for only a moment more, then the rain became a wall that blocked her view.

She thought about heading for her cabin but knew she'd be thoroughly soaked no matter where she went. In spite of the rain, Sophie still needed to eat. She dashed for Sophie's enclosure, soaked within seconds, her clothing stuck to her and her hair plastered to her head. Struggling to see through the streams of rain pouring down her face, she sidestepped torrents of rushing water that had already begun tearing ravines into the road that had only moments earlier looked like the surface of the moon. Could she still let Sophie wander freely for the afternoon, let her enjoy the rain? *No.* It took one heartbeat to decide against it. The lightning would strike the tallest object, sometimes an elephant. Ali's right ear still showed the scorch marks of a near miss last year. Then there was Sophie's PTSD. She'd easily spook if the thunder was amplified by the mountains around the sanctuary. *Nope, not a good idea.*

She'd guessed correctly. When she reached the enclosure, Sophie and several of the other elephants were huddled *en masse* under the roof. One of the younger elephants jogged back and forth, then turned around and around in anxious circles, despite the rest of the herd's trumpets of admonishment. Obviously, Sophie wasn't the only elephant with a history of pain.

It surprised her that the elephants had found their way to the enclosure. Where were their mahouts? And had they all suddenly decided to befriend Sophie?

Natalie moved into action, straight into the center of the group, speaking to each individual elephant in Thai, as a mahout would. Siriporn once told her that elephants possessed a designated *devata* or a deity that guarded him/her. In order to get the elephant to understand a mahout, that mahout meditated on the deity and gave that deity *metta* or universal love.

She focused, concentrating on each of the elephants and using her mahout commands to get them to move. She didn't think about it, didn't wonder whether they would understand her. She simply stepped into their line of sight and trusted them to follow her. If she had thought about the process as a doctor, or as a scientist, she would have called it insane, but through the months, she had seen it work. Sophie had become something of a therapist, sensing when Natalie was upset or frustrated. She'd lay her trunk over Natalie's shoulder. Sometimes Natalie hadn't realized herself that she'd become anxious, but Sophie knew. They had come to some type of understanding that deepened and became more natural as time went by.

"Thaya! Mai!" Natalie called the two younger females who were always together. They fed off each other and were now anxious about the ever-increasing storm. They pushed against the edges of the overhang and nudged the other elephants as if wanting to incite an escape. Natalie stepped in front of Thaya and gave the command to stop. "*Hou! Hou!*" She placed a hand on each female's trunk, letting them get her scent, forcing herself to breathe slowly, calmly. She shushed them both, the universal sound for an animal to calm down and one the mahouts didn't have to teach her.

As she passed by, she touched each of the other elephants. Five in all, milling around, eyes wide, ears flaring. Any one of them could charge at any moment. She had to trust that they wouldn't. Remaining calm and confident was key. Again, she took a deep breath.

Sophie stood in her enclosure, her forehead pressed against the back wall, her butt facing the railing, as if begging for a release from the anxiety the other elephants raised. Natalie released the gate and quietly entered the pen. She worked her way over to Sophie's good side, knowing that if Sophie saw her, it would help keep the elephant focused.

"*Mai pen rai. Mai pen rai,*" Natalie murmured. Siriporn

would have rebuked her if he had heard her tell Sophie, "it's okay, it's okay," but Natalie could think of nothing else to say to the distraught animal.

As she had so many times in the past couple of months, Natalie began singing "Michelle," the Beatles song her mother had sung to her throughout her childhood, substituting that song for the traditional lullaby. It always worked. When the boys were little, Natalie sang it to them, substituting their names for "Michelle." They loved it, even as they grew older, and so did Sophie. Natalie sang it over and over as the storm raged through the compound, roaming among the small group of elephants, touching each one of them, singing directly to each, keeping them engaged with her so that they wouldn't notice the winds and the pouring rain. Surprisingly, the rest of the small herd seemed to find the song soothing as well.

Natalie stayed for two hours with the ellies, listening to the monsoon rattle through the mountains and, eventually, disappear into the jungle. Unsure whether it had truly ended, she sat for a while longer, wondering whether the worst of the storm had passed, but she had a feeling it was simply a lull in the action.

When the elephants drifted away from the enclosure one by one, Sophie finally lifted her head and began eating the fruits and vegetables Natalie offered her. Natalie had no idea what time it was, but it didn't matter. She wanted nothing more than to retreat to her cabin and get into dry clothes.

She finished feeding Sophie, talking to her quietly all the while and promising the old girl that she'd be back later on that night. They took a short walk up the road and back again, Sophie ever vigilant as if the boogie man might pop out of the banana trees alongside the road. As they headed back to the enclosure, Natalie remembered Andrew's comment earlier that they were to have company. She debated with herself about whether to head up to the administration building for dinner, but when her stomach growled nonstop, her hunger won the argument. Back to her cabin she went, where she took a quick shower and dressed.

Whoever these visitors were, they had experienced firsthand

the weather challenges the sanctuary had to face. She wondered whether they'd understand the other challenges as clearly.

Thirty-One

How dull it is to pause, to make an end,
To rust unburnished, not to shine in use,
As though to breathe were life!
-Alfred, Lord Tennyson

NATALIE WOVE HER WET, waist-length hair into a braid, took a deep breath, and headed up the muddy road to the administration building. Truth be told, her bones ached for some aspirin, and she would rather be in bed with the magazines Maman had sent in her latest care package, but Andrew had insisted. As she slogged against the rain that had picked up again, she thought, *this better be good.*

"Speak of the devil. Here she is!" Andrew spoke loudly, competing with the monsoon that had reappeared. It threatened to rip the overhang clear off the building. Natalie paused a moment to let her eyes adjust to the dim light. It amazed her sometimes how casually the people who lived in this region of the world accepted wild weather.

Five people sat around one of the picnic tables that had been pushed deep into the pocket of the platform underneath the overhang and against the only corner. It offered some protection from the rain, but not enough. The winds blew the rain sideways, soaking everyone at the table. Natalie peered more closely. A single fat candle flickered, casting shadows on their wet faces: Andrew, Mali, Karina, Hatcher, and a man she didn't recognize.

She sat down and looked around the table. The new guy, the man Andrew had referred to earlier as "company," flashed a smile at her so bright she would have been able to see it in the dark. He reached out a hand. "I gather you're Dr. DeAngelo." He, too, raised his voice but his was smooth rather than strained, as Andrew's had been. "I'm Seth Vincennes."

As she shook his hand, she realized she'd heard that name before, and he looked vaguely familiar, but she couldn't place him. He wore a white shirt, sleeves rolled up to reveal forearms the same rich walnut color as Mali's skin. A bit taller than Natalie, he was slim but sturdy. His handshake was strong. Warm. And his accent was definitely not Thai. He had grown up speaking English. *Indian, maybe.* She'd figure it out later.

"Andrew forwarded your article, and I'm quite impressed," Vincennes said. "You must be one of the first western women to become a mahout—and to rehabilitate a pachyderm others considered, well, violent. Wasn't she?" He turned to Andrew for confirmation.

"Dr. Hatcher was ready to put her down," Andrew said.

Hatcher adjusted his fogged-up glasses and kept silent.

"I'm not a mahout," Natalie said.

Vincennes's mouth opened a bit as if he was trying to figure out what to say.

A crack of lightning lit up the meadow and outlined the jagged mountain peaks in the distance. Natalie glanced toward the enclosures, straining to hear any trumpeting, but the rain and wind obliterated any other sounds.

"Is this Sophie now back with the herd?" Vincennes asked.

Does this guy not notice we are in the middle of a storm? Natalie wrapped her arms around herself, told herself to be patient.

Mali and Karina huddled together on the other side of the table, obviously miserable. They weren't best friends, so to see them, shoulders touching, seemed odd. But what was even stranger was that neither Andrew nor Hatcher seemed to register the women's discomfort. Instead, they continued to chat with Vincennes as if they'd finished nine holes and were enjoying a whiskey sour on the veranda of the Pinehurst Country Club where women wore big straw hats with their pink-and-green Lilly Pulitzer sundresses.

Vincennes had the steady gaze of a man who'd never doubted that he was anything less than pertinent to the conversation. He wore a slight smile and had straight shoulders he pulled back slightly. He appeared confident, sure of himself. She could see why Andrew wanted to prove something to this man even though she still couldn't figure out who he was.

Thunder rolled again, then for a split second, silence prevailed. In the distance, she heard a series of trumpets. The herd.

She stood. "I'm sorry, but Sophie and some of the other elephants are having a hard time with this storm, so if you don't mind, I'm going to beg your forgiveness and go calm them."

Vincennes rose as if preparing to pull out her chair like he would if they were at a dinner party. The perfect gentleman. She wanted to laugh; instead, she simply moved aside. *Who the hell is this guy anyway?*

"Of course you need to tend to your animals," he said. "Is there anything I can do to help?" His words and accent were distinctly British, yet some other accent flickered beneath the British.

This time she did laugh. Aloud. "No, no, but thanks. You're in dry clothes. Maybe you can come meet them tomorrow."

In a swift movement Natalie didn't see coming, he stepped out past the overhang. "No need to worry about me." He spread his arms wide as he stood in the pouring rain, and within a heartbeat, he was soaked. "Not like I'm going to melt." He laughed as if getting wet was the highlight of his day. "Besides, I want to meet this Sophie."

Natalie caught Andrew's eye. "Don't look at me, dearie," he said, throwing both hands up as if in defeat. "The only place Mali and I are going tonight is the cabin. If you want to bring this crazy man to meet Sophie, it's up to you. I'm sure Karina has had it for the night, too. Right, love?" He glanced at his sister.

Karina nodded and stood, shifting to the right and placing both hands on her lower back. "I've done my duty. A four-hour one-way ride down and back to the Bangkok airport is enough for me for one day. I thought we'd need a boat on the way back. Right now, a cup of sherry and dry clothes is all I want. Mr. Vincennes, why don't you meet me here tomorrow morning, and if it's cleared up, I'll take you on a tour?" Her voice rose, becoming high-pitched and falsely cheerful.

"You can take me tomorrow," Vincennes told Karina, "but tonight I'm going to meet Sophie."

Without asking for permission, he grabbed Natalie's hand and said, "Let's make a mad dash for it! Lead on, Dr. DeAngelo!"

Two seconds later, they splashed through running water, heading for Sophie's enclosure.

Neither spoke as they dashed down the muddy road, slipping and nearly falling several times. Still, Vincennes's grip on her hand stayed strong, and when they reached the enclosure, Natalie felt almost reluctant to release it.

The enclosure reeked of elephant dung. "Looks like this storm has literally scared the shit out of someone," Vincennes said, waving a hand in front of his nose. He laughed good-naturedly, and she shared in his laughter as if she'd known him since high school.

The elephants—Ali, Pahpao, Thaya, and Mai—that had decided to join Sophie outside her enclosure were female with the exception of Ali. The females would not have included him in their group if he'd been in *mustph*. Thankfully for him, he'd experienced his *mustph* last month. But because he wasn't currently raging with testosterone, he acted like the biggest baby in the herd and needed company during thunderstorms. Even now, though he stood at least two feet taller than the other elephants, he frantically tried to squeeze into the middle of the group. Sophie reached for him with her trunk, but the rest of the females ignored him, bumping him with their butts as if he was one of the adolescents.

Vincennes stood a step or two behind Natalie under the overhang, yet not out of the rain. It didn't seem to bother him. The wetter he became, the tighter his jet black hair curled. It created commas around his forehead and the tips of his ears, shining with the moisture.

"So who are these beauties?" he asked.

As Natalie introduced him to each of the elephants, she watched his face. His eyes, almost black and rimmed with long and feminine kohl eyelashes, squinted a bit as he studied each elephant, his gaze roaming over their faces as if appraising them. But she suspected it was more than that. It seemed he knew he must silently assure them that he was both confident and non-threatening. He aroused her curiosity.

He must be a philanthropist of some sort, one of Andrew's friends, perhaps one of the people who funded the sanctuaries. Maybe that's why his name appeared vaguely familiar. And maybe that's where his self-confidence came from. The few people she knew who were immensely wealthy had an air about them that was difficult to describe as if every one of their physical needs had been met so now they recognized and enjoyed their passions. On some people, that air became an obnoxious and selfish black cloud, while others reflected their passion and embraced new experiences joyfully, like a child, making them appear the golden people. Andrew was like that and Seth Vincennes seemed to be as well. He also wasn't afraid to get wet.

"And the bull over there who's a scaredy cat is Ali," she continued. "He's Sophie's best friend." Natalie gestured toward Ali who had his head tucked against Thaya's butt. "He's not a big fan of storms. He's also a strange male. Usually the boys don't hang out with the girls in the elephant world."

"Has he been trained using protected contact, too?"

"No, Sophie's the only one. The other vet who's here isn't quite sold on the technique yet, so Sophie was an experiment. He still believes the mahouts need to use the *ankus* to direct the elephants. We don't agree on that. Obviously." She moved further under the enclosure and reached for Sophie, whose ears were at full attention, a sure sign of her heightened anxiety. Sophie didn't know Seth Vincennes—and didn't always trust men. Even though Natalie was sure the storm was the source of most of Sophie's anxiety, she suspected Vincennes's sudden appearance in the enclosure hadn't helped.

"How long have you been working exclusively with Sophie?" he asked, leaning against the gate.

"Almost six months. Every day," she answered. She stood in the middle of the circle of elephants now, touching each of them and talking to them quietly.

"What treatments is she still getting?"

"The leg wound has pretty much healed, so I work with a salve, for the most part." Natalie angled herself back so she could see him and kept her voice even. This wasn't exactly the right time for an interview, but it appeared she didn't have a choice.

"What about Sophie's history? Any chance of a relapse into her previously violent reactions?"

"I don't think so," Natalie said. She told him the little she knew and the ways she treated Sophie's PTSD. As she spoke, Sophie watched her, as if she knew Natalie was talking about her. "I'm convinced 90% of Sophie's reactions were due to the incredible pain she was in."

Natalie stroked Sophie's ear as she spoke, willing the elephant to calm. "She'd worn a hooked chain on two legs for most of her life. The infection in her front leg had started to eat the bone. We're lucky we were able to aggressively treat it—and I really credit the protected contact technique with giving us the capability of moving her leg and administering medicines in a way that was safe for us and calming for her." As if on cue, Sophie shifted and leaned on her good leg. "Man, once those medicines started working, she calmed down, and I was able to get her to follow the commands the mahouts taught me. It was like magic. Even now, she loves being in the enclosure. She feels safe, I think."

The thunder abated a bit, though rain still pelted against the roof like machine gun bullets.

"Your article said something about her being insecure around men." Vincennes took a few steps toward Sophie. The elephant turned her head a bit so she could watch him with her good eye.

"It amazes me that you actually read my whole paper," Natalie laughed. "When I was regularly publishing, the only people who read my papers were my editors."

"Of course I did. Why do you think I'm here? In fact, a lot of people are going to read it. Don't you know you'll be the talk of the veterinary world? All over the blogs. Your work with PTSD is going to help so many elephants. Hasn't Andrew told you? I'm here to get the scoop. You're going to make news in the animal world." He stood now with his feet spread and his hands on his hips, a flirtatious smile pulling at his mouth.

"No, I didn't know, to tell you the truth."

"Then you don't know who I am, do you?" He laughed as if totally delighted that she wasn't impressed with him.

"No, I don't. Should I?"

"Well, a lot of people do."

She shook her head in apology.

"Do you watch Nat Geo?"

"I haven't watched television in a long time. And I purposefully haven't used my cell phone since arriving here. The only time I've used technology is for research." She waved a hand to indicate the area around them. "We don't get great reception. And to tell the truth, I haven't missed it."

He laughed, a deep, rolling laugh that indicated he had taken no offense.

In the light from the gas lanterns hanging from the enclosure's poles, she studied Seth Vincennes once again. When he watched the elephants or glanced her way, it was with those black fringed eyes, made serious by a squint, as though he spent a lot of time in the sun. A ragged, short beard, kept close to his chin and a sketchy moustache served to punctuate full lips. It was an attractive face, a deceptively serious face, until he smiled, then everything changed, and she was disarmed. Unnerved. Uncomfortable. When he stood near her, she was aware of how tall he was. Six foot two or three, she would guess, and he carried that height comfortably. In another life, he'd be a basketball player or a cowboy. Here in Thailand, he was an anomaly.

Who the hell was he anyway?

He turned to her, only six inches or so away. So close, she could smell his minty breath.

"We're on TV. My show . . . it's . . . uh . . ." For a moment, he stammered, which wasn't exactly what she expected. Could he be a bit embarrassed? She watched him duck his head and run his fingers through his thick wave of hair. "I have a show on Nat Geo. *Exotic Beasts of the World.* A combination travel documentary and animal reality series. I'm kind of . . . well, I'm the host. I think they chose me because of my vet experience, and I happened to be in the right place at the right time." He grinned modestly. "Each week we focus on a story about human interactions with animals. You know, who's doing something great with an endangered species or breaking ground with new research." He paused and flashed her one of his smiles and arched one eyebrow flirtatiously, "Or who's raising the most adorable baby tiger kittens."

Her eyes widened, but she didn't say anything though she had to clamp her mouth shut to do so.

"That was a joke. You can laugh," he said, though he wasn't laughing himself.

If she didn't know better, she'd swear he was nervous.

"My road crew will be here tomorrow. I always get to the location first to scope out the place where we're going to shoot, and once we're pretty set, I bring my guys in. Always works out better that way."

"A television crew," Natalie repeated slowly. "Cameras and sets and crew members." She ran her hand absent-mindedly along the edge of Sophie's trunk. The elephant rumbled and drew her trunk up Natalie's arm. She could sense Natalie was getting upset.

He nodded and cocked his head to the side. "Andrew didn't tell you, did he?"

"Not really, but he doesn't have to, does he? I understand."

"Hope you do, because Andrew gave me his permission to be here for a month and the wherewithal to shoot what I wish."

The back of her neck prickled. Had Andrew thought about what this might do to the elephants, particularly Sophie? Why hadn't he spoken to her about this? Maybe she shouldn't have written that paper, but how could she have known how much attention it would garner?

A month. The words reverberated as if a gong had been sounded next to her ear.

A television crew.

Thirty-Two

Of all African animals, the elephant is the most difficult for man to live with, yet its passing—if this must come—seems the most tragic of all. I can watch elephants (and elephants alone) for hours at a time, for sooner or later the elephant will do something very strange such as mow grass with its toenails or draw the tusks from the rotted carcass of another elephant and carry them off into the bush. There is mystery behind that masked gray visage, an ancient life force, delicate and mighty, awesome and enchanted, commanding the silence ordinarily reserved for mountain peaks, great fires, and the sea.
-Peter Matthiessen

BESIDES THE CLICKING INSTRUMENTS, the only sounds in the clinic were an occasional grunt. The mask over Natalie's nose and cheeks itched as a drop of sweat trickled down her forehead. She pointed at Anurak who sat on his haunches in the far corner. He never sat in a chair, but that was fine with her. Tucked in a corner, he was less likely to be in the way. He jumped up immediately and dabbed her face with a cloth. In a few more years and with a bit more training, he would be an invaluable veterinary assistant.

Hatcher had awakened her at five that morning, banging on her cabin door and hollering that he needed her immediately. Without posing a single question, wiping the sleep out of her eyes, or throwing on a bra, she'd gone to the clinic in the t-shirt and boxer shorts she'd worn to bed. Four hours later, she still stood next to him helping repair the damage from an early morning dog-and-elephant fight. Thankfully, this time Sophie wasn't involved, but Thaya and Olan, the oldest bull at the sanctuary, and five dogs were. No one knew exactly what started it, but two of the smaller dogs had broken legs, one of the lab mixes had a crushed front paw (Olan had stepped on it), and the other three had open wounds from being caught up in the melee.

Natalie and Hatcher speculated about the cause of the battle. "It's got to have been that black lab mix. The one with the white front paw," Hatcher said. He knew the dogs much better than she, since she had to ensure they didn't get entangled with Sophie. In fact, she knew that at least four of them lived in his cabin with him. "What did the kids name him? Bonzo? Banzai? He's a banshee, that's what he is. Always acting dominant, no matter who's around."

Natalie grunted as she concentrated on putting the final stitches into a cut on the eldest lab-mix who answered to the name Salé. She slipped her mask down for a moment and relished the coolness of fresh air against her sweaty skin. "I wouldn't be surprised if it was one of the little ones. They move too fast around the ellies' legs. Bet they were chasing each other like they always do, and the rest of them joined in. The ellies were probably dancing, trying to get out of the way and the dogs were caught in between."

Olan never went far from the feeding platform. He was older than Ali and much less sociable. An injury to his right leg had resulted in severe arthritis that got worse every year, making it hard to move more than a couple of feet. Once in a while his mahout brought Olan to the river, but those trips became fewer every month.

The elephants weren't badly injured—just scratches. They milled about anxiously, yet to settle down. Natalie and Hatcher had been setting bones, stitching wounds and operating all morning, and even worse, they'd had cameras in their faces the whole time, one of the reasons for being soaked in sweat.

The only one who seemed to be enjoying the drama of the whole event was Anurak. He hadn't stopped grinning since the cameras came into the room. Even now while wiping her brow, he grinned with his missing front tooth and the cowlick that stubbornly stuck up in the middle of his head. He actually posed for the camera any time the crew was in sight, hand on his hip like a model. If not for being so immersed in operating, she would have laughed at his goofiness.

Rob, a chunky and happy-go-lucky guy from China, spoke perfect English. He'd told her when they first met that he learned the language by watching American TV. Even now, idioms crept into his conversation. Sidecar was the exact opposite of Rob: a small and skinny guy from southern India, he wore wire-rimmed glasses that he constantly pushed up the bridge of his nose. He was serious, where Rob always joked. The two of them constituted a great pair, partners who worked in perfect concert with each other, an artistic coupling.

"Closing up here," Hatcher said, pulling some thread through his needle. "We're almost done."

She flexed her fingers, working out a wrist cramp, and pulled off her gloves and mask. She needed to soak in the shower. Cleaning up the countertop where she'd been working, she dumped the surgical instruments into the sink, filled it with disinfectant, then motioned for Anurak to scrub them.

When she turned, ready to leave, she spotted Hatcher and Seth in the far corner of the room, standing head to head, talking animatedly. She had a feeling the conversation had nothing to do with the surgical procedures they had just performed. If circumstances had been different, she might be curious, but right now, she was done. Everything was under control.

She told Anurak that he and Decha should leave, and the boy's face was as crestfallen as if he'd been told Santa wasn't coming this year. But when she made the sign for lunch, his face brightened a little, then his head cocked as it did when he sensed something out of the norm.

"What is it?" she asked.

He shook his head as if to silence her and lifted a finger. She opened the door and felt the rumble at the same time she heard the roar.

Sophie trumpeted, again. The screaming, high-pitched sound she made when upset. The trumpeting turned into a roar, and Natalie took off running toward the elephant's enclosure.

Even before she saw Sophie, Natalie heard Chanchai, the mahout, screaming at the top of his lungs. She pumped her legs faster, pushing herself to gallop, certain she would find a devastating scene.

As she came to the curve in the road where the enclosure loomed into sight, she saw Chanchai, *ankus* high above his head, waving it menacingly at Sophie. The *ankus*. The one thing that terrified her. The elephant's screams were full of that fear.

"What the hell are you doing?" Natalie yelled. She reached for the *ankus* as Chanchai pulled back to strike Sophie again. The sharp tip caught Natalie's palm, and she cried out and doubled over. Still, she had to stop him. She screamed again, "Chanchai, what the hell are you thinking? You know you can't use the *ankus* with her! Do you want to get yourself killed?"

Wild-eyed, he ignored her and yelled another command. A garbled word. Another slash with the *ankus*.

Sophie surged forward.

THE WOMAN *grabs for the howling mahout's red and black shirt but misses. Ducking out of the way, the mahout pokes and yells at the elephant, trapped in the enclosure.*

Sophie hates this man, his violence, his unfathomably black eyes. She wants to flee, to run far away from him, but her back is against the columns that support the enclosure's roof. She has nowhere else to go, and the mahout is taking advantage of it, poking the silver-sharp pole at her through the bars. She widens her eyes, her large pink ears flare, she pushes against the bars, flails her trunk everywhere, tries to reach the mahout. Trumpets, then trumpets again, as loudly and ferociously as she can. She could kill this mahout easily, could stomp on him or gore him with her tusk, but she has been taught to fear the men, to fear the ankus, and since she has not tried to defend herself against anything but the dogs, she has no true idea of her own strength.

Still, the mahout screams and pokes, jabbing the ankus at her every time he's within reach. He yells commands, but none of them make sense, nor does he give the elephant a chance to accomplish what he's asking.

Behind her, the elephant hears humans running and voices shouting but she instinctively knows that if she looks, she'll lose control over the greatest danger: the mahout waving the ankus. Another roaring trumpet travels up through the elephant's vocal cords, almost ripping them, she has exerted so much power. Her throat tightens. The cry comes out strangled, high-pitched, full of terror.

Finally, the woman catches the mahout's shirt and swings him around to face her.

"Stop! Put the ankus down. Now!" she screams.

The mahout stares beyond the woman to Sophie, his eyes still as black as a rock, but he lowers the ankus even while he ripples with anger like the currents of the river.

Sophie rocks forward and back, then side to side on her back legs, her nerves still unsettled. She feels trapped. She smells the other men behind her. They are not mahouts. They don't smell like mahouts, don't sound like mahouts. Still, they are men.

"Leave. Now." The woman points to the road, and nods at the mahout, expecting him to respond to her command.

The mahout seems to know what Sophie does, that there will be a great price to pay if he rouses her once again: his life. He scurries up the road like a spider, as if afraid Sophie might follow him.

But the other men do not leave. They speak quietly with the woman, holding their giant cameras on their shoulders, sometimes pointing them at the elephant, sometimes at the woman, but never coming any closer to Sophie than the enclosure's gate.

They finally move away, and woman comes into the enclosure, touches Sophie's trunk, speaks quietly, and when she softly sings into Sophie's right ear, the elephant begins to relax.

Thirty-Three

Grief can take care of itself,
but to get the full value of joy,
you must have somebody
to divide it with.
-Mark Twain

CHANCHAI WAS GONE, BUT nothing helped Sophie to quiet down.

Seth, Rob, and Sidecar were the only people left around the enclosure, so Natalie quietly said, "Please back away from the elephant."

She waited for them to move themselves and their camera equipment, then she slipped in closer to Sophie, put her hand on Sophie's ear and felt for her pulse. It wasn't as rapid as she thought it would be. Only then did she place her hands on Sophie's head and take some deep breaths, deliberately calming herself.

Breathe in, breathe out. When she felt Sophie begin to emulate the rhythm of the breath, she began softly singing "My Funny Valentine," the only song she could think of at the moment. Andrew had been whistling it all day yesterday, making her complain to him that he'd provided an ear worm she couldn't shut off. He'd laughed. Little did he know that the song that had bothered Natalie so much yesterday was the exact balm Sophie needed today.

Within ten minutes—and four repetitions of the song—Sophie's pupils returned to normal, she'd accepted some food, and she rumbled gently. She'd made great strides, Natalie felt, but there were still some triggers that aroused Sophie's PTSD. Natalie would never be able to make those triggers disappear, but she could help Sophie learn that her own actions made the bone-crushing fear worse. It surprised her sometimes that she often applied what had worked for her own PTSD when dealing with Sophie's. Sometimes the remedy worked, sometimes it didn't.

She was lucky this time.

Convinced Sophie was fine, Natalie began to move to the gate, still humming under her breath, planning to walk to her cabin and take as hot a shower as she could manage. She was completely drained.

Behind her, Seth coughed.

She stopped mid-step. "I'm sorry," she said, turning to him. She had forgotten all about him and his cameramen throughout the time she'd sung to Sophie, so engrossed in getting the elephant calm.

"Mind if I walk with you?" He matched his steps to hers before she had a chance to say yes. His white, cotton shirtsleeves were rolled up to his biceps. A set of sunglasses hung out of the breast pocket.

Behind him, his two-man camera crew continued filming. They'd never stopped, she figured. Her shoulders tensed with the memory of other camera crews that filmed her every move. Their endless questions. Their demands for her time. Their intense curiosity about how she was handling her grief. Now she would be on film with Sophie. She still wasn't sure she was comfortable with that.

With a superhuman effort, she shut down the memory that threatened to overtake her. She was getting good at doing that.

"That was amazing." Seth's eyes were wide open, excited. "You were like a hypnotist back there. The damn elephant whisperer. Whatever made you sing to her? It was magical. I wouldn't have believed it if I hadn't seen it myself." He swung his arms, walking sideways to talk to her, his lips curved in a smile so wide, every one of his white teeth were displayed.

She laughed wearily. "Right." A stray thought about how dirty she was ran through her mind. *Too late for that*, she figured and wondered why it had ever been important to her that her hair and makeup were perfect.

"Have you sung to her before? Does it always have that effect?"

"I used to sing to my—" She caught herself, almost gave herself away. She had sung to the boys all the time. When nothing else worked, an old Beatles standard would calm them down. They had their favorites, and most times, she sang the wrong words. They didn't care. Neither did Sophie.

"It's nothing," she told Seth. "Just some white noise to calm her down."

"No, you don't understand. It's the singing, but it's much more than that. Your connection with that elephant is like you're communicating without speaking. It's amazing," Seth said. "We shot the best raw footage with you right now, better than anything else we've done since we started here. So glad that happened."

"Listen, this might be my exhaustion talking," she said, her words tumbling out before she thought about them being caught on camera, "but I'm not setting up moments like that one with Sophie so that you can get a few sound bites. I've been working long and hard with her, and I'd appreciate it if you wouldn't be so delighted when she backslides like that. Jesus, she could have done some damage today! Would you have liked that? Would it be exciting to get a rampaging elephant on tape?" She glanced behind her, and Rob and Sidecar, caught in the act of filming her, looked sheepishly away. "Turn the damn cameras off," she said. "Can you give me a break, for God's sake?"

"Wow, I'm sorry. I—I . . . you know, we're . . . I mean, we really didn't do anything except to film." Seth threw his hands out to the side, palms up. "I'm not in this business to create drama. I just want to report it. There's enough natural tragedies and excitement in the animal world without inventing more. Besides," he laughed a little sarcastically, "I want to live a while longer. Not interested in getting trampled by a rampaging two-ton gray beast."

She let out a breath, realizing she had taken out her frustrations on the wrong person. That's what happened when she was stressed. "Listen, I'm sorry. I'm wiped out. I need a shower and some sleep. It's not your fault about what happened. I'm protective about Sophie. She's come so far."

"I understand." He touched her gently on the shoulder, so lightly that it felt as if he was afraid to touch her at all. Then he took a step backward and shrugged his shoulders, as if caught doing something he'd be ashamed of later. "You've had a long day. I'll let you go and rest."

With a half-hearted wave, he turned and followed Rob and Sidecar up the road.

She watched after them for a moment, a bit stunned that his simple touch on her shoulder had made her stomach flip. She hadn't expected that. Yes, he was attractive and dynamic and personable, but that stomach flip meant she was physically attracted. When was the last time that had happened?

They disappeared around the corner, and she let her shoulders slump. Suddenly the adrenaline left her body and her exhaustion rooted her to the ground as if her legs had turned to granite.

When she finally could lift her legs to walk, she made it to her cabin, but never to the shower. Hours later, she woke up, still fully-dressed atop the bed, and simply rolled over.

The last thing she thought before going straight back to sleep was: *Why would Chanchai be trying to handle Sophie with an ankus?*

Thirty-Four

A mother's hardest to forgive,
Life is the fruit she longs to hand you,
Ripe on a plate. And while you live,
Relentlessly, she understands you.
-Phyllis McGinley

A WARM WHISPER OF a breeze wiggled the leaves above
Natalie and rustled the bushes next to her, bringing her attention back to the road beneath her feet. She was on her way to the
administration building to try to convince Andrew to help her,
though she wasn't sure he would. She sighed. Knowing Hatcher,
he had already gone to Andrew and convinced him to get rid of
Sophie after yesterday's interaction, yet when she ran the scene
through her mind, she remembered Hatcher had appeared angry
enough to hit Chanchai. She couldn't figure him out anymore. If
she'd ever had even the slightest clue what kind of a human he
really was, she had absolutely none now.

Sophie hadn't been that riled up in a long time, and the way
she had reacted to the mahout made Natalie rethink her training
techniques. What would happen when she left the sanctuary?
Sophie would need to work with another mahout, and Siriporn
probably wasn't an option. She'd hardly seen him during the past
couple of days and suspected he and his group of Red Shirts might

be planning a demonstration or rally. During the last one, twelve people were injured or killed in political rallies in Bangkok. If he didn't get himself hurt, she would be willing to bet he'd be moving into the city to take a more active role in politics. No. He wouldn't be around to take care of Sophie.

What were the options? Chanchai? Hell, no.

Chanchai was pretty typical of most mahouts who relied on brute strength and the *ankus* to control his feisty female, Mai. He'd told Natalie early on that he didn't think protected contact would work.

In his broken English, he'd said, "Elephant too big for woman. *Ankus*, Dr. Natalie! *Ankus!*"

The ankus set Sophie on fire, but without it, most mahouts or elephant handlers would not take the chance working with her.

Natalie wanted to tear her hair out. Somehow, in some way, she needed to get it across to everyone at the sanctuary that Sophie only needed the soft pole she used in protected contact. A slight touch on the leg and Sophie would move. She knew the commands for walking and turning and backing up and bending. She was smart. Responsive. Nothing else was necessary but the commands and the pole. Unfortunately, the mahouts didn't understand.

Even before Natalie approached the stairs to the administration building's platform, she heard arguing. At the back of the building near the kitchen entrance, the camera crew sat, talking to Mali. Rob and Sidecar glanced over at Natalie but continued their conversation. Mali waved and smiled at Natalie. She raised her eyebrows, an unspoken question about the raised voices coming from the other side of the platform. Mali shook her head. Unsure what that meant, Natalie stood at the base of the stairs for a moment, debating about whether to enter the lion's den.

The men who were arguing sat on the platform. She couldn't see the three of them clearly, but one of them sounded like Hatcher. He had a full head of steam. She wasn't sure she wanted to be anywhere near him. The other two: Andrew was one; the third hadn't said anything, but she would bet her last buck it was

Seth. Yes, she was about to enter the lion's den and began questioning her own sanity for doing so.

As she mounted the stairs, the voices became clearer. She heard her name and froze.

"And I can't be everywhere on the compound, but damned if I haven't been accused of bugging you folks when the truth of the matter is that certain people are ruining it for the rest of us," Hatcher said, his voice rushed and uneven.

"Peter, that's enough." Andrew's strong baritone struggled to maintain control.

Natalie wondered how long he would be able to remain that way. The thought flew through her mind that she should leave, but curiosity kept her feet planted on the stairs.

"Why? Why do I need to stay quiet? What have I done wrong?" Peter said. "Andrew, tell me. What in God's name have I done wrong?"

A hot breeze swept along the tree line and stole Andrew's response. The banana fronds rattled.

"And if his people don't stay out of my way, I'll—"

"You'll what?" Andrew boomed.

She moved a few feet, stood in full view of them now, but nobody noticed her.

Hatcher stood at one end of the center table, his shoulders pushed forward, fists clenched by his sides, his normally-pale cheeks flushed. At the opposite end of the table, Andrew leaned forward, his beefy hands balanced on the table as if ready to launch himself. And Seth stood in the middle, one foot propped up on the seat, elbow on his knee and his face leaning against his hand. A casual stance but Natalie could tell, even from where she stood, that the conversation was far from casual.

"Andrew, listen to me," Hatcher said.

His voice had that soft, even-pitched tone she remembered hearing in her own voice the night Parker announced he wanted to leave. Quiet desperation. A plea. She had tried to appear reasonable but rapidly lost control. She remembered the cold tightening of her own larynx the night she fought the urge to plead with her husband. It was the sound of someone who'd become terrified about what they might lose.

"I'm sorry," *Parker had told her that night. He leaned against the kitchen counter, caught in the corner, trapped. By her.*

She stood in front of him, a dish towel in her hands, snapping it. Her stance was wide, unmoving.

"I'm not doing a good job at this." *He looked at the kitchen floor.*

"At what? Good job at what?" *she'd said, though she knew exactly what he meant.* "Doing a good job at being a father? A good husband? Good at being a man?" *Ironically, in that moment, she had felt a rolling surge of pity for Parker. It must have been a heavy and painful burden to find you weren't good at the very basic of basics. How could you not be good at being a person?*

Now, standing on the platform, she felt the same type of pity for Hatcher that she'd felt for her husband. The back of her neck prickled with sweat. She lifted her heavy braid and swung it over her shoulder. That movement caught Andrew's eye, and he registered surprise at seeing her, an emotion Hatcher must have discerned because he turned, and all of his anger shot through his eyes and pierced her like a well-placed javelin.

"If it wasn't for you," Hatcher began, directing his comment toward her.

Andrew rose. "Peter, that's enough. You're not making sense anymore, old boy. She had nothing to do with any of this. Listen, why don't you sleep it off, and we'll talk about this tomorrow morning when we're all rational? You've had a bit too much scotch. That's all."

"No, damnit. I've kept my bloody mouth shut long enough." He swung back to point a finger at Andrew. "I've given you years of my life, Andrew. Nine fucking years. I've been here when there was no damn electricity. I've held down this place when you were gallivanting across the ocean, and I've made sure the animals were cared for and that the people were fed. I did a good job. I know I did."

"Yes, you did, Peter. I never said you didn't . . ."

"We worked well together. Then all of a sudden, you go off on

255

one of your trips and you come back with bright and shiny new ideas without even consulting me." Hatcher's mouth scrunched up. "Without talking to me about them! Without sharing anything at all . . . without giving me credit for what I've done. Without offering the respect of asking for my opinion, for God's sake! I told you before you left that I needed an assistant, and I knew exactly who would fit the bill. Why the hell didn't you listen to me? Christ, man, training her has made my life ten times more difficult!" He shot Natalie another scathing glance. "And to make matters worse, she focuses on one animal. One goddamn elephant! I could have gone without her . . . without her help." Hatcher curled his lip back like a comic book villain.

She almost laughed, but he hadn't finished.

"For all the good she's been to me, you could've saved yourself a bunch of money, Andrew, but no . . . not only does she concentrate solely on Sophie, but she concocts some hare-brained scheme for special training that brings the sanctuary to a standstill to do her bidding, and—I want to underline that word—*and* it costs us a cool sixty thousand dollars to build the enclosure and buy new equipment."

He paused for a breath, and in that two seconds, Natalie registered Seth's discomfort and Andrew's growing rage. She wished she had turned around and run when she'd first heard the men arguing, but she could no longer stand by dumbly. "I raised part of that money. I found several grants . . ." she said in a weak voice that made her hate herself.

"Shut. The. Hell. Up." Hatcher took a menacing step toward her.

Both Andrew and Seth reached out to stop him, but he backed up, both hands in the air as if to say they needn't worry, but he kept talking.

"Then, as if more salt in the wound is necessary," he continued. "She's now the darling of Thailand and this damn TV crew is following her every move as if she's a dyed-in-the-wool movie star." He swished his hips, mocking her. "Now I can't move more than two steps without a camera up my ass and Mr. Jungle

Jim here parading around like he owns the bloody place."

"Hold on." Natalie held up her hand.

Before she could protest further, Seth rounded the table and grabbed Hatcher's collar. "That's enough," he said, lifting Hatcher a little, as he would a misbehaving dog.

"Andrew asked you nicely to quit a few moments ago," Seth continued, his lips a mere inch from Hatcher's ear. "I'm not going to be so nice. Shut up now or I'm going to make sure you don't speak clearly for a couple of weeks."

"Take your hands off me," Hatcher said through gritted teeth.

Seth didn't move. A standoff. Between two strong dogs.

One more breath, and Hatcher erupted. His fist caught Seth's jaw with a resounding *thwack*. Seth stumbled, then rose halfway to stumble once again, this time against Hatcher.

Hatcher swung again, his fist coming from his knees, landed another thudding punch against Seth's cheek, then another. Seth brought up his knee, and the two men fell to the ground in a tangle of fists and angry shouts.

From out of the night, the sanctuary's dogs stormed the platform, barking and snarling, and surrounded the men scuffling on the floor. Andrew shouted.

Natalie grabbed the dogs' collars, yelling for everyone to stop. Somehow Andrew got between the two men and separated them, standing like a granite statue, each of his hands holding a man. Still, they fought and clawed at each other. They grunted and spat blood. The sound of the fight brought out the kitchen help and the mahouts. The lady cooks stood near the wall, a safe distance away. Their hands over their mouths, their eyes wide, they watched with a mixture of fear and excitement.

Finally, Andrew's considerable bulk prevailed, and he released Seth, forcing him to sit on a bench. Andrew held both of Hatcher's hands in one of his against the small of Hatcher's back, as tightly as if he'd just clapped on a pair of handcuffs.

"You're done now," Andrew wheezed. "This is finished. I won't have any of this at my place. Sit. Both of you."

Natalie's heart pounded as she, too, took a seat, still holding two dogs by their collars. Someone ran for cloths and ice. A small group of women surrounded each man, debating the wounds and how to care for them.

Hatcher seemed oddly relieved and quiet, as if happy to have released his anger. Blood trickled down his face. Seth and Andrew breathed hard and watched Hatcher closely, as if afraid he'd erupt again.

"We could've talked about this, you know. Reasonably. It didn't have to turn into a fight," Natalie said. She released the dogs and watched them leapfrog over each other before running into the night.

Hatcher stared at her. "No, we couldn't. You wouldn't have understood. Probably still don't."

Her adrenaline still pumping, Natalie spun on him. "I understand more—much more—about your selfishness and idiocy than I want to, Dr. Hatcher! From the moment you accused me of ruining your life because I critiqued your damn dissertation, you've acted like a bratty two-year-old who hasn't gotten his way, and I, personally, am damn tired of your barbed and often incorrect comments."

She took a breath, aware that Andrew and Seth had frozen, but she kept staring at Hatcher's shocked face, and she couldn't stop. "I worked three jobs with two little kids who needed me when I was reading dissertations like yours. I devoted all my nights and weekends to reading seven-hundred-page manuscripts about cat hernias and gestational cancer in camels, and whatever yours was. I gave up my kids' childhoods to help people like you, to give you my honest critiques, and to help shape some of the best research I've ever read. And I fucking hate you for punishing me for giving you what I thought was positive feedback. For God's sake, grow a pair of balls and get over it! There are far more important things that we need to take care of."

She leaned against the table and pointed a shaking finger at him. "I don't give a good goddamn if you don't like me, but if you're going to continue this battle, I will no longer lie down and play dead like some apologetic, weak sissy. Bring it on, Peter

Hatcher. Bring it on."

Hatcher lunged. His face, brilliant red. His eyes, iceberg blue. His hand reached for her as he clattered across the top of the table. Andrew thrust out a beefy arm like an iron gate, stopping Hatcher from going further.

"Seriously, Hatcher? You'd hit a woman?" She thrust her face closer to his. Taunting him, angrier than she'd been in years. "Why does it not surprise me that you're a bully?"

"Okay, that's enough," Andrew shouted as Hatcher struggled to get past him.

Behind her, Seth grabbed her arm. "This isn't making anything any better," he said in her ear.

"I don't give a shit!" she hissed. "This bastard isn't going to get the best of me."

"As long as you're as upset as you are, no one wins." Seth's arm wrapped around her shoulders. "You need to give yourself some breathing space. Talk to him when you're both calm."

"That'll be never."

Andrew pulled Hatcher away, talking to him the whole while. Natalie stood and watched until they were out of sight, then sunk to a squatting position. A wave of anxiety spread over her. She shook. The back of her neck soaked her shirt. Prickles went up the sides of her head. She forced herself to count. *Breathe. Breathe.*

Thirty-Five

Do not let your fire go out, spark by irreplaceable spark in the hopeless swamps of the not-quite, the not-yet, and the not-at-all. Do not let the hero in your soul perish in lonely frustration for the life you deserved and have never been able to reach. The world you desire can be won. It exists . . . it is real . . . it is possible . . . it's yours.
                                                                    -Ayn Rand

SHE TRIED NOT TO look into the audience. It felt like thousands of people had crammed into the meeting room where she was to deliver her paper, but in reality, she knew it was more like a hundred. Still, that was at least ninety-five people more than she was used to speaking to at any point in time.

She swallowed, tapped the microphone, and said, "I'm Dr. Natalie DeAngelo, and currently, I'm volunteering at The Lotus Animal Sanctuary, about five hours north of here. We rehabilitate elephants, dogs, and other small animals, with more than one hundred and fifty to two hundred animals on the compound at any point in time. Currently, we have more than a dozen elephants, most of whom came to us from the logging or tourist industries." She took a breath. The hand holding her notes still shook, but it would stop. Once she got started, she'd be fine. "Most of them have been abused and also have serious physical conditions. What I'd like to talk about today is the use of the protected contact technique with a violent elephant plagued with both PTSD and a traumatic captivity wound."

The room quieted, the lights lowered, and her video of Sophie's treatment history began in the background, sound off. Like Andrew's presentation had done to her many months ago, her audience was immediately drawn in. And like Andrew's presentation, the audience stood and honored her with a long ovation afterwards, and people lined up to speak to her about her work. To Natalie, the whole event felt like a blur.

She floated through the rest of the day, barely listening to the other presentations she attended. Fragmented thoughts and plans for future research kept her off balance, inattentive. It had been a long time since her research had been vetted by her peers, and the recognition gave her a high that was almost tactile.

Though she was proud to claim some success with Sophie, the number of other abused elephants she'd heard about from the audience rose into the hundreds. And all of them could use the same treatment or some iteration of it. *I have to help*, she kept thinking. *But how?* Exhausted, she pushed the thought out of the way toward the end of the day when she caught up with Andrew and Seth.

"You're the rockstar of the conference." Andrew looped an arm around her and pulled her in for a bear hug. He'd already loosened his tie. "You'll be plenty busy offering advice to the colleagues who'll be pounding at your door."

"It might not work for everyone," she said, holding the door for Seth, who came behind her with his arms full of photo equipment. "If there's one thing I've learned, it's that every elephant responds to treatment differently. Like us."

"Yeah, but an aspirin is an aspirin is an aspirin. They work on pain and inflammation, not cuts and burns. Know what I mean?"

"So many others need our help." She dropped her shoulder satchel on the table. They'd rented a suite of rooms that included a small sitting area where they had gathered last night for a glass of wine after arriving at the hotel. During their time at the conference, it had become the spot where they checked in with each other. Natalie slid into one of the chairs at the table, not intending to stay long.

"And you can start by helping the ones we have right at the sanctuary," Andrew said as he poured himself a scotch. "Or better yet, you can come with me to Kenya the next time I go and spread the word there, too. Plenty of vets and trainers and behaviorists would want to know about the technique."

The thought of traveling right now made her tired. In fact, she realized she'd been tired for months, but this air conditioning was accentuating it. Andrew continued talking, excited about the possibilities, until her head started to droop.

"Hey, love, you need a quick nap before tonight?" He touched her elbow gently.

She didn't need to be asked twice. "Just a half hour?"

Two hours later, she was roused by a knock on her door. She hadn't even realized she'd fallen asleep, but she knew one thing for sure as she opened the door to Andrew: she could have used a dozen more hours in the comfy and luxurious hotel bed.

Andrew bustled in and deposited a big box on her bed. "Go ahead. Open it."

The white box was edged with gold and lettered with the tailor's name in Thai, a gorgeous curlicue of a name that looked elegant even though Natalie had no idea what it meant. Inside, a confection of crepe and chiffon, layers of dove gray silk and pale pink chiffon, coupled with a pair of silk gray sandals embellished with sequins embroidering the toe strap.

"I feel like 'Pretty Woman,'" she said, lifting the dress up to her shoulders. "When I packed to come the sanctuary, I never thought I'd need evening wear."

"And I wouldn't have suggested it." Andrew wiped a bead of sweat from his forehead. Outside, the humidity made the ninety-three degree weather feel like the thermometer had shot over one hundred. Even though the hotel's air conditioning kept the rooms much cooler, Andrew still dripped with moisture. "But we couldn't have you enjoying a formal dance in your T-shirt and Bermuda shorts, now could we, love?"

Normally, the International Society of Veterinarians didn't host a gala on the last evening of the conference, but then again, there had not been a fiftieth anniversary of the Society up to this point. And the gala attracted the philanthropists interested in adding more to the sanctuary's coffers. Others would be pitching their own projects, and Natalie supposed she wasn't the only vet uncomfortable in evening clothes, but she might be one of the only ones who had an evening dress specially tailored by one of Bangkok's famed tailors. Andrew had pulled a couple of strings to have the dress made overnight after discovering that Natalie was at least two inches too tall for anything off the rack.

Amidst a flurry of thank yous and fumbled hugs, Andrew left her alone with the dove grey and sunset pink gown. She'd chosen the colors on a whim, thinking that they mimicked Sophie's skin colors—and that would be good luck. After all, if it wasn't for the paper Natalie had written about the old girl, she wouldn't have been invited to speak at this conference to begin with. She lifted the dress, resisting the impulse to sigh when the cool silkiness of the gown slipped over her head and slid like water down her body.

It had been a long time since she'd worn a gown, and she had to admit it instantly made her stand up straighter as she checked herself in the floor-length mirror. She hadn't realized it, but now that she could see her full body, she knew she'd lost some weight. Her arms were strong, muscled from months of hauling giant, heavy buckets of food for the elephants and from the days in the clinic where she lifted dogs who needed vaccinations and treatments. She often spent afternoons helping the volunteers cut sugar cane in the hot sun, so her skin had darkened, and constant walking had toned up her long legs.

And her hair had grown. Every morning, she'd simply slapped it atop her head with a couple of clips, but now that she had loosened it, it hung down to her waist in a mahogany cape, contrasting sharply with the pale grey gown. She already coated her lashes with some black mascara and applied a swipe of dark pink lipstick. For the past seven months, she'd been lucky if she could get a warm shower at night. Today, she'd spent more than an hour under a sizzling spray, luxuriating in the billows of steam and hoping that the good soaking would get the last vestiges of dirt from under her fingernails. Though she hated to give in, she let Andrew talk her into getting a mani-pedi in the hotel's beauty salon, and felt totally decadent sitting in the chair doing so, especially since she knew the polish wouldn't last long once she returned to the sanctuary.

Slipping her feet into the pair of silver sandals, she checked her reflection one last time and gave herself a pleased smile. The pedicure had been worth it, because the simple pink polish actually made her look polished and more than a little glamorous. It had been a long time since she felt . . . well, pretty.

Seth and Andrew were waiting near the lobby's elevator, and when she stepped out, Seth gave her a long low whistle. Behind him, the camera crew paused for a moment, glancing at each other in a moment of shock before focusing the camera and going back to work. Tonight was supposed to be their final night of filming, and Natalie couldn't be happier. She was tired of tripping over the cameramen, Rob and Sidecar, every day. They were good guys, but they were in the way on a regular basis.

"You look like a bloody movie star," Andrew boomed in his gravelly voice. He wore a black tux with a crisp white shirt with black buttons, his tie undone, the buttons on the shirt straining to stay fastened across his massive chest.

Seth stood next to him and held out his arm for her, the epitome of gentlemanly manners. He held himself with the ease of a man quite used to wearing a tux, a slim James Bond in glasses. Unlike Andrew, Seth's buttons were all properly fastened, his tie meticulously bowed, and his glossy black hair sexily mussed. Natalie noted several women checking him out as the three of them moved to the hotel's ballroom.

"I hope you don't mind me saying you're the most dazzling vet I've ever seen," Seth whispered to her when he pushed in her chair at their assigned table.

He smelled warm and spicy. Hot. She felt a ripple in the base of her stomach, something she hadn't experienced in quite a long time. It surprised her.

They shared their table with a couple of vets from Zimbabwe who worked with large cats, and several others from India who also worked with elephants. Conversation moved along in a lively and interesting fashion, and Natalie felt complimented that several of them had attended her session the day before. They asked questions about how she'd fared while training to become a mahout. Had it been difficult to break into a traditionally male profession? Especially being a white female? Had she encountered prejudices? How did she manage to get the elephants to listen to her?

She told them about Sophie's bumpy road to success, how she had often back-peddled into unacceptable behavior and what had to be done to counteract it. She retold the stories of Sophie's horrid interactions with dogs, about her love for submerging herself in the river so long that Natalie had to be sure she hadn't drowned and how every time she waded in to check to see whether Sophie was still alive, the elephant would emerge long enough to spout a shower of water at Natalie, her personal elephant joke. She told the table full of rapt listeners about Sophie's love for Beatles songs and listened as intently when the group from India shared their own stories about elephants who loved sitar music, and who were often lulled to sleep by an old mahout whose singing was so bad that everyone but his elephants wore earplugs.

There were other stories, too, that she filed in her brain for future reference. Stories about the type of cream that worked best on an elephant's open foot wound and what foods were best for a lactating female. They talked about "protected contact," a technique that most had heard of, yet Natalie appeared to be the only one at the table who'd used it successfully. And they shared contact information for the pharmaceutical industries who had recently developed new antibiotics designed to work almost overnight on the worst infections.

The talk would have continued all night except the band struck up after everyone had finished eating, and Seth stood and reached out a hand to her.

At first, she felt confused. The last time she had danced with a man was before Danny's birth, so she'd forgotten the simple body language that indicated a man's interest. But she realized that he was inviting her to dance and, abashedly, she accepted.

In spite of the fact that she wore heels that added three inches to her five-foot-seven stature, he was still a bit taller than her, and she leaned into him, noting her chin could rest against his shoulder. She caught another whiff of his cologne and let herself drift into it as the orchestra played a jazzy version of "My Funny Valentine." She found herself grinning against his shoulder at the memory of singing the same song to Sophie.

They lasted another four songs on the dance floor, then she needed a break.

Back at the table, Andrew had disappeared as had the group from India. The only people left were the folks from Zimbabwe, and they were clearly there for the duration. The two men, Dr. Mugame and Dr. Batope, bobbed their bald, black heads to the music and smiled at Natalie as if showing their approval of the orchestra.

"It is so good to be kept abreast of the ways in which veterinary personnel in other countries are attending to their businesses, don't you agree, Dr. DeAngelo?" Dr. Mugame asked her during a pause in the music. His English-educated voice boomed deep and rich as he folded his hands over his round belly. He wore a royal blue suit with a multicolored shawl around his shoulders like the ones people wore at graduation. His colleague, Dr. Batope, was as thin and tall as Mugame was short and fat, but both wore the same type of glasses: square rimmed, perched high on the bridge of their noses. And both were equally intense, immersed in their work and committed to learning about other vets who'd dealt with the same types of issues, no matter whether on the other side of the continent of Africa or the other side of the world.

The three of them shared information about what they'd learned in the various seminars they'd all attended throughout the conference, and Natalie was impressed by the abundance of information they had gleaned about elephants, though their specialty was big cats. All three leaned into each other to listen and talk though they had to compete with the music, and Natalie found herself excited by the conversation, engrossed in it until Seth returned.

She got a whiff of his cologne, the scent enticing and insistent. Her attention wavered from the conversation. When he held out his hand toward her, it felt natural to rise and drift into his arms for another round of dancing, but by the second dance, she stifled a yawn.

"I'm sorry. I haven't been up this late in almost a year. We're all usually headed for bed shortly after the sun sets at the sanctuary. But you know that." She pulled back from Seth's shoulder, amazed to see his clear black eyes less than a couple of inches from her own. His gaze drew her in, and she puzzled at what it meant. An emotion. A question. A chemistry that she could not—and did not want to—deny. Then a sliver of doubt crept between them. She backed off, and he turned away, gave a little cough.

"Let me take you to your room, then." Seth steered her back to the table, now empty, and they collected their belongings and headed for the elevator.

She leaned against the back wall of the elevator, her palms against the cold steel, her eyes fixed on the flashing light as they rose to the sixth floor, her room. She tried to ignore the way he'd held her elbow as they walked through the hotel's hallways, could still feel his touch, though he had let go when they stepped into the elevator. He pressed the floor, but he hadn't moved away, and if she had flexed her little finger, she could have touched him now. Out of the corner of her eye, she could see his eyelashes flicker, the edges of his nostrils flare as he breathed. She wondered whether he felt the same curiosity she'd been fighting.

What would it be like to kiss him? It both terrified and thrilled her to think about the touch of his lips against hers, their breath intermingling, his hands on her waist. She pressed the small of her back against the cold elevator wall, rebuking herself for being a silly romantic female, then the elevator stopped and he turned to her, smiling, his nose millimeters from hers, and paused for what seemed like long moments though only seconds had passed.

She shifted to the side. "My floor."

"Mine, as well," he said and swept his hand in a gallant half circle. "Ladies first."

Her gown made a shushing sound as she stepped off the elevator then fluttered soundlessly against the carpeted hallway floor. Without speaking, they walked down the long hallway to her room, and as she fumbled for the card key, he reached out and touched her hand with the tips of his fingers. She glanced up and this time, there was no denying the look in his eyes and no doubt that as he lowered his head, his lips reached for hers. Gone were the thoughts of what to say and how to say it, gone were the worries about what she would do if this moment came to pass, gone were the doubts as old as her high school memories. Instead, his soft lips touched hers, gently at first, and then with an intensity that matched the way his arms wrapped tightly around her, and she realized that they had been moving toward this moment from the first time she studied the angles of his face in the dim light of Sophie's enclosure. She realized that her curiosity and imagination were only one miniscule piece of reality, and that now, this moment, this warm rush of blood flooding from the depths of her belly and throughout her chest, her hips, her heart, and the back of her throat was so welcome and strange and recognizable and true that she wanted more.

And then the door to the room swung open and he followed her inside, pressed her against the wall, dropped what he'd been holding—she was no longer sure what it had been—and murmured her name and that he wanted her and that she was more beautiful than anyone he'd ever known and would she, could she.

Her gown slipped to the floor slowly and his hands traced her shoulders, the tight muscles of her arms, all the way to her fingers, and as they palmed both hands, he pressed her arms above her head against the wall, and left breathless kisses down the sides of her face, in the hollow of her throat, along her breastbone, tracing the laciness of her bra and slipping along the soft skin of her belly to the concaves of her hip bones, and his warm tongue found the edge of her panties, pushing them down, and all the sounds in the world went silent, and she was his.

Thirty-Six

Never doubt that a small group of thoughtful, committed,
citizens can change the world.
Indeed, it is the only thing that ever has.
-Margaret Mead

NATALIE PEERED OUT INTO the darkness. What was the sound that had awakened her from a sound sleep? Where were the cars and lights from other buildings? Her room was on the sixth floor, not that far above the city streets. When she'd been getting ready for the night's festivities, she could hear people calling to each other in the street below and the sounds of traffic going by. Now, nothing. Across the river, the golden spires of the Grand Palace reminded her of the day she and Parker and the kids had wandered through the maze of buildings to see the golden and emerald statues, so much grandeur, such opulence. Danny had been fascinated by the statues of the gods and when they reached the Temple of the Emerald Buddha, he acted his age and said, "That's it? All the other statues are much bigger than this one." She'd had to shush him because heads turned.

Surely something had woken her up. She glanced back over her shoulder at Seth still sleeping soundly and a ripple of butterflies erupted in her stomach. He'd made love to her for several hours before they finally succumbed to exhaustion. His desire for her had aroused her own needs, and she'd met his every thrust, his kisses, his strong embraces. She had surprised herself, because it had been years since she'd even thought about making love to a man, and that long period of abstinence seemed quenched in one night. She'd known from the moment they met, when he first grabbed her hand to run into the rain, that she was attracted to him, but she'd gotten good at keeping up walls through the years. Tonight, they'd all come tumbling down. And it felt good.

Seth slept peacefully, a mere shadow in the evening light from the window. Moments from their whispered conversations during the last few hours repeated in her mind. He'd told her about growing up in Mumbai, the son of a local seamstress and a schoolteacher. The oldest of five kids, he made breakfast for everyone on a daily basis, got them ready for school and helped them with their homework every night, but he lived for his vacations when he could escape to his grandparents' farm near Seoni. His grandfather, one of the village elders, knew every creature who lived on or passed through his land. He had spent years studying them, and Seth told Natalie that Papaji knew more about animals, their migration, and social habits than any other person—educated or not—that he'd ever met.

Papaji had imbued Seth with a curiosity about the animal world that he'd translated into a business over the years. Seth started as a veterinary assistant at one of the local zoos, then took some classes and worked his way through university, dropping out only a couple of months before graduation because his money ran out.

"I had to be creative," he told her, so he relied on his wits, became a tour guide for a state forest and liked it so much that he applied for a job at the local TV station. "The rest is of historical significance." He grinned.

Though his grandfather had died suddenly of a heart attack while tending to his herb patch, at least he had seen Seth's first appearance as a guest on a local TV news show, and he'd been confident that Seth would succeed.

"Every time I see the green light on a camera, I think of

him and send up a prayer," Seth had said in a reverent whisper. He absently played with a long strand of her hair, then brought himself back to the moment and smiled into her eyes. "He would have loved to meet you and Sophie."

She smiled back and almost told him about Danny and Stephen, but she wanted at least this night, this weekend, with him before the story of the school shooting came out and her reality started seeping back into her daily life. She'd managed to step out of her media nightmare for a long while. This had become a place to start healing, which both surprised and pleased her. But she still needed more time.

She placed her hand against the window now, and its clammy coldness reminded her that this moment was very real and that hiding from life wouldn't last forever. She sighed.

She turned, watching him sleep, and took a silent step toward him.

With one finger, she tentatively reached out and touched him to make sure the moment was real, that she was still there. In the act of making love, she'd discovered she was, indeed, still alive. Still there.

She smiled and sighed and looked back out the window.

On the street below, she saw movement. Several people running. Then more came after them, and within moments, the street was full and the sounds that must have woken her up filled the canyon between the buildings. She opened the window and a warm current of humid air made her draw back her face. She'd become so used to air conditioning for the past couple of days that she'd forgotten how hot Thailand had become over the last month or so.

Now she could see a group of people—red shirts, protestors in the same group Siriporn had been following—and behind them, at least half a dozen military.

"What's going on?" Seth stood behind her, the sheet wrapped around his waist, the contrast between the white sheet and his brown body so enticing that she wanted to crawl back into bed with him, then another shout brought her attention back to the window.

"I'm not sure. I think this must be part of the demonstration everyone was talking about earlier. I know that there's been some problems with the government, but I must admit I haven't really been following it. When you're at the sanctuary, you're pretty much cut off from the rest of the world."

She watched as the group of red-shirted people scattered into the darkness below, some followed by the militia who appeared to be carrying guns. It all seemed a bit surreal, like a scene from an action movie.

"Something's obviously going on. Let's turn on the television and see if there's anything on the news." Seth headed for the remote on the bedside table and perched on the edge of the bed as he scanned the channels. "Well, I never . . ."

"What is it?"

"The TV stations have all been shut down. Looks like the military has taken over."

"What does that mean?"

"I have absolutely no idea."

Natalie moved from the windows to peer at the television. No matter which station Seth flipped to, the message appeared the same: The Center for the Administration of Peace and Order had temporarily halted broadcast. She'd never been in a country that had the power to shut down the television stations. But for that matter, she'd never experienced a military *coup d'état*.

Within moments, the phone rang. Andrew had heard the demonstrations as well, and had called the front desk. Nothing they could do tonight, he told her, but they must be on the road back home first thing in the morning.

She hung up the phone and told Seth, who'd already begun gathering his clothes and getting dressed. All the warmth and passion of only a few hours ago had dissipated.

"Don't go outside," he warned her a few moments later as they stood at her door. "I'll see you in a few hours." He paused long enough to drop a lingering kiss on her lips, touched her cheek, then disappeared down the hallway.

When she turned to the window again, the sky had brightened a little. She stood, watching a few pairs of headlights cutting through the early dawn light, and. for the first time, she wondered about Siriporn and worried about both him and Mali. That must have been on Andrew's mind when he called earlier. She made a mental note to ask him whether he'd heard anything.

Thirty-Seven

He that has eyes to see and
ears to hear may convince himself that
no mortal can keep a secret. If his lips
are silent, he chatters with his fingertips;
betrayal oozes out of him at every pore.
-Sigmund Freud

As soon as they pulled into the sanctuary's drive, Mali caught up with the truck and stuck her head in the window. "Natalie, your mum has called at least ten times. She's frantic. You should call her immediately."

Without taking her suitcase to her cabin, Natalie went straight to the office phone and called home, trying in vain to explain to her mother that the situation in Bangkok wasn't as dangerous as the international news stations reported.

"Natalie, I insist you come home," Maman's voice crackled over the phone. A bad connection. "We didn't want you to leave to begin with. Your father thought you were running away, and you know you can't run away from life. *Rien ne pèse tant que un secret.* You know that, Natalie darling. Nothing weighs more than a secret. It'll follow you, my sweet."

Natalie crossed her arms over her chest. "I wasn't . . ."

"CNN is showing pictures of military patrolling the streets, Natalie. Enough of this foolishness. Come home!"

"Maman, I'm five hours from Bangkok, a very long distance from the uprising." She'd never tell her mother she'd just come home from the capital city or that she'd seen military patrolling the streets below her hotel window. And even if she did tell the truth, the events in Bangkok didn't affect the highly-isolated sanctuary. No matter what Natalie said, she couldn't convince her mother that she didn't see or hear or experience anything like what was going on in Bangkok.

Somewhere behind her, Natalie heard Andrew make a crack about how hysterical American women can be. She turned and put a finger to her lips to shush him. No way would he understand that Maman's worrying had a different edge. Maman felt more upset that her daughter wasn't dealing with her grief than she was about the uprising.

Natalie sucked in a deep breath, but before she could utter another word, her mother was off and running, rambling about Natalie's inconsiderateness and how she could travel halfway across the world to an unstable country when she had family back in North Carolina that were also going through the grieving process, didn't she understand what she needed to do? She had to stop running away. Natalie felt her lips and shoulders tighten and turned her back on the other people in the office as she tried to stop Maman-the-runaway-train and get a word in edgewise.

"Maman . . ."

She kept on chattering, not hearing Natalie at all.

"Maman, it's like going from Wilmington to Asheville. That's how far away Bangkok is from where I am . . ."

Again, Maman rolled right over Natalie's words, still harping on how Natalie ignored her own grief, how she should be there with family who understood rather than halfway across the world, that this uprising in Thailand was dangerous and that it was imperative that she come home.

"Maman!" Natalie didn't normally raise her voice, but sometimes it seemed necessary.

No answer on the other end of the phone. Finally, Maman listened.

"I know you're worried, but I'm sure Nonna and Boppy worried about you when Pop brought you to the States, and I know for a fact that you didn't go back to Provence until I was ten, so how is that different from what I'm doing? You were only a teenager! I'm thirty-six years old. Big difference. I'm not a child anymore. I own a business. I've been divorced and supporting myself for years. I'm level-headed and smart and well-traveled. Please, please, please calm down about this. I'm not going to step in the middle of machine-gun fire, believe me."

Natalie paused for a moment, expecting a response. Getting none, she jumped right back in and continued. The words pummeled out of her mouth.

"Remember how the reporters made my world a fish bowl after the shooting?" Her throat constricted and the space behind her eyes itched and watered. "The pain of losing a child never abates, Maman. It's indescribable. And you know that sometimes the grief is . . . well, it's like a freight train without brakes. Uncontrollable. Even you, my own parents, cannot possibly understand the impossible agony of . . . putting one foot in front of the other." She swallowed hard. "There's nothing more difficult during the first year after a child's death than just . . . living."

When Natalie found herself smiling—even painful smiles—that first year, she felt guilty. Here in Thailand, she had been able to smile again. No guilt. Yes, she thought about Danny and Stephen all the time, but she persisted, attempting to live again.

"I'm doing what they would have wanted. I'm trying to help save some of the most sensitive creatures on earth." She knew in her heart of hearts that was true, and it should make sense to Maman, too.

Still nothing on the other end.

"I'm still grieving, Maman. I always will be. But being here and being able to help others has proven to me that I still have something left to give. Do you understand?"

Maman sighed. "Of course, I understand. We are grieving with you, my darling. That's why I want you home. Please. Come home."

Natalie closed her eyes, and Seth came to mind. She wished he were by her side, offering his sympathetic shoulders and that thought surprised her. Normally, she wouldn't long for a man's strength to complement her own. And since he wasn't there, she leaned against the door jamb and picked at a piece of peeling paint. She heard her mother sigh and knew she had meant no harm. What she said and did came from a place of love, yet Natalie knew that being home would mean prolonging the grief until Maman felt it was over. And lord only knows when that would have been.

"Are you sure it's safe there, Natalie?" Maman's voice softened, yet she still sounded nervous.

"I'm fine, Maman. I have more of a chance of being hit by lightning than shot by a protestor. Believe me, I'm in the middle of nowhere. In the jungle. In the mountains. So far from Bangkok that most people here have only seen pictures of the city."

Finally, Maman seemed convinced, so they spent a few moments catching up on family news, then Natalie reminded her mother how much this phone call would probably cost, which convinced Maman to say her goodbyes. Natalie hung up the phone in its cradle and rubbed her eyes before turning around to leave.

Seth sat facing her, his back and elbows resting against the table, his legs stretched out in front of him. He smiled at her sadly. She caught her breath. How much had he heard?

He patted the seat beside him and beckoned her over.

"Will you forgive me? When I arrived, you were in the middle of your conversation and I wanted to talk to you, so I sat and waited." He wore a khaki shirt, sleeves rolled up, tail out, unbuttoned to the third button, and he hadn't shaved, but instead of looking scruffy, he looked sexier than he had in that tux in Bangkok, if that was possible. She refrained from touching him.

"I was talking to my mother."

"I got that."

"What else did you get?"

"That she's worried about you."

"Hmmm. And?"

"That there's something—no, someone—you haven't told me about."

He'd heard more than she wanted anyone here to know. *Damn.* "That's true, but it's not another man." She took a deep breath and turned away. *Tell him,* her inner voice said. *He's going to find out anyway.* But another part of her refused. "They're my children, and they're not something I want to discuss right now. I haven't even had a chance to unpack."

"I know this might be a bit too soon, Natalie, but I do care for you and . . ."

"—Natalie, I need to talk to you." Mali suddenly stood behind them, wringing a cloth in her hands. Her face was streaked with tears.

Without thinking, Natalie left the tense discussion with Seth and went straight to Mali, enveloping the smaller woman in a hug. For several moments, Mali simply cried, but when she could finally get her breath, they sat down. Natalie glanced over Mali's shoulder to see that Seth had left, always the gentleman, so they had privacy.

"What in the world has you so upset?" Natalie wiped Mali's last tear away with her thumb, then caught Mali's hands in hers. To see the normally strong and cheerful Mali disintegrating made her want to cry herself.

"Siriporn's gone. He disappeared right after you left for Bangkok, and I know he's probably down there . . . but now they're saying that some of the protestors are dead, and he's not bloody answering his phone, damn him, and none of his friends . . . none of them have seen him for the past couple of days. I talked to one of them only an hour ago." She blew her nose and raised her black eyes to Natalie.

Natalie had seen that type of pain before. In the mirror.

She knew what it felt like to lose a son, whether to a senseless act of violence or to a choice the son made, a loss was a loss. "The last time they saw him, the army had begun . . ." Mali's voice cracked again. "Oh, God, Natalie, they were raising their guns!"

"No, no, no, Mali. Don't think that way. Listen, let's sit down. Talk. Calmly. Tell me what happened."

She steered Mali to the seat Seth had vacated. Mali wiped the tears from her cheeks with the flat of her palms.

"Right after you left, Siriporn came to me and told me he needed to return to Bangkok. I did not . . . I did not handle that news well. I'm afraid we got into a bit of a tiff." She inhaled in a jagged fashion like a child who'd been crying for a long time. "He left without speaking to me. You weren't here. Andrew had left. The only person I could talk to was Karina, and you know she's not particularly fond of my son."

Natalie restrained herself from grimacing. One thing she knew for sure about Karina was that she probably had never had a compassionate thought. Andrew, her older brother, had practically raised her, and she'd been by his side throughout the time he'd built his philanthropic empire. She believed his word was gospel, though everyone knew Andrew and Siriporn barely tolerated each other. Mali might have had no one else to talk to about her heartbreak, but she would have received more sympathy from one of the elephants than from Karina.

"I overheard her talking to Peter about my concerns later on after I'd asked her to keep it to herself, and you know me, Natalie, I prize my privacy so I confronted them. I'm afraid I could have used a bit more tact."

"Tact? Do you really need to be tactful with those two?"

Mali shrugged with her palms up, ducked her head and gave Natalie a tearful grin. "Truth is, I was downright crude. I read them both the riot act for not being sympathetic. I believe I called them sub-human. By the time I finished, neither one of them would look at me straight."

Natalie giggled. "I think I would've paid money to see that."

Mali shook her head. "Maybe you won't think it's so funny if I tell you what happened after you all returned."

Not much else would have surprised Natalie, but she sat back, folded her arms across her chest and said, "Try me."

"When I woke up the next day, this place was pretty much a

ghost town."

"What do you mean?"

"I'm afraid I ran everyone off. Karina and Peter were gone. Siriporn was gone. You and Andrew were gone. I've been running the place by myself ever since." Her chin quivered.

Natalie realized now that Mali's tears weren't all about Siriporn's disappearance—though she definitely had a right to worry. Mali was purely and simply exhausted. No one could run this place alone.

"To put the kidney in the crust, Andrew blew his stack when I called and told him what happened." That admission brought on a fresh onslaught of tears. "Can you please talk to him for me, Natalie? He's the only one who can find out what's happened to my son, but right now, he's not talking to me."

Though Natalie doubted she'd get any further than Mali had with Andrew, she promised her friend she'd do what she could. They hugged, a hard and affectionate embrace, and Mali headed for the kitchen. Natalie went to her cabin to unpack and while taking her shower thought long and hard about the best way to approach Andrew.

When she was dressed, her hair still damp, she headed for Andrew's cabin, the meeting weighing heavily on her mind. There were a million things she'd rather do other than to talk to her boss about the sanctuary's missing personnel.

Thirty-Eight

This is a night when kings in golden mail
ride their elephants over the mountains.
-John Cheever

Sophie stood in the enclosure and watched Natalie out of her good eye, waiting patiently as Natalie watched Seth and Rob and Sidecar set up to film, laughing and joking with each other, confident in their new project. As much as Natalie wanted to show Sophie off to the world, she fought a "what if" feeling. What if the guys spooked her? What if Sophie suddenly forgot everything she'd learned in the past six months? What if having Ali and Thaya and Pahpao waiting outside made her suddenly stubborn and more interested in heading off to the mud pits with them?

"*Sok*, Sophie! *Sok*!" Natalie barked the command to walk backward, her voice as deep and authoritative as she could make it. She touched Sophie's hip with the pole, a medium push, a flea touch compared to the stinging dig of the *ankus*. Sophie inched back, taking her time, but following Natalie's commands.

"Good girl, Sophie." Natalie's voice softened. "Good girl."

Under the heavy weight of her hair, Natalie's neck and back were soaked with sweat, both from nervousness and the day's sweltering humidity. Filming would end soon, and she was happy to see it end, though the end of the project also meant that Seth no longer had any reason to stay. They'd talked about it late into the night as they faced each other in her twin-sized bed.

"I can squeeze in a couple more days here," Seth had whispered as he wiped a curl of her hair from her forehead with a gentle finger. "But we have an assignment in Borneo I need to get to. They'll understand me needing a couple of days' break before I start, but no more than that."

He adjusted his arm beneath her shoulders and slid his leg down hers until their ankles locked. Their bodies fit together perfectly, and when she glanced down at the contrast between them, she was struck by the fact that it was a very subtle difference. Her own skin had become so tanned that she was only a few shades lighter than he was. Mali called them "handsome as movie stars."

Handsome, Natalie thought. The right word for Seth, but for her? No one had ever called her that.

With the previous evening's memory still fresh in her thoughts, she eyed him, in his bright white cotton shirt, his black hair curly and shining with the day's humidity, his mouth straight and serious, intent on getting a good day's shooting done without incidents.

And so far, Sophie was cooperating perfectly. She backed up a few more feet and was clear of the enclosure.

"*How*, Sophie!" Natalie gave the order to stop. She leaned toward the elephant and breathed in Sophie's warm scent, a combination of bananas and dung and sweet potatoes and mud. Earthy. Heavy. Elephant.

Sophie stopped and reached out her trunk to touch the pole, as if reassuring herself of its location since it was behind her and out of sight. To the right side by a grove of palm trees, three mahouts watched from atop their ellies. Natalie and Siriporn had talked about getting the mahouts off the elephants' backs, but changing their mindset was still a work-in-progress. All of them—humans and elephants alike—watched Sophie intently. None of the mahouts held their *ankuses*—Natalie had won that argument—and Chanchai, his legs straddling Ali's neck, finally appeared comfortable without it.

This was the third time they'd all joined together, working the elephants with only their voices and the protected contact pole. As Andrew pointed out, Ali, Thaya, and Pahpao were always well-behaved, as long as Ali wasn't in *mustph*. They knew each other well, having spent the past ten years together at the sanctuary. They really didn't need to be retrained. It was the mahouts who needed an education. They believed using the *ankus* was the only way to get an elephant to behave, but at least they were trying and that was major considering how ingrained their beliefs were.

Natalie watched the mahouts working their elephants and wished Siriporn was here. He had been a convert to protected contact and was a valuable partner, but he was still missing in action. Andrew had checked with his contacts in the Bangkok military after Natalie talked to him, but he found out nothing. Mali had barely spoken to Andrew after that. It was clear that her son's well-being came first, and Andrew knew it. The problem was that neither of them would budge when it came to their opinions about how to raise Mali's oldest child.

Natalie couldn't blame Mali. No matter what kind of issues Andrew and Siriporn had, the least Andrew could have done was to offer her some comfort. After all, he was her son. But Andrew wasn't going out of his way to help. Mali called him a *wanker*, the closest she came to vulgarity.

Seth checked with his production company to get a list of those protestors who'd been shot or arrested. A day later, he received a phone call. Siriporn hadn't shown up on either list. When Natalie relayed the info to Mali, she wordlessly grasped Natalie's hand. Still, no word from Siriporn, and the protests throughout the country continued, even though the military had taken control of the government.

And neither Karina nor Hatcher had contacted Andrew. No one knew where they'd gone nor had anyone heard from them. The mahouts gossiped that Dr. Peter and Mr. Andrew's sister had run away together for a romantic tryst, but Natalie highly doubted it. It was more likely that Hatcher figured his disappearance might remind everyone of how much he did at the sanctuary. Andrew growled more often than he spoke these days.

He did that now, as the elephants moved together in a tight little pod with her on the ground amidst them. She peered up at Pahpao. Khalan sat atop the middle-aged female's neck, wearing a Yankees baseball cap that Seth had given him last week. Rumor had it he didn't remove the hat even when he took a shower, that's how much he loved it.

The elephants parted, and for a moment, Natalie saw Rob and Sidecar pointing their cameras right at her as she commanded Sophie to move forward. She smiled contentedly when Sophie did exactly as she was told.

"I'm proud of you, ol' girl," she whispered and patted the elephant's wide foreleg. Sophie flapped her ears and lay her trunk against Natalie's arm as she always did when she knew she was going to get a treat.

As Natalie fed her some bananas, she heard a familiar sound: the clicking of a camera lens close to her ear. She froze and glanced up, half-expecting to see a gaggle of news photographers and journalists, yelling questions about her sons and gun control and demanding to know whether she even thought of the other parents who'd lost children. She was prepared to bolt, but the knee-jerk reaction receded when Seth lowered his camera and said, "I've never seen anything more beautiful than you two girls."

Natalie ducked her head, embarrassed at the emotion welling in her eyes, but Sophie shifted, forcing herself into Natalie's view. Sophie's big brown eye stared right into Natalie's, then the long fringed lashes closed and opened as if Sophie had just winked.

THE BULL *they call Ali pushes his way to Sophie's side. He is taller than all of the elephants and wider than most, but he doesn't cause problems and is respected for that. He's mild and quietly confident. Noble.*

Sophie lifts her trunk and touches the inside of his mouth in greeting, then stands with him, quietly eating. He is the only elephant she recognizes from long ago. Everyone else is gone, but the big bull is part of that old memory.

Long ago, he led the trail of logging elephants up and down the rocky, jungle mountain road every day. She followed behind, smelling his scent in the dirt and on the small trees they uprooted as the herd traveled single file up and back, up and back. Every day for many seasons, she followed him up the mountain, then back down. Together always, the elephants were attached to each other by a chain that wound through the iron ring encircling each elephant's ankle. It was that ring that created the pain Sophie has endured for so long.

She did not share Ali's food pile or even the same grazing area when they were in the logging camp, because females were always separated from males, but she knew him. He became the patriarch of their logging family, taking the place of the large matriarchs that normally led the herd. Nothing in their captivity was normal, nothing was the way nature intended. Mothers and calves were separated. Large bull elephants who hadn't yet mated worked side by side with females whose scent drove the bulls wild. Every season, at least one of them had to be killed. Some charged right off the skinny mountain roads, pulling several other elephants with them.

Sophie was in her thirtieth year when Ali vanished in a big truck that usually arrived to remove one of the fallen members of the herd. Another bull took his place on the line the next day, another bull left his scent on the trail and the trees.

One season later, the big truck came for Sophie. The iron ring remained on her ankle. Another chain was attached to it, and the pain stole Sophie's memory of the following couple years. She now remembers only pain. No sounds. No family. No delicious mouthfuls like the zucchinis the woman had given Sophie earlier. There was no memory of life between the truck and this moment.

Throughout the long time between the days she'd worked with Ali and her arrival here, she had not thought of him, yet she searched constantly for the family she'd known long ago. She yearned for the day she would find one of them. Then she arrived here, and when she caught the scent of her long-ago friend, she recognized him immediately. He represents family for her.

He bumps her now, rubbing his hip against hers, finally bumping her out of the way so he can steal some of her food. He chews loudly, and from the crunch, he is eating some palm fronds. Relishing them. Sophie presses her hip back against him, feeling his solidness, and she sighs with the contentment of an aging grandmother.

Thirty-Nine

Let me not pray to be sheltered from dangers,
but to be fearless in facing them.
Let me not beg for the stilling of my pain,
but for the heart to conquer it.
-Rabrindranath Tagore

NATALIE AND SETH WALKED in silence, hand-in-hand. Their shoes scuffed along the moonlit dirt road, the only noise other than an occasional night bird. Natalie thought about the comments that had been made about Hatcher and wondered how she could have missed the tender side of him that Mali and the others described. Had she been blind to it or had he changed so drastically when he came into her company that he acted like a true Jekyll and Hyde? Did he hate her so much that he couldn't even be himself when she was around?

The flickering light cast shadows on Seth's face. She couldn't see his eyes, but she felt them on her. He turned her to him and held both her hands in his. Tightly.

"I have something I need to tell you, Natalie." He said her name softly. Seriously.

He's going to say it, she thought, and her stomach quivered. *He's going to tell me he loves me.* Many years before, she had stood in front of another man who'd said the very same words, and she'd felt almost the same emotion, but the passage of time had colored her life and instead of feeling like the world was going to be delivered to her feet, she felt as though taking a step into a new world would be the bravest move of her life. She held her breath and fought hard not to swallow because she was sure there'd be an audible gulp.

He paused for what felt like five minutes, though she knew it was only seconds. "I don't know how to say this . . ."

Now she could see his eyes and knew deep in the pit of her stomach that he wasn't going to say what she expected. "Say whatever it is, Seth. I don't do well with suspense."

"Well, there's something I know . . ." He dropped her hands and wiped his hair back, then peered up at her through his eyelashes, his face fully illuminated in a shaft of moonlight. "I know about the Lakeview School shootings. Natalie, I know everything."

Her hands dropped to her sides like stones. She swayed a little and a thrumming filled her ears. He continued talking, though she only heard every other phrase or so.

"We have to . . . research team . . . necessary to your story . . . so sorry . . . overruled by the producer . . ."

She caught her breath and talked herself into listening. *Focus, Natalie. Damn it. Don't act like a freaking baby. Focus.*

"You can't tell the whole story," she blurted. "This program that you've shot . . . it's not about me. It's about Sophie. About the sanctuary. Why the hell is what happened in my life even important?"

"I agree with you, believe me, but I also understand the producers' plight. We fight an ongoing battle with hundreds of shows that viewers can choose to watch. Sometimes you have to dangle a carrot for them to choose yours."

"A carrot? A school shooting where dozens of people died is now a *carrot*? You know, I left North Carolina to get away from people like you. And now you're as inconsiderate of my feelings as they were. I thought you were different, but you're all the same, aren't you?" She pulled her shaking hands away from him. "The goddamn story is number one. You never consider the people who are in the middle of what could be the most devastating moments of their lives. You never think about what happens when you leave. You never think about grief and sadness and . . . and the tragedy that knocks you in the stomach like a baseball bat. You never think about the people left behind."

"I don't want to do this," he said, reaching for her face. "Believe me. This is not my decision." His eyes glistened.

"What *do* you want?" she asked. "It feels like I'm being ambushed. I'm the one who's going to be in the limelight. My boys . . ."

"I think you're in it anyway, Nat. But people will sympathize. You have to strengthen your backbone."

She took a step back and shook her head from side to side. Her cheeks burned, but her thoughts had never been clearer. "That's strange that you say that because that's what I've been doing for more than a year. Almost two, as a matter of fact. Strengthening my backbone. Healing. Dealing with nightmares and paralyzing anxiety. PTSD. And it takes a helluva lot more than a couple of years to recover from losing a child. I'll never recover. No parent who loses a child does. But you and your producers don't care about that, do you?"

She swiped a hand over her mouth and avoided looking at him. "I've been trying to balance everything in my life, but reporters keep butting in and reminding me of what's going to be repeated over and over and over. That's why I came here. I didn't want to hear it anymore." Her hands tightened into fists, and she faced him squarely, as she'd faced so many other people from the media. Angrily. Fearlessly. "I want it to stop."

"I'm so sorry for everything you've been through, baby." Seth stepped forward and reached out to hug her.

"Why is it that I hear a 'but' in your voice?" She dodged him. Her jaw hardened.

Without another word, he turned on his heel and started to leave.

"Wait, Seth. Wait."

He stopped, but he didn't turn around. She could see he was breathing heavily, obviously upset. He wasn't the only one, but nothing in her life had ever seemed so clear. It was time to trust someone with her story.

She sat on the stump of a giant tree they came to, and in short, hesitant bursts, she told Seth about the hordes of journalists who drove her from home and to this remote part of Thailand. She shared the dreams she'd had of the boys since coming to the sanctuary, the visions of them when she least expected to see their faces. And when she finished, she sat with her face in her hands and felt him patting her shoulder like any friend would.

A touch, a hug, a shoulder. That's all it took.

The machine-gun-like blasts of forbidden memories pummeled her, beating her relentlessly. She couldn't breathe.

Stephen, the gurgling baby with a sharp fringe of impossibly long eyelashes, gazing up into her face with an impossible innocence.

Danny in third grade, a crooked tooth from a recent bike accident, a cowlick that simply would not stay down, proud as a rooster about his first science project.

Stephen asking to hold the baby when Danny was born, insisting it was his, she had told her it was his, wanting nothing more than to be part of his brother's life.

When had it changed? When had Stephen become a stranger? When did I lose him?

She didn't realize she was sobbing until Seth kneeled before her and held both of her hands in his sturdy fingers and coaxed her to answer his questions about her Stephen.

"He thought I hated him. I didn't hate him," she told Seth, emphasizing the words as if not only trying to convince him but to also convince herself. "I didn't hate him."

Seth simply nodded. He knew. He had told her he knew. No one ever knew what to say. That's why she hadn't told the story, but she'd started now. It was coming as surely as water does when you open the faucet.

"He loved his brother. I know he did. That's why . . . that's why . . . .." A wrenching breath caved in her chest. Seth kept holding her hands in his and didn't say a word. "That's why I didn't understand. I don't . . . I don't understand why."

"Go ahead, love."

"How could he have done it?"

"Done what?"

She stared straight ahead, no longer in Thailand. She was home. North Carolina. It was two years ago, once again, on that devastating day at Danny's school.

She had felt the tension in the group of parents who surrounded her, all of them kept in place by a piece of flimsy yellow police tape. She heard the crackled vibration of silenced cell phones that rippled from one end of the crowd to another. Then those shots. Those horrible shots. And the pandemonium that took over after that. Each parent, each family member in that crowd cried out for their own child, the child trapped in the Lakeview Middle School with shooters who'd kept the whole school captive. So many shots. Then the long silence. The loudest, longest silence. And, suddenly, the pounding boots of the SWAT team as they found their way to the cafeteria door entrance. Shouts from inside the school. Bright flashes of light. More shouts. Then another silence. Never-ending. Moments later, ambulances and fire engines. Sirens. Screaming. Panicked voices. Often, she awoke screaming when she dreamt of that sound in the middle of the night. In fact, Sophie had heard Natalie scream so often that she came to the bars and threw her trunk over Natalie until the screaming stopped.

God.

Stephen.

Danny.

Her sons, her babies. Her heart.

A fresh wave of emotion. She shook so hard it felt as if her body would split apart.

"Are you alright, love?"

"I'll never be alright. Ever."

"Talk to me. Keep telling me the story. Cry, if you need to. I'm here. Sometimes giving a voice to the pain is the only way to get past it."

"There's no getting past it." She didn't want to talk about that day, but it wouldn't be the first time she'd been forced to. There had been so many interviews, then the month-long court proceedings. And no one could comfort her. No one could explain why it happened. No one could give her back her boys. Even her own family couldn't offer any answers. She had long ago given up on God.

"I know, love, but you have to talk about it." Seth held her upper arm and had one palm to her cheek. His eyes were moist.

"You know already, don't you?" She stepped back and her hands flew to her throat. "You know."

"I always have."

His simple answer floored her. Yet, as she wrapped her mind around it, it made sense. Of course he knew. The story had been in all the newspapers: *Teenager Shoots His Own Brother in School Shooting.*

What no one seemed to understand, though, was that Stephen would never have shot Danny. He couldn't have. She always knew that, but no one listened.

"The newspapers had it all wrong, Seth. I was sure of it. But then I talked to Stephen's friends."

She paused, picked at an insect bite on the back of her hand. Kept scratching the bite because it kept her focused, reminded her where she was. The present. Now. Thailand. Almost two years later. Two years after. She pulled her nail over the bite one more time and drew blood.

"It was an accident, they said. No one even realized it was Danny until it was too late. I knew Stephen wouldn't have done it on purpose."

Stephen had gone to school that morning with his friends. Kyle had driven, as he usually did because he was two years older. He had an old beat-up Ford. The perfect car for tailgating and riding Main Street looking for girls on weekend nights. Unfortunately, it had broken down that day, and the guys who'd driven with him—Stephen included—had to walk almost two miles to make it to school. Stephen was supposed to give a speech to the Student Farmer's club during first period, but he was late. The teacher sent him to the principal's office, but he never made it there. Instead he joined his friends and groused about the school principal and their teachers, and the kids created a plan for getting out of their classes. Permanently.

They all sneaked out into the parking lot, went back to Kyle's car, and smoked a joint. Then Kyle showed them what he'd taken from his father's closet: two revolvers and three shotguns.

"Let's scare the shit out of them," Kyle said to his friends. "There's one for each of us. Here." He handed them out and the boys stood there, the weight of the guns heavy in their hands, a ripple of forbidden excitement bubbling in each of their chests. "They'll never fuck with us again when today is over."

Kyle was right. The principal and teachers would never fuck with him again. He lived in jail now. Natalie had watched him sob on the witness stand, the only one of the four boys to survive. And in front of her, his parents held tight to each other, watching their only child as he was sentenced for the murder, the cold-blooded murder, of children and teachers. The courtroom filled with the moans and cries of those family members, but Natalie couldn't cry that day. She sat on that courtroom pew as still as stone, her heart barely beating.

Kyle had been Stephen's best friend, had been to Natalie's house more times than she could count. She'd known him since his fifth birthday. Seeing him walk out of that courtroom in shackles was like losing a third son.

She forced herself to visit him a month later when the night-mares wouldn't stop, and Dr. Littlefield had told her the only way she would find out the truth was to ask Kyle himself. She went to the prison alone, jumped every time a lock clicked, squeezed her fists so tightly that her fingernails scored her palms.

"The boys went back into that school, and Kyle started looking for the principal," she told Seth, breathing carefully and choosing her words. "They meant to scare him. A stupid prank.

But someone saw the guns. The other kids heard the screams. Someone called the cops. They got scared. He and Mark and Jeremy started shooting. Just shooting. Shooting and shooting and shooting. None of them had held a gun before but they'd played video games like Slasher III and they knew how to aim for the head. The heart. They called to each other as they shot, claiming twenty points, a hundred points. A bonus. Kyle said they heard someone yelling, Danny yelling at Stephen, he said, and Kyle said he told Stephen to point his gun at a group of kids, and Danny . . . Danny stepped out in front of them. He tried to protect them. I think he thought . . . I think he thought Stephen would stop. He wouldn't shoot."

She wound her fingers together in her lap. A drop of wetness fell on the back of her right hand. She wiped it away with her thumb.

"I should've seen it," Natalie said. "Stephen was miserable after his father left. He blamed himself. And when Parker never called again, Stephen sunk deeper and deeper into a depression. I should've taken him to a therapist, but I thought he'd get past it like Danny had. Danny was fine, so I thought Stephen would be, too. And I was so busy trying to keep myself together and trying to put food on the table that I fooled myself into thinking everything was . . . everything was going to be okay. It's a mother's instinct to protect, and as long as I fed the boys and put clothes on their backs, they would be fine. At least that's what I wanted to believe, but I couldn't protect them. I couldn't protect either of them. I failed. That shooting . . . all those deaths . . . I could have done something. I should've known. I'm as guilty as those boys were."

Seth reached for her again and hugged her, whispering in her ear, "No, no, no, my sweet Natalie. Horrible tragedies like that are never someone else's fault. Life is a series of heartbreaks and joys. You know that. We all struggle. We all fail. Sometimes we find the light of happiness, but most days we simply move on through life's moments. Through the pain. The suffering of being alive."

He kissed her forehead. Above them, several monkeys played

tag in the tree's branches. From a distance, one of the elephants trumpeted. He gazed toward the sound, softly chuckled. "You know, I think sometimes that humans are conscious of the causes of our emotions. But animals . . . well, animals simply react to them. They feel pain and sadness and grief like we do, but they also know that life goes on, and they do not feel guilty for living. All you have to do is live with elephants for a while to see that. They feel the importance of family and of bonds, of supporting each other and working together. But they don't make that a difficulty. They don't make it dramatic or anxiety ridden. They don't feel guilt." He took her face in his hands. "You shouldn't either, dear one. You shouldn't either."

Forty

> He who gains a victory over other men is strong; but he
> who gains a victory over himself
> is all powerful.
> -Lao Tzu

TELLING SETH ABOUT THE boys had set off an anxiety episode that made Natalie want to find an old empty tree, crawl inside, and turn into moss. Her chest squeezed tightly, her lungs struggled for breath, her sight swam as if she had drunk way too much.

She retreated to Sophie's enclosure, slept very little that night, imagining the Pandora's Box that had been opened and all the ills in the world being visited upon her like an upset bees nest. She dreamt of flying things that hit her body like icy projectiles, bringing up boils on her skin, blinding an eye, crippling a finger. More than once, she woke herself screaming from that time right between fully awake and deeply asleep.

Reality hit her the next morning that the truth was that the story released another type of evil upon her world. As soon as Seth's show aired, her family would be on the receiving end of the media's desperate need to make more of her story. They'd speculate about her life, follow the blog she'd started to write about Sophie, steal away what little privacy and normalcy she'd built. Everyone wanted to figure out what the mother of a mass shooter was like, especially a shooter who killed his own brother, her other son.

There. She said it.

She spent the day with Sophie and was grateful when no one tried to find her. She suspected Seth might have kept them away.

Now, the sunset created colors they might not yet have named, and she was exhausted. She wanted nothing more than a few hours of sleep in her own bed, but the argument with Seth marched back and forth through her mind like the foreign legion had marched through the Sahara.

Yes, she'd escaped any human interaction by spending the night in the enclosure, it was not a good place to sleep. Now, she rolled onto her right knee, enjoying the safe cave Sophie's body made.

She thought about her conversation with Seth and it took on a different light. Had he thought she would be fine about sharing such a painful story with the world? On the other hand, why would she understand his need to add the drama of a school shooting to a story about elephants? Wasn't the story of Sophie's transformation enough? He was producing a TV show about animals for chrissakes, not people. No need to learn anything else. Especially about her boys. And now that he knew her story and cared about her, wouldn't it be all the more reason to leave her personal life out of the production?

She leaned against Sophie's leg and looked up. The elephant's trunk and head created a dark, cool shadow against the orange-and-yellow sky.

Closing her eyes, she imagined Seth's face as they made love. "Do you know how good you feel to me?" he'd said. "How long it has been since I've felt this way about a woman?" His black eyes softened as he lowered his head to take her mouth, the warm moistness of his lips on hers. And she remembered the surprising hardness of his shoulders and back beneath her hands as the magic built up in her lower stomach and exploded throughout her body.

She forced herself to inhale to the count of eight, exhale to the count of ten. Painfully. Slowly. Opened her belly with the breath. Exhaled every last wisp. Three times. Four. Her body started to relax. She concentrated on the breath, the way her yoga instructor had taught her. Tried to empty her mind.

Life is about change, she told herself. *Endings are beginnings. Life is a series of cycles: birth, death, rebirth, and so on.*

"Dr. Natalie! Dr. Natalie!"

Natalie heard the distant call and wanted to ignore it.

"Dr. Natalie! We must needs you!"

"Who's there?"

"I am Khalan. Hurry, Dr. Natalie. We must needs you!"

She moved from beneath Sophie. "What's going on?"

Coming down the road, she heard Andrew's voice and realized the light was coming from his truck's headlights. Khalan grabbed her arm and pulled her toward the truck, then unceremoniously shoved her inside. Andrew threw the truck into reverse and the tires spat dust as they wheeled around, then switched into a forward motion. She waited a couple of moments, then asked again.

"What's going on?"

Andrew glanced at her. "Got a call from one of the elephant handlers we work with in the village. Some people call him Sammy. Remember him?"

She nodded. She'd treated his elephant, an ancient matriarch that Sammy and his family treasured like a family pet. Sammy, short and bow-legged, laughed about everything. She liked him and appreciated how he took such good care of his ellie, Pira.

Andrew continued. "Pira started getting upset tonight, so Sammy followed her to the edge of the forest on his plantation. He says she led him to three females and a male. All dead. The male's tusks were gone. Sawed off." He spoke too evenly. Calmly. Andrew spouted off regularly, his temper tantrums legendary throughout the area, but what most people didn't realize was that it was his silence you needed to fear. When he seemed calm, he was actually at his most dangerous.

At that moment her foot hit something cold and steely. She leaned down to move it and traced it with her fingers in the dark.

The long, cold barrel of a rifle. She shivered.

Poaching elephants happened regularly, but she hadn't expected to be thrust into the middle of it. Part of her wanted off this truck right now, as strongly as another part of her wanted to hold the "Save the Elephants" banner high overhead and follow Andrew into battle. That mix of fear and anger and disgust and uncertainty silenced her. She fixed her eyes on the dark road in front of them and felt her blood pulsing in the base of her throat, a slight tremor in her hands.

She didn't know how long they'd been driving when someone pounded twice on the hood of the cab. Andrew slowed down, then took a left down a dirt road that wove through a messy tangle of downed branches and ropes that looked like ivy. A voice that sounded like Khalan's told Andrew to cut the lights and the engine.

Suddenly Natalie couldn't see the trees or the dashboard or Andrew's profile or her hand in front of her face. She heard him breathing and the stifled cough of someone on the truck bed behind them. They sat there in silence for about fifteen minutes until a thin ray of light broke the darkness to her right.

A flashlight.

Khalan jumped off the truck and into the light, greeting what sounded like a group of men. More flashlights sent cones of light into the dark. The jungle came alive with faces. Men, all wearing baseball caps and bandanas over their mouths, came to the driver's side of the truck and spoke to Andrew. He seemed to know several of them and clasped their hands as they spoke with him urgently in Thai.

Then the truck started moving again, slowly following the streams of light as the men led them through the undergrowth and into a clearing. The faint reddening of the night sky and the horizon in the distance told Natalie it was almost dawn. They'd been out all night.

Almost time to have morning tea with Mali on the platform, Natalie thought, and the routine brought a pleasant warmth to her chest.

Andrew stopped the truck when all the lights converged in front of several greyish-black rocks. As Natalie got out her side, she was instantly struck by a smell that reminded her of low tide on a brutally hot day on the Outer Banks. The closer she came to the rocks, the more it became clear they were not rocks at all. The "rocks" were elephants. Brutally beaten elephants. Elephants sliced raggedly as if someone had taken a chainsaw to their limbs. A year ago—even a month ago—the scene would have made Natalie throw up, but now it roused a hot stream of anger in her belly. She stepped in something sticky and slipped, putting her hand to the ground to stop her fall. The blood had spilled and made small ponds around them. Her stomach flipped and brought its contents into her mouth. She blinked rapidly. *Get it together, girl. Get it together.*

The patriarch lay in the middle, two bloody holes where there were once a massive set of tusks.

Natalie paused, wanting to scream, but she told herself to control the anger. She fought with her emotions as she stood with the others in stunned silence. Flashlights shot unforgiving spotlights on the bodies.

Then instinct kicked in. She ran from one elephant to another, head to each chest, listening (hoping) for a heartbeat, her fingers searching the back side of each elephant's ear flap for a pulse, her cheek to each mouth sensing for breath and sniffing for signs of life. One large male and two grown females, one with still-full teats meant for nursing. Natalie palpated the uterine area.

"There must be a young calf somewhere. She gave birth not too long ago. A week. Maybe two," she told Andrew. "Can you check to see if the baby's under one of these elephants? It's either here . . . or it got away with the rest of the herd. God, I hope it's close by."

"I don't know if there is more to this herd." Andrew moved around, shining his flashlight on the ground. "We don't see any other large footprints. All I can see are smaller ones. That baby has to be hiding. Probably petrified. Looks like it circled these larger ones over and over. Something must have scared the humans away or they would have taken the calf with them. They're worth some serious money on the open market."

He swung the flashlight around erratically. "Listen up, everyone! We need to find that calf and get it onto the truck so we can bring it back to the sanctuary before it dies out here. It's probably spooked, so if you do find it, please call me and give me your location. Whatever you do, don't scare it. Remember not to stare or to reach out for it. Let's take it slow and easy. Got it?"

Everyone answered, then fanned out. Their flashlight beams disappeared into the dense grasses and brush.

Natalie followed Andrew, trying to walk as soundlessly as possible, but with every step, she crunched. Finally, she stopped and listened. The guys had gone off to the left, Andrew to the right, so she backtracked to the elephant carcasses, her heart breaking. She stood there and held her breath. In front of where she stood, she heard leaves move, twigs break, and the faint hush-hush-hush of something breathing. Then a cry. Quiet and scared, but a cry. She froze, wondering why she'd been left without a flashlight. In the total darkness she sensed rather than saw an animal. Something half her size.

God, a wild boar. Shit. They're drawn by the smell of blood.

Again, she heard the cry, then realized the sound was closer and as she peered through the darkness, she saw a moving shadow and instinctively knew that it was the baby. The poor thing stood beside what she imagined was its mother. Crying.

Slowly, excruciatingly slowly, Natalie moved in the direction of the calf. She reached out her hand, searching blindly for the orphaned elephant, unsure how big it would be. With only a cursory exam of the mother, Natalie couldn't be quite sure. Her heart beat hard. She held her breath. Again.

Then a warm wetness met her fingers. The tip of a baby elephant's trunk. It trembled. Natalie's eyes watered and she stood still, let the baby come to her. The trunk explored her arm. A squeak escaped, and the trunk disappeared. Natalie exhaled and said, "It's okay." She knew the elephant didn't understand, but she hoped the softness of her tone and her smell would reassure the baby. Another squeak.

Natalie called out softly, "I found it."

Relieved voices answered from all directions. The flashlights started coming closer. Natalie reached out in the direction of where she last heard the baby's cry. It seemed like it was calling for reassurance. A hand brushed against the baby's hide and in the ever-lightening shadows, she saw its silhouette and stood, then pressed her hip against the calf. The baby leaned against her with a deep exhale. Natalie leaned back and wrapped her arm around the little one's neck. It shivered.

"Andrew, walk very slowly," Natalie said, keeping her tone conversational, concerned about spooking the calf. She anchored herself, letting the calf explore her with its mouth. If she had known where they were going or what to expect, she would have brought some cream or milk or something liquid, but how could she know? "I have the baby. If you can come over to the side, we can put the baby between us. Slowly, though. This little one's scared out of its mind."

Andrew whispered to the other guys to go slow. Their flash-lights dimmed and the circle became smaller as they all drew back to the place where Natalie stood. Within another couple of seconds, the men surrounded her and their flashlights shone on the calf in the middle of the human circle. She was small, barely a couple of weeks old, and her eyes were rimmed with fear.

Khalan came up behind Natalie and whispered in her ear, "Baby lost mama. Baby not live long."

"You're wrong," she returned. "You're wrong." But she knew his experience proved otherwise. One of the greatest challenges to any elephant camp was keeping orphaned babies alive. Often they died for no apparent reason. Feeding them the correct formula of mother's milk and providing a social environment as soon as possible was paramount. She wouldn't lose this calf. She couldn't.

Andrew and the two other locals joined Khalan and Natalie. The five of them encircled the baby, someone found a blanket and threw it over the shivering infant's back, and they all worked together to get the baby on the back of the truck. Natalie pulled out a hypodermic filled with a tranquilizer and shot some of it into the calf's hip, whispering, "God, I'm going by my guts here. I'm not even sure how much I've given this little guy. Hope it's not too much."

All the way home, she cradled the baby's head in her lap, listening for her breath and praying to whatever god would listen to her to keep this infant alive.

When they arrived at the sanctuary, the sky, striped with low-hanging pink and orange clouds, felt optimistic.

Forty-One

Any wild elephant group is, in essence, one large and highly sensitive organism. Young elephants are raised within a matriarchal family of doting female caregivers, beginning with the birth mother and then branching out to include sisters, cousins, aunts, grandmothers, and established friends. These bonds endure over a life span that can be as long as 70 years. Young elephants stay close to their mothers and extended family members—males until they are about 14, females for life. When a calf is threatened or harmed, all the other elephants comfort and protect it.
-Charles Siebert

By the time they arrived back at the sanctuary, morning had broken and the place buzzed with people at work. Since Andrew had called Mali and told her to ask the other mahouts to prepare a space for the calf, Seth and Mali ran down the platform stairs to meet the truck. Natalie felt her stomach rumble as the mahouts loaded the baby onto a big, blue tarpaulin and carried her carefully down the road. Her own hunger reminded her that the baby would be hungry and disoriented when she awoke from the sedative. Determined to be by its side when the calf came to, Natalie stayed close.

Mali had thought ahead and prepared some food for everyone. She passed around some bowls of *larb gai,* a spicy salad eaten with one's fingers, while Natalie questioned Khalan—with Andrew and

Mali's help—about what the calf would eat and how they could best introduce her to her new home.

"We could very easily lose this little one, you are aware of that, aren't you?" Andrew folded a piece of lettuce in half, spooned some *larb gai* into it, rolled it between his fingers and practically inhaled it. They only had about ten more minutes before the calf woke up.

Natalie nodded.

For the first time, she missed Peter Hatcher's knowledge. She'd heard him speak fondly—and proudly—of several foundling calves he'd helped raise successfully. He would have known what to do. But . . . he was gone because of what he did to Seth and to her, and she hated him. *How immature that sounds,* she thought, *but it's honest. Still, if he'd been here, he could have helped.* Andrew had some practical experience, but he lacked the veterinary knowledge.

Twisting his Yankees baseball cap on his head, Khalan told them in fits and starts about the calves he'd fed and cared for during his career. He knew how to train them and how to care for various ailments, even how to introduce new calves to adult elephants, yet he'd never actually prepared food for a newborn nor had he cared for an orphan. Even without understanding most of his words, Natalie could tell by the way he pursed his lips and looked to the sky before answering that he was unsure of his own knowledge. Though he was normally a self-assured mahout, Khalan was still a teenager looking for approval and sometimes he'd make up stories to gain attention. She hoped this conversation wasn't one of them.

"What about the other mahouts?" Andrew asked Khalan. "Chanchai? Jabari?"

Khalan put a dirty finger to his temple and thought about the question. "Chanchai maybe know."

They finished their breakfast as they walked toward the shed where the calf had been moved. Andrew asked one of the children to find Chanchai. Three of them, along with several dogs, ran off to do the errand, treating the task as if it were one great adventure. A trail of giggles followed them, floating on the air and echoing as they disappeared into the trees.

"If Rob and Sidecar were around, at least we'd have some valuable extra hands," Seth said.

She'd be willing to bet that was not what Seth was thinking. He wanted their cameras and sound equipment. Seth's first thought would be to record the event, to get the story of the dramatic rescue. He was the consummate journalist, and this was a good story. But he'd have to record this one using old school tools: pen and paper.

"Babies in peril always make great stories." Her voice sounded louder than she'd meant it to be. She avoided Seth's glance, thankful they had arrived at the shed, and that she wouldn't need to clarify her remark.

The calf now stood on her feet, her eyes wide, trunk swinging from side to side like an out-of-control snake. Natalie moved into the enclosure leaving everyone else at the door. The shed was a tin box barely three-feet wide by six-feet long. Not meant for animals. It had been used to store gardening equipment, which now lay nearby on the ground. The rakes and hoes and shovels had been quickly tossed outside so the baby could be contained. The interior steamed with the morning's heat. It wouldn't do to leave the little one in here for long.

"Hey, sweetie. Shhh . . . shhh . . . I know you're scared, but I have to look you over, then we'll get you fed." As she talked, Natalie visually checked the tiny pachyderm and then gently traced over the baby's body, checking for any injuries. "Looks like you're in pretty good shape other than being awfully scared. Can't say that I blame you . . ."

The calf trumpeted loudly in Natalie's ear and tried to head butt her, but there wasn't enough room in the shed to move around. Natalie placed her open palm at the end of the baby's trunk and called for some soft bananas.

"Mush them up really good," she said, "and see if Chanchai's coming! We need to make a bottle of some kind. She has to nurse. We have to get something into her *soon.*"

"I'll go up to the kitchen," Seth said. He'd been filming her with his cell phone, but pocketed it as he sprinted away.

Chanchai's face replaced Seth's. His wild eyes looked to the right, though he spoke directly to Natalie. He ordered her to do something in his gravelly voice, though she had no idea what he said since he only spoke Thai. But whatever he said must be important because he kept repeating it.

"Will someone please tell me what the hell he's saying?"

"He says 'no bananas.'" Mali stood behind Chanchai like a ventriloquist would stand behind her puppet, her hand on his shoulder. "Make a bottle with baby's formula and honey and calcium pills. No cow's milk, he says. Definitely no cow's milk. And I have no idea if we have any baby formula either. I'm going to have to see if there are any leftover cans in the back of the kitchen shelves . . ."

"Are you sure? I read somewhere that the mixture should be goat's milk and something else."

Mali translated, and during that short pause, the calf reached its pink-tipped trunk for Natalie's face. Natalie turned and looked the little elephant straight in the eye. Her innocent gaze reached for Natalie's heart and squeezed it. That single look pleaded on a more elemental level than any animal's she'd ever met. Of all the dogs and horses and cats and cows she'd medicated and operated on, the lives she'd saved and the ones she'd put down, this one reached into her soul and made her see its pain.

Mama, save her, Danny's voice whispered in her ear.

She gasped.

Danny. Her eyes darted into every corner. She searched the faces peering in the doorway, but her son wasn't there. Her shoulders folded forward, and she went to one knee, her forehead falling against the calf's flank. She fought for breath and squeezed her eyes shut.

"He says he'll mix a formula for the baby and bring it to you. I have bottles we can use, and Seth is going to the clinic to get some rubber gloves," Mali said. Her voice reminded Natalie of the present, and she raised her eyes, faced the task at hand.

Suddenly, everyone disappeared to help. No more faces at the doorway. Then Anurak's dark head and Decha's blonde snout appeared. The boy and his dog were small enough to fit into the shed with Natalie and the calf. Anurak stood on the other side of the calf, stroking its head and making a guttural noise, his way of soothing the baby. Decha sat at the calf's feet, sniffing its legs as if to make sure it wouldn't step on him. Still unsteady on its feet and bewildered by its own trunk, the calf flailed around and bumped into her and the shed wall.

Natalie smiled at them both and wrapped her arms around the baby's neck, knowing that at that moment she was not a veterinarian. She was only a woman, only a mother who knew that this baby needed as much mothering as she could possibly muster.

Anurak and Decha helped her to comfort the calf during the fifteen minutes it took for Chanchai to arrive with the bottle of food. Khalan and Mali and Andrew stood outside the door while Natalie and Chanchai worked together to get the baby to take the nipple Mali had fashioned out of some cheesecloth she'd found in the kitchen.

Andrew gave Natalie a blanket. "Put it over her shoulders. It'll comfort the little bugger like her mother would've."

Salty sweat ran into Natalie's mouth. The space had grown way too small to accommodate all of them, and the day became hotter by the minute. It took a lot of coaxing and Natalie literally had to hold the calf's mouth open, but finally, she started to suckle and as soon as the concocted mixture started flowing down her throat, little moans of contentment filled the tiny shed. Chanchai caught Natalie's eye above the calf's, and he started talking quietly. Mali interpreted.

"He says there always must be someone with this calf. We cannot leave her alone. And she must be fed every couple of hours like a baby."

"The first couple of months are critical," Andrew added from outside. "I can't tell you how many orphans we've lost at Doba. The handlers would think the calf was out of the woods, then overnight the little one would seemingly give up." He sighed. "It's heartbreaking. For a long time, we didn't even know what to feed them, but thanks to the Sheldrick people, we all got a lesson."

"The Sheldrick people?" Natalie measured the contents of the bottle as the calf took a breather from suckling. Almost half gone.

"Dame Sheldrick. She and her husband, David, worked together at the Royal National Parks in Kenya for years. When he died, she kept going. Now she and her son have what they call an orphanage. They're pretty much heroes in Africa. Saved hundreds of orphans. Elephants, rhinos, giraffes. All kinds of African beasts. But she lost a lot of ellies until she finally figured out what she was doing wrong. It was the food. She figured out a formula for baby ellies and rhinos. Now she has a nursery full of them. Twenty or thirty strong at any point in time, I'd imagine. Dame Daphne's a force to be reckoned with."

In the distance, a trumpet and an answering rumble reminded Natalie there were other mouths to feed. She handed the empty bottle to Khalan. "I think this one's had a successful first feeding. Let's get out of here before I pass out with this heat."

Outside, the air felt positively blissful. With the elephant leaning her little body trustingly against her, Natalie told Khalan to find the sunscreen lotion they bought by the case. Since this little one would have no mother to shelter her, Natalie would need to ensure her sensitive skin had the extra protection it needed against sunburn.

Mali and Andrew disappeared to take care of kitchen and administrative business, promising to return as soon as they were done. Khalan left to feed his own elephant, Pahpao. Natalie was about to lead the calf to an area where she could sit with it for a while, when another trumpeting split the air.

"That's Sophie," she told the calf. As if she understood, the calf reached her trunk out and tentatively touched Natalie's fingers.

"I think your old girl might be wondering what's going on." Seth came from behind, a Nikon video camera in his hand. He pointed it at the baby. "Maybe you should go reassure her that you haven't deserted her."

Natalie thought for a moment, then turned to Seth. "Maybe we should introduce them."

Seth's face lit up. Within moments, they were walking down the road, the calf between them.

"I'm going to name her Apsara," Natalie announced when they arrived at Sophie's enclosure. She was at the gate, like an old lady waiting for them to join her for a cup of tea.

"That's Thai for angel, isn't it?" Seth stood behind Sophie, filming her reaction to the little orphan. Seth moved forward, his attention focused on the calf.

"Far enough," Natalie warned. Sophie had begun rumbling in the back of her throat but stopped when Seth came into her line of vision. The calf stood on shaky feet, her ears wide, as if unsure whether this big elephant was one of her family.

"What do you think, old girl? Do you want to meet Apsara?" Natalie whispered.

Sophie stopped swaying and stared at the baby. Stretching her trunk straight out, Sophie appeared to check the baby's fingerprint, her lineage. Apsara, innocent and trusting and curious, trotted over to the fence and shakily lifted her own miniature trunk up to try to meet Sophie's. Sophie backed up a few steps and reached for Natalie, grabbing Natalie's arm, then dropping it, as if to say, "Who is this? Her smell has been on you."

"This is Apsara, Sophie. Can you be friends?"

Sophie rumbled and leaned forward as if considering the question. She reached her trunk over the fence, and Apsara skipped backward, stumbling a bit. The tiny elephant kicked up her back legs and chortled, playing, then reached out her trunk again. This time hers and Sophie's touched.

Natalie's throat constricted. In her heart of hearts, she knew that she was watching a very special moment. She smiled at the obvious pleasure Apsara got out of actually touching another elephant, and Natalie's pride in Sophie filled her chest. She glanced at Seth to see if he was getting everything on video and caught him wiping his own eyes.

THE WOMAN *stands next to her, holding Sophie's trunk and talking quietly. Sophie inspects the woman thoroughly, her large trunk inserting itself in the food bag the woman carries. She smells the woman's hair, touches her arms and legs, searching for hidden treats. Only after her inspection is complete does Sophie reach down for the little one next to the woman's side.*

"This one is very small, Sophie. You must be patient with her."

Sophie's eyes flicker from the calf beside the woman and back again.

The memory of the one she lost fills her mouth with a sour taste. Her dried up teats ache with a phantom infant's suckle. It has been many seasons since she's seen a little one, and many more before that since she had one of her own.

Her trunk reaches in the calf's direction, its pink-freckled tip stretching. Opening. Closing. She shifts from one foot to the other, deciding whether to move forward.

The baby has yet to learn how to use her own trunk. It flaps and flops uselessly as she dances around.

The woman takes the makeshift teat from the calf's mouth. With her feed removed, the little one instantly catches sight of Sophie and gives a whistle and a chirp.

In seconds, she's between Sophie's legs, searching for what Sophie cannot give her. Still, Sophie wraps her trunk around the baby's belly, huffs, feels for the calf's mouth. She cannot remember the last time she has known joy.

Forty-Two

Better to live alone; with a
fool there is no companionship.
With few desires live alone
and do no evil, like an elephant
in the forest roaming at will.
-The Pali Canon, Ib. 23.330L

ANDREW CAME INTO THE clinic, Sivad behind him like a
shadow. She wore a little, pink dress and clutched a ragged, eyeless
teddy bear to her chest. Her brown feet were bare and dusty.
When she saw Natalie, she ran to her. Natalie instantly swooped
her up and nuzzled her neck, bringing a delighted giggle from the
little girl.

"Seth's packing up," Andrew announced upon settling himself
in the office chair. "He let me see the rough cut of the episode this
morning. It's outstanding!"

He slapped an open palm on her desk. "Sophie's story is going
to put the sanctuary on everyone's radar, and we're sure to be able
to raise the funds we need to repair the perimeter fence and add
more protected contact enclosures. I'm here to thank you, love. For
everything."

She hugged Sivad closer. "You don't have to thank me. Actually, I need to thank you, Andrew. This place . . . and Sophie . . .
have been wonderful for me." The comments felt very much like a

goodbye, and she realized in that brief moment that she'd have to face the reality of going back to her true life soon, and she wasn't sure she was ready for that. Or wanted it.

He laced his hands over his ample stomach and raised one bushy white eyebrow. "I think that one man's appearance—and another's disappearance—might have more to do with the smile on your face than this place and Sophie." He grinned wickedly. "You've seemed pretty content lately, but I've a feeling I'll see a different look on your face tomorrow."

Sivad squirmed so Natalie released her to the floor and gave her some pencils and a piece of paper to draw on. The girl lay on her stomach on the cool tile, her teddy bear beside her, instantly in her own little world. The couple of moments it had taken to get the little girl busy gave Natalie enough time to compose herself before answering Andrew.

"I knew Seth wasn't going to be here permanently." She searched carefully for the words to explain the complicated feelings she'd been experiencing during the past month. "I'm not even sure I would want something permanent with him, but it's been . . . I don't know how to say it. It's been many things, but I think the best is that it's been lovely."

"Lovely is always a good word." Andrew's voice and eyes were unexpectedly soft. "I like that word because it's got round edges to it. No stress to the word 'lovely.' And it's respectful. Kind of dignified, don't you think? Plus, it holds the word 'love' inside it, without the ties of commitment like, perhaps, the word 'special.' Did you know that word—love—has been around for about five thousand years?" He nodded emphatically in response to her raised eyebrows. "Yes. And all of the words that combine with it or create another subtle meaning came along from thereon. Good Old English word it was: *lufu*. And almost a holy word. God was a god of love. A being that showed great affection. And, of course, that being would be described as lovely. It's a good word—lovely is—to describe a relationship that's temporary yet treasured."

They sat in silence for a moment. She hadn't pegged Andrew for a romantic. Both of them tenderly watched Sivad drawing a cat and a dog, then some flowers and a stick tree. Natalie mused that all children must draw the exact same images at some point in their lives, no matter where in the world they lived.

She remembered looking down on Danny's head from above. He was drawing a red and blue snowman with crayons she'd stuck in his Christmas stocking when he was five. With all the big mechanical gifts he'd received that year (it was the year he wanted nothing but "choo choo trains"), the crayons were what he played with most. She had told Parker then that she wanted to keep Danny this age always, she never wanted him to grow up. The innocence and curiosity, independence and gaiety, fearsome courage and tender friendship—all were so genuine and precious. She knew, even then, that with each year, he'd grow away, and she needed to capture the memories when they happened.

"You know, it's funny that we often don't know what we're going to remember and treasure and which moments are fleeting glimpses we'll forget as soon as they pass," she said to Andrew.

"So true," Andrew sighed. "The older I get, the more I remember from the past. I was thinking the other day about my great aunts and how they would bake pound cakes on the weekend and invite all the nieces and nephews to the kitchen for milky tea and lemon pound cake. We'd sit around the little wooden table like right proud adults, sipping tea and eating our cake as if we'd been born with crowns on our heads. Those aunties made us all feel as special as the kids who lived in Windsor castle. We were a solid little army, right we were." He sighed and glanced up at the ceiling, his eyes a bit glassy. "Lord, I loved that stuff, and I hadn't thought about that for many a year."

"Daddy, draw me an ellie?" Sivad stood at her father's knee, handing him a pencil and a piece of paper. He glanced up at Natalie and smiled.

They sat together, Natalie helping Andrew with the requested drawing for his daughter, and they laughed about how bad it was. When the dinner bell rang, the three of them strolled down the road, Sivad in the middle with Natalie and Andrew each holding a hand as the little magpie chattered on about what she wanted to eat for supper.

That night was the first time since they'd returned from Bangkok that Mali sat with them for dinner. As they all sat around the table and celebrated the last evening they would be together, wine and brandy flowed as freely as the conversation, and when the talk turned to what Andrew called "telling tales out of school," the evening of libations oiled the way for lots of laughter. Andrew and Seth competed to tell the most outrageous stories, the tales getting taller and taller as they passed the virtual storytelling baton back and forth.

Finally, Natalie pleaded for mercy with her hands on her sides and big hysterical tears flowing down her face. The men acquiesced, someone brought over a pot of tea, and Seth's hand found its way to Natalie's thigh. She felt the color rise in her cheeks and was happy that the only light on the platform came from half a dozen candles scattered around the group.

Once the laughter died down completely, talk turned to the political situation in Bangkok. Everyone shared the most recent tidbits of news and their personal opinions. Rob had heard from a fellow cameraman that everyone except the people who ran and frequented the nighttime outdoor markets, was complying with the curfew. Andrew said there had been another verbal confrontation between the military and the protestors. That comment made Mali grimace, and she backed her seat away from the table. She fidgeted and played with her hair, yet she didn't speak to anyone.

"Isn't there someone in charge of the protestors? A spokesperson of some sort?" Natalie asked of no one in particular.

Mali looked at Andrew. He glanced across the table at Seth, who instantly shot an unspoken question to Rob and Sidecar. Both shrugged their shoulders as if to say, "Not guilty."

"I find it hard to believe that no one's in charge," Natalie continued. "Even when there's an unruly mob, there's someone with a bullhorn. There's always a leader. If you folks don't know, I'd be willing to bet there's a journalist somewhere who does."

"I'm sure there is," Seth said. "I'm not necessarily in those circles, but if you want me to find out . . ." He looked directly at

Mali as if posing the question. She nodded. "I'll see if anyone at the station can find out."

An uneasy silence hung over the table for a couple of moments, then Andrew asked the cameramen if they'd noticed anything strange the day Siriporn, Peter, and Karina disappeared.

"I was in the river most of the day," Sidecar admitted, pushing his wire-rimmed glasses up his nose. He sweated constantly and was more often than not peering over the top of them. "It was a steamer that day, and I took the day off. Just floated in the river. It was the only time I've had to relax in quite a while. Took advantage of it. Got to admit it. I did see Dr. Hatcher earlier in the day with some of the kiddos. Now that I look back on it, well, it did look like he was saying goodbye but can't say I thought much of it at the time. No, I didn't."

"He always talks to the children." Mali studied her fingertips as she spoke. "They love him. Sivad thinks of him as her uncle. He taught her how to say her ABCs. And if it wasn't for him, half the dogs in the village would've been rounded up and on their way to the slaughterhouse. He's not the easiest man to understand, but his heart is huge."

"I always blamed him for giving me extra mouths to feed," Andrew laughed.

"You're talking about him like he's gone permanently." Rob took a long drag of his Chinese-made cigarette, a smelly type of herbal combination that made Natalie nauseous. "He didn't strike me as someone who'd abandon his job. I wouldn't be surprised if there's another motive."

"Well, there's the lady," Sidecar said with an elbow and a wink at Rob. He pushed his wire-rimmed glasses up on his nose. "Love Boat." He sung the words as if starting the theme song for the classic television show of the same name.

"They were always close." Andrew leaned forward on the table, his face full of unanswered questions. "But I can't see either of them abandoning their responsibilities."

"Love makes you do crazy things," Seth said. His tone was serious and his dark eyes slid to Natalie and stayed there. She held his stare a beat longer than was comfortable, then glanced away. Confused.

Seth's comment surprised Natalie. Though Hatcher and Karina did have an ongoing flirtation, she'd be shocked if the two of them had planned a passionate tryst and had run away on romantic pretenses. It had always seemed to her that the bantering they had was Hatcher's way of passing time and that their relationship consisted of gossip and teasing. No passion.

"Neither of them left a note," Andrew said. He pushed a hand through his hair, a habit born of frustration, Natalie thought. "I can't believe they wouldn't tell me why they were leaving. I feel like it was a last minute decision. You sure you didn't see or hear anything that day?" He addressed the last question to Rob and Sidecar, but once again, they mutely answered with a negative headshake.

Everyone at the table glanced away once again, all in different directions as if avoiding each other's eyes. The conversation was definitely over. Natalie fought the urge to ask for more clarification, but she knew she wouldn't get it.

Forty-Three

Mrs. Darling loved to have everything just so, and Mr.
Darling had a passion for being exactly like his neighbours;
so, of course, they had a nurse. As they were poor, owing
to the amount of milk the children drank, this nurse was a
prim Newfoundland dog, called Nana, who had belonged
to no one in particular until the Darlings engaged her. She
had always thought children important, however, and the
Darlings had become acquainted with her in Kensington
Gardens, where she spent most of her spare time peeping
into perambulators, and was much hated by careless nurse-
maids, whom she followed to their homes and complained
of to their mistresses. She proved to be quite a treasure of a
nurse.

-J.M. Barrie

NATALIE WASN'T SURE WHAT had awakened her, but it probably had something to do with Sophie's farts and Apsara's wet
trunk flapping in her face.

"Seriously? When did sleeping with elephants become part
of my chores here?" She flipped onto her side, shoving away the
dirty, smelly blanket rubbing her cheek. She'd never felt dirtier or
smelled worse, but she had to admit there'd been few moments in
her life when she'd felt as happy.

Sophie had taken on Apsara, the orphan, as though the little
one were her own kin. No one at the sanctuary could believe the

transformation in the old cow. Though Sophie had improved both physically and emotionally, Natalie hadn't seen such softness in the elephant since they'd first met. If there were such a thing as pachyderm love at first sight, it had manifested itself in the relationship Sophie and Apsara had formed from the very beginning. Yet with the bond they had, Apsara still wanted—and needed—Natalie around. And Sophie had no problem sharing both her young charge and her human friend. Over the span of a few short weeks, the three of them became inseparable.

Deep into the summer season, the relentless Thai sun burnt skins more quickly than a hot toaster burnt bread, so Natalie, Khalan, and Chanchai took turns feeding the infant elephant and covering her with a constant coat of sunscreen. She needed round-the-clock attention and feeding, one thing Sophie couldn't do. Though she tolerated the mahouts when they invaded her space to feed Apsara, when the other elephants were around, Sophie acted like the proud aunt, sheltering the precocious baby and making sure to guard her against the other adult elephants.

Natalie and Mali often sat and watched the herd as they encircled the baby in the mud pit. The two women entertained themselves by taking turns attributing human voices and commentary to the elephant group's antics, dissolving in hysterical laughter on more than one occasion when their fabricated commentary almost matched the movement of the elephants' mouths.

Like any toddler, Apsara endeared everyone to her, and as the only baby at the sanctuary, the group spoiled her—and she loved it. The only cloud over the baby's arrival was that Sophie would not let Seth—who'd postponed his departure date over the past couple of weeks—anywhere near Apsara. For some reason, Sophie didn't trust him, and her determination to keep him away from the baby convinced Natalie that it truly was dangerous for him to stay. Sophie's maternal instincts ruled her now, and Natalie knew better than to leave Sophie with someone like Seth, who couldn't read her noises and body language.

When the hour finally came that Seth meant to leave for

good, Natalie joined everyone else in wishing him good fortune. She stood at the back of the small crowd as everyone said goodbye and felt torn. He had done nothing mean to her. She couldn't fault him for doing his job, even though using her past as "color" for the show about Sophie truly ripped her in half. Still, he'd opened her up to the possibility of love, and that was something she hadn't considered as an option for the rest of her life. That was a positive take-away. There would be times they might run into each other at conferences or seminars. He'd be a good friend.

He climbed into the truck, and she reached for his hand through the window. "Can't wait to see the show. Thank you, and I wish you the best."

He smiled, that same dazzling smile she'd noticed the first night they'd met. "You'll be the first one to see the edited version. Hope you like it, Natalie." His eyes searched hers for a deeper conversation, but finding none, he smiled resolutely.

"I'm sure it'll be fine," she replied and withdrew her hand as the truck started. She stood with the rest of the group in the road as the truck left them in a cloud of dust, and she remained there when everyone else dispersed for a long while before heading back to Apsara's pen.

It was days later when Natalie glanced out at the pouring rain from inside the enclosure and told the tiny elephant, "Seth got out of here just in time."

Though the baby couldn't understand what she said, she had started to understand the word for "come," and whenever they walked, Natalie repeated, "*Ma, ma, ma.*" Whether she came because she had learned the word or because she was playing, Natalie couldn't tell, but at least Apsara responded.

Sophie spent most of the day with the calf, rescuing the little one when she slipped on the slope into the river and making sure she didn't wander off when it was time for her feeding. She'd become a wonderful surrogate mother, though she had nothing to give to Apsara from her dry teats.

Sophie now stood outside the enclosure, clearly enjoying the soaking that the afternoon rains provided. She lifted her trunk occasionally to the roof, knowing exactly where to place herself to get the steady runoff. She drank as though her trunk had become one large straw. It wouldn't last much longer, according to what Natalie could see of the sky. By the way the dark clouds moved quickly over the mountains, the rain would stop for at least a couple of hours. But it never stopped for long during rainy season, which made everything at the sanctuary slippery and moldy. At least Natalie didn't need to worry about Apsara getting sunburnt.

As she awaited the end of the storm, Natalie fed Apsara and ran over her chores in her mind. Next week, she would conduct the monthly dog clinic that she and Peter used to do together. She mentally reviewed what meds she had on hand and planned what inventory she'd need to replace after the clinic. She also made note to order replacement parts for the large freezer and talk to Andrew about what he wanted her to accomplish while he was in Africa. He departed next week for almost three months, which left her in charge of the sanctuary until she was ready to go home. Originally, her year would have ended next month, but since no one else could take over in Andrew's absence, she agreed to stay until his return. Maybe by then, Apsara would be more stable and the other mahouts could take on her feedings and care.

Andrew had been in regular contact with his people in Africa, asking for advice, especially regarding the ingredients for Apsara's formula, and for the warning signs to watch for that might indicate the calf was on a rapid downhill slide. He reminded Natalie that caring for infant elephants was risky, at best, but Natalie refused to think about how she would deal with the sudden death of baby Apsara.

The rain stopped as Sophie came toward the fence. Somehow she sensed that Natalie had waited for a pause in the rain to walk with Apsara, and Sophie wanted to tag along, though she thought she led the pack.

Apsara skipped ahead, giving karate-like kicks as she chased birds and tossed her trunk. The rain had invigorated her senses, evoking happy squeaks. Natalie couldn't help but smile at the little girl because everything was always new to her. She could sit for hours exploring Natalie's face with her bristly little trunk, then she'd be off down the road, mock-charging whoever might be coming the other way. Sophie, on the other hand, moped along, in a way that made her appear blasé and indifferent.

At times, Natalie thought of Sophie as lifting one eyebrow when she looked at the world, like a French gallery owner might look askance at a beginner's imitation of a Monet water lilies painting. Like the gallery owner, she had seen it and experienced it all, but she, too, was enamored by the happy baby elephant frolicking before them.

Content and preoccupied by her thoughts, Natalie had almost tuned out her surroundings, so Sophie's abrupt right hand turn caught her off guard. Then she saw Apsara trotting in the same direction, and when Sophie's big rear end shifted, Natalie could see why both elephants veered off the path.

Decha and Anurak trotted toward them. Apsara did her happy dance, tripping on her feet and tooting an imitation of Sophie's much louder trumpeting. Sophie, not happy at all, would never be friendly with any dog, and barely tolerated Decha. The only reason she didn't trample the yellow mongrel was because Apsara played with him as though he were another baby elephant. Usually Anurak gravitated directly to Apsara and would press his face right against the elephant's head, but today he headed for Natalie, his bare feet slapping against the muddy path. The closer he got, the more evident that he was upset.

His hands gesticulating wildly, he grunted and squeaked, the only sounds he could make, and frantically pulled on her hand, pointing again and again, as if demanding she come with him.

"Okay, okay, sweetie. Let me take Sophie and Apsara back to the pen. They'll only be in the way."

Anurak and Decha followed them back down the road, waiting impatiently while Natalie got the elephants settled. Anurak danced from one foot to the other, pantomiming the whole time, though she still couldn't understand what he tried to tell her.

Hand-in-hand they ran up the road, sliding in the mud and almost falling several times. When they rounded the corner by the clinic, Anurak grabbed her arm and pulled her inside, pointing to the medicine cabinet. She got it now: there had been some sort of accident.

"What do I need? I have no idea what's happened. Goddamnit, I wish you could talk." She grabbed the bag she always kept packed, knowing it contained a tranquilizer, some antibiotics, bandage materials, and a splint. "Do I need something else? Crap, you couldn't tell me even if you knew . . ."

Anurak's dark eyes widened and his brow knit for a moment, then he brightened as if he'd had a brilliant idea and ran to her desk, grabbing a pen and paper. In seconds, he'd sketched something, then held it up for her to see.

Her heart stopped.

A cobra.

She grabbed some syringes and a bottle of the anti-venom always on hand from the fridge, shoved them in her bag and the three of them flew out the door.

Forty-Four

Courage is not the absence of fear, but
rather the judgement that something
else is more important than fear.
-Ambrose Redmoon

NATALIE WAS OUT OF breath when they reached the rice fields. In the distance, she heard screams. She fought to grab another breath, forced herself to keep running.

Christ.

She knew the results of a snake bite, knew what to do, but what would happen if she had to deal with the cobra itself? She hated to admit it, but unlike most of her veterinary colleagues, she'd always had a deep fear of snakes.

The impossibly green marshes stretched out to the mountains beyond, a natural boundary. In the distance, a group of thatched huts rose above the fields on wooden poles set deep in the rice paddies. A small group of people gathered near one of the huts, several of them wearing the bamboo bucket hats that the rice workers wore to keep off the sun. Probably members of Anurak's family. She followed the boy through the water-logged rice paddies. Anurak lived on the outskirts of the fields and would have been working with them today, which is probably why the edges of his pants were still wet when he came to her.

She kicked off her sandals and continued wading down the paths between the paddies, keeping to the mud as much as possible and watching closely in front of her for the telltale squiggles that the big snakes made. Her heart beat hard in her chest, and the sun blurred her vision. Within a few moments, she saw that one of the people was a blonde man dressed in Western clothing.

Peter Hatcher? When did he come back, and what the hell is he doing in this rice paddy?

"Oh, thank God, Natalie!" He shouted to her, his hand over his eyes like a visor. "I hope you brought the anti-venom. It's Anurak's dad!"

She held up her bag. "I have it." She waded into the calf-deep water toward Hatcher. Behind him, Anurak's mother cradled her husband in her arms. As Natalie drew closer, she saw Anurak's dad struggling for air, though Hatcher had tried to open an airway with a homemade tracheotomy. She jogged the last couple of steps, then bent to check on the man.

"I have no idea where that damn snake went," Hatcher whispered to her. "Watch yourself." He pulled open her bag and grabbed one of the vials of anti-venom, plunging the needle into Anurak's dad's arm. Immediately, he began breathing more easily.

"Get him out of here!" Hatcher told the men. Then he said something in Thai. Immediately, they hoisted their friend up and scurried toward dry land. Natalie and Peter started following, but the sound of heavy breathing stopped them in their tracks. A deep growl followed.

"Fuck . . ." Hatcher pointed to his right.

An impossibly long, angry cobra, its burnished tan and black body raised, its yellow and white hood wide, coiled only two feet away from Hatcher.

Natalie's breath caught when the cobra struck. So quick. Hatcher cried out.

A struggle, some splashing, and he screamed again.

Natalie's legs zippered through the watery rice paddy toward where he now leaned forward as though he were about to plow into the shallow puddles of water.

Was the cobra still holding on? She caught him by the arm, pulled with all her strength and heard another hiss nearby.

Whirling, she saw a flash, and heard Sophie's roar, then her angry trumpet.

In the sunlight, Sophie sprinted down through the paddies toward her. *How did she get out?* A shadowy figure sat atop her shoulders. The sunlight blurred for a moment, then the person came into view. Long skinny legs, a glossy brown head of hair. Huge smile.

Danny! Natalie lost her grip on Hatcher's arm. His groan pulled her from the unbelievable sight of her son on the back of her elephant and grounded her in the moment. She grabbed Hatcher's arm again, instantly realizing she couldn't move him.

"You've got to stand, Peter. Stand. Then, lean on me. We've got to get out of here!"

She frantically worked with him until she could get him to stand, his face white and his legs wobbly. To her left, Sophie, still trumpeting, wrestled with something Natalie couldn't see. She shaded her eyes.

Danny. Where's Danny? A trick of the light through the rushes alongside the rice paddy. A wish on Natalie's part. A visit from beyond. Whatever Natalie saw was no longer there. She shook her head and concentrated on Peter.

He struggled to get to his feet, mumbling something about the anti-venom. Natalie checked his hands quickly, found the needle he'd been using on Anurak's father, and quickly shoved it into Peter's right arm, hoping beyond hope there was enough still left in the vial to stop the venom. At least to pause it. The cobra bite on his upper left arm looked way too close to his heart. She had to get him back to the clinic. She called for Sophie. She came immediately, her bulk casting a shadow around them.

"*Nung long!* Sophie, *nung long!*" Natalie yelled.

Immediately, Sophie lowered her head to the ground as Natalie had commanded. Together, Natalie and one of the rice workers pushed and pulled Peter's body until he lay over Sophie's lowered shoulders. They slid him down so he was cradled against her neck, then Natalie commanded her to stand up, and Sophie did.

"Loog khen! *Sophie, loog khen!" the woman says, so Sophie rises.*

A strange buzzing fills her ears. Her legs are unsteady, but she slowly lumbers down the road, the man's inert body slumped over her neck. She holds her head erect. She needs to hold him in place, knows that he cannot hold on, so she moves carefully when she feels him slipping. They pass under the cashew trees. The only sound: the birds overhead. Slowly. Carefully. Finally, the white building is in sight. She lifts her legs a little higher, walks a little more quickly.

The woman yells something. Two men run inside.

Then the woman is by her side and orders Sophie to lower her head to the ground. All the elephant sees is the woman's face. All she hears is the woman's voice. She ignores the tightening in her chest as her legs stiffen, and she lowers her head, feeling the man slide over her forehead, past her eyes, landing in the curl of her trunk. She stays perfectly still until the woman and two male humans take the man off her, and she tries to stand. Sways. Finds it difficult to catch her breath. Forces her good leg straight.

Then she stumbles.

GLANCING UP to scold the elephant, Natalie notices the bites. Multiple bites. All around the healing scar on Sophie's leg. She'd been bitten by more than one snake. Bad enough the big cobra had still been agitated enough to attack, but Sophie must have disturbed the nest. *Oh God, no.* Baby cobras didn't know how to temper their release of venom like the adults did. The chances of dying from multiple baby cobra bites could be much higher than dying from an adult's single bite. And God knows how many of them had bitten the big elephant. "Jesus." Natalie looked into Sophie's eyes, silently begging her to wait for a few moments while she cared for Peter. "I'll be right back, ol' girl," she said softly.

Turning to the volunteers now rushing around, Natalie shot quick orders. "I need more antidote, a clean bed, a bowl of hot water and fresh towels, and someone get some anti-venom for Sophie, too. Load it in a super large syringe, and as soon as I get Peter set, I'll be right out to take care of her. Now, go!" The students stood around her in wide-eyed shock. "Go, for chris-sakes! Go!"

Forty-Five

Life will break you. Nobody can protect you from that, and living alone won't either, for solitude will also break you with its yearning. You have to love. You have to feel. It is the reason you are here on earth. You are here to risk your heart. You are here to be swallowed up. And when it happens that you are broken, or betrayed, or left, or hurt, or death brushes near, let yourself sit by an apple tree and listen to the apples falling all around you in heaps, wasting their sweetness. Tell yourself you tasted as many as you could.

-Louise Erdrich

NATALIE QUICKLY INJECTED PETER with two more doses of anti-venom and lifted his arm above the wound, making sure it was elevated above the heart. Thankfully, he'd been wearing long sleeves, so the venom hadn't gone directly into a vein. Still, if they hadn't gotten back to the clinic as quickly as they had, he surely would have died. Satisfied he was safe, she flew back outside.

As soon as Natalie came out onto the clinic stairs, Sophie pitched to the right and shivered. She lowered to the ground in slow motion, releasing a long, ragged sigh, as if she were very, very tired. Her sides heaved. Every breath became a struggle.

Respiratory paralysis.

"Sophie!" Natalie vaulted the stairs to the elephant's side. In her hand, she held the giant syringe she'd asked the volunteers to fill with eight vials of anti-venom. She jabbed it into the elephant's upper thigh near her chest and watched Sophie's eye flicker. The elephant looked at Natalie, as if saying, *I trust you.*

Holding her breath, Natalie placed her shaking right hand over Sophie's heart and lowered her ear near the elephant's mouth. Sophie's breaths were shallow and short. Labored. Her limbs started convulsing uncontrollably.

"Get me another eight vials. At least thirty thousand units. Now!"

The blonde girl—Natalie couldn't remember her name—ran back into the clinic where Peter laid on a cold steel gurney that had last been used as an operating table for a dog who'd been caught in barbed wire and needed 42 stitches. Natalie knew she should be in there with Peter. After all, weren't human lives worth more than elephants'? Yet, through the clinic's window she could see at least four people attending to Dr. Peter Hatcher. Out here in the muddy pathway lay the heroic elephant who had done all she could for a human who had not wanted her to live.

Natalie angrily wiped away the tears that ran down her face unabated.

The blonde girl popped back through the clinic doors and wordlessly shoved the refilled syringe into Natalie's hand.

"Hang in there, Sophie. Please." Natalie jabbed the needle into the same area she'd just hit. Emptied the vial. Plugged in another. Repeated the procedure over and over.

Sophie's body quivered. Her breath came in big gulps, then one last, long shudder.

Natalie froze. She scrambled over Sophie's leg and flipped back her ear, searching blindly with her fingers for the ear artery. She placed her hand there, keeping as still as possible, holding her breath, hoping against hope she'd find a pulse. Each second felt like an eternity. She remained still, reminding herself the cardiac output in an elephant was only 25-35 beats a minute. In a healthy elephant. It would be much slower in Sophie's state.

"C'mon, Sophie," she whispered. "Please, girl."

Still nothing.

Natalie flipped the ear back. Sophie's eyes closed. Her mouth hung open, tongue lolling. Her breathing stopped. Frantic, Natalie pounded under Sophie's leg in the heart area, a vain attempt at CPR.

"No, Sophie. No," she told the elephant, as casually as if they'd been on one of their walks and Sophie had taken a wrong turn. "Sophie. No. No. No."

No response. No breath. No heartbeat.

Natalie glanced around. Khalan and the nameless volunteer stood beside her. They didn't know Sophie as well as she did, yet their faces reflected their sadness. She turned away.

"No!" she screamed. "Oh God, Sophie, no!"

She fell against Sophie's legs, her head rubbing the elephant's bristly skin, her arms around the legs she had often leaned against. "Goddamn you, Sophie. Get up. *Look. Look!* Get up. Get up!" She flailed at the elephant with fists that had no strength. She wailed and cried and screamed and sobbed until her throat felt raw. She slumped against the elephant's huge body. Spent. Exhausted. Defeated.

Natalie didn't know how long she lay against her friend. When she finally opened her eyes, the sky had dimmed. She sensed she was not alone.

She turned her head and saw Ali, his magnificent tusks dragged the ground near Sophie's head. Next to him, Thaya stood, her trunk fondling Sophie's as a human being would hold another human's hand.

A low, vibrant rumbling surrounded Natalie, a sort of hum, the kind of sound that soothes and calms and makes you feel the wonder of nature. Like a hymn. A lament. A dirge.

She stood and watched the rest of the elephants moving silently down the road toward them. Ten of them. A long, graceful line of gray titans. A funeral parade. They made a half circle around Sophie, each coming to her, one at a time, using their trunks to smell her, lifting their feet, and touching her body with their sensitive foot pads.

How many stories could be processed that way: where someone had come from, who their family was, what they ate, whether they had given birth, how old they were, how they had died?

As they felt Sophie's head, touched her feet, ran their trunks along her backbone, touched the spots where she'd been bit, they rumbled gently and snuffed through their trunks.

They encircled Sophie, including Natalie in that circle, occasionally reaching out the wet tip of a trunk to touch her hair or her shoulder or her face, as if to comfort her. She let a new wave of tears wash her face, silently, and the herd also became silent for several moments. Then Ali and Thaya moved aside.

Anurak came forward through the elephants, his eyes large and full of tears. He touched Sophie's now-still ears, lifting them gently to rub his face with them. Behind him, Decha led the baby Apsara, then he disappeared around the corner of the clinic, as if he knew this wasn't his place.

Thaya and Pahpao rumbled as they sidled next to the baby, who lifted her head to Sophie's leg and ran her tiny trunk along it. She bumped it with her forehead as if begging Sophie to rise, then backed off with a cry.

Immediately, Thaya and Pahpao reached their trunks to encircle the baby like aunties comforting a niece who had lost her mother.

"They'll be your nannies now," Natalie whispered as Apsara nestled beside her. "They'll take care of you, little one."

Ali lifted his head, his trunk straight up in the air and rumbled strongly, loud and long. The sound vibrated in Natalie's chest, moving her heart and stirring the breath that had stopped moving through her muscles. He'd been Sophie's best friend. He had led this mourning parade to her.

As he turned his massive, wrinkled, dove-grey body, Natalie stood. He paused for a moment and lowered his creviced head, his beautiful golden-brown eyes regarding her with a solemnity that felt both wise and compassionate. She reached her hand out to him, and he responded with his trunk. They touched for a brief second, her fingers to the finger-like growths at the end of his trunk. Gently. Softly. *A salute*, Natalie thought. *An understanding of our common grief.*

Behind him, Thaya and Pahpao gathered Apsara into the herd and the rest of the elephants followed, each of them pausing briefly, touching Sophie's body in their own individual way, giving her their respect, sharing their sadness.

Together, the herd walked soundlessly and slowly toward the river, leaving Natalie with Sophie. Anurak hugged Natalie's waist hard, then he, too, left her.

It was only then that Natalie raised her head to the sky, letting the soft rain that had begun to fall wash her face.

Forty-Six

Three things cannot long be hidden:
the sun, the moon and the truth.
                                    -Buddha

"It's only been two days. I think it's going to take at least a couple more weeks before you start feeling back to yourself." Natalie took the blood pressure cuff off Peter's arm and sat back in the chair.

It felt strange to be treating him in his cabin, seeing his clothes strewn around on the floor, smelling his morning breath, and feeling the cool smoothness of his skin as she took his vitals. No, that was an understatement. As she studied him now, pale and weak, lying back against the pillows, she wondered how she could have ever been intimidated by him. He was so thin and white that he was almost transparent.

"I've got a question for you," she said.

He glanced up at her a bit fuzzily and reached for his glasses on the side table. "Shoot."

"Where have you been for the past . . . what is it? A month? Where did you and Karina go?"

"Karina?"

"You both left the same night. Where did you go?"

"I didn't leave with Karina. I left with Siriporn."

"Really?"

"Yes, Siriporn. He wanted to go to Bangkok. For the protests, you know? Karina wanted to go home, so we gave her a ride to the airport." He adjusted his glasses, then fell back against the pillows. "Must admit I was curious. We had lots of, you know, conversations, Siriporn and I. Yes, conversations," he said, addressing the surprise on her face. "Political conversations. He told me about all his beliefs. I wanted to know more, so we went to Bangkok together. We protested. Actually, got arrested." He laughed a bit. A wheezy laugh. It was still hard for him to breathe.

"Arrested?"

"Yes, didn't Mali tell you?"

"No, I've been preoccupied with other things." She slapped the blood pressure cuff onto the table and turned away. "Is he home?"

"No, he stayed. Said something about continuing . . . I don't know." He wheezed again.

A long pause. Natalie looked out the window. Her work was done here. She needed to be heading for Apsara's enclosure.

"So the day of the cobra . . . you had just come home."

"Yes. In fact, I wasn't here for more than an hour when one of the kids ran up to the office looking for help. I had no clue what was going on, so I went out there."

Another pause. The warm breeze rustled through the windows and flipped the pages of a book on his bedside table.

"When Sophie came, you yelled for Danny. Who's that?" Peter closed his eyes and groaned a little.

She had never been so grateful that someone's eyes were closed.

"Danny. That's my son."

"Your son? Didn't know you had a son."

If you hadn't been so intent on destroying me, maybe you would have found that out, she thought. She rose from the chair and made for the door. "I have a few things to do. Talk to you later, okay?"

"No, wait, wait. Come back here." He patted the chair.

Natalie shook her head and forced a shaky smile. She didn't want to go back, didn't want to sit on the chair. Didn't want to talk. Couldn't. Not to Peter. Not to anyone. If she was going to talk to anyone, it would have been Seth. But he wasn't here, and part of her was glad he wasn't, though she thought about him late at night. Missed him in a way that didn't give her any heartache. She was glad she'd spoken to him, but she still didn't know what the final film would be like. She'd come to the conclusion that it would be whatever Seth needed it to be, and she had to be okay with that.

"You know, Natalie, we haven't exactly had a friendship, but I feel like I can say something to you." Hatcher pulled the sheet up to his chin and pointed at her. "You're a very sad woman, Natalie DeAngelo, and I think it's because of your Danny. Tell me about him."

It was a command. She didn't do well with commands. She reached for the door again.

"Sit, Natalie. Come, come. Sit. Tell me the story of your son. Tell me about Danny."

She shook her head. "I really don't want to. Not now, Peter." She'd repeated the story to Seth. She wasn't ready to do it again, especially to a man she'd spent the better part of this year despising, the man responsible for Sophie's death.

He peered at her over the rims of his eyeglasses, then glanced away, smoothed his sheet, thought for a moment and turned back. "I understand, believe me. I know what it's like to lose a child."

That caught her off guard. *How could he know? He'd never had a child.*

"I know what you're thinking," he continued, a slight rasp in his words. "You're thinking I could not understand since I have not had a child myself. Well, you're wrong. You've not heard me speak about my daughter, but that doesn't mean I didn't have one." He stopped and took a deep breath. "Twelve years ago. A horrendous auto accident. My wife. My daughter." He stopped again, searching for another breath, but this pause wasn't because he couldn't breathe. This appeared to be an emotional pause, not a physical thirst for air.

"Yes, I was married when you read my dissertation. Happy. But when I had to rewrite it, I became angry. I threw myself into it. Was horrible to live with." He took a deep breath and let it out shakily. "They went to a birthday party that night. I was too busy to go with them." He polished his glasses with the corner of the sheet, gave himself a moment to compose his thoughts.

"For years, I couldn't talk about them. I sunk myself into work. I performed more emergency operations as the vet on call in North Yorkshire than anyone since World War II. Worked twenty-four hours a day sometimes. Surprisingly, it didn't take away the memories to work that much." He laughed, a hoarse and painful sound. "Even now, I can still see the flames that engulfed their car."

She let out a short, involuntary moan.

"Yes, I saw the accident. That's always been the worst part. Wish I hadn't, but I did."

Natalie studied her fingertips instead of staring at Peter. Suddenly, he wasn't the man she knew a month ago, and she didn't know how to handle that. "You blamed me for the accident, didn't you?"

"I did. I could never point the finger at myself. I guess because it's easier to blame someone else for something that . . . that . . . horrible. But now I know. It was an accident. No one's fault."

She let his confession sink in, and when it did, she wordlessly reached for his hand.

"Now, tell me," he said softly. His tone kinder, gentler than it had ever been when he spoke to her.

She watched his face as he listened to a shortened version of her story. She found it easier to tell this time, easier than telling Seth, and thought that maybe this is what Dr. Littlefield meant when she said, "You have to be the sailor, Natalie. You have to tell the albatross story over and over again. Lessen its power over you. Get used to the emotions. Dig deep into them. Expose them. Eventually, you'll see the story no longer has control over you, is no longer something you fear."

When she finished, Hatcher placed his dry hand atop hers. Something in that cold, dry touch awakened her anger and lit another candle under her grief. Sophie's life for his. Natalie's story of grief would not include her best friend. Because of this man.

Swallowing back a sob, she pointed at him, the man she'd just treated. "There was no one—no one, no human, no other animal—who was more humane than the elephant who saved your life. Sophie saved *your* life. And you wanted to take *hers*. You wanted to *kill* her! Do you remember that? Do you?"

He hung his head. When he looked up again more than a minute later, tears ran down his pale cheeks. "I remember. I know, believe me."

"I fucking hope that you never forget that, Peter Hatcher. I hope you live the rest of your life thinking about how Sophie gave up her life for you. I hope you never forget it. Because I won't."

He turned his head against the pillow and shut his eyes. "I won't. Believe me, I won't."

"Enough. We need to stop this. Nothing will come of two people hurting each other." Andrew voice came from behind. "You both have been through enough pain. You strike out, thinking that others don't understand. But you do. You both do. It's time for you both to stop."

Natalie turned to look at him as he spoke and felt as though she'd had the life drained from her. She had no fight left.

"I'm sorry, Natalie," Peter said quietly. "I'm so sorry."

She shook her head slowly and didn't respond.

Beyond the cabin, an elephant trumpeted, then a very small one answered, reminding the three of them that there were many important lives to protect.

Andrew stood, facing Peter and Natalie with a wry smile on his face. "You know, one of the reasons I started this sanctuary is because the best way to treat broken animals is with broken people. Each fixes the other."

He placed one hand on Peter's arm and the other on Natalie's shoulder. "The dogs here would be lost without you, Peter, and you, Natalie. Don't you think your life has changed—and so had Sophie's—as a result of coming into each other's lives?"

Natalie knew he was right. She rose and hugged him, then glanced at Peter and nodded. There was nothing more to say.

Forty-Seven

Outside the open window
The morning air is all awash with angels.
-Richard Purdy Wilbur

DOWN THE HILL, THE rooster and his chickens crowed and clucked. Apsara answered with a trumpet and shook her head, flapping her ridiculously large ears. Even at four months old, she'd already developed a bit of an attitude and that made her all the more lovable. The sanctuary crew each scheduled a moment in their days to come and visit her, sometimes to sit and watch, sometimes to take her for a walk, and most often, to share a food treat. The children took turns with Natalie and the mahouts to sleep with the calf at night. But the nannies determined who could see her and when. They took her into their embrace and kept her there, in the middle of their tight group, rebuking her when she misbehaved, saving her when she fell, loving her every hour of every day. As Natalie did.

When Natalie came into the pen, Apsara came running, swinging the trunk she hadn't quite learned to control yet, tripping on her feet as excited as a toddler. Every time she did so, Natalie felt like she'd become a grandmother who could easily spoil the delightful child, yet she forced herself to remember how important it was to discipline the rambunctious youngster, even though the calf got her feelings hurt regularly.

"Elephants not forget," Khalan told her. "Make friends again. Not be mad."

She listened to him and allowed him to teach her that taking care of adult elephants was often easier than caring for babies.

When she told her parents about what had happened, about rescuing Apsara and about the cobra attack, Sophie's death, and what she'd learned about Peter, it was easier for them to understand why Natalie couldn't leave the sanctuary when her time was up. She had to stay. Though Maman cried, she told Natalie, "I know you're happy. I know you have to be around the animals, so we understand." And a month later, Maman called to say that she and Pop wanted to come for what she called "a vacation to Bangkok" in the fall. Natalie couldn't wait to introduce them to everyone who'd become her Thai family.

Not a day went by when Natalie went to the pen to help the other mahouts that she didn't think about her old girl. Her brave old girl. The program that Seth and his crew had shot aired a couple of weeks ago, and the last moments were dedicated to her in memoriam. Since that time, hundreds of people had called or emailed, wanting to send their abused elephants to her or to learn her training program. Andrew often joked that he'd be quite happy if they'd send him their cash so he could continue his work. He was opening another sanctuary and wanted Peter to run it, which made Peter giddy and proud. Though he and Natalie had come to terms with their relationship and could even work side by side, it was best that Peter be in charge of his own reserve. Ironically, the first thing he'd asked Andrew was whether he could have several protected contact buildings at the new place.

She adjusted the blanket on Apsara's back now, and the calf naughtily snatched it off with her trunk. She'd become more adept at using her trunk within the past month and had yanked Natalie by her braid so many times that Natalie finally cut it off. She shook her newly-shorn hair now and giggled as she picked up Apsara's blanket, tied it around the calf's neck and wagged her finger at the baby. "Don't do that."

"You need to make your voice a bit stronger if you're going to discipline her. I would laugh at you if I were her." Mali was behind them, leaning against the fence that surrounded Apsara's pen. She pulled the black turban from her head and rolled it in her hands. "Have you seen Siriporn? He's supposed to bring Sivad to see her new school."

"He was taking Ali to the river then heading your way." Natalie popped Apsara's bottle into her mouth and stood beside her, holding to the railing as the baby leaned her whole three hundred pounds against her human nanny. "How long's he staying?"

Mali screwed up her mouth. She still wasn't happy with Siriporn's decision to stay in Bangkok to take on the leadership of the Red Party's base there, but he was an adult, and she was trying to learn to let go. She was trying to work off the guilt she felt for not being there for her sons when they were younger, trying to make up for lost time. Besides, since becoming one of the Red Party's leaders, he'd become determined to infuse some of the good and bad he'd learned about American history into the party's structure. And he was equally determined to work toward freeing the elephants who'd been in chains, serving humans, for most of their lives. It would take a while, he'd told Natalie, but it gave him a focus.

"Maybe a week this time, then he's going back," Mali said. "I told him he needed to be here for his sister's first day at school. She won't know what to do without him."

Natalie raised an eyebrow. "Neither will his mother."

Mali grunted, her favorite way of not engaging in a subject she didn't want to discuss.

"Do you want to have tea when I'm done?" Natalie asked, adjusting Apsara's bottle so the calf wouldn't pull it away.

"I'd love that. I have something to tell you." Mali smiled mysteriously.

"Why not tell me now?"

"Over tea."

"You always do that to me," Natalie said, adding a little

childish whine to her voice.

They shared a laugh and some chit chat until Apsara finished her bottle with a burp and a sigh, as a toddler would. She followed them up the road to the platform, wandering off with Anurak and Decha to play with the big tire Andrew had given them. The women sat on the platform and watched, marveling that three species could play together as though they were all siblings: a dog, a little boy, and an elephant.

"I think if Apsara hadn't had the friendship of those two, and nannies like Thaya and Pahpao, she would've died after Sophie was killed. She really needed to be with other youngsters. Other elephants." Natalie sipped a bit of the hot, sweet tea Hom had brought over to the two of them.

Mali nodded and studied her friend. "You're okay, aren't you?"

"I'm better than I thought I'd be," Natalie answered. "I've done a lot of thinking, and I've come to one conclusion."

Mali waited.

Natalie wrapped her hands around her cup. "I've come to the conclusion that what Oscar Wilde said about the truth being rarely pure and never simple pretty much sums up life."

Mali nodded again and the women simply sat with each other.

"What did you want to tell me?" Natalie asked.

Mali smiled and held a hand over her stomach. "Andrew and I are getting married. There's another baby coming . . ."

Natalie reached to hug her friend. "That's wonderful!"

"And I want you to be maid of honor and godmother."

Natalie's eyes filled. "I'd be honored."

"Good," Mali said. "Good."

In the distance, Apsara gave a baby elephant roar and Decha barked. And further away, the rest of the herd grazed in the meadow near the mountains, a tableau of grayish-pink humps against the lush green of the jungle. The denim-blue sky rippled with the heat of a late morning thunderstorm in the distance. Several of the mahouts, their brightly-colored rugby shirts a shock of red and orange and blue against the dark green vegetation, called their elephants together, then the herd started moving through the gently swaying grasses, heading for home.

Acknowledgements

It is true that the first people I want to thank are the members of the incredible Amberjack Publishing team. From the moment I spoke with Dayna Anderson and Kayla Church, I knew they were the publishers for me, and my editor, Jenny Miller, has been supportive and helpful throughout the process, as has Cami Wasden, the office assistant. Sometimes you think you're going in the right direction, but you're not sure. With the Amberjack crew, I'm definitely home, and I can't thank them enough for their editorial direction, help with marketing, and their overall spirit.

Throughout the process of writing *The Mourning Parade,* my writing community supported me. I started the novel while in the Algonkian Novelists Workshop, and Michael Neff, the founder, and I had several long conversations about where the story was going. Literary agent and developmental editor extraordinaire, Elizabeth Kracht, suggested the new title and helped me reshape the story's arc. Damian McNicholls and Laura Rennert also made suggestions that were helpful in developing the story.

Ron Jackson inspired at least two of the scenes that made the final cut and his rich way of interpreting scenes strengthened my words. Carolyn Burns Bass, Christine Mojica, Shannon Capone Kirk, and Lolita Guevarra have all heard bits and pieces of the story or have read the entire novel (sometimes several times). I don't know what I would have done without them! Carolyn's voice rang through my head as I wrote, Shannon boosted my ego when I needed it, Christine read the early drafts of the book, and Lolita sat with me when I wrote the final draft. And my Facebook family has cheered me on, helped me choose photos and graphics, and listened to all my trials, tribulations, and celebrations. My heartfelt thanks to each of you.

The folks at the Elephant World in Kanchanaburi, Thailand taught me more than they'll ever realize. Their old bull, Rom

Sai, was my inspiration for Ali. Lek Chailert and her sanctuaries have done an incredible job bringing attention to the plight of elephants in Chiang Mai, Thailand. She's well known all over the world for what she's done for Asian elephants. In a different part of the world, Dame Daphne Sheldrick is equally as well known in Kenya for her work with saving baby elephants. These incredible women formed the basis of my research on elephants, and I counted on their expertise – as well as my experience at the elephant sanctuaries in both Thailand and Africa—to complete this work.

The Weymouth Center for the Arts and Humanities gave me space and time I needed to finish the final draft of the book, though I needed to compete with spooky stories to do so! Thank you, thank you, thank you!

And finally, my family and friends have put up with my crazy work schedule and habits of disappearing to jot something down on a napkin for too many years. You all know I love you.

About the Author

A writer, theater critic, mosaic artist, and educator, Dawn Reno Langley has devoted her life to literature and the arts. Born an Army brat to a WWII and Korea vet and his wife, Dawn spent her childhood scaring her younger siblings with stories of monsters under the bed. Her first published works, an essay on the Cuban missile crisis, revealed a deep sense of social justice that has never waned. Since then, she has written extensively for newspapers and magazines, has published children's books, novels, nonfiction books, short stories and poetry, as well as theater reviews and blogs.

A Fulbright scholar with an MFA in Fiction and a PhD in Interdisciplinary Studies, Langley lives in Durham, North Carolina, a small city where people present her with new stories every day. She is always amazed that one finds most stories in small places rather than large cities, and she appreciates the warmth of the friends she has made in the town she calls "funky/artsy."